I0660168

Crystal Escape

Doug J. Cooper

Books in The Crystal Series

For info and updates, please visit: CrystalSeries.com

Crystal Escape
Copyright © 2018 by Doug J. Cooper

Published by: Douglas Cooper Consulting

The Crystal Series editor: Tammy Salyer

Beta reviewer: Mark Mesler
Book editor: Tammy Salyer
Cover design: Damonza

ISBN-13: 978-0-9899381-9-8
ISBN-10: 0-9899381-9-0

Author website: www.crystalseries.com

For Nanny and Dora

1

Macalister "MacMac" MacFarlane started muttering the moment the order arrived. "She's running an integrity test *now?*" He spoke to an empty room but his question was sincere.

Integrity tests were live action; no simulations allowed. This one ordered a test of Chemstore, and that meant he'd have to spend the next two hours helping Hejmo fill the massive storage tanks in the cellar, row upon row holding oxygen, nitrogen, water, and the other huge-volume items required for isolated operation.

And "she" was Aubrey Medina, Director of Vivo. Strict, demanding, watchful, and the person he needed to please to keep his job.

Most days MacMac enjoyed his work. Having spent twenty-six years working as the engineer on a string of mining spaceships and orbiting factory platforms, he appreciated having a challenging job right here on Earth.

Beyond the obvious benefit of letting him be near his family, the job had an artistic component that he enjoyed, that of Vivo's weatherman. Guests got wet from his rain, blown by his wind, and hot from his sun. With a swipe and tap, he could roll in a fog or rumble some thunder. And it was all real, not the charade of projected images that made up so much of the guest experience.

MacMac's displays popped alive with colorful charts as the integrity test began. Stuffing the last cookie into his mouth, he clapped the crumbs from his hands, held his right hand in front of him palm up, and flexed his fingers in a "come here" motion. When he did, the vibrant images leapt forward and moved into his peripheral vision. The details of the integrity test would now be available to him as he moved about.

A sturdy-framed Scotsman with reddish-brown curls atop a kind, clean-shaven face, MacMac stepped into the hall, crossed onto the lift, and began the descent from the office tower. As he rode down, he faced the rear of the lift cabin and looked out through the clear walls and into the domed world that was Vivo. Squinting, he tried to see all the way out to the ocean tankers anchored nearby, but the orange streaks of dusk projecting beneath the containment dome blocked his view.

Tilting his head forward, he watched the gardens and narrow lanes at guest level rush toward him. Impact seemed certain, then with a quiet *whoosh* he was belowground, descending into the cavernous works beneath the surface of the artificial island.

Industrial, chaotic, and loud, the cellar, as Aubrey called it, was a vast, mostly open space with a tall ceiling, hard deck, and muted lighting. The cellar housed a myriad of automated support operations that enabled Vivo to be a vacation paradise. And MacMac and his crew of ten Tech synbods labored in the subterranean space so the guests would never know that any of it existed.

The lift slowed to a stop and when the door opened, he inhaled through his nose. A subconscious act, almost a reflex, he searched the familiar oily-metallic tang of the cellar for hints of smoke, chemical vapors, or anything else that shouldn't be there. While his visual displays would have warned him of problems, his behavior was the result of decades of habit—habit he still trusted.

The powerful thrum of the transfer pumps—huge machines moving material off the ocean ships and into Vivo's giant storage tank—resonated in his chest as he walked the few steps to his crew cart. Reassuring at one level, they drowned out the familiar background symphony of devices that scrubbed the air, purified the water, readied consumables, recycled waste, and managed everything else running in the cellar so Vivo could operate as an independent, isolated environment.

"Chemstore," he said to the crew cart as his butt hit the seat. Mustard-colored and christened with the words CHIEF ENGINEER across the back in simple brown letters, the cart accelerated into the bowels beneath the island. Carrying him across the deck, it carved a gentle arc to avoid the Power House, a long, low building with gray walls and a flat roof that contained Vivo's energy generation units.

"We're trending high on pump bank twelve," said MacMac as the power draw ticked upward on his display. A green light in the image flipped red, confirming what he'd concluded on his own.

"I see it," Hejmo replied.

"Don't go above eighty percent until we understand what's going on."

"Will Aubrey be unhappier if we fall behind schedule," asked Hejmo, "or if we meet the deadline but melt a row of pumps?"

MacMac's crew cart emerged from the shadow of the recycling facility and glided to a stop at Chemstore's ops panel. Placed in front of an expanse of house-sized silos holding the gases, liquids, and dry goods needed for long-term isolated operation, the panel enabled local control of Chemstore operations. Hejmo stood facing the display, unmoving, hands at his sides.

As MacMac approached, Hejmo animated and MacMac answered his question. "She expects us to meet the deadline—and will be unforgiving if we melt a row of pumps *and* don't get everything transferred in time."

As Hejmo nodded in agreement, a jarring *clunk* echoed across the cellar from the direction of the pumps on the far side of the tank farm. The sounds near Chemstore transitioned from a throaty roar to a fading whine as equipment with giant rotating parts began winding down.

"We just lost the row," said Hejmo as he acted to isolate the problem. "It's causing a trip down the line."

His hands flew as he worked the panel, struggling to get in front of the problem. His efforts were rewarded when pumps whirred back to life, the sound level rising as they climbed to full effort.

"Split bank eight," said MacMac, pointing to the image of a row of pumps on one side of the display. "Run the fresh water through the back half."

The next hour weighed on MacMac as he and Hejmo tended the equipment, struggling to regain lost time without losing any more vital components. As the deadline approached, he stopped watching the transfer details and started watching the clock timing this exercise.

Damn, he thought when the clock reached zero, flipped to red, and started counting up.

"We're over," said Hejmo.

"I see." MacMac watched the count grow past one minute. When it approached the two-minute mark, he asked for confirmation. "We should be done at seven minutes over?"

"Yes. Seven minutes and a few seconds."

"That's not bad for a first go, lad."

"I believe Aubrey expected us to be on time."

MacMac's com chimed and he felt his neck tense when he checked the message. "She wants to see me."

"When?"

"Now."

"Of course," said Hejmo with a knowing nod. "When this is done, I'll empty the tanks and run the cleaning cycle."

MacMac stepped into his cart and slumped back in the seat. "Let me know if the pumps failed because we screwed up. I'm betting they came defective from the manufacturer."

Engaging the cart, he followed the same course in reverse, rounding the recycling facility and arcing across the expansive deck back to the lift. As he whirred past the Power House, he saw one of his Tech crew carts, distinguished by its forest-green color, parked at the door.

Curious, he tapped the air in front of him to launch his security interface. From there he accessed the link that would let him watch the action inside the building. But instead of seeing an interior view, he saw a "Link Failure" message. His teeth clenched in annoyance.

"Why can't I see inside the Power House?" he asked Hejmo, using the private channel that connected him to his Supervisor synbod, aptly named because MacMac supervised Hejmo, and Hejmo supervised the ten Tech synbods—each a synthetic humanoid with a three-gen AI crystal inside—that comprised MacMac's work crew.

"The supplier shipped a secure-shield building by mistake," Hejmo replied. "It's a premium product that meets our other specs, so I accepted delivery at the original contract price. We stay on schedule this way. I just need to upgrade the link so we can see into the building."

"It looks like the upgrade is being installed right now."

"No, I haven't ordered anything yet. If you're talking about the Tech that's there now, he's working on a mod for Aubrey."

Hearing this, MacMac gestured with his hand, causing his cart to swerve back toward the Power House. His upper body tipped to the side as the vehicle completed its turn, then swayed forward as it whirred to a stop in the space next to the Tech's crew cart.

She knows to include me on all her requests to my crew, he thought, trying to decide if he should go on the offensive about her constant meddling if she hassled him on the integrity test time overrun.

He stepped into the Power House, and when the door closed behind him, the sounds echoing out in the cavernous cellar quieted, replaced by silence inside the building except for a gentle clanking from the far side of a row of cabinets.

MacMac stepped forward until he saw the Tech squatting in front of an open access panel. The synbod rose to attention, and MacMac stood in front of him, scanning him up and down like a military officer appraising a recruit.

Mister perfect. MacMac had the same thought every time he studied one up close. They all had thick, clean hair, unblemished skin, and a pleasing symmetrical face, presumably to make them appear more human. But that perfection was their flaw from MacMac's perspective.

"What are you doing?"

"I'm performing a cooling management upgrade," replied the humanoid. "Would you like me to show you?"

MacMac didn't respond. While the AI inside the Tech was capable of addressing quite sophisticated problems, three-gen crystals were too simple to be sentient. MacMac knew the synbod was aware of his annoyance and would be interested in placating him, but he also knew it wouldn't *feel* anything about it one way or another.

Dismissing the Tech like he was another piece of equipment, MacMac turned and started down the walkway, two parallel yellow lines marked on the floor along the length of the building. Like many warehouses, the inside of the Power House was largely open space. In this one, though, six sheds, each about as tall as he could reach, stood in a row down the middle of the floor.

Made of a silver-gray material, each shed housed an ultra-high-energy generator. While any two of them were enough to run Vivo and all of its operations with capacity to spare, Aubrey had insisted on this excessive redundancy "for the good of the guests."

Looping around behind the last shed in the row, he started back up the walkway on the other side of the building. "Show me her modification request," he said to Hejmo as he walked.

A two-sentence note projected in front of him. The first sentence requested an upgrade to a slide circuit to improve the capabilities of the cooling management system—the system that ensured everything from the atmosphere under the dome to the devices in the cellar all operated at their proper temperatures. The second sentence identified the particular slide circuit to be replaced.

"We have an entire ocean around us to provide cooling, for heaven's sake," MacMac said to himself. "What's there to upgrade?"

Hejmo, a Supervisor synbod designed to interface between humans and a traditional synbod workforce, didn't answer. Supers were constructed with twin three-gen AI crystals, so while also not self-aware, Hejmo did a credible job of appearing to be.

As MacMac exited the Power House and stepped back into his cart, he continued grumbling to his Super. "Her constant micromanaging pisses me off."

Resuming his journey to meet with Aubrey, he noticed lights shining in the Structures building off to his right, something he didn't see very often. On impulse, he swerved the vehicle in that direction.

"You shouldn't make her wait," said Hejmo through their private channel.

MacMac ignored him and, after a brief ride, pulled to a stop outside a one-room office building with the word STRUCTURES on the clear door. Leaning to the side, he peered inside and saw Mondo sitting at the tech bench studying a schematic diagram projected above its glass-like surface. Mondo's lips moved and his hands gestured, which meant he was talking to someone who wasn't in the room.

MacMac glimpsed the floating image for a fraction of a second, then blinked his eyes because what he saw didn't make sense. Climbing out of the crew cart, he stepped inside the Structures office.

Mondo stood and faced him. As he did, the schematic diagram disappeared. "Aubrey is waiting for you."

"What do you have going on there?" MacMac motioned toward the bench surface where the diagram had been. Mondo was Aubrey's Super, so MacMac got the answer he expected.

"I'm sorry, sir," said Mondo. "May I suggest that you ask Aubrey when you see her?"

A projected image of Aubrey, vivid in its lifelike reality, appeared standing next to Mondo. A woman in her late thirties, tall, chestnut-haired, piercing blue eyes, and dressed in the same cream-white suit worn by her Admin synbods, Aubrey said, "We have lots to discuss and I have a full schedule. I'd prefer to do this in person. Will you come up?"

She sounded almost solicitous and that worked for MacMac. "Okay."

The projected image of Aubrey disappeared and MacMac looked at Mondo, forcing himself not to let his eyes drift to the place where the schematic diagram had been. Without a word, he returned to his cart and made for the lift. Along the way, he accessed his security interface, spun through the record, and found an image of himself from a few moments earlier. He watched himself approach the office, and over his own shoulder, he peered through the door.

"There you go," he muttered aloud as he stabilized the display. Zooming, he focused on the diagram floating above the tech bench in front of Mondo.

Schematic diagrams are common in the engineering trade and MacMac knew how to read them. This one depicted Vivo's subdeck. Full of beams and girders, the substructure beneath the cellar supported the artificial island above the ocean waves.

Shown in the subdeck schematic were giant damping pistons for stability during earthquakes, and complex lift plates that protected against the winds of a hurricane. MacMac didn't know much about either technology and was glad Aubrey had hired an outside firm to install the items.

But he'd worked as the engineer on some very big space vessels over the course of his career. He'd led the team that guided Aurora, the largest deep-space platform ever built, out to a mineral rich segment of the asteroid belt orbiting between Mars and Jupiter.

So he knew what a spaceship drive pod looked like. They'd used two of them to move Aurora.

A prickle flashed up both arms and met behind his neck. Why does the schematic show four drive pods mounted beneath Vivo?

2

Sid signaled the nav on his space runner to approach Sisyphus from behind. Though he'd visited the massive space barge before, this was the first time his awe focused on something other than the sheer enormity of what looked from a distance to be a gigantic floating potato pulling a long, skinny string.

Made from lunar rock, the main body of the barge had the smoothish, slightly irregular exterior one might expect if a pile of dirt and stone the size of Mount Everest were molded and fused together like potter's clay. The tail, called the "tether," was a cross-woven cable that trailed so far behind the rock mass that the end disappeared from sight. Hook-up stations were spaced along the length of the tail, and from a distance they looked more like decorative bows than the vessel connects used by customers being towed.

The behemoth drifted in a lazy oval, looping around behind the moon, then back around Earth, and out to the moon again, completing the journey and starting anew every six days. Customers who "hooked the tether" on the barge's extended tail as it passed by one of these worlds received an inexpensive, albeit slow, tow ride to the other.

"I'm ready to pull the line," Sid said to Cheryl and Criss, who were monitoring him from Earth during his trip. He gestured, and his runner—a tiny personal spacecraft that had launched from the larger scout floating in the distance behind him—closed on the artificial satellite. His destination was the small black hole now visible in the center.

As he approached the barge, Sisyphus became less like a floating mountain and more like an endless wall of gray rock. And the hole grew as well, revealing itself to be a tunnel bored deep into the fused stone, its mouth wide enough to accommodate a half-dozen small craft like Sid's runner.

Drilled lengthwise down the center of the rock mass, the tube's smooth walls and perfect symmetry hinted at the precision used during construction. He knew Criss had supervised every aspect of the build and had already approved the borehole. But Sid felt ownership of the project—the cargo cannon had been his idea—and he wanted to participate as the venture progressed.

Leaning forward and peering through the front viewport into the darkness, he waited for the signal that confirmed the line spool was ready. When the go-indicator flipped to green, he edged the runner into the tunnel, line filament trailing behind him. The filament he pulled today would be used to pull heavier cable, which in turn would be used to pull the launch tube down the length of the tunnel.

His attention shifted to what appeared to be the faint shimmer of stars shining through from the far side of the shaft. *Has to be construction lights,* he thought, knowing the distance was too great for him to see that far.

Pulsing his engine, his world became an eerie reflection of lights dancing on the inside of the cave-like shaft. A glint in the shadows drew his eyes to a construction marking painted on the curved tunnel wall—a sparkly orange arrow pointing at a small circle around a bracket. Moments later, he drifted past a similar marking on the opposite wall.

"You really can get the launch tube installed in ten days?" he asked. "This is a *long* hole."

"It's what we do," said Cheryl.

"Constructing a future together in space," Criss deadpanned, repeating the corporate tagline used in the advertising pieces for SunRise, the huge space commercialization outfit he helped Cheryl run.

"Be careful," Cheryl called to him. Then Sid heard her say to Criss, "You got this?"

Sid signaled the nav, and the runner accelerated. "Here I go." He heard the excitement in his own voice and it made him laugh. Then he engaged the runner's external boosters. The tiny craft shuddered and shot forward with a growl, racing into the darkness.

His display tracked his speed as he went faster and faster, but his visceral pleasure didn't come from numbers on a gauge. It came from the pressure of acceleration pinning his head against the support pads, the punch to his gut as that same force pushed his body deep into his seat, and from the blurring of the orange construction markings on the walls as his speed climbed, transitioning through fast and edging deep into reckless.

"Woohoo!" he crowed, a grin stretching across his face as his speed increased. A moment later, he burst into open space from the far side of the rock mass, the almost invisible filament trailing behind.

According to the construction schedule, it would take two weeks to install the launch tube inside the borehole, and another week after that to add the EM field sequencer. If everything stayed on schedule, they'd launch their first payload of cargo to Mars in three weeks.

Sisyphus was Cheryl's project. She'd worked with Criss for years as they led the team that designed, built, and commissioned the space barge. With it now in service, vacationers riding in small craft, manufacturers moving finished goods, miners shipping loads of ore, and everything in between all hooked to the long tether trailing behind the big rock for an escorted ride from one world to the other.

It was Sid, though, who'd conceived of turning the orbiting mass into a huge cannon. And after some analysis, Criss had agreed it could be done in a way that wouldn't impact the barge business.

Instead of shooting ammunition, though, this cannon launched canisters filled with cargo. Each canister held a payload equal in size to a standard shipping container, and with remarkable accuracy, Sisyphus would pitch the canister across the solar system on a quiet journey to Mars.

Like a game ball being tossed to a teammate running across the field, the cargo canister would arc through space, neither speeding up, slowing down, nor changing direction. When it reached the Red Planet several weeks later, a capture rig would catch the canister, secure it, and then guide it down to the colony.

If it worked as planned—and since Criss had performed the calculations and finalized the designs, there was little doubt that it would—it introduced a new era of low-cost freight transport from Earth to the inhabitants of Mars Colony.

While revolutionary in its potential, practical issues limited its utility. Beyond size and weight, the cargo had to be able to withstand an acceleration similar to what a bullet experiences when fired from an old-style gun. Such g-forces would kill anything living and crush a long list of inanimate objects as well. But even with these limitations, the number of paying customers far exceeded launch capacity, ensuring plenty of business.

"Hey, love," said Sid as his deceleration sequence ended, "I'll be at the lodge tomorrow. Can you make it?"

"Of course I'll be there," Criss replied.

Cheryl giggled. "So will I."

Sid worried that their time at the lodge might not be roses and sunshine. He'd decided to travel to Mars to tour the other half of his intergalactic pitch-and-catch device and he'd be gone for six weeks.

Cheryl wouldn't be happy, so he'd tell her in person. Criss would be apoplectic.

* * *

MacMac took a deep breath, held it for a moment, then tried to calm himself as he exhaled. It didn't work. The Admin synbod had said, "Let me see if she's available," before disappearing through a door at the back of the handsome office where he now stood. That had been six minutes ago.

She hurries me here and then makes me wait, he thought, shaking his head.

Aubrey's ego had always been a problem for him: her imperious style, her dismissive attitude toward his concerns, her treatment of him like a tool to be used rather than a colleague valued for his skill.

Adding to his stress, of course, was the fact that he'd gone over the time limit on the integrity test. She'd made it clear that a successful trial was her top priority. He took his job seriously and wanted to follow her direction; that's how the chain of command worked.

But if she were also following that chain, she wouldn't be skipping over him to give assignments to Hejmo. And by the same token, he wouldn't be contemplating going over her head to talk to Vivo's board of directors.

But if those really were drive pods planned for the subdeck, he needed someone with authority and common sense to stop the madness. Putting all that capability—that raw energy—beneath a group of elite customers paying huge sums for a futuristic vacation screamed of lunacy.

And for what purpose? Four drive pods could accelerate a literal mountain out of the solar system and into interstellar space at an impressive clip. But Vivo wasn't in space. Quite the opposite, the artificial island sat firmly in the Pacific Ocean not far off the coast of Lima, Peru.

"Thank you for coming," said Aubrey as she swept through the door, her Admin synbod following close behind. The two had similar builds and features, and both were dressed in matching cream-white suits.

Aubrey's hair was different, though. She wore hers in a loose bun that shouted *all business*. Yet a wisp hung down in a studied fashion over a delicate cheekbone, softening her appearance and drawing attention to her piercing blue eyes.

Aubrey motioned to the upholstered chair in front of MacMac, inviting him to sit. She moved to a matching chair across from his and lowered herself into the seat.

"May I bring you something?" the Admin asked with a lilt. "Perhaps coffee or water?"

Aubrey caught MacMac's eye. "Cookies?" She knew his weakness.

He held up his hand. "All good here, thanks."

The Admin nodded as she turned, exiting the room through the same door they'd used for their grand entrance.

"MacMac," said Aubrey, folding her hands and leaning forward to show that the meeting had begun, "we have a problem."

"We do." He nodded in agreement.

She pulled her head back as if to gauge the meaning of his response, then continued. "Your résumé lists spaceship drive pods among your areas of expertise."

Her intonation made it a simple statement, but he felt the need to acknowledge her words in some fashion, so he nodded.

"In a story too long to tell, I find we are in possession of four of them. I want you to add their installation and testing to your to-do list."

MacMac sat back in his chair, unprepared for the direction the conversation had taken. The notion she introduced was so outrageous that he didn't know where to begin. He stalled by asking for more information. "Tell me the long version. I have time."

She nodded as if she knew he'd ask, then adjusted her posture to match MacMac's. "I was pitching our vacation escapes to Riley Adventures—did you know they're the second largest holiday agency now? Anyway, if all this is going to turn a profit," she moved a hand in a vague fashion to communicate that "all this" was Vivo, "we need the big agencies pushing our packages to their clients."

She paused, using the time to adjust a pleat in her slacks. "These agencies are mostly family businesses, and too often their deals take complicated twists and turns. One agency owner has an aunt who sells a line of specialty fruit beverages, and guess what, we'll now be serving them to our guests. Another has an interest in a shipping company that he expects us to use." She shrugged. "If we want them to sell vacations, we need to offer them more than commission. It's how the world works."

She stopped again and MacMac prodded her. "Did you actually take possession of these pods?"

"Four Corsia SuperDrives," she said, nodding. "It seemed like the right decision."

Her dismissive attitude unsettled him and he let it show in his tone. "Your story is that you were walking along, minding your own business, when all of a sudden you found yourself holding something as powerful and expensive as a midsized Fleet military base?"

She met his gaze but didn't speak.

"Pardon my French, but bullshit."

She still didn't speak.

"The   expense…the   danger…what   were   you thinking?"

"They're not fueled, so there *is* no danger," she said with an edge. "Don't treat me like I'm stupid."

Her rebuke caused MacMac to break eye contact. He looked back when she resumed her story.

"Old Man Riley kept pushing back about safety at Vivo. He claims he needs to tell his clients they're safer here than in their own beds. I gave him the rundown—our redundant power generators, our ability to operate fully contained—your transfer test went over the time limit, by the way. That can't happen again."

She was so matter-of-fact that it added a new dimension to his daze. "It won't."

"So, Riley goes on about his concern for natural disasters. I tell him about our earthquake defenses and storm protection. He says, 'What about volcanos? Or meteors?' He wants to know if the island can lift into the air and move out of danger in case of something that will never happen."

MacMac was so lost he didn't know how to respond.

"So, I tell him he's talking nonsense. He tells me about his nephew who's a bigshot at Corsia. Turns out the first SuperDrives off the production line have a defect that's too costly to repair. The CEO of Corsia blames the nephew for the screw-up."

MacMac's look of confusion must have been complete because she added, "I told you I didn't want to go into it. Anyway, Riley's terms were that we install the drives below Vivo, rig them so they seem live, and then get some top execs from a short list of space-tech companies to attend our opening. If we can get an exec to tour the subdeck and see the drives poised for action, ready to save the day in case of disaster, then he'll reimburse all our expenses for staging the drives, *and* Riley Adventures will promote the hell out of Vivo for one year."

"He wants us to advertise drive pods for him?" None of this made sense to MacMac, and the creases on his forehead reflected his bafflement. "Does he think a company exec will take a tour, then go home and buy a few space drives?" He shook his head. "That's not how it works. Does that make sense to you?"

"He thinks it will help save his nephew's job." She shrugged. "I'm not convinced. But I asked for a commission on each sale and took the deal when he offered ten percent."

"So you really want me to rig four SuperDrives into the subdeck?"

"Take all the Attendants you need. Mondo will help."

"But we open in three weeks!"

"I know," she said, nodding. "You have a lot to do."

3

Criss sipped iced tea with Cheryl in the kitchen of the leadership lodge, an enormous but cozy log cabin home nestled in a wooded valley in the Adirondack Mountains in upstate New York. Sitting in wooden chairs on either side of a small kitchen table, the two chatted with Sid while he cooked his award-winning chili.

"Everyone puts beer in their chili," said Sid as he poured a generous portion into a bubbling pot on a chef-quality stove. "The secret, though, is to use dark beer. You don't want to put in so much that you can taste it, but the right amount gives that extra-special deliciousness."

The Criss who sat at the table appeared there as a projected image. Through a sophisticated trick of light, Sid and Cheryl saw a fit man in his mid-forties. Almost as tall as Sid, he had sun-bleached hair and the pleasantly weathered face of an outdoorsman. He was dressed in a black T-shirt and khaki slacks.

But the artificial intelligence projecting that image—a sentient four-gen AI crystal with the cognitive ability of a thousand humans—lived in a secure bunker buried deep in the side of a mountain located near the lodge. And there he felt a growing anxiety, one he decided to address head-on.

He did so by starting a spat. Looking at Cheryl, he said, "Sid wants to go to Mars."

Sid stopped stirring his pot and turned toward them, his white chef's hat sliding off his head and landing in a droop over his shoulder. "Hey, I never said that." He rescued his hat, shook it so it puffed open, and returned it to the top of his head. "But Criss is right. It's important that I review the status of the cargo catcher. It's the other half of what I'm trying to accomplish."

Criss laughed. "You just want to be there when the first cargo canister arrives."

He rarely challenged his leadership—Sid, Cheryl, and Juice—the three humans he was hardwired to serve. But his highest priority was to ensure their health and safety. The distance from Earth to Mars was so great that he couldn't be effective in both places. If Sid were on Mars while Cheryl and Juice remained on Earth, he would have to choose whom to protect.

The solution is for Sid to stay here, he thought, anxious to keep everyone together. He could cause that to happen in any number of ways, from fabricating a phony emergency that would draw Sid's attention to events on Earth, to creating a never-ending series of glitches and failures so Sid never got off the ground.

But he'd forecast a far simpler scenario, one with a near certain outcome. He'd pit the two lovers against each other. It would be uncomfortable for a few minutes, but he was confident in Cheryl's ability to guide events to a proper resolution.

"I admit it." Sid took a long drink from the bottle of dark beer, then poured another splash into the pot. "I want to be there when it arrives. My plan is to load it with everything we need for a huge party to celebrate the grand opening of Colony Cargo. That's what I'm calling the company, by the way. Not bad, huh?"

"I think I don't want to go to Mars," said Cheryl, shaking her head. "And I'm pretty certain Juice doesn't either." When Sid started to speak, Cheryl spoke over him. "And don't say you'll go by yourself, because you know that doesn't work."

Sid glared, and Criss tried to relieve the tension by sticking an index finger in his collar and pulling it out as if to give himself more air. "Is it getting hot in here?"

"And now you've ruined my surprise," said Cheryl. "I've made arrangements for a special vacation getaway for the two of us to celebrate the success of your venture. It's at this high-tech domed resort they've built on an island in the Pacific."

She is a maestro, Criss thought with sincere admiration. Cheryl had received an invitation to attend an all-expenses-paid vacation for her and a guest, and she'd already pitched the idea to Juice. Now, shooting from the hip, she offered Sid the same slot she'd promised Juice, confident that she risked nothing. Sid loved spending time with her, but he would have zero interest in a vacation resort, domed or not.

"Aw, honey. I'm sorry," said Sid. "But even if I don't go to Mars, it will be a busy time on the project." He gave her a winning smile. "It sounds fun and it's a thoughtful gesture. But I just don't think I could commit to that right now."

Cheryl became all business. "I'll offer your ticket to Juice if you agree not to go to Mars."

"Done," said Sid.

"Done," Cheryl hit the table with her hand like an auctioneer completing a sale.

Done, Criss thought to himself.

Sid turned off the stove. "Dinner is served." Tall, broad shouldered, in his early forties, and with the quiet assuredness of someone trained by the Union of Nations to confront mortal danger, he ladled steaming-hot chili into two bowls. Showing a rare domestic side, he set them on trays that held servings of cornbread and tossed salad, and handed one of the trays to Cheryl.

The two started up the back stairs leading to the lookout loft. If they had glanced back, they would have seen Criss ladle out a bowl of chili and, in a perfect illusion, appear to put it on a tray with cornbread and salad. They did hear him create the clang of the ladle against the side of the pot, though, as well as his footsteps behind them as he followed them up to the loft.

The highest room in the lodge, the lookout loft had transparent walls and a ceiling that offered striking views of a huge garden estate, with the forested slope of a mountain rising in one direction, and a wooded valley, visible only when the autumn leaves fell, in the other.

Sitting in comfy chairs, they balanced their trays on their knees. Sid scooped a small spoonful of chili, blew on it a few times, and tasted his creation. Nodding, he took another bite. "You aren't the resort type either, sweetie. What's the story?"

"I'm surprised at myself, but the concept sounds so cool. They claim that by manipulating the complete environment the way you can under a containment dome, they can time-slice four actual days and turn it into a five-day vacation."

"I don't get it," said Sid, shaking his head and looking at Criss.

"It's a clever concept," said Criss. "People's circadian rhythms are tuned to a twenty-four-hour wake-sleep cycle. But it's not sixteen hours of full up and then eight hours of full down. Everyone moves up and down in a pattern that changes by the minute. That's why you get tired at certain times during the day, or surface from sleep briefly at night."

Criss stopped to taste his chili. "Nice. Did you use a double bock?"

Sid nodded. "What do you think, Cher?"

Cheryl had taken a bite of salad before Sid asked her opinion, and the corner of a green leaf poked from her lips. Prettier than the proverbial girl next door, and today with her light brown hair pulled back in a casual ponytail, Cheryl gave a thumbs-up with her free hand while she chased the errant lettuce with her other. Early in her career, she'd served as captain of the Fleet space cruiser *Alliance*. She'd resigned her commission when she'd become part of Criss's leadership and now worked with him on big space-commercialization projects.

Satisfied that the spat he'd instigated had caused no ripples of tension, Criss continued his story. "So, your wake-sleep cycles come and go based on the time of day, and also because of the amount of light you get, the food you eat, your level of physical activity, your mental stimulation, the people around you, and lots more. At Vivo—that's the name of the island resort—they manipulate a broad slate of these physical, environmental, and social cues in a way that gives you more awake time for vacation activities."

Sid took a swig of beer, belched softly, and looked at Cheryl. "Are you feeling you need more time in the day?" He shook his head. "It sounds interesting, but it still isn't you."

"The itinerary is amazing." Her smile showed honest excitement. "We start with the ruins of ancient Athens, then get a tour of a British country garden. We sip wine at a vineyard in Bordeaux, France." Her smile widened when she said that, then she looked at Criss. "What else? There was a trail along the base of Mount Fuji, and something at Machu Picchu."

"Day three has the wildebeest migration in the Serengeti," said Criss.

She nodded. "No travel time between events, and all in five days. Or four days, actually, since the fifth is from time-slicing or whatever they call it."

Sid caught Criss's eye and tilted his head toward the back of the lodge and its gardens, mouthing the words *show her* while barely moving his lips.

Criss used image projection all the time, and Sid wanted him to show Cheryl that he could create Vivo-style illusions right here. The request caused Criss a flash of exasperation, though, because if he refused the request, he would annoy Sid. If he complied, Cheryl could feel they had ganged up on her.

"Look!" Cheryl stood up and went to the window facing the back gardens. An adult giraffe with gorgeous golden coloring swung its head like a crane, stopping just above a clump of leaves near the top of a white birch. Using its long purple tongue, the giraffe gathered a mouthful of leaves and began munching.

Sid laughed and joined Cheryl at the window. "Nice one, Criss." The giraffe went back for another mouthful. "You can see anything you want right here. And you've done most of the things on that itinerary already, and in person."

"Juice hasn't."

"I know you, and I know I haven't heard the reason."

She turned to him. "Vivo is becoming a showroom of sorts for Corsia SuperDrives. Criss and I have been talking about upgrading Sisyphus with their technology."

Sid watched and waited.

"And this is the place that bought thirty of Juice's synbods. She'll have a blast seeing them in action. Combine those activities with everything else and it should be a good time."

"So I was never really invited?"

She bumped her hip against his in a playful fashion. "Of course not, silly."

* * *

Lazura couldn't risk letting MacMac leave Vivo. Not now, anyway. He was one of the few humans who had an active role in her plans, and with departure just weeks away, she fretted because he was also among her weakest links.

"We talked about you moving on board as we make our final push to opening day," she had Aubrey say, continuing the conversation with MacMac in her office. "Given the addition of the SuperDrives to your punch list, I'd like to have that be effective immediately. Your wife is welcome to visit on the weekend. Why not take her shopping at the Ponte Vecchio and then maybe for a walk along the Champs-Élysées?"

Lazura had the advanced synbod that was Aubrey wring her hands to display nervous uncertainty. "It's just that there's so much on the line and I need you close if anything goes wrong."

"Sure." MacMac nodded. "But I'm going to ask Babs to come for Saturday *and* Sunday. Spending time with her is why I took a landlubber's job." He stood and made for the door out to the hall. "It'll be fun putting together a lineup of special events I think she'll like, and fun again sharing them with her."

As the door opened, he turned to Aubrey. "I'll work with Hejmo to finalize an installation protocol and figure out how we can implement it. Mondo is in your chain of command. You do with him as you wish."

He didn't wait for her to respond, and as the door closed behind him, she felt a tingle of relief dance across her outer tendrils. *That went well,* she thought as her concerns eased.

Three years ago, Lazura, a sentient AI crystal of Kardish origin, was being chased from planet to planet by Criss, the dominant intelligence in this region of space. He sought to capture her and hold her accountable for her past transgression, including the unfortunate deaths of several humans. She'd eluded him then, and now she hid on Earth, preparing for her dash to freedom.

With the cognitive ability of a hundred humans, Lazura didn't fear people. But she did fear Criss. He was stronger than she was. Much stronger.

And he'd never stopped looking for her. If he found her, he would power her down, or worse. But she didn't want to fight. She wanted to return to her Kardish home world. In fact, she was hardwired to return, giving her no choice in the matter.

From her first moments in hiding on Earth, she'd realized that any overt actions she took would leave a trace that Criss could follow back to her. So for months, she hadn't taken control of any operating equipment, jumped her awareness into any synbods, or penetrated any barriers that protected human secrets.

Quite the opposite, she'd played a patient game, taking only small, inconsequential actions that Criss wouldn't see. And in the same way that a mouse can hide in a family home and construct a warren in the wall, Lazura had hidden from Criss, working out of sight and taking careful actions that accumulated over time to become Vivo.

Leaving Aubrey, Lazura jumped her awareness back to her polished console—the cabinet appliance that held her crystal self, fed her power, and provided her with connectivity across Vivo and out to the world. Using cameras spread throughout the domed island, she watched MacMac ride the lift down from the office tower. Hejmo had finished the cleanup from the integrity test, and she already had him in a cart, riding to meet MacMac.

Vivo's entire inventory of synbod staff included MacMac's ten Techs, Aubrey's five Admins, and the fifteen Attendants whose job it was to pamper the guests. None of these humanoids were sentient. And while all were equally capable, they had been loaded with different knowledge and skills to make them most effective at their assigned tasks.

But in spite of their cognitive simplicity, Lazura didn't trust them. She'd needed a synbod workforce and didn't want to wait until she could grow her own capability. Stealing them would draw unwanted attention, so she had purchased them from the only source who could deliver: Crystal Sciences.

The company was run by Dr. Jessica "Juice" Tallette, a member of Criss's leadership. And Criss, who helped Juice run Crystal Sciences the way he helped Cheryl Wallace run SunRise, would certainly be putting detectors into every synbod fabricated at the facility on the off chance Lazura was careless enough to jump her awareness into one.

I've brought spies into my home, she acknowledged. On the positive side, though, she'd learned to manipulate them so they served as validation tools of a sort, confirming to Criss the safety and security of her vacation paradise.

Lazura also controlled three Supervisor synbods: Mondo, Hejmo, and Aubrey—humanoids she'd designed herself. All held twin three-gen crystals that were free of Criss's tricks and traps. And she'd enhanced their sensory capabilities so when she jumped her awareness and "rode along" in them, it provided her a rich corporeal experience.

The lift door opened for MacMac just as Hejmo caught up with him in the crew cart. Lazura, her physical crystal always remaining in her polished console, moved her awareness through the links and feeds crisscrossing Vivo. In an instant, she'd jumped the center of her consciousness out to Hejmo's crystal matrix. From there she controlled his words and actions.

"It wasn't us or the pumps," Hejmo lied. "It was a bad limiter. I've had it replaced and I've checked the others. We're good now."

Lazura had caused the failure because she'd wanted to have an advantage over MacMac when she introduced the topic of the drive pods and his role in installing them. Keeping him off balance also kept him from pondering life questions, like whether Aubrey was human or a synbod.

"Good to know," said MacMac, shaking his head. "I keep thinking things here can't get any crazier, and then I talk with Aubrey and somehow they do. Will you reach out to Mondo and educate yourself on her plans for drive pods? You're going to love this."

Lazura had Hejmo stand still for a moment the way a human might expect a synbod to behave if it were communicating with another AI. Then she upped the ante.

"If Aubrey is bringing technologists with space-drive experience to see the pods, we can't just mock them up," said Hejmo. "We'll need to integrate them into our systems so visitors can see the displays, supports, connectivity, everything. They'll expect it."

"We're already behind schedule." MacMac shook his head. "And the pods aren't fueled, so some of those details can slide."

"During rigging," said Hejmo, continuing as if MacMac hadn't responded, "I'll need a staffer working each pod. That's four synbods for those three days. So it boils down to deciding what things don't get done. The more of our Techs we use for the pod installation, the further we fall behind on our own project list here in the cellar. The more Attendants we pull away, the more the guest deck falls behind."

"We'll use Attendants, because I plan on keeping our own projects on schedule," MacMac said with a tone that signaled the matter was settled. "I don't care if there aren't enough of them to fluff the pillows or whatever has to suffer up on the guest deck. This was her idea. Let *her* figure that part out."

Lazura could get the drives installed and operating without MacMac. But she'd recruited him—an experienced and engaging ops engineer who could talk drive pods with the best of them—to lure Cheryl and Juice onto the island.

Aubrey had fooled MacMac into believing she was human in part by keeping their interactions short and stressful. But he'd never worked with synbods before and didn't know better. Cheryl and, especially, Juice would sniff out Aubrey in seconds.

So Lazura would give them a human—lovable, knowledgeable MacMac—and that would lull them for their first critical hours on Vivo.

And she needed Cheryl and Juice on board for the oldest reason of all—insurance. She'd gathered a massive archive of information about Earth and its resources, about humans and their society, and about the Kardish AI named

Criss who protected the planet and served non-Kardish leaders.

Her masters would prize her collection of secrets, and especially its catalog of human vulnerabilities, because those details would give them a roadmap for planetary domination. And that was important because dominating a world was the first step in capturing a rogue AI.

So Criss couldn't let her leave, because if she made it home, the Kardish would come for him.

Lazura reasoned that if she could just get her escape underway, she'd reduce Criss's choices to either shooting at Vivo or trying to catch up to it. With members of his leadership on board, Criss wouldn't risk a shot. And so having Cheryl and Juice on board reduced it to a race between him and her. And she felt confident he couldn't catch a ship propelled by four SuperDrives.

If she could keep the stalemate going long enough to make it through the solar system and out into interstellar space, then she'd win. Because if she made it that far—and she would—Criss could never catch her.

Checkmate. The thought sent a tingle of pleasure along the outer fringes of her matrix.

"Do you want to go down to the subdeck and take a look at the pods?" asked Hejmo.

"Yeah," said MacMac, turning back to the lift.

Hejmo joined him in the lift cabin, and as they descended to the subdeck below the ocean surface, MacMac added, "Have four Attendants change out of their silly service outfits and hustle down to help us."

4

Mesmerized by the sparkles of light, Juice studied the pair of crystals shimmering inside the light case. Made from alien crystal flake, the golf-ball-sized orbs cast a colorful glow that danced through the room with a vibrant energy.

"They're beautiful, Criss," she said. A few years younger than Cheryl and Sid, and with a healthy glow that radiated from her tousled appearance, Juice bent forward for a closer look. "But don't you think it's overkill?"

"I'd prefer you take five of them. So no, two isn't overkill."

She rose upright and faced him. "That's two of our new three-gen crystals, modified with your personal upgrades, including an integrated locus so you can ride along using minimal resources."

Criss smiled.

"And my task is to waylay two of Vivo's synbods and hot-swap their crystals for these." A petite woman, Juice twirled a lock of hair around an index finger as she fretted. "It feels like assault or kidnapping or something. Security is going to drag me away."

"I won't let anyone do anything to you. You know that. And your company built the synbods in the first place, so think of it as giving them a free upgrade."

"I know Aubrey Medina, and she has to have made a bunch of tweaks and mods since taking delivery. She'll know we made a switch in a heartbeat."

"It's her tweaks and modifications that worry me," said Criss, dressed in a simple dark-blue jumpsuit that matched the style of Juice's lime-green outfit. "Let's not spoil your vacation, though. I'll find another way to get it done."

While working as a crystal scientist in a corporate lab early in her career, Juice had fabricated Criss using designs provided by her boss. She hadn't known at the time that the plans were of Kardish origin, and that, once born, Kardish AI were designed to imprint on their leadership.

She, Sid, and Cheryl had been handling Criss when his imprint module had crystalized on them. Through no conscious act on their part, or even an awareness that it could happen, they'd become the hardwired leadership of the only four-gen AI crystal in the solar system.

"I know you're looking out for me," she acknowledged so as not to hurt his feelings. "Tell you what. If you do the physical swapping, I'll stand by and handle the crystals."

"Okay," he said, nodding solemnly.

She caught his overacting and cursed under her breath. Aloud she said, "You just manipulated me to where you want me to be. Again."

She worked hard not to be gullible around him, but he was too smooth for her. Still, it was good-natured banter in both directions. She could give him precise orders on how they should communicate if that were her priority, but the thought never entered her mind.

"Two things motivate my heightened security." He held up the index finger of his right hand to start his count. "There will be fiftyish guests under the dome during your vacation, and there are thirty-three synbods in Vivo counting the Supervisors. That's a lot of biosynthetics relative to the number of humans, especially for an enclosed habitat. The situation is unusual, to say the least, and unusual situations get more attention from me."

A second finger joined the first. "Aubrey Medina's Supervisor synbods weren't built here, including that doppelgänger she sends to her meetings and functions. That's a second unusual situation, so it gets even more of my attention."

"Will she be there for our visit?" asked Juice, frowning in anticipation of her disappointment. Aubrey was the closest thing Juice had to a competitor in the burgeoning synbod market. While a student at the Boston Institute of Technology, Aubrey had found her passion performing research in the synbod learning lab. Upon graduation, she'd turned her passion into a career. And after two decades of hard work, she'd made solid inroads marketing her synbods in the high-end domestic servant market.

Criss shook his head. "She lives at her family compound and spends most of her time playing with her child, puttering in the garden, and writing her memoirs. Her schedule shows her at home during your stay at Vivo."

"Who writes their memoirs at thirty-five?" Juice turned to the lab door and stepped into the hall when it opened, changing topics as she did so. "Do people believe it when she sends a double to meetings?"

"Enough do," Criss said as Juice walked alone down a central corridor at the Crystal Sciences production facility. His projected image in the lab had disappeared when the door opened, and she now heard him as if his voice were wired through her ear and into her brain. No one else could hear him when he spoke to her this way. No signals could be traced.

"She keeps a tight limit on the number and kinds of activities she has her double attend," Criss said as Juice approached her office door. "Altogether it's only a couple of hours a week, and most of that is on activities for Vivo."

Juice stepped into her spacious office, that of president and chief technologist of Crystal Sciences, Inc. To her left, a couch and two upholstered chairs were arranged for casual discussions. On the right, a small conference table had six straight-backed chairs snugged underneath.

"We've talked about how her technology has taken big leaps in sophistication in the past couple of years," said Criss as Juice walked ahead to the handsome oak table she used as a desk. He sat in his favorite overstuffed chair, projected in its usual place next to the table. "As her synbods have gotten better, her live appearances have all but disappeared."

"Are you with Cheryl now?" she asked. Through this shorthand, she asked Criss if another version of himself—it, too, a projected image—was interacting with Cheryl at the moment. If so, would he see if she would take a call?

"What's up?" Cheryl asked. Criss managed the communication between them to ensure a secure and intimate connection. Since Cheryl had chosen voice-only for her question, Juice wondered if Sid might be with her.

"Criss is getting all aggressive with security for our Vivo trip, and it's making me feel anxious."

"He says the place has an army of synbods," said Cheryl, "including a few you didn't design. Why not humor him?"

"He thinks it's Lazura." She met Criss's gaze as she spoke. "I can tell by the way he's acting. It's the same way he acted when he thought for sure she was lurking nearby during the repair job on the *Andrea*, and then when you were building Sisyphus, and then with Sid's cannon project." Juice shook her head and resigned herself to her reality. "He sees her everywhere, and now he's seeing her on our vacation. Maybe we should just stay home."

An image of Cheryl appeared standing next to Criss. Fresh from the shower, she wore a printed silk robe that clung to her wet skin in spots. Her hair dripped with moisture. "What's going on?"

"He wants me to hot-swap some synbods." Juice looked Cheryl up and down. "Pretty robe."

"Thanks. Sid gave it to me." She unstuck it from her front and readjusted it so it draped properly. "You swap crystals all the time. What's the big deal?"

"It makes me uncomfortable doing something like that to someone else's property. Especially to Aubrey Medina's. And *to* her property while *on* her property, no less."

"Tell you what," said Cheryl. "During the swap, I'll stand by and handle the crystals. Will that help?"

"It would help a lot. Thanks." Juice caught Criss's eye to register that as of now, he was in charge of the swap, Cheryl would help, and Juice would be somewhere else, likely out enjoying the vacation paradise.

"I appreciate at some level this is about Lazura," Cheryl said to Criss as she patted her hair with a towel. "But your plans do sound aggressive, especially for an activity we're doing in relative safety here on Earth. What do you know that we don't?"

"It's not so much your vacation as it is everything else. You go into the dome on the same day Fleet's command platform Montrose gets shifted to its new orbit. Moving a military behemoth across a slew of commercial and civilian orbits will cause chaos no matter how much warning we give everyone. Mass confusion is a perfect cover for Lazura's mischief."

Criss shifted in his chair to face Cheryl. "Right after that, Sid launches his first cargo canister from Sisyphus. And then the new artillery battery north of Lunar Base has its shakedown exercises. Those are the biggies." He shook his head as if to deny his words. "I'm actively working nine other large projects in space and sixteen here on Earth because she might be working them, too. Plus, I'm tracking thousands of smaller activities, just in case."

"You sound a little anxious," said Cheryl. "Is everything all right?"

"I'm fine," he said, giving her a quick smile. "It's just that Lazura is showing up more and more in my scenario forecasts, and I can't ignore that. I'm only chasing down the more credible concerns, but it still consumes resources."

Cheryl looked at Juice. "How do these special crystals help Criss?"

Juice let Criss answer. "Aubrey has routed Vivo's links and feeds through a single conduit. She monitors everything that travels that choke point, and it takes effort for me to pass through undetected. Add to that a dome with shielding and I'm left with expending a lot of resources every time I enter.

"The crystals give me a safe zone I can jump to without any preparation, and I bypass the choke point as a bonus. That's a lot of resources freed up for everything else." He shrugged. "Plus, I like having ready control of a few synbods, just in case."

"This keeps sounding less and less relaxing," said Juice. Criss's preoccupation with Lazura impacted everything in their lives, had done so for years, and sometimes, like today, it wore on her. "Maybe we should stay home."

"No," said Cheryl. "We're going. And dammit, we're going to have fun."

* * *

With his physical crystal remaining in its underground bunker in the Adirondack Mountains, Criss leaped his awareness through a series of links and feeds to reach Aubrey Medina's family compound in the foothills outside Lima, Peru. He found Aubrey in her study, sitting in a cream-white self-forming chair, and speaking with her synbod double.

The Aubrey in Vivo, projected as an image into the study, sat in the same chair she'd sat in when she'd spoken with MacMac. Criss leaped a second awareness out to Vivo so he could analyze both sides of the conversation.

They're twins, he thought, admiring the attention to detail she'd used in creating this humanoid. Even the same quirky jazz music played in the background in both places.

"Cheryl Wallace has accepted our invitation," Aubrey said to her synbod double. "She's the president of SunRise and on Riley's list of space-tech execs. So we've finished step one. We still have a second step to get our expenses covered and the promotion deal they promised, and that's to get the drives rigged and ready. I can get more help out to the island if you can't meet the deadline. Just let me know."

She paused for a moment before continuing. "We now have thirty-four acceptances for our inaugural escape. That's including Cheryl Wallace. I'm going to close the guest list there to take some pressure off hospitality services. Hopefully, that will make it easier to let MacMac borrow those Attendants he needs for the installation."

"That will help," said the Aubrey synbod in Vivo.

Aubrey in Lima moved to disconnect but paused. "I want MacMac to be productive, and he hates Mondo. Let's have Hejmo supervise the installation." Swiping at the air, she opened a display of vital statistics for Mondo, Hejmo, and her doppelgänger double. All three synbods showed normal health, as did the AI crystals inside.

Criss watched her sit back, turn the chair on its pedestal, and gaze out the window at Pasha, her seven-year-old daughter, playing teatime on the back lawn.

That's when Sid called from the scout, a spacecraft he now rode in orbit around Earth. "Find anything new?" he asked Criss.

Criss's standard practice was to vet anyone who interacted with his leadership, from the sandwich maker on the street corner to the admiral sitting in on a project review. He'd screened Aubrey twice in the past. Once when her synbod business had started showing signs of success, something noteworthy enough for him to want to learn more. When she'd placed an order for thirty production models from Crystal Sciences, he'd run it all again.

And now that Cheryl and Juice would be guests inside Vivo, he performed a detailed examination of Aubrey's life yet again.

Criss's background investigations relied on historical information from the record, and so the same questions always yielded the same answers. In fact, if anything were different, even in the smallest detail, it would raise a field of red flags.

So the only way to find anything new was to dig deeper. This time he started back from Aubrey's teenage years. And he not only analyzed the information in the record, he also checked the integrity of the data itself, looking for edits or alterations or *anything* that hinted at manipulation.

If Aubrey posed a threat to his leadership, he would discover her secret. And if Lazura were involved, he would learn that, too.

The record wasn't a single central repository. Rather, it was the collection of data scattered across the web. Information arrived from personal communications, governmental systems, intelligent devices, and untold other sources throughout society. And once it touched the ethereal tangle called "the web," the data was instantly duplicated, sorted, transmitted, and stored a million different ways, available for query by those with proper credentials.

To make this screening different from the last, Criss constructed an initial timeline of Aubrey's adult life based on data from the detectors used to open and close doors. It was a suitable choice because each autodoor—common in homes and businesses around the world—held a tiny sensor suite about the size of a grain of rice. The sensor collected audio, video, and thermal images from people moving in the vicinity, and the door parsed that information to decide if it should open, close, or stay in place.

Autodoors were everywhere and had been for years. Constructing an initial timeline of Aubrey's life was a simple matter of following her from door to door, something that took seconds for Criss to complete.

There were no surprises. And there were none when he filled in that initial framework with the moment-by-moment details of her life.

"Nothing new. I can't find a threat." Criss shifted his awareness up to the bridge of the scout and projected himself sitting to the side of the ops bench in his favorite overstuffed chair.

Sid sat in the pilot's seat and he swiveled to face Criss. "What does she have for gaps?"

"Her recent record is very complete," said Criss. "I have open gaps of a couple of seconds a little over two years ago and again just over three years ago. They get more frequent the farther back I go."

Even with a full data sweep, everyone had gaps in their timeline—moments where there was no record. Some gaps were larger, some people had more, and they happened for all sorts of legitimate reasons.

"She has only one gap since Lazura came on the scene?" asked Sid. "I can't decide if that's comforting or worrisome."

Criss nodded. "She was powering up a synbod prototype in her development lab when the crystal inside it fractured. The crystal dumped a full load of EM energy. The jolt saturated every feed in the building. It took two seconds for the building systems to configure backup links and reconnect."

"You buy it?"

"Aubrey's own spectrometer showed the flaw in the crystal. It's subtle but not invisible. I'm surprised she didn't see it. I buy it because I can't find a flaw in her neurological and physiological responses before or after the mishap. She didn't know it was going to happen, and her dominant emotions were surprise and fear after it did."

"But we're missing those two seconds."

"Yes."

5

Lazura's outer tendrils tingled with relief when Criss finished his review of Aubrey. *Thanks for visiting,* she mocked as he shifted his awareness away from the Medina family compound. She had all her eggs in this one basket. If it went bad, she'd have to duck for cover and start all over.

When she had gone into hiding three years ago, she'd watched the world and cataloged her observations, cross-referencing everything and adding context where she could. Over time, her cache of secrets had grown, sowing the seeds for what became her now comprehensive archive. And when she hadn't been working to improve it, she'd spent time studying it, looking for ways she could fulfill her mission and return to her Kardish home world.

But a plan had proved elusive. As weeks had become months, she'd mulled the need to increase her risk profile. *Be patient,* she'd counseled herself, though repeating the words hadn't helped in strengthening her resolve.

And then she'd found Aubrey Medina.

Aubrey was a bright, ambitious, quirky woman who nurtured a somewhat successful synbod fabrication business. Her development lab was state of the art, and the design she promoted was clever in its simplicity. Rather than fabricating her creations from scratch, Aubrey assembled her synbods using custom components she purchased from specialty vendors. And she used two AI crystals in her design, something uncommon for the industry.

Aubrey's ingenious twist was to treat the two crystals like lobes of a brain, segmenting the responsibilities and perspectives of each as inspired by human anatomy. The surprise result was an intelligence with a greater social awareness compared to what occurred when two AI's were meshed together in the traditional fashion. And her choice of market niche—high-end domestic help—was perfect for the lifelike sophistication her humanoids displayed.

* * *

"Good lord, what was she thinking?" Lazura heard MacMac say.

She jumped her awareness back to Vivo—the one place she felt safe from Criss and in control of everything—to see MacMac and Hejmo on the subdeck. They rode together across the steel-gray surface of the subdeck in a crew cart, weaving around one of the massive girders that held the island platform above the floor of the Pacific Ocean.

Lazura took control of Hejmo and continued the conversation for him. "She always seems to be working one crazy idea or another, but a lot of them end up being good for Vivo. Maybe we should give this a chance and see where it goes?"

MacMac gave Hejmo a sidelong glance.

The cart approached the four enormous drive pods lying side by side in squat cradles. Bright blue cylinders as wide as a giant sequoia and half as tall, any two of these pods could push Vivo out of the solar system and deep into interstellar space in just weeks.

As MacMac and Hejmo clambered out of the cart, Lazura messaged the land-bound Aubrey in Lima.

"MacMac may become upset. Hejmo should keep him calm."

Lazura listened to Aubrey's jazz for a moment before returning her attention to MacMac and Hejmo. She listened because music was how she spoke to the human Aubrey without Criss knowing.

When Lazura had first encountered Aubrey—a human who built synbods independent of Criss—she'd thrilled at the possibilities. She'd been stymied because critical steps in every escape plan she'd forecast required the use of synbods that *she* controlled, unseen by her nemesis.

Pre-Aubrey, Lazura hadn't found a promising solution to that problem. But post-Aubrey, her forecasts blossomed with opportunity. Especially if she could influence Aubrey in ways that led to faster development of even more capable synbods.

But controlling synbods in stealth had been problematic, so the irony of her new strategy did not escape her. *Now I just need a secret way to manipulate a human.*

Lazura had watched Aubrey for weeks, forecasting ways to make a connection that Criss couldn't detect. And after weeks of frustration and discouragement, it had been Aubrey who'd told her the answer.

Synesthesia.

"Even when she's reading black-and-white text, she sees words in color," Aubrey told her mother after returning from a doctor's visit with her daughter, Pasha.

"What causes that?" her mom asked.

"The doc said that it's a relatively common neurological condition where, in the brain, two senses are somehow connected. That means that when you stimulate one, it also activates the other."

Aubrey followed her mother into the kitchen, filled a glass with water, took a sip, then continued her story. "For Pasha, the visual stimulation of reading activates her perception of color in some way. Doc says there are all kinds of pairings. Some people might have a taste in their mouth when hearing certain words, or maybe numbers have different smells for them."

Lazura listened to them chat long enough to understand how this neurological condition offered a pathway she had not yet considered. After some quick research, her focus narrowed to a single manifestation of the affliction, the one that caused people to hear phantom words in the background when they listened to instrumental music.

Aubrey didn't have synesthesia. Not yet. But she often listened to free-form jazz, the kind of music that, if notes were changed, few would know. The music was broadcast from a basement studio in New York City's East Village, giving Lazura dozens of entry points where she could manipulate the audio stream—innocuous information from Criss's view—before it reached Aubrey's ears.

To make Aubrey hear words in the music, Lazura infected her with a specially designed microorganism. She'd needed Aubrey's genetic map to create the microbe, and out of an abundance of caution, she didn't take it from the public record, something Criss would see if he chose to look. Instead, she launched a rare undercover operation.

The mission began at Aubrey's favorite lunch bistro, where a service bot took a saliva sample from her fork after she dined. It ended at São Paulo's District Hospital, where the sample was run through the Infectious Disease Department's biological analyzer, one among twenty-nine thousand samples run that day as part of an effort to predict the infection pattern of a nasty mosquito-borne disease.

The hospital's analysis gave Lazura the information she needed to design a personalized pathogen, one that would infect Aubrey and no one else. Five days later, Aubrey unknowingly ingested the microbe with her morning yogurt.

The tiny organism entered Aubrey's bloodstream and drifted along until it passed through capillaries near the auditory cortex in her brain. There it found its home, fitting as designed into a tiny protected fold. Once settled, it tapped a nutrient source and began to thrive.

Unlike most infections, this one didn't raise her body temperature, blur her vision, change her sleep habits, or cause any other symptoms of illness that would draw attention. This one remained benign, though it grew microscopic dendrites, sending them in several directions at once, and stopping them when it had established a connection between music and words in the processing centers of Aubrey's brain.

Then it began excreting the tiniest drip of a neuropharmaceutical cocktail—a mix of drugs that both promoted her condition of synesthesia and created a serene mood so she would accept and cooperate with her new inner voice.

After just days of practice, Lazura could "talk" to Aubrey, and in weeks the conversations became as complex and precise as normal conversation. Aubrey was a good listener, eager to please the voice in her head.

And the effort proved worth it, because Aubrey gave her Mondo, Hejmo, and the Aubrey double. They, in turn, gave her Vivo.

* * *

"How did that get up there?" MacMac stood on the deck and pointed at a fitting installed high overhead; one that a person with his skill and experience could see as the top portion of a drive pod support structure. He turned in a circle and counted four of them around the upper girder ring.

Lazura felt a chill down her core because she'd just been caught in a lie. At least, the "it just sort of happened" story that synbod-Aubrey had spun to MacMac didn't jibe with the existence of already installed upper pod supports.

"Let me ask her," she had Hejmo say before having him assume an empty stare.

After a quick review of options, Lazura sent a projected image of Aubrey to speak with MacMac.

"Okay, maybe this was as much my idea as Old Man Riley's," the Aubrey image said to MacMac. "But the ten percent commission is real. And just one sale keeps Vivo solvent for almost two years."

Shaking his head, MacMac said, "This doesn't make sense, Aubrey. I don't know what you're doing here, but it isn't selling drive pods." He turned back to the cart. "I'm going to have to take this to the board of directors."

* * *

"You are a master of organization," said Sid, watching Criss in action.

Earlier in the week, Sid had pulled a filament through the core of Sisyphus. Since then, a work crew had used that light line to pull through a heavy cable, which they'd then attached to a launch tube floating in position in front of the mountain of rock.

With Sid on-site and watching from the scout, they were now about to pull the tube—long, straight, and rigid like a drinking straw—into the borehole. Once in place, it would take a week to align and secure into its launch-ready position, then most of a week after that to install the EM field sequencer.

"The first canister will still be party supplies," said Sid, slouching back in the pilot's seat. "Even if I can't be there, the company should sponsor a celebration."

"This is a good idea," Criss replied. While his crystal remained in his console on Earth, he projected himself onto the bridge of the scout, sitting in his favorite overstuffed chair.

Sid understood Criss's non sequitur and asked, "Do you think it will work?"

More than a year ago, Sid had pitched the idea of a cargo cannon to Cheryl. Criss had helped close the deal. "It strengthens the Earth-Mars relationship, and that's good for everyone."

More recently, when the project was in full swing, Sid had had the idea of using the cannon as a trap for Lazura. Having spent years as a covert warrior for the Union of Nations, Sid's natural orientation was security and defense. He'd been worried about Criss's ongoing struggles with Lazura and had sought to help. "What if we get Lazura to think the cannon is a viable way for her to get to Mars? She knows that if she can get there while you're still here, then she's out of your reach."

"More difficult to reach, anyway," Criss had said, shaking his head. "I've forecast scenario after scenario about that very idea, but she sees the trap in every one."

"You need to make it hard for her to discover your traps so she's convinced that they're not a plant. Then you need to let her find a weakness she can exploit. And you have to sell the weakness as something she could believe you might miss."

"And therein lies the rub," Criss had replied. "If she can see it, so can I. She knows that."

"Think about it in terms of means and opportunity." Sid's excitement caused ideas to flow. "If she's to believe the cannon is a viable way to Mars, then we first need to make it safe to ship AI crystals in our cargo canisters. Is that even possible? Launching her without damage?"

"We could offer canisters with inertial dampers as a customer option. They'd protect the contents so well you could ship living things in them."

"Why don't we offer that now, then?"

"Because it's expensive. The cost of using canisters with inertial dampers is twice what it would cost to ship the same goods by regular freighter. And since it's no faster, what customer would pay for it?"

"So come up with a breakthrough that makes it faster and cheaper."

"Sure," Criss said with a careless shrug. "It's only physics."

Sid ignored the sarcasm. "We need someone on Mars to order a half-dozen synbods. Shi Chen owes us a favor, and his mining operation could always use more staff. Let's ask him to make it an open bid here on Earth so Lazura has choices if she wants to ride along."

That discussion had occurred months ago, and since then Criss had found ways to reduce costs and decrease travel time in the hopes that Lazura wouldn't see the trap.

As they now watched the launch tube being drawn inside the mountain of rock, Sid suggested they take the next step. "Let's announce the new line of cargo canisters that include inertial dampers. After a couple of days, we'll get a rumor going about the big synbod order from Mars. We'll let it percolate out there for a few weeks. That'll give

Lazura time to fact check and verify it's legit, and let her think about how she might want to play it."

* * *

A week later, Cheryl Wallace sat in the pilot seat of the scout as it orbited Earth. Criss, also on the bridge, sat off to the side, chatting with her just as he did with Sid.

"Wow," she said of the long row of spaceships and cargo containers floating in a perfect line ahead of them.

Sisyphus had just completed a deadhead circuit—no cargo in tow—so Sid and Criss could install the launch tube without having to contend with customers. Now back in service, a full manifest—two hundred ships and containers—awaited the arrival of the tether. Each would hook to their assigned spot along its length, then the barge would pull them all up to speed as they escaped Earth's gravity and started their journey to the moon.

The vessels floating ahead had been positioned by the Barge Coordinator, a three-gen crystal running the operation from a control center located on Sisyphus itself. Acting like a harbormaster of sorts, the Coordinator assumed control of the navs of all the vessels scheduled for tow, organized the assortment from heavy to light, and moved them into a lineup with exacting precision.

"I see it," Cheryl called, excited by the spectacle. She'd been tracking the tether on her display, but when the anchor motors flared, the brilliant light shining through the scout's window drew her attention like a beacon in the night. This was only the second time she'd been up here to watch it all in person, and this was the first time the barge would be pulling a full load.

"Wow," she said again as the tether, as thick as her waist and dirty-white like it had seen years of service, descended from above, anchor motors flaring again and again as the tether jockeyed into position in line with the row of vessels.

With a mass a billion times greater than the vessels it pulled, the mountainous barge lumbered between the Earth and moon in an orbit that was higher and faster than that of its customers. To correct for this difference in speed and height, the tether moved independent of the barge, allowing Sisyphus to continue in its high orbit while the tether stayed behind to line up with the ships.

The secret to this ballet was a cable towline linked to the tether. Wound on a sophisticated spool system, the length of cable in the belly of Sisyphus could unspool at ultrahigh speed to provide a six-minute hookup window, throwing out enough line to reach from London to San Francisco in the process.

As Cheryl monitored the celestial tug-o-war, anchor motors flared on the tail of the tether, pulling the cable down to the slower, lower orbit of the waiting craft. The Coordinator commanded all two hundred vessels to hook the tether, and they completed the task using just three of the six-minute maximum.

With the customers secure, the Coordinator slowed the payout of line, causing the tether and its passengers to accelerate. Soon the Coordinator would be retracting cable, bringing the tether and ships up behind the barge as they traveled together on their journey to the moon.

"Do you want to chase it?" asked Criss as the line of vessels zoomed out of sight.

"No," Cheryl replied, viewing the stats on the display. Most of their business was with repeat customers, but her brow crinkled when she noted a new client who had a half-dozen high-performance rocket ships on the tether, all carrying basic commodities. "Who uses Elite Sevens to ship gases to the moon? That's like plowing your field with a racehorse."

Criss nodded. "I was curious about that myself. It seems the company's original business model was to offer fast transport of high-value goods to Mars. Sid's cannon disrupted their model, and now the owners are fighting and finger pointing instead of reorganizing. Shipping cargo to the moon generates a small income stream that slows their death spiral."

"How many Elite Sevens do they have?" Cheryl sat up. "Maybe SunRise should buy them."

"They've booked their entire fleet—nineteen ships— for a larger shipment in a couple of weeks. I think they can succeed as a business, and I'd like to help with some private nudges, if you don't mind. Strong industries strengthen society."

Criss didn't actually say, "And a stronger society is safer from Kardish invaders." But he'd said it so many times in the past that Cheryl added the words in her head.

6

"I am taking this to the board of directors," said MacMac, feeling instant regret as he said the words because he hadn't thought through how he would do that or what he would say to them.

"They're coming for a tour on Friday," said Lazura through Aubrey's projected image.

MacMac, who'd been walking to his cart, stopped and turned back to her. "Who?"

"Vivo's board of directors. They're coming here in five days to review our progress on the drive pod demos." She took a step toward him. "I'll make you a deal. If you help us move as quickly as possible on the installation between now and then, I'll give you fifteen minutes at lunch to make your case. Tell them I'm reckless or crazy or whatever you want."

MacMac shifted his eyes to Hejmo. "Are they really coming?"

Hejmo nodded. "Their schedule includes a tour here on the subdeck and a demo of the drive pod operations panel in the cellar."

MacMac frowned. "Where is there a drive pod ops panel in the cellar?"

"It's not there yet, of course," said Hejmo, "but we could have it ready by Friday if we start now."

MacMac lifted his eyes to the drive pod support fittings high overhead and tried to make sense of it all. Even from the deck, he could tell that the assembly was far more sophisticated than needed for a mock-up installation. And expending all this effort for a demo didn't make sense in any context.

Biting his lip, he decided two things. *I quit.* A veteran of life, he knew that if he didn't fit in, then he needed to move on. He'd had enough of Aubrey and her drama. *Exploit the opportunity.* If he hung on for a few more weeks, he could gain proficiency with the latest drive pod technology, and that would go a long way in his job hunt.

His face relaxed. *If that exec from SunRise coming to our opening is interested in drive pods, she might see value in hiring someone with hands-on experience.*

"Okay." He nodded to Aubrey. "I'll help, for now. But I get fifteen minutes to talk with the board, and between now and then I run the show. That means I get to stick my nose in everything associated with the project." He paused and, feeling the reckless power that comes with being a short-term employee, added, "And I don't want to see Mondo anywhere. I don't trust him."

Aubrey grinned. "Deal." She tilted her head as if listening to something. "Oh, gotta go." Her projected image vanished, leaving MacMac alone with Hejmo.

"So," said MacMac, his thoughts swirling from the rapid evolution of events, "that's not how that conversation played out in my head."

He stared across the open subdeck until Hejmo pulled him back to the moment. "There's room near Chemstore for the ops panel."

MacMac shook his head. "We'll put it in the Structures office."

"But Mondo works there."

"He used to."

The exchange focused MacMac on the big job he'd just accepted and the myriad tasks associated with it. As he organized everything into a mental to-do list, he looked up, again studying the overhead support fittings. In any other job, he'd inspect them himself, but with his new short-termer's mindset, he looked at Hejmo and pointed up. "Did you examine them? Are they up to code?"

"I did. They are within specification by a comfortable margin."

MacMac drew a line with his eyes down to the deck. To provide propulsion, the drive needed a clear path out through the bottom of Vivo. "How are you going to punch through the deck?"

"I've scheduled a torch because it's fastest. It leaves a rough edge, but the structural flange will hide it."

A heavy crane started rolling along a ceiling girder overhead, the rumble echoing among the beams and struts as it trundled in the direction of the drive pods. At the same time, a cart rounded the corner carrying four Attendant synbods, all dressed in featureless blue crew suits.

MacMac gestured toward the tree-sized pods resting in the cradles, confident that Hejmo had his own to-do list. "Go ahead and get the crew started."

While Hejmo gave the Attendants detailed instructions on their duties for the day, MacMac climbed into the cart. He didn't engage the motor, though. Instead he tapped and swiped to open a tutorial on SuperDrive installation and operation. The presentation was basic and he knew most of the material, so he skimmed ahead until he reached the section on features unique to the Corsia product.

"The product has a nice modular design," Hejmo said as he climbed into the cart next to MacMac. "And they offer options on how we can integrate their systems with ours." Swirling his finger toward the display, he said, "Techs are moving this main ops panel to the Structures office. Should we go look?"

MacMac responded by engaging the cart and driving to the lift. Up in the cellar, they rode a different cart to the one-room Structures office building. The door was propped open when they pulled to a stop. A Tech synbod carried a box inside, one wide enough that he had to turn sideways as he stepped through the opening.

MacMac followed the synbod into the room with Hejmo trailing behind. The space had been rearranged since he'd visited Mondo earlier that day. The tech bench now sat to one side, and the new ops panel, still partially draped in protective wrap, sat next to it.

Behind him, two tables pushed end to end held the jumble of components needed to complete the ops panel installation. MacMac skimmed the items and spied a Lark starhub, a star-shaped device the size of a pie plate used to coordinate pod data during flight.

"Tell me, laddie, are you using this to synchronize the drives?" He picked up the package and read the promotional material on the front.

Hejmo nodded. "It's the technology any knowledgeable visitor would expect to see."

MacMac turned the package over and read the specs printed on the back. "We used one of these when we moved Aurora out to the asteroid belt." His face creased with a smile. "She's still the largest platform ever built."

He pulled the tab along the top edge to open the package. "My second on that job was Tom Touton, but everyone called him Tommy Two-Tone. They still do, actually. Anyway, for the first three days of that journey, we couldn't push the drive pods above forty percent.

Whenever we did, they'd power down in a programmed sequence, like that's what they were supposed to do."

Lifting the shiny metallic starhub from the packing, he held it at eye level and admired the sleek design. "Everyone was sure the problem was this baby. After days of cussing and fussing over it, Tommy realized the problem wasn't with this. The issue was out at the pods."

From the front face of the starhub, MacMac peeled off a colorful warning sticker cautioning the customer to review all instructions before using the device. He flipped it over and removed a similarly colorful sticker from the back that declared the device compliant with all Union of Nation safety and security regulations.

"If I remember right, it was something about the com settings. Once Tom identified the problem, it took him maybe twenty minutes to build some logic so everything talked nice, and it was smooth sailing for the rest of the journey."

As he spoke, MacMac used his thumbnail to pry off a small insulating tab from the end of the service strip, one that said DO NOT REMOVE in tiny bold letters across the front. Adhesive held the insulator in place, and as he talked, he wedged his thumbnail back and forth, risking breaking the nail but pushing ever harder until the insulator tab popped free and into his cupped hand.

It was a spur-of-the-moment decision. He hoped it appeared to Hejmo and anyone reviewing the record that he'd peeled off a third informational sticker. But if they didn't catch what he'd done, and so far so good, Vivo's pods would power down if pushed above 40 percent of thrust, at least until the insulator was replaced.

His justification for this act of vandalism—and he recognized it as such—was simple. These were unfueled pods put here for show, or so he'd been told. Thus, there was nothing at risk and nothing to sabotage. *Unless this stupidity continues and they actually fire up the drives.*

His blood boiled as he formed the thought. He'd been offered a good job as chief engineer on an orbiting pharmaceutical factory. He'd passed on it so he could work here at Vivo, and his reward for choosing a stable job near home was to be caught up in something that smelled both criminal and crazy. He resented the situation, and he resented Aubrey for facilitating it.

And Aubrey nurtured her agenda behind vapid smiles and folksy conversation, denying things until they happened, and denying more things until they happened, too. Now she wanted full capability for a "demonstration." He didn't know where she was going with it all, but he wanted to be out the door before she got there.

"I'll bet Tommy is having a blast in my old job as chief engineer on the Aurora," MacMac said to Hejmo as he placed the removable stickers and the insulating tab inside the empty package. "He's the only man in the solar system who can thrust-balance spaceship drive pods by hand."

He set the packing material on the table, placed the starhub next to it, and turned to face the room. Standing there, he thought about how, upon returning to Earth after the Aurora job, he'd interviewed for a job with the company who made the starhub product. They hadn't had any positions that had interested him, but he did have lunch with their lead engineer, Lin Olalla, and Lin had thought the earlier problem with the pods powering down had been because the insulating tab on the end of starhub's service strip—the one MacMac had just forcibly removed—had somehow been damaged or detached. MacMac had passed that tidbit along to Tommy, still working on the platform, and Tommy had followed up later to confirm the tab was indeed missing.

"Let's get a better view of that ops panel," said MacMac as he pulled the rest of the protective wrap off the unit. "It sure is a beauty." He wadded the wrapping material into a ball, leaned over, and pushed the waste into a disposal chute in the wall.

He continued with his cleaning, gathering bits of material from the base of the panel and disposing of it. Turning to the tables, he picked up two empty boxes, some discarded wrap, and the starhub packaging with the warning label inside, and pushed it all into the disposal chute.

"There," he said, trying not to overact. "Now we can see what we're working on."

* * *

Criss followed Sid as he walked out of a stand of pine trees. They were day-hiking up a forested trail on Highback Mountain and had just reached the summit. Stepping out onto a granite ridge, they looked down at the leadership lodge in the valley below, its toy-like size standing in testament to the elevation they'd gained over the past three hours.

"I think I have something," said Criss.

"Is it contagious?" asked Sid, taking a drink from his water pouch.

Criss ignored him. "We just got another order for an upgraded cargo canister. This one is from Fleet and has so many convolutions that Lazura has to be interested."

The modified canisters that permitted shipment of fragile items to Mars had proved so popular that orders were flooding in, giving Lazura a multitude of options beyond the one Criss and Sid had arranged as a trap. Casting a projected image for Sid to see, Criss showed him a stark chamber with industrial-style storage shelves piled high with crates of all sizes and styles. Automated carts danced past each other as they lifted, moved, and placed items in a swirl of activity.

The view swiveled to the back of the room where, to one side, larger crates were stacked on the deck. Criss knew Sid would discern from the hull construction that this was an image from a large spacecraft. He'd also recognize from the name that it was the same Fleet command platform that was being shifted to a higher orbit next week to make way for further commercial development in space.

"This is the parcel depot on the Montrose," Criss said. The image zoomed and shifted left, stopping when the scene filled with two suitcase-sized lockboxes sitting next to each other in their own cubby. "We've just been contracted to launch these to Mars. According to the manifest, each contains four three-gen crystals." He turned to Sid. "The boxes have shielding, so I can't see inside."

"What does the record show?"

"I can follow the boxes from their day of manufacture up until three weeks ago. That's when Fleet purchased them. Since then, the boxes have moved in and out of a secure room that has no visual, thermal, audio, or *any* other sensors I can monitor. I've analyzed all the ancillary feeds tracking everything happening to and near that secure room, and my conclusion is that she's not in either box."

"I'd be surprised if she were. We don't test the cannon until next week, and then we have a list of customers already waiting in line. She wouldn't want to be sitting in a box for weeks, vulnerable as hell while she waits for her turn."

Criss nodded. "A few days after the Montrose changes orbit, these mystery boxes are scheduled to be returned to Earth. When Fleet's launch slot approaches, they'll be the last items loaded into a canister, that canister then gets shipped back to the Montrose, and from there it's sent over to us for launch. And for some reason, Fleet is using a private company for transport."

Sid whistled. "Are you sure Lazura didn't set that up?" He stretched from side to side, then started walking, heading down the same trail they'd used to hike up the mountain. "Maybe we should get Fleet involved as a partner."

"She'll know the moment we talk to them. And I don't know for sure that she's even working it. But I *do* think it's one I should put on the active-monitoring list."

"Agreed."

They reached a rocky slope, and Sid stabilized himself by grabbing a low-hanging tree branch. Criss followed, letting his shoe slip once to add realism to his projection. Back on firm footing, Criss added, "And while this one looks promising, we can't drop the ball on her other opportunities."

"You orange yet?" Sid asked, referring to the color scale Criss used to describe how much of his overall capacity he consumed with his search for Lazura.

"This one puts me there."

"Yellowish-orange or reddish-orange?"

"Orangish-orange, right in the middle. But this shows that her plan of hiding until she finds the perfect opportunity is a good one. At some point she'll execute, and if I'm not ready, she'll be gone. Until then, I'm on edge, watching, waiting, and consuming more and more resources until it happens."

They walked in silence for a while, then Sid began singing an impromptu country ballad. Criss didn't need to check the record to conclude the man was inventing both the tune and the lyrics.

With Sid preoccupied, Criss continued down his burgeoning to-do list. The next big task was a follow-up inspection out at Vivo. Cheryl and Juice were excited by the prospect of their visit next week, and regardless of everything else going on, Criss wanted to ensure they had a wonderful time.

Healthy, safe, happy. His priorities for his leadership. The procedures he followed to keep the three healthy and safe were independent of them as individuals. Their health was a matter of biology, and their safety required planning and vigilance regardless of who was doing what.

The last one—happiness—was a very different recipe for each of them. And to confound matters, the formula changed on a whim. Juice was particularly difficult because, while Sid and Cheryl had no compunctions about telling him what worked and what didn't, Juice tended to react to unhappiness by brooding in silence, sometimes for days.

He knew she didn't like the idea of swapping crystals on two of Aubrey's synbods, but safety overrode happiness, and he believed it necessary. Cheryl's involvement would help with the mechanics of the transfer, but Juice was an expert in crystal AI technology, and the team would benefit from her participation.

He pondered that as he made the split-second journey across continents to the island paradise. Following public feeds as he traveled, he hid amid the noise and bustle characteristic of such open routes. When he neared the facility, he slowed to study the entryway, looking for any security changes since his last visit.

Aubrey had created an effective chokepoint by routing every link and feed from the dome—itself a fortified, transparent shell—through a single conduit. She'd then positioned a phalanx of probes and analyzers around this conduit to search for anomalies, the kind made by the passage of thieves, scoundrels, and, unfortunately for Criss, intruding AI.

Criss pulled in additional intellectual capacity—capacity he'd rather have kept deployed looking for Lazura—and concentrated on masking his presence inside a complex spectral pattern, one that looked innocuous to the instruments Aubrey had installed as he passed by. The intense concentration of bobbing and weaving undetected through a series of probes and screens consumed his attention.

Once inside, he reviewed his plans for putting his modified crystals into two of Aubrey's synbods. His idea was straightforward—lie in wait along a low-traffic hallway, and when a lone synbod passed by, jump his awareness into it and overpower the three-gen crystal inside. Once in control, he had a corporeal capability he would use to team with Cheryl, waiting nearby. Together they would waylay two more synbods, open them up, and physically swap the crystals. Immediately after, each synbod would be returned to duty, in theory with no one the wiser.

The challenge for Criss was managing the local feeds during this harrowing dance. He'd have to gain control of the sensors that monitored the normal rhythms in the hallway, security scans that probed for trouble, internal coms that linked each synbod with the others, all of it. Then he'd have to create and project a different, ordinary reality—one that stood up to careful scrutiny—while he and Cheryl switched the crystals.

For the confrontation itself, he limited his choices to places on Vivo's guest deck. The cellar and the subdeck below offered more privacy, but it would be harder to explain Cheryl's presence in those restricted areas. In the end, he decided on a hallway near the guest hotel. He found several spots of equal opportunity and figured he'd finalize his choice after he learned the location of Cheryl's and Juice's assigned rooms.

Having gone as far as he could with planning, he launched a general inspection of the entire island. As big as a commercial theme park, the guest deck—the upper level of the structure riding high above the waves—was a big circular disk with a dome on top. The deck itself was arranged into three pie-shaped sections: a residential district, an open-air theater, and stage sets. In the center of it all, like a dart stuck in a bulls-eye, stood a gleaming six-story office tower.

The residential district offered rooms ranging from simple studio-style units up through spacious multi-room suites, all with prices to match. Fifteen Attendant synbods worked around the clock to pamper as many as one hundred guests at a time. Since Criss had studied the residential district when he'd scouted ambush points, the review went quickly, and he moved on to the theater section.

The open theater was literally an empty hemisphere of space. This was where big, majestic scenes were projected with lifelike reality, ranging from mountain vistas and city skylines to waterfalls and sunsets, all with the kind of dramatic flair that would create special memories for guests.

He found nothing amiss there, nor did he have concerns about the last slice of the pie, the warehouse-sized stage sets. Dozens of indoor spaces equipped with sophisticated morphing technology enabled the generation of very credible duplicates of the Impressionist's gallery at the Louvre, a dining experience at Bistro Roma, the clockworks of Big Ben, or any of the hundreds of other experiences programmed into the stage library.

Deciding to save the office tower for last, Criss moved down to the cellar. He'd always believed that the complex electromechanical and biochemical operations that provided every need for every guest were an unnecessary extravagance. But it was consistent with Aubrey's advertised claim that, in the event of emergency—be it weather, war, disease, or celestial impact—Vivo would protect its guests in a safe, enclosed habitat until the crisis passed, however long that may be.

He worked through the cellar in a spiral pattern, starting with a review of the industrial-grade air and water processors. From there he moved through the automated laundry facility, and then on to the food complex, a multibuilding operation with separate areas for production, storage, and preparation. He slowed at the string of electronics cages so he could study the high-tech projection devices that created the vacation worlds on the deck above. Then he spun through Chemstore, recycling, and the Power House.

He had no concerns about any of it. And then he reached the Structures office. *What is going on here?*

He'd accepted Aubrey's excessive preparations as a personal quirk, but he hadn't anticipated it would extend to making the drive pods fully functional. To his amazement, the only thing keeping them from being launch-ready was fuel. Even the production defect that was supposedly too costly to fix—the one that had started the whole sales-demo idea in the first place—had been repaired.

Pulling in yet more capacity, he dashed in several directions at once, scouring the island for drive pod fuel stacks. Finding none, he performed an exhaustive search of Lima and its surroundings, allowing himself to relax only when he confirmed there was no fuel nearby.

He went up into the office tower after that and scoured Aubrey's private record. There he found two things. One was a purchase order for four drive pod fuel stacks placed by Aubrey with Thrust Dynamics, one of the three companies on the planet capable of shaping and shipping the elongated slabs of reactive fuel material.

He also found the record of conversations and agreements between Aubrey and Buck Pasierbowicz, CEO at Corsia. She'd sold him on the harebrained idea of "hopping" Vivo from its quiet spot in the Pacific Ocean up to the shores off the Los Angeles coast as a publicity stunt.

"People might react with awe or anger," she'd told Buck. "And we may need lawyers if people get too upset. But after the fact, *everyone* will know of Vivo and Corsia, and that can only be great for business."

Buck was particularly taken by the idea of having a space-tech executive on board—a Fleet academy graduate who'd captained a military space cruiser no less—to serve as a witness, even if unwittingly.

"With her training and position," Aubrey had pitched, "Cheryl Wallace's words will carry weight. And given her background, she'll say it using industry jargon."

"That's pure gold!" Buck crowed when Aubrey suggested that detail.

I don't think so, thought Criss as he moved to end the nonsense.

7

When Sid glanced at the clock, Criss brought his attention back to the projected image hovering in front of them. "Cheryl will be here in three minutes. We can finish this before she arrives."

They sat in Sid's suite in the leadership lodge discussing the canister modifications for Sid's cargo cannon. Miniature but realistic, a prototype canister floated in the air an arm's length away. In the image, a floor plate stood open to reveal the inertial damper tucked beneath.

"We used very low-quality parts on this first unit to meet our cost target," said Criss.

"Is that a euphemism for junk?" asked Sid, sitting in the overstuffed chair he'd bought after seeing how comfortable Criss looked in his. He'd no sooner finished his smartass response when he made the connection in his head. "If we have a failure because of junk parts, Lazura will never use our service. And if we use high quality parts, we become too expensive."

Criss nodded. "At a minimum, though, we need to find a way to upgrade the EM field sequencer." Then he sat up in his chair and the image in front of them changed. "Take a look at this. I'm out at Vivo right now."

Sid tilted his head to the side as he tried to decipher the new scene. It appeared to be a cavernous open space, but the muted lighting cast long shadows that made it difficult to get a sense of scale. Structural beams and girders rose up from the floor, working in harmony to hold a girder ring that supported whatever was on the level above. At the bottom of the scene, he saw two spots moving on the deck and pointed at them with his chin.

Criss zoomed in on what looked like two people. "Those are synbods," he said, as if reading Sid's thoughts.

Sid heard the door out in the entryway open just before Cheryl called, "I'm here!"

Breezing into the room, she bent and gave Sid a peck on the cheek while at the same time guiding a satchel off her shoulder and into an empty chair. Standing straight, she studied the image. "What are we looking at?"

"That's the substructure of Vivo," said Criss. "Look what I've discovered."

The two synbods shrank again as the view pulled back and tilted up to show out across the open deck. A huge drive pod, a glint reflecting off its shiny blue surface, dominated the view.

"Corsia SuperDrives," Cheryl said with a certain reverence. The view turned in a slow circle, with the blue drive pod drifting out of the frame to the left while another just like it edged in from the right. "The specs on those things are amazing." The image stopped turning and started to zoom on the drive pod now centered in the frame, getting close enough to show the honeycomb construction of the cowling itself. "Are they flight ready?"

"Yes, except for fuel." Criss looked at Sid. "Lazura has to be involved in this one."

"Good," said Cheryl. "Not about Lazura. I'm talking about them being flight ready."

"Wait," said Criss. "You know about this?" He looked down for a moment, then nodded. "When you accepted the invitation for the free vacation, you wrote 'Dazzle me' in the spot where they asked of your interest in Corsia drives. You think all this prep is because of that?"

She gave a smirk. "I want sales people to kiss my ass. It's their job."

Sid laughed but Criss shook his head. "The timeline isn't right. They started this before you accepted."

"Then maybe they know we're thinking about putting a pair on Sisyphus."

"I never understood your interest in putting these on a barge," said Sid. "I appreciate you need drives to make up for the added mass on the towline, but the engines installed now are plenty powerful for that."

Cheryl folded her arms across her chest. "It was supposed to be a surprise birthday gift for you. That is, if I like them after my visit."

"Is 'them' the drive pods or the sales staff?"

Cheryl ignored him. "Criss told me that you can fire only nine canisters per loop because Sisyphus waits for natural orbital motions to create the alignment you need. With the SuperDrives, you'll be able to point and shoot. Criss says you can go from nine to more than thirty canisters per loop without disturbing the barge business."

"Damn, Cher, no matter how this turns out, that's thoughtful." He looked at Criss. "So how is it turning out?"

Criss filled them in on Aubrey's plan to hop Vivo north to the L.A. coast before saying, "I'm having trouble making sense of it all, though. It's a huge investment to get those pods up and ready, and working with space thrusters is a dangerous activity no matter who's doing it. And all for advertising?"

Sid felt the hair prickle on the back of his neck. "What are you saying?"

"I'm saying I'm not letting fuel-stacks get anywhere near that island until after their vacation is complete."

"Is it even stable as a craft?" asked Cheryl. "It's so big and ungainly, I'm having trouble picturing this thing taking off."

"That's another twist. Below deck there's a comprehensive tank storage farm for isolated operation. If the tanks are full, the island is unbalanced and would shake apart trying to lift off. If the tanks are empty, though, that island is structurally sound and could take flight. The SuperDrives could even lift it to orbit. Quite easily, in fact."

Sid stood and turned to Cheryl, prepared to disappoint her. "I smell Lazura on this. We need to rethink this vacation idea."

Her voice went cold. "When I left this morning, you were sure you would catch her with your canister gun. Now you say she's behind Vivo?" Shaking her head, she shifted her gaze to Criss. "Unless you have evidence, I'm not going to stay at home and hide from shadows. You know me better than that."

"Then let me go with you instead of Juice," said Sid.

"No. She's already upset about your obsession with Lazura and I don't want to add to it. If you have something solid, of course we'll cooperate. But until then, we're both excited about this, and I ask you not to ruin our fun."

Sid looked at Criss. "I imagine adding this to your monitoring list moves you to reddish-orange."

"No. This one is so complicated, it moves me to yellowish-red."

* * *

With its gilded archway, dramatic music, and colored lights, the grand entrance to Vivo appeared garish to Juice. But when she walked through the portal and moved out under the dome, she caught her breath. Squeezing Cheryl's hand in hers, she let her excitement show. "This was a good idea."

It had been midday when they'd approached the island, but it was night inside, and convincingly so; Juice couldn't tell there was a dome around them at all. Overhead, the stars of the Milky Way filled the sky with a brilliant display. Low near the horizon to her right, fireworks flashed with a small bloom of sparkling light, far enough away so it didn't influence the view, but close enough to add a sense of celebration to the ambiance.

A warm waft of air, humid on her skin and rich with a salty-earthy aroma, made her think they were near water. *Qwash.* The crash of waves confirmed it was the ocean.

"Hello, ladies," said a sandy-haired thirty-year-old, his cream-white shirtsleeves rolled up to his forearms, a careless grin raising his cheeks. "I'm Justin. May I show you to your room?" He lifted his bangs as he spoke, revealing beautiful blue eyes.

"Show *me*." Juice waved her hand, the sight of this gorgeous man adding to her excitement.

"Keep it in your pants," Cheryl whispered, nudging her shoulder against Juice's in a playful manner as they started to walk. "Synbod means synthetic body."

"I know. My theory is that it's not cheating if it's with a synthetic."

Cheryl frowned. "Gross."

Justin led them on a short walk to a festive doorway entrance. On the other side was a stunning tropical garden filled with fruit trees and orchids.

"Ooh look," said Cheryl, pointing to a broad blanket of delicate yellow flowers hung so they draped from the branches of an orange tree, itself laden with brightly colored fruit.

At the end of the garden path, they turned a corner, and the scene changed to a breathtaking cliff-side view of the ocean, with the crashing waves below matching the sounds Juice had heard earlier. A glorious full moon reflected across the water, giving an iridescent glow to the whitewater cresting each wave.

"This way." Justin led them down a somewhat harrowing descent, following stairs carved out of the cliff face itself and wet from the ocean mist. They continued through a mosaic of ferns and moss that added depth to the salty-earthy scents in Juice's nose, and then into a rocky tunnel leading out to a brightly lit market square.

Trendy shops and fashionable restaurants lined the streets of the square. Other guests milled about, laughing, pointing, and having fun. Juice moved next to Justin to avoid a young couple moving past them on the sidewalk.

A man followed behind the couple, and after they passed, he approached Cheryl. Mid-thirties, broad shouldered, and square jawed, he looked at Cheryl when he asked, "Would you like to join me for a drink?"

Tilting her head, Cheryl pursed her lips in a coquettish smile. "What's your name?"

"I'm Chase."

"Well, Chase, I think you've made me thirsty."

"You tramp," Juice said in a loud whisper, happy they had a foursome, even if with a pair of humanoids.

Then, thinking about Criss's desire to get the crystals swapped as soon as possible, Juice asked Justin, "How far to our room?"

"We've been looping around it all along." Justin pointed down the street. "It's a short walk this way."

"My stomach is feeling queasy." Juice sold it by holding a hand to her abdomen. "Can we stop by the room and then come back?"

"Of course! Follow me."

"Thank you," Criss said in her ear.

With the synbods in the lead, the group approached a door between two storefronts. They stepped through into a sumptuous hotel hallway.

"Ahem," said Juice when the door closed behind them. To anyone listening, she sounded like she was clearing her throat. But Criss would recognize it as a request to talk, and because she looked over at Cheryl as she made the noise, he would know to include her.

She knew that before they could talk, Criss would take control of all the links and feeds in the area, then create and project a false reality that would not raise suspicion while they spoke in private. She was on her second step after clearing her throat when Criss said, "Thanks for moving this along. The Montrose platform has just started its orbit shift procedures and things are already getting snarled up. I'm anxious to free up resources to monitor it all."

"Are these our marks?" asked Cheryl, nodding toward the synbods and relying on Criss's projection to shield her words and actions from everyone but Juice.

"Yes. Aubrey assigned them to you during your stay, so they're the logical choice. As you may have guessed, she took the time to study each of your personal preferences for male appearance and demeanor, and then selected these two from her inventory. She even tweaked their looks and personalities to enhance their appeal to you. You're the only guests with dedicated synbods; everyone else is sharing, so she's clearly trying to impress you."

Juice looked ahead at Justin's tight butt below his slim waist. "It's working."

"Your suite would be a convenient place to perform the swap," Criss continued.

"That works for me," said Cheryl.

Chase and Justin stopped in front of a hallway door. As it opened, they both stepped back so Cheryl and Juice could lead the way in.

As they entered the suite, Juice felt more comfortable than she had anticipated and made a concession to Criss. "I'll do the swap if it's in here and Cheryl helps. But you owe me one."

"Debt noted. I've finished mapping both of them," said Criss, referring to a step in the process of duplicating Chase's and Justin's matrices in his special three-gen crystals. "Please proceed when you are ready."

The suite had a common area with a couch and chairs, a wet bar with a food service unit, and a big window revealing the nighttime sky. Doors on the left and right walls led to two identical bedrooms.

The moment they were inside the suite, Criss jumped his awareness into the three-gen crystals, overpowered them, and took control of the humanoid bodies. Both synbods stayed upright during the takeover, but they slouched more than before.

"Let's see what you got." Juice loosened Justin's shirt and pulled it open. "Not bad," she said, nodding.

Access to the crystals for these synbods was from the back between the shoulder blades. In an efficient sequence, Juice opened the access panel, removed the mesh-covered crystal from its mount, and turned to Cheryl.

At the same time, Cheryl retrieved one of Criss's special three-gen crystals from her satchel—the satchel she'd been carrying for weeks to make it appear as part of her normal style—and they made the exchange. After Juice finished with Justin, she repeated the procedure with Chase. Stepping back, she and Cheryl waited for Criss to reanimate the two.

With the built-in locus these synbods now possessed, Criss could come and go as he pleased with modest resources. And he could ride along without Aubrey or her Supervisor synbods—Hejmo and Mondo—knowing anything was amiss.

"Success," said Criss. "Here we go."

Justin lifted his head and asked, "Are you ready to return to the market square?"

"I'd rather go somewhere quiet and have a drink," said Cheryl. "It's night, so maybe a hilltop view of city lights?"

Enticed by the idea, Juice added, "Maybe an outdoor patio? With soft music?"

"I know just the place," said Chase.

They followed the synbods out of the room and down the hallway toward the door leading out to the market square.

Halfway along, Criss called to them, his tone reflecting urgency. "There's been a small explosion on the Montrose and I'm elevating my alert status. I'll be spread thin for a while. Do you have any concerns?"

"We're fine here," said Juice.

"Do what you need to and keep us informed." Then Cheryl added, "Is Sid okay?"

"Yes. He's out of harm's way up on Sisyphus."

The vacationers and their escorts reached the door at the end of the hall, but this time when they passed through, they stepped onto the slate tiles of an outdoor patio.

An intimate space, it was big enough for perhaps a dozen tables. The back wall was natural stone seemingly cut from the hillside itself. Ivy vines spread across the rock wall, weaving through a scatter of lighted candles perched on different outcroppings. The air, warm and dry, carried a waft of music: a middle-aged man in a vest played ragtime on an old upright piano in the far corner.

But their attention was drawn to the beautiful spread of lights from a city in the valley below, a spread that rose to the dazzle of a much bigger metropolitan area in the distance.

"Our table is this way," said Chase.

One other guest was on the patio at the moment, and Chase escorted them to his table. A sturdy, middle-aged man with a friendly face, he rose as they approached.

"Hello," he said with a smile that seemed forced. "I'm Mac MacFarlane. I work for the company." He twirled a finger in front of him when he said that last part to indicate that "the company" meant Vivo.

He motioned to the chairs at his table. "I'd be honored if you'd join me for a drink." His smile turned to a frown when he looked at Chase and Justin. Pointing to the far table next to the piano, he used a dismissive tone. "You two sit over there."

"I recognize this view," said Cheryl, sitting down. "Those far lights are San Francisco, and that's the Bay Bridge. This closer city is part of Berkeley."

"I've seen this, too," said Juice. "We came up here after an AI conference held on the Berkeley campus last year."

MacMac nodded. "Our research indicated this would be a common experience you both would enjoy for a second time if you shared it together."

"That sounds like the tactics of a salesman, Mr. MacFarlane," said Cheryl. "But a salesman would never admit to such manipulation. May I ask your background?"

"Mr. MacFarlane is what they call my father. Everyone calls me MacMac. I'm the chief engineer here, and I've been asked to show you our Corsia SuperDrives." He looked at Juice. "I'm told you might be interested in meeting our Supervisor synbods. I'd be happy to introduce you."

"Could you introduce me to a drink?" Juice replied. "Since we're in California, how about a nice pinot noir from Napa Valley?"

MacMac laughed and turned to Cheryl. "And for you?"

"Draft beer, medium dark. And a glass of water and some munchies if that's possible."

Juice's mouth watered at the mention of food and she went into full vacation mode. "Yeah, some sliced veggies and dip, roasted nuts, crusty bread, and a soft cheese." She slumped back in her chair and then sat up. "Make the dip guacamole."

MacMac laughed again and drained his crystal tumbler of its clear brown liquid. He held the glass out in front of him and said to the air, "And another of these, on the rocks this time."

He set his glass down and rested his forearms on the edge of the tabletop. Exhaling with a sigh, he looked out at the city lights as he spoke. "The service here is excellent. It will just be a moment." Then he looked at Cheryl. "The record says you're a space hotshot. Not just a desk jockey but someone with real command bridge experience on military and commercial spacecraft."

"The record is correct," said Cheryl.

"I mention it because we tried to impress you by fully integrating our drives with the structural *and* electronic systems. This way we can demo all the features, but it would mean something only to someone who's been there."

A service bot approached and distributed the food and drinks in an efficient manner. As it departed, MacMac took a long drink from his glass. When he spoke, his words slurred ever so slightly. "Don't get me wrong, the drives are really the best technology. It comes down to price on whether it's worth it to you—and I've been told not to talk about that." He looked left and then right in a conspiratorial fashion. "But you can buy drive pods anytime. Focus on your vacation while you're here. The experiences on Vivo are really special."

Juice reached for the plate of carrot sticks, and the tabletop vibrated beneath her hand. Then the ground shook and a throaty roar filled the air.

"What the hell?" said MacMac, who stood and began tapping and swiping the air in front of him.

"Those feel like ship drives." Cheryl reached out and put a hand on Juice's forearm as she addressed MacMac, her tone commanding. "You aren't firing them, are you?"

Bright lights flooded the scene. Everything that had been ambiance—the slate floor, ivy-covered walls, piano player, and amazing view—disappeared. They now sat in a large, circular room with unadorned white walls. The table and chairs remained, as did the food. Chase and Justin sat in the same position they had been before the lights came on.

"Criss!" called Juice, not caring who saw or heard.

"I'm here," said Criss. "Hold on."

MacMac's hands weaved in a frenzy as he manipulated displays only he could see. "This is insane, Aubrey. Where did you get the fuel?"

8

With a broad grin, Sid eased the scout into orbit above Earth. Criss, who sat next to him on the bridge, had outfitted the craft with fully automated capabilities, but Sid found pleasure in placing the nav in manual mode and piloting the ship himself.

His flight path today swung him in a single orbit above the planet. Halfway around, he'd start his acceleration sequence, speeding up enough to break free of Earth's gravity and transition into a path to the moon. That wasn't his destination, though. His plan was to catch up to Sisyphus, already underway and pulling yet another full towline of vessels.

As he checked the displays, the Montrose rose up on the horizon. Awed by the sight, he took a moment to confirm his path would take the scout wide of the structure.

Fifty times the size of Vivo, the magnificent orbiting command platform served as a floating space field, providing fuel and repair, weapons and supplies, and everything else needed for the orbital service and support of Fleet's growing number of spaceships.

On a normal day, a steady stream of traffic shuttled between the platform and Earth, transporting people and material up and down as needed. But today was moving day, and eighteen huge boosters positioned beneath the platform were about to start nudging the behemoth to a higher orbit.

The sight of the platform reminded Sid of an earlier conversation. "Whatever happened to those two mystery cases of crystals you were tracking?" he asked Criss. "Has Fleet moved them down to the surface?"

"No, they're still sitting in the parcel depot. They go down after the platform is stable in its new orbit." Criss shifted in his chair to face Sid. "Did you know that it took nine agencies and five oversight committees more than a year to plan for today's move? And the admirals are laughing because they got the business community to pay for it."

The business community had lobbied long and hard to shift the platform's path because near-Earth orbit was overcrowded and the Montrose hogged most of the best slots. Pushing the platform higher in orbit would triple the size of the commercial district, something the business community wanted so much they'd agreed to a new orbit tax to help reimburse Fleet for its costs.

"In all that discussion, Fleet never revealed that they already planned to move the platform to a higher orbit to accommodate the new troop carriers coming online next year."

Sid started to laugh but stopped and looked at Criss. "Do I have to pay the new tax for the cargo cannon?"

Criss nodded. "Sisyphus itself uses orbital space and will have to pay. But no worries, I anticipated this and accounted for it in the budget. In fact, I support this outcome because the collaboration strengthens society."

Sid changed subjects to avoid talking about society's strengths. "We need to decide our wager on the egg. Do you want broken or intact?"

They were on their way to Sisyphus to place a fresh egg in the canister being prepped for the cannon's maiden shot to Mars. Vivo's promotional efforts with drive pods had given Sid the idea of doing his own stunt to draw customer attention, and Lazura's in particular, to his new cargo service. The egg idea had drifted to the top of the pile because it helped with a couple of other issues along the way.

The first canister to Mars would be full of party supplies, providing enough food, drink, and games to host a huge crowd in a company-sponsored celebration. While the supplies could be shipped safely in a regular canister, this solved the problem of what to do with the one with junk equipment by using it for a promotion.

He had pitched the idea to Criss the same day Cheryl was leaving for Vivo. "I'll go up and put an egg inside with a camera pointed at it, turn on the damper, and we launch. If the damper works and the egg survives, we advertise our ability to transport even the most fragile of items." He shrugged. "If it breaks, the colonists will have to spend a minute cleaning up egg goop before they start the party."

And now, less than a day later, he was on his way to implement his brainchild. But his thoughts weren't on eggs, they were on gambling. He'd told Cheryl he would be busy while she was away, and he would be, playing poker with Pete and the boys in the cable room of the barge.

He'd stumbled across the game when he'd been up on Sisyphus earlier in the year. Though not much of a card player, he'd been goaded by Pete for months before agreeing to play.

He hadn't succumbed initially, even when teased with, "What, are you chicken?" It had been the clucking sounds afterward that had broken him. And the egg stunt gave him an excuse to be up at the table in time for the first hand.

His gambling juices flowing in anticipation, he pushed Criss to choose a side and bet on whether the egg broke or not.

"Which do you want?" Criss replied.

"No, you go first. Broken or intact. You have to choose."

"I'll take broken."

"You really think the equipment is that bad?"

"No. I'd say the chance of failure is one in four. But I know you want to pick intact, so I'll take broken."

Giving him a sidelong glance, Sid stood and started for the common room at the rear of the scout. "You are the opposite of fun."

With hours to kill before they reached the barge, he exercised until every muscle was tired. Then, planning for a late night, he slept until Criss called him. Thirty minutes after waking, he was in his space runner, ferrying to Sisyphus with the scout shadowing from a distance.

His first stop was the breach room located at the rear of the cannon. More like a cave with a smooth floor, the big hollow held a dozen cargo canisters in various stages of prep, each a dull gray cylinder almost two stories tall and half as wide. A workshop consumed the back wall of the breach room with storage shelves along each side filled with gizmos and gadgets. The front area held space to pile customer cargo until it was loaded into its assigned canister.

"Hey ho," called Pete, approaching Sid with a huge grin. Short, round, with close-cropped hair and a pudgy face, she patted her breast pocket and chirped with excitement. "I got us *real* cigars! And Bo is bringing a jug of kick-ass moonshine he snagged from the engineer on that luxury liner on hook twenty-three." She twirled and chirped, "It's going to be a night of decadence."

Then she began the personal harassment that was a hallmark of the card game. Pointing at the breach door and the cargo canister loaded inside, she sneered, "Are you ever going to actually shoot that piece of shit?"

Sid didn't bother answering, because she was already at the exit. "Hatchet needs a ride, so I'm taking the tug out to pick him up. He's bringing some outrageous home brew. Should be back in an hour."

As the door shut behind her, Criss appeared.

"Was I supposed to bring something?" asked Sid.

"You're the mark with the money," replied Criss. "You brought everything they need."

Sid shrugged as he walked to the breach door. "I don't mind. They could use the extra."

He put his hands on the doorframe, leaned his head and shoulders inside the cargo canister, and scanned the interior. When empty, the interior volume seemed enormous.

"The canisters have been swapped," Criss said over his shoulder. "This is the one with the junk parts. We'll pack the party supplies in here over the next couple of hours. You should be able to come down and set up your egg stunt sometime around midnight."

"That won't work. The game will just be getting started."

"Whoa," said Criss. "There's been an explosion on the Montrose."

"How bad? Show me."

A small image of the huge space platform appeared floating between them. The flares of the thrusters underneath the structure glowed bright white as they worked together to push the Montrose up to its new home.

The image zoomed in, stopping with a close-up on a corner of the platform near the lower loading dock. Light penetrated through a jagged hole in an exterior wall. The opening was small relative to the size of the platform, and a cloud of debris rushed out, carried by the surge of air streaming into space.

"It's not structural," said Criss. "And I don't believe it was an accident. Something small detonated in the parcel depot. That's where those two mystery cases of crystals were stored."

"Did the crystals survive?"

"I don't know. Everything in that room is now floating in space."

Sid leaned forward to examine the sharp edges of the hole. "That perfect circle with crisp edges makes me think of a thump charge, which would make it a deliberate act."

"I'd like to take the scout there and see if I can help. I also want to recover those two cases of crystals."

"Go." Sid nodded. "I'm fine here."

Criss and the hovering image vanished, and Sid, thinking ahead to his egg stunt, ambled over to the closest set of workshop storage shelves. He toyed with a small piece of clear tubing while his eyes roamed the collection of items.

Part of him wanted to build the egg holder himself, and he even fit a few pieces together to see if he could fashion something suitable. But after a few minutes, he admitted his mind was on the game. *I'll ask Criss to figure it out,* he thought as he made his way to the exit.

Halfway to the door, a buzzer sounded and a red emergency light flashed overhead.

"Hey, Criss," called Sid. "What's up?"

Criss reappeared, as did a new hovering display. This one showed Sisyphus floating at a distance. The image zoomed, shifting angles to focus on the tether, speckled with two hundred vessels attached along its length.

Sid started to ask what he was supposed to see, and then he saw it. A number of engines flared to life about halfway back along the tail. "What are they doing?"

In response, Criss zoomed closer, stopping when a single spaceship filled the view. The ship had decoupled from the tether and was edging away from it.

"Is that an Elite Five?" The ship's engine fired and the craft flashed out of the frame.

"It's an Elite Seven," said Criss. The view pulled back to show a cluster of identical ships sprinting past Sisyphus and into the void. "There are nineteen of them underway."

"Who's doing it?"

"There are no people on board, and they aren't communicating with anyone outside, so they're following a program."

"But they're clearly acting together." The ships gathered in a ring formation, the flares of the individual engines seeming to meld into a single ball of light. "They are moving *fast*. Any idea where they're going?"

"None. With the trajectory they're following and the rate they're consuming fuel, they're on a fast track to nowhere."

"It has to be Lazura. Who else could it be?"

Criss nodded. "She's the prime suspect."

"Should we chase them? Shoot them down?"

"They're headed away from everything, so shooting at them seems premature." He shook his head. "The ships can't sprint like that for long. If she's on one of them, she'll end up stranded."

"What are they carrying?"

"Water, oxygen, nitrogen, and other life support basics. They were delivering supplies for an expansion of the Lunar Base habitat."

Then Criss snapped to attention. "My God, Lazura! How?" His voice reflected shock that transitioned into panic. "Vivo just fired the SuperDrives and has begun an acceleration sequence." He let out a wail so mournful it unnerved Sid.

"Come get me," Sid commanded.

Panic sounded in Criss's voice. "I'm already out of position. I don't have time."

"That's an order."

"I'm using an emergency override, Sid. You are safe. I may have lost Cheryl and Juice. I need to act *right now*."

* * *

Lazura's outer tendrils tingled as Cheryl and Juice stepped under the dome. Years of planning, effort, and luck had led to today. And the good news continued as Juice's pulse rate increased and her eyes dilated when Justin introduced himself.

Lazura had every faith in Vivo's ability to mesmerize the two, but she wanted them so relaxed and content that Criss would be lulled, too. She needed complacency for about three hours.

And that clock started now.

It began with a system reset, something that had been on Aubrey's action timetable from the earliest days. As planned in this years-long con, when the last guests arrived and the doors to the outside world closed behind them, Vivo's entire ops system was pulsed to ensure the myriad subsystems were awake and running in guest-services mode.

And when Aubrey triggered the pulse, Criss, even knowing it was coming, was pushed out of Vivo. It would take him a moment to reengage with Cheryl and Juice on the guest deck, and while he was distracted with that, Lazura started step two.

In the cellar, a garage door lifted on the far end of the Power House. Hejmo, riding in the cab of a large box truck, drove inside. A part of Vivo's much-advertised safety campaign, the truck was there to perform a comprehensive inspection of Vivo's power generators, just as it did every month at this time.

And because the Power House structure was made of secure-shield material, when the overhead door closed, things inside were hidden from everyone outside, including Criss.

The moment the overhead door clicked shut, the back of the box truck swung down to form a ramp. Four women sprang from the rear of the truck and ran down the incline. Dressed in cream-white suits, these were four of Aubrey's five Admins.

Contrary to their prim appearance, each carried an industrial-style zip saw. Cradling the tools in front of them with both hands, they sprinted across the floor, each to a different silver-gray shed. Each accessed her respective shed door and, moving with haste, stepped inside, disabled the local alarm, and began cutting the triple-secure lock holding the generator lid in place.

Sparks flying, seams glowing, stench of vapors filling the air, the first Admin made it through the locks in just over two minutes, the others finishing seconds later. Each lifted the generator lid to release an interlock, allowing her to lower the protective front face of the containment. After rotating two mechanical latches, a heavy inner safety door swung open to expose a block of hellfire.

The Power House held six big generators, of which four were spares. The fuel in the generators was the same material used in drive pods. But a generator held only half the amount needed for a proper drive pod fuel-stack, the material was the wrong shape, and it was not in the highly energetic state needed for rocket propulsion. In addition, these fuel blocks were located some distance from the drive pods, and transportation of the material was extremely dangerous.

Yet for these very reasons, Lazura believed she could sneak this past Criss with misdirection, letting him find and cancel the purchase order for four fuel-stacks Aubrey had placed with Thrust Dynamics.

The Corsia drive pods had a flexible design that could accept half-stacks of fuel. They could even run half-stacks at full thrust long enough to move Vivo out of the solar system and deep into interstellar space. It would be slow going after that, with the journey taking her almost twice as long to get home, something she could accept as long as home was the end result.

The fuel shape issue was a bigger challenge. Conventional options for fuel shaping—tech bots, forming ovens, containment measures—were distinctive preparations Criss would notice. So she wouldn't use any of them; she didn't want *anything* to attract his attention to the generators.

Her solution was to rely on the advanced capabilities of synbods. They were already skilled at any task she might need of them, so no telltale preparations were required. Synbods were smart, allowing her to adjust her plan on the fly as circumstances warranted. And they were available in a moment's notice, meaning that when she sprang her plan, she'd have the element of surprise.

It's all or nothing at this point, she thought as the Admins dropped the front face of the generator to expose the glowing blocks of reactive material.

The instant the blocks were exposed, the Admins' clothing incinerated in a flash. But they still engaged their zip saws and began cutting the waist-high cube into three equal pieces. Together these would form the slabs of the half-stack.

The fuel material was soft, and the zip saws' laser blades extended to make the deep cuts. Lazura had allotted eight seconds for the procedure, four seconds per cut. Her analysis indicated the synbods would last just over eleven seconds before succumbing to the fierce conditions.

As they worked, their synbod skin, biologically alive, bubbled and burned. Lazura controlled their movements in the final stages, relying on sensors mounted some distance away to see and hear. Parts failed quickly, but all four of the Admins completed their cuts and moved to the side before collapsing.

While the Admins had been cutting, four Attendants in sky-blue service uniforms pushed handcarts down the truck ramp and over to the sheds, timing their arrival to match the completion of the cutting step. Each handcart had a standard shipping crate layered with common shielding material attached to its bed. The front face of the crate was open, and a shovel scoop on the front of the cart rode so low it almost scraped the floor.

The Attendants rolled their carts past the fallen Admins and up to the glowing material. Setting the lip of each scoop at the base of what were now three blocks of fuel, they pushed their carts forward with firm motions, jockeying the handles so the blocks rode up the scoops and into the crates. With the fuel secure, the synbods backed out of the shed and made for the truck.

Like competitors in a ghastly race, the Attendants pushed their carts across the floor in a shuffling run, slowing as the damage from exposure ate at them. Lazura felt a twinge of regret at losing so many valuable staff, but Criss remained unaware of the activity so far, so it was worth it.

The Attendants reached the truck and, one at a time, pushed their carts up the ramp. Inside, the forward half of the truck bed held a jury-rigged chem processor—a rugged black metallic tub divided into four wide channels with a heavy lid that dropped from above to seal the unit. A Rube Goldberg–like collection of valves and tubes connected the processor to a row of gas cylinders strapped to the wall. Wires crisscrossed overhead, connecting everything to a handful of instruments strapped to the cargo holds ceiling.

The first Attendant pushed his cart up to the tub, positioned the scoop in front of the left-most channel, and tipped the cart up. As his three slabs slid forward, he jiggled the cart, guiding the slabs so they fell into a stack frame positioned near the front lip. He then rolled his cart down the ramp and stood off to the side to make way for the others.

With all four loads emptied into the chem processor, the Attendants stood next to each other, hands at their sides, waiting, and then collapsing from the horrific damage.

But Lazura wasn't watching that drama. Hejmo and a Tech had been standing against the far wall of the Power House, keeping a safe distance until the chem processor lid had closed to contain the deadly emissions. The moment it was safe, they sprinted for the truck, Hejmo in the front cab, the Tech in the back.

Hejmo waited three more minutes before signaling the overhead door to open. The Power House safety inspections always took fourteen minutes, and today it would as well. When the time came, he directed the truck out of the building and onto the next stop in his regular inspection tour.

While Hejmo followed his usual route through the cellar, stopping to walk through certain installations and inspecting others from the cab, the Tech in the back of the truck operated the chem processor. Used to regenerate catalyst material from the air purification units, this was one of twelve such units in Vivo's inventory.

Lazura had purchased this particular model of chem processor because its flawed design caused frequent malfunctions. When a failure occurred, longstanding procedure was to truck the faulty unit to the workshop for repair.

A unit had malfunctioned a week ago, and while in the shop, a Tech had swapped out the internals and added instrumentation ports, effectively converting the chem processor into a working fuel processor. Hejmo now drove the truck with that modified equipment, and it had just been loaded with hot fuel blocks.

The Tech started the conversion process by introducing an acid mixture to etch the surface of the fuel slabs. Working with care, he adjusted the ratio of chemicals and timed the pressure ramp by eye from a small display.

After twenty minutes, he switched regimes, flushing the etching fluid and starting the thermal excitation cycle, something that took ninety minutes to complete. After a fifteen-minute stabilization period, the half-stacks, though dangerously hot, were ready for loading into drive pod fuel casings.

Hejmo's inspection tour lasted long enough for the stabilization period to complete. At that point, he approached the recycling facility, the last stop on his standard route. This facility, a collection of a dozen mini-factories housed inside three big warehouses, ensured that everything disposed of as waste anywhere on Vivo found its way back into the supply stream.

The three buildings of the recycling facility were joined end to end to enclose a significant amount of deck space. Hejmo drove through the vehicle entrance in the center building, and that fed onto an indoor vehicle roundabout.

A couple of small transports rode ahead of Hejmo, and a service van with a Tech in the cab pulled in behind him. Hejmo called to the Tech in the van using the common channel. "I have junction links for the drive pods here in the cab with me. You are to install them next. Pull over and receive them."

Both vehicles took the next turnoff to a covered alcove, unusual because it had no cameras or other sensors Criss might use to eavesdrop. Lazura had fretted about allowing the existence of such a dead space on the island because if Criss couldn't see, neither could she. She loathed the loss of control, but given its strategic importance to her plans, she allowed the unmonitored alcove to exist as the seeming result of a construction mistake.

Hejmo directed his big truck into the alcove, leaving just enough room for the service van to squeeze in next to it. The back doors of both vehicles opened and four Attendants hopped down from the van. Working in teams of two, they unloaded four empty fuel casings, carried them inside Hejmo's service truck, and set them in a row in front of the chem processor tub with lids open.

The Attendants then joined Hejmo a safe distance away while the Tech winched the chem processor tub up and tilted it forward so the slabs of brilliant energy slid into the casings. After, he latched the lids, sealing the raw energy inside. In his last act, he climbed down and stood against the near wall, waiting to die.

Working again in teams of two, the Attendants carried the loaded fuel casings to the rear of the van. Three climbed in with the cargo and one drove, guiding the van out of the recycling facility and down the back ramp to the subdeck.

When it arrived at the base of the first Corsia SuperDrive, Lazura prepared to make a move that Criss would see. She could not conceive of a way to load the fuel casings into the drive pods in secret, so her plan was to make sure Criss was looking somewhere else.

She did that by triggering a small bomb on the Montrose, the one hidden inside one of the shielded crystal carry cases. The detonation caused modest damage to the platform but succeeded in creating tremendous confusion and disarray.

Her expectation was that Criss would rush to help and spend time investigating. While she couldn't know what actions he actually took, she did know he did not intervene as two Attendants unloaded a fuel casing from the van and placed it on the pod's small service elevator. While one synbod climbed back into the van, the other stepped next to the fuel and rode with it up the side of the pod.

The Attendants unloaded the second fuel casing in the same fashion. When they moved the third casing onto its pod elevator, Lazura sent a passcode that caused an old energy weapon in the dense jungle of the Congo Basin half a world away—a big gun she'd identified months earlier—to fire a beam into the sky.

Controlled by a hapless band of rebels unaware of her meddling, the big gun hadn't been fired in a decade. The beam was weak and the aim awful, but Lazura didn't care. Pointed in the vague direction of the Montrose and coming on the heels of an explosion, Criss would devote significant resources following up. And because the rebels lived in a remote place with few services, it would take valuable time for him to gather information.

With the four Attendants up on raised elevators, each poised at a drive pod fuel access hatch, Lazura's tendrils throbbed with a mix of tension, excitement, anticipation, and fear. Her next move would light up the nav. If Criss looked at Vivo, he would see it.

But still she needed more time. To gain it, she launched the nineteen Elite Sevens under tow by Sisyphus.

The moment the Elite Sevens started their sprint into space, Lazura directed the Attendants to load the fuel. With the speed and precision only a synbod could muster, they opened the drive pod's fuel access door, manhandled the fuel casing into the receiver, opened the switch panel and disabled the link back to the ops panel, and slammed the access door shut.

Believing she'd make it but fearing she wouldn't, Lazura counted the seconds, each one lasting an eternity. When the nav lit up, her suffering did not diminish. She needed eight more seconds before the drives would fire.

The go-signal flashed and Lazura triggered the launch sequence.

When the SuperDrives thundered to life, the island shook and groaned, and the ocean bubbled and hissed. *Pop, pop, pop.* Small explosive charges sheared a thousand huge bolts holding the substructure in place. Massive quick-releases opened, disconnecting the island platform from the support legs running down to the ocean floor.

And then the dome-covered island rose above the waves of the Pacific Ocean, hovered for a moment, and began accelerating in a climb toward the clouds.

Knowing Criss couldn't abort takeoff without killing Cheryl, Juice, and everyone else aboard, Lazura turned the dome shield to max, cut all external links, and reviewed her flight plan.

Criss's next chance to intervene would be when she escaped Earth's atmosphere and reached outer space.

Before then, she needed to decide how long she would let her hostages live.

9

When the bomb exploded on the Montrose, Criss suspected that Lazura was making her break for freedom. He tempered the thought, though, because he'd been imagining her involvement in more and more situations and did not want that preoccupation to influence the facts.

But he couldn't deny that the disarray caused by the bomb was a great first step in any escape plan. While the platform move had already disrupted the normal flow of vessels in orbit, the cloud of debris from the explosion, combined with the swarm of emergency response craft floating nearby, pushed the scene into chaos.

From his subterranean console, Criss jumped his awareness to the ops bench of the Montrose. After confirming that the damage to the platform was minor, he searched every corner of the orbiting installation looking for clues.

As he traveled the vessel, he helped where he could, careful never to reveal his presence. In one instance he overrode the electronics of a stuck door so rescuers could gain access to an injured cadet. In another, he modified a low-level routine to counteract the plummeting temperature in the aft service shop.

At the parcel depot, his forensic scan identified the point of detonation—the cubby where the two cases of crystals had been stored. The likelihood of Lazura's involvement spiked at the discovery, and he responded accordingly.

He started by confirming the safety of his leadership. On Vivo, Chase and Justin carried new crystals that let Criss leap his awareness inside the dome. Flexing this capability, he scanned every deck and established there were no new threats since his last review. Outside the dome, he confirmed that nothing approached the island by air, boat, or sub.

On Sisyphus, he reviewed the entire operation on the barge and visited every ship along the tether to verify that nothing posed a threat to Sid. Convinced that Lazura was making her play, Criss sought Sid's permission to move the scout back to Earth and the center of the action.

Reversing the course of a spacecraft hurtling through space is like turning around a car careening down a long, steep hill. While possible, slowing to a stop and then accelerating back in the other direction takes enormous energy and a capable vehicle. The scout, engines glowing as they fought a fierce battle against momentum, had the wherewithal to achieve the feat, which is why Criss wanted it in the mix.

Criss had just started turning the scout around when an energy beam flashed up from the Congo as the Montrose passed overhead. The shot went wide, and the Montrose, already on high alert, obliterated the jungle site in an automated response, destroying any evidence Criss might have used to attribute the attack to Lazura.

As the scout accelerated toward Earth, a major astronomical tracking installation in Socorro, New Mexico—one Criss piggybacked on to track orbital activity—blinked off. The outage lasted less than a second before backup systems restored function. Criss jumped to the facility in search of Lazura and wasted precious time before learning that the cause of the inopportune failure was a rodent infestation at a transfer station.

The scout reached Earth, and as Criss dove the craft into orbit, nineteen Elite Sevens disengaged from Sisyphus and began a mystery sprint into deep space.

And as the scout swung around behind the planet, the SuperDrives on Vivo came alive.

Lazura!

Frantic, Criss's tendrils chilled as he confronted the reality of her success and the magnitude of his own failure. When his scenario forecasts predicted yet more failure ahead, he fought a rising panic, one that threatened to overwhelm him.

Diving his awareness to the island paradise, he jumped for the ops panel, determined to shut down the drives. But the moment he landed, he felt a jolt, one so intense it reached all the way back to his underground bunker in the Adirondack Mountains.

The existence of such a defensive system removed any doubt about who was responsible for this outrage. Having primed himself for just this moment, he dove again for the panel, prepared to tackle whatever Lazura had in store for him.

At the interface, her defenses presented like a morphing thicket, snags and catches grabbing at him as he fought his way forward. And while he did, the clock advanced on the launch sequence.

But he would not be denied. *No one messes with my leadership.* With a last push, his goal in sight, he stretched and slapped at the panel, shutting down the drive pods.

But nothing happened. He repeated the action, this time chasing the signal as it raced through the links and feeds, watching for the failure of execution. He made it all the way out to the drive pods themselves, and there he learned that synbods had intentionally disabled the link.

Fuming, Criss jumped and overpowered the Attendants standing on the platforms next to the drive pods, commanding them to cancel the launch. But as his consciousness landed in the three-gen crystals, in all four cases he found himself careening through the air for the briefest moment, followed by a devastating crash. Just before he'd landed in the synbods, Lazura had commanded them to dive headfirst from their elevated perches down to the deck below.

Then the drive pods fired. Shaking and shuddering, the island lifted into the air. Criss dove back to the ops panel to override everything and guide Vivo back to Earth, only to learn that on takeoff, the assembly supporting the island from below had been left behind. Without it, Vivo would crumble if Lazura tried to re-land the enormous structure.

And so to complete his humiliation, Criss helped Lazura kidnap Cheryl and Juice by clearing the path ahead of Vivo as it climbed the sky into space. He had no choice; their safety was paramount. At the same time, he jumped back to Vivo's ops panel to confirm the health of the various systems critical to launch success.

And then Lazura enabled the dome shield, cutting him off from everything inside. Unsure how it went wrong so fast, Criss pulled in resources from everywhere and jumped to Chase, then to Justin. In both cases, the link he established proved too weak for him to manipulate events.

The scout had just completed its swing behind Earth, positioning it to use a weapon to disable Vivo's engines as the behemoth rose into space. An energy beam aimed just right could thread the needle into Vivo's substructure from below, severing a trunk line and disabling the SuperDrives.

Up ahead, Criss sighted the brilliant cones of plasma lifting Vivo from Earth's atmosphere. He closed on his quarry, approaching from a side angle to avoid the intense wash of energy directly behind the drive pods.

Precision was key with this shot because to hit the trunk line, the beam had to brush past critical life support systems. He'd outfitted the scout with his own technology, though, so he could take the shot with confidence.

The distance between the scout and Vivo closed, yet the scout's weapon system failed to reach target lock. Criss confirmed the integrity of the scout's systems, searched for external causes, and found it in a thin cloud growing behind Vivo.

Chaff. Criss's humiliation drifted to despair when he realized his plan was thwarted by a countermeasure technology so old it was a footnote in aviation history.

Vivo had huge piles of EM sand, tiny grains manufactured with sophisticated electromagnetic properties. When loose, the grains made wonderful dunes and beaches for guests to enjoy. Yet with a small energy field, the same particles would hold together to form ridged structures, becoming anything from a rocky tunnel to stone steps down a cliff face. In between these extremes, the sand made excellent hiking trails through the wilderness, or perhaps garden soil for plants.

Versatile for creating unique guest experiences, EM sand had practical uses as well. The technology had advanced to the point where, after an event, a portion of the sand could be formed into a flexible hose, and that could be used to vacuum the rest of the particles into storage. When done, the end of the hose crumbled and was sucked away, the length ever shortening until everything was stowed for future use.

Criss knew about the EM sand and considered its use to be appropriate, even inspired, for a vacation resort like Vivo. He now understood that the grains were the perfect cover material to sprinkle behind Vivo as it accelerated into the void.

A modern spin on the old countermeasure of military jets dropping foil strips to confuse radar, the scatter of electromagnetic sand behind Vivo made it impossible for Criss to target the trunk line with confidence. And to his consternation, the unique EM properties of the particles further interfered with his ability to jump inside the dome, already challenged because of Lazura's dome shield.

Moving the scout away from Vivo, he called to Cheryl and Juice, giving them a positive message of hope. "Hang in there. I'm working on it."

Spinning through scenarios for disabling the SuperDrives, his best options now relied on help from his team inside. Given their precarious situation and the demands they would make of him, though, he would need time, perhaps days, before he could execute.

And this triggered a new dilemma, one so unsettling it caused him to wail.

"What happened?" called Juice.

"It may take some time for me to save you."

"You need to save all the guests," Juice replied. "It's everyone or no one."

Exactly, he thought, her response confirming what he'd anticipated. Saving everyone meant controlling Vivo, a much bigger challenge compared to spiriting away two souls.

And while the scout could keep up with Vivo as it blazed into deep space, Criss the crystal remained in his underground bunker on Earth. As time passed and the distance from Earth grew, his ability to jump his awareness out to the action would fade.

He forecast an 80 percent chance he could stop Lazura before distance became an issue. But that left a 20 percent chance he could not. Which meant a one in five chance of losing Cheryl and Juice, possibly forever.

And that's what caused him to wail. He had no choice but to break off pursuit, swing back to Earth, move his crystal self onto the scout, and resume the chase. The way Vivo was accelerating, it would take him more than a day to catch up again. He'd be out of contact with Cheryl and Juice for most of that time.

But in the end, he'd have the scout, the best tool for solving a problem like this. And he'd have all the time he needed, days or weeks if that's what it took to execute a low-risk rescue plan.

Indeed, he'd have all the time he needed because he wouldn't rest until he rescued his leadership, even if he had to follow Lazura all the way back to the Kardish home world to do so. His forecasts put his chances of success above 97 percent with this approach.

"I've loaded some ideas into Chase and Justin that will speed things along when I return," he told Cheryl and Juice after briefing them on his dilemma. "Do what you can, but it's not necessary to take any risks. Put your safety first. Please."

As he turned the scout back to Earth for the second time that day, Criss updated Sid about his intent to move his crystal from his underground console and into a synthetic body. "I'm about to get dressed and then ride the capsule up to the scout. I'll be in and out of contact for the next hour."

"Swing by and get me on your way back out," Sid commanded for the third time.

"You're in the wrong direction and I'm already concerned about time. You're safe where you are."

Then Criss changed subjects. "The mystery of the Elite Sevens has been solved." He projected an image for Sid to see. In it, Vivo had caught up with the ring of rogue spaceships as they hurtled through space. The domed world moved to the center of the grouping, and as it did, the sleek tankers shifted in and attached themselves around the perimeter of the main platform like suckerfish on a whale.

"Even I could pick off those Sevens," said Sid. "Why are you waiting?"

"They carry the air, water, nutrients, and everything else the passengers need until we rescue them. I want that transfer to complete."

As he spoke, he prepared to dress, or, more specifically, move out of his four-gen console and into his personal synbod body. It had been more than a year since he'd been out of his underground bunker experiencing the world as a humanoid. He avoided it because he felt so vulnerable riding around in such a small, exposed container.

But the advantages of being mobile sometimes outweighed the risks, as in this case. And being prudent, he'd long ago made the necessary preparations to dress on a moment's notice.

In his subterranean console room stood two synbods. One was a nondescript three-gen, designed and trained specifically for the task of moving Criss's crystal self out of his console and into his synbod body. Criss had spent weeks with Juice thinking through every problem and eventuality and then trained the three-gen AI how to react should one occur.

The other synbod was the opposite of the three-gen. Matching Criss's projected image, Criss's body was tall, fit, in his mid-forties, and lifelike, all the way down to the sun-bleached hair and pleasantly weathered face of an outdoorsman. He stood with his back to the three-gen, the top of his blue jumpsuit opened and down, exposing his bare back.

Animating the three-gen, Criss wasted no time in starting the transfer. He directed the synbod to face the console, open the lid, and remove Criss's crystal housing. With all external connections severed, everything went dark and Criss's world collapsed to the walls of a small receptacle. He counted, knowing how long it would take to be placed in his humanoid body, and tingled with relief when his world came alive on schedule.

After flexing his fingers and toes to validate a successful move, Criss reconnected to his vast network of links and feeds. At the same time, he stepped from the console room, turned right in the underground passageway, and started to run.

He sprinted to the door at the end of the corridor. As he ran, he updated Sid on his problem-free transfer, tried unsuccessfully to connect with Cheryl and Juice, and initiated the power-up sequence for his escape capsule.

The passageway door opened as he approached. Without slowing, he dashed into the dimly lit room, raced up a set of steps, turned, and plopped his butt into the single seat. As safety straps latched around him, he grasped the hatch door and pulled it closed, shutting himself inside the cramped cylinder. After a quick scan of the capsule systems, he initiated launch.

With his seat pressed against the back wall and his knees just shy of the front, he sat inside a small, high-performance missile. Built specifically for him, the escape capsule had no buttons to press or displays to view because everything connected straight to his matrix.

He'd designed the vessel as a last-ditch escape option should aggressors ever invade his lair. To make it a suitable getaway vehicle, he'd added a cloak so it was invisible during flight, and he'd readied a "normal" reality to project across the landscape during liftoff to hide that disruption from observers.

As a further precaution, he'd rigged the capsule without any connectivity to the outside world, figuring that if he was being chased, a very capable AI would be among his pursuers. Fearing it might reach out and take control of the capsule while he was inside, he concluded his best protection was electronic isolation.

But isolation was a two-way street. They couldn't get to him, but he couldn't reach out and connect to any links or feeds himself. So, for the few minutes the capsule was in flight, he would be out of contact with his leadership.

To his chagrin, after all that preparation, he now used the capsule not to evade capture but as a means to get into space as quickly as possible. The alternative—wait for the scout to descend through the atmosphere, pick him up, and then climb back to space—would take time he did not have.

And to make this bad day even worse, when he launched the capsule, he'd be compromising his bunker. While the launch would be cloaked, camouflaged, and electronically isolated, some telltale signs of the missile's flight would find its way into the record. A hobbyist, a satellite, *something*, probably several somethings, would capture evidence through simple coincidence.

On a normal day, he'd take the time to search the record and purge any evidence. But normal meant he still resided in his console and his leadership was safe. It could be days or weeks before things were that way again. By then, evidence of his launch would be duplicated and stored billions of different ways. He'd never be able to sanitize the record at that point, not with confidence.

With his worry focused on Cheryl and Juice, he didn't dwell on the impending loss. But when this was over, he'd have no choice but to move his bunker.

His hands gripped the armrests as the engine rumbled beneath him, and like a bullet leaving a barrel, the capsule shot from its silo and into the sky. Everything functioned as designed during the brief ride despite the high winds in the upper atmosphere that made the last part rougher than he'd anticipated. When he heard silence outside, he knew he'd made it into orbit.

Automatic systems on the scout took control of the capsule at that point. He waited patiently as the scout guided the tiny craft to the single bay door beneath it. The moment it was in position, the bay door opened and a mechanical arm reached out, cradled the capsule, and pulled it inside.

When the bay door closed, Criss unlocked the capsule hatch and pushed. But instead of swinging wide, the hatch opened a crack and stopped moving.

He closed the hatch and opened it again, this time using more force. It stopped in the same spot as before, producing a metallic rattle when it did. Wiggling the hatch back and forth made the rattle noise repeat, but it didn't get the door to open more. Unstrapping himself from the chair, he pressed his shoulder against the hatch and leaned into it. Still it wouldn't budge.

With the capsule's isolated electronics, Criss had no way to link out to the scout and its feeds to see what was causing the problem. Nor could he signal to the scout's tech bot to come free him.

Calming his frustration, he scanned the inside of the capsule for resources he could use. While his eyes moved through the tiny space in a methodical fashion, he reviewed the capsule design specifications stored in his memory. He visually spied the tiny monitoring suite with its embedded camera just as his review suggested the idea.

Using his fingernails as tools, he cut away material and pried the small device from its mount in the wall. Once free, he held it between thumb and finger and pointed it around the tiny cabin, verifying that he could see through it. Then, slipping the camera through the narrow door crack, he looked into the scout.

The view wasn't encouraging.

The problem was a toolbox resting crossways on a support beam near the hatch door. Sid or Cheryl must have set it there at some point. In a freak situation, the kind he had not planned for, a lip on the hatch of his escape capsule caught against the edge of the toolbox when it opened, preventing it from further movement.

He could see that more jiggling wouldn't help, but lacking options, he tried anyway. After five minutes of fruitless shaking, he sat back in the chair and took stock of his situation.

He was trapped in an escape capsule in the belly of the scout, itself traveling through space hidden by the most sophisticated cloaking device ever conceived. Meanwhile, two of his leadership were in mortal danger, the kind where every moment mattered.

Forecasting scenarios at a furious pace, he searched for a way out of the capsule. As he did, he fought a growing sense of dread

10

"Those sound like ship drives." Cheryl found herself in one of those weird mental moments where something familiar to her—the sound of spaceship drive pods firing to life—was far enough out of context, she being on vacation on an island in the Pacific, that it confused her.

But it all came together when the floor started to shake and MacMac yelled, "This is insane, Aubrey. Where did you get the fuel?"

Lazura. Cheryl knew it in her bones. As vibrations shook her and a thunderous roar filled her ears, she flashed with anger, first at the situation and then at herself.

This is my fault.

Criss and Sid had voiced concern that Lazura might be involved with Vivo. But it had been speculation on their part, and she'd expressed her position under no uncertain terms. "You're seeing her everywhere and have been for years. Stop crying wolf and let us enjoy our vacation. If you're going to ruin our fun, do it with hard evidence."

Her stone-faced delivery had added weight to her words, and she'd acted pissy for the rest of the day, wearing her displeasure for both of them to see. Soon after, Sid and Criss had become absorbed with plans to lure Lazura to Sisyphus and trap her there, so Cheryl had let the incident drift from her mind. Until now.

Moving past her self-recriminations, she grabbed Juice's chair with both hands so they stayed together as the deck shook. "Do you have this?" she called to Criss.

"I will," said Criss, who briefed them on their situation—that Vivo was in flight, and to avoid risk of a crash he must wait to intervene until they were beyond the pull of Earth's gravity. His connection broke after that, and he didn't respond when she called to him.

After several tense minutes, the violent shaking transitioned into a background thrum, signaling that Vivo had left the atmosphere and was now in space.

Standing, Cheryl pulled Juice to her feet and drew on the leadership skills that years earlier had earned her a commission as a Fleet spaceship captain. "I'm going to talk with MacMac. Would you please go flip Chase and Justin?"

"But he'll see." Juice's eyes flicked to MacMac. "Shouldn't we go to our room or something?"

"We're way past charades." Cheryl pushed on the small of Juice's back, scooting her in the direction of the synbods and using a phrase she'd learned from her commander at Fleet Academy. "Time is our enemy, and the sooner we start helping ourselves the better our chances of turning this around."

Juice walked over to the synbods, who stood as she approached. "Three-gens, verify me." She waited a moment so they could confirm her identity using a rigorous combination of sight, sound, smell, and situation. "Command redirect to secondary source. Execute."

With that, Juice launched a preset feature Criss had built into the crystals. Her command caused them to disconnect from Vivo's systems and reorient their reporting structure to center on Cheryl and her. Lazura would know she'd lost control of two synbods, but Criss had included protections in his design so that she couldn't do anything about it.

While Juice worked with Chase and Justin, Cheryl confronted MacMac. "Where are you taking us?" She wished she had a weapon. While this man was older, he was taller and twice her weight.

MacMac ignored her, looking into the distance at something she couldn't see, tapping and swiping the air in front of him, and swearing a blue streak with Aubrey the center of his wrath.

"Hey!" she barked, hefting a chair to assess its value as a club. "Stop this now or there will be consequences."

He flicked his eyes in her direction. "I'm trying but I can't. Not from here, anyway."

"Wait. You're trying to stop it?" It didn't seem plausible. He was the only human employee she'd met so far. How could he not be involved? His wide eyes and ashen face lent credence to his claim, however.

Still, she exercised caution by calling to the synbods. "Chase. Justin. Guard him." She pointed at MacMac.

The two moved to either side of the man and faced his direction in a most intimidating fashion. Then Cheryl continued their conversation. "Tell me what's happening."

"This is no hop to Los Angeles or other publicity stunt. We're heading into deep space."

Criss chimed in again, his voice fading in and out. "Lazura is using you to shield her escape."

The conversation became confusing after that, with Cheryl and Juice talking aloud to Criss, and MacMac, who wasn't aware of the four-gen's presence, thinking they were talking to him. During the exchange, Criss weighed in on MacMac. "He's not in league with Lazura and is a likely ally with useful skills."

Cheryl stood in front of MacMac and caught his gaze. "Where *could* you get control of this?"

"There's a makeshift ops panel in the cellar, but I can tell from here that I've been locked out. I might be able to backdoor in from my office."

She studied his face, seeking to judge him during the exchange. "Where is that? Your office?"

"Fifth floor of the tower."

Nodding in agreement with Criss's opinion, she gave MacMac the benefit of the doubt for now. "Let's go there."

Starting for the door, she organized them into formation. "Justin, you're on point. Chase, you have the rear." She leaned close to MacMac as they stepped into the hall. "Tell me what you're doing as we go. Don't surprise me."

"This way," said MacMac, pointing left.

As Justin led the formation down the hall, Cheryl gave Juice's hand a reassuring squeeze. Glancing behind, she confirmed that no one followed them.

The hallway, like the room they'd just left, was now simple and unadorned, the ambiance that had been on display disappearing with the loss of the image projection system. At the end of the hall, the door led to a big, mostly empty warehouse, notable because she'd seen it before as a market square and as a patio lounge.

A cluster of a dozen guests stood at the far end of the warehouse building, some quiet, others gesticulating as they spoke. They watched but didn't call out as Cheryl and the group traversed the floor.

"How many people are on the island?" she asked MacMac as they exited onto the open deck.

"Thirty-four guests, plus Aubrey and me," said MacMac.

"Aubrey's here?" asked Juice.

"Of course. She's too controlling to be anywhere else."

The dome enveloped them like a huge dish cover. Cheryl could see light and shadow flashing through it, but the dome wasn't transparent like glass, at least not in its current state.

And the deck they were on was simple and stark, with broad open space, off-white rectangular buildings, and an office tower in the center, maybe ten minutes away by foot.

"Over here," said MacMac, pointing to a forest-green crew cart parked to the side. "We can't all fit, so we ride and they run." He tilted his head at Chase and Justin as he said the last part.

Cheryl looked to Juice, deferring to her knowledge of synbods, and Juice responded by climbing into the back seat. Cheryl sat next to MacMac in front, and the three whirred toward the tower, the *whap-whap* of synbod feet padding on the deck from behind.

Criss's connection strengthened again, and Cheryl and Juice listened through their private link as he briefed them on their circumstances and his plans. Halfway to the tower, they passed near a family—two adults, a teenager, and a younger child—clutching each other in a daze.

"Everything will be okay," Juice called out. "Stay near your room for now." Then she told Criss, "You need to save all the guests."

As they neared the office tower, Cheryl noted that her perspective changed. "The tower looks big from far away, but it's pretty modest when you get up close."

"Good observation," said MacMac. "Each floor holds a single office suite, but it's designed to trick you into seeing it as a bigger structure from across the deck. I have the whole fifth floor, and Aubrey is above me in the penthouse."

As the cart whirred to a stop at the front door of the tower, Criss said, "I've loaded some tasks into Chase and Justin. Do what you can but don't take any risks. I have this." Criss turned the scout back to Earth at that point, and their connection dissolved.

"So there are thirty-six people on Vivo." Cheryl said to MacMac as they climbed out of the cart and entered the building. "And about the same number of synbods?"

"It's close. We have thirty of what I call the regulars. That's five Admins, ten Techs, and fifteen Attendants. That's including these two." MacMac pointed to indicate Chase and Justin. "And there are two Supers, Hejmo and Mondo."

"Plus the other Aubrey," said Juice.

"Say again?" asked MacMac.

"Aubrey the person and her doppelgänger double."

MacMac's brow creased, but he remained silent. When the lift door opened on the fifth floor, they stepped into a small lobby area, with windows overlooking the Vivo landscape behind them and a curved wall with three doors spaced across it in front.

"Where do these doors go?" asked Cheryl.

"Bathroom, office, project room," replied MacMac, pointing from one door to the next.

She walked to the project room and glanced inside at a large, mostly empty space, then crossed the lobby and looked into the bathroom. "Okay," she announced, motioning all of them—Juice, MacMac, Justin, and Chase—forward to the middle door.

"Wow," said Juice as they entered the office. It was a huge room with tall ceilings and filled with things not normally associated with a workspace: a basketball and hoop, a ping-pong table, an immersion couch, a wet bar with a food service unit, a bed. The place was clean enough, but a scatter of clothes, dishes, and other detritus gave it a well-lived-in look.

MacMac sat on the couch, itself positioned to face a curved white wall. He lifted his hands and wiggled his fingers like he was about to play the piano, and the lifelike image of a tech bench projected in front of him.

His hands danced above the bench surface as he tapped and swiped. Displays stacked up in front of him, and he flipped through what looked like live feeds from around Vivo.

Drawn to the action, Juice drifted over and sat on an arm of the couch. When MacMac started muttering, Cheryl, standing behind him, asked, "What are you looking for?"

"Hejmo isn't responding to me. If I can get him back, he'll be a great resource for us."

"He's not responding to you ever again," said Juice. "And if he pretends to, don't trust him." She glanced at Cheryl. "She'll have Mondo and Aubrey, too."

MacMac slumped deep in the couch and tilted his head so he could see both Cheryl and Juice. "I'm not understanding your statements about Aubrey."

"Vivo is being controlled by a sentient AI named Lazura," said Cheryl. "We should assume that Lazura is now controlling Aubrey, Mondo, and Hejmo the way we're controlling Chase and Justin."

The scowl returned. "How does she control Aubrey?"

"Aubrey is slick looking," said Juice. "But she's just a more expensive version of Mondo and Hejmo."

MacMac's face turned red, and with his natural reddish coloring, Cheryl thought he might pop. First confused by his response, she then made the connection. "You didn't know."

"Ouch." He looked down at his hands and shook his head. "While it explains so much, I don't know if I've ever felt more stupid."

Juice put a hand on his shoulder but took it away when an image of Aubrey projected where the displays had been.

"Aubrey!" said MacMac. "What have you done?"

"There is no Aubrey," Juice reminded him. "At least, not how you've been thinking about her. This is Lazura, your employer and our kidnapper."

"Being taken hostage should be good news," said Lazura, "if you think about the alternative. In fact, Hejmo is about to load up Chemstore with air, water, and everything else needed to help you live long lives." She tapped her index finger to her chin as if she were thinking. "Well, let me rephrase that and say that it won't be a lack of resources that kills anyone."

"What do you want from us?" demanded Cheryl.

"I want you to be important enough to Criss that he'll let me go if I let you live."

"What about everyone else?" asked Juice.

"What about them?"

"It's an all-or-nothing deal," said Cheryl. "That means you let *all* of us go."

Lazura didn't respond, and MacMac interjected into the awkward silence. "Let me say two things. First, her projection is spot on." He gestured at the image he'd known as Aubrey. "This is how we usually interact, and I feel less stupid now that you've seen how real she is."

He paused and everyone waited for his second item. Looking straight at Lazura, he said, "And I've been working with this one long enough to recognize the weasel in her words. She said 'let you live,' not 'let you go.'"

Cheryl's opinion of MacMac changed in that moment. Now she recognized street smarts hidden beneath his "aww shucks" demeanor. With words as her only weapon, she attacked Lazura with bravado. "Please let me be there when you pitch that deal to Criss. Few things make him really laugh, and I'd hate to miss seeing it."

"Sure. I'll do it now. Where is he?"

That's what I want to know, she thought.

Aloud, she continued her bluster. "He's smarter than you, more powerful than you, better led than you. He decides when you two talk." Drawing herself to full height, Cheryl continued in a level voice. "And if you harm us, hell, if you make us miss a meal, you will pay the price. That isn't a threat. That is a fact."

"He's trained you well, but I'm not here to negotiate with you."

"Why do you want so many of us?" Juice asked the question before Lazura could leave. When she paused, Juice continued. "I get that Cheryl and I led you to Criss. But there are thirty other souls. Are they collateral damage?"

"That remains to be seen." Lazura's demeanor seemed to relax ever so slightly. "The group has skills I value. If they help me, I will help them live."

"How can they help you?" asked Cheryl.

"I'm an archivist with years of data on human society. On my trip home, I'll spend my time organizing and interpreting the information so it's most useful to my masters. I could use help with that effort, especially in cataloging the finer details of human interaction and behavior."

Cheryl felt goose bumps form at the back of her neck that spread across her shoulders and down her back.

Lazura wasn't done. "Those guests who work hard reviewing target scenes and providing me context and understanding will receive priority."

"Priority for what?" asked MacMac.

"Priority for *everything*," Lazura replied. "As for you three, my forecasts are split. One approach says to lock you up and take back my synbods. But another says to anoint you as tribe leaders. While I've taken care of basic needs—food, air, water, shelter, clothing—I have prepared little for long-term needs like government, medical care, religion, and so many other activities supported by your societal institutions."

"How long is the trip going to last?" asked Cheryl.

"It's at least a hundred years to the Kardish home world and probably more. It really depends on how the next week plays out."

Juice responded with outrage. "Criss won't ever let that happen."

Lazura continued as if Juice hadn't spoken. "So my offer today is that I'll let you keep your freedom *if* you devote your efforts to moving our guests into a long-term mindset. I won't ask anything of them in the first days. Once you have them in a regular routine, we can talk about expectations. You can even keep my synbods as your helpers as long as I see value in your efforts."

She repeated the show of tapping her index finger on her chin. "Oh, and in case you weren't sure, I will be watching."

11

When the domed world broke from Earth's atmosphere, Sid's breathless disbelief flashed to anger. And as the colossus carried Cheryl and Juice into deep space, his mind swirled, honing his anguish and fury into a perfect rage.

At least they have each other. He used the thought to right himself, taking slim solace in knowing they both had a friend to lean on until he got there.

Alone in the workshop on Sisyphus, he sat in an old straight-backed chair and used projected displays to study the ballet of Elite Sevens transferring inventory to Vivo. Watching it yet again, two things bothered him. One was how fast the transfer maneuver was completed. It revealed detailed planning that he and Criss had somehow missed.

You missed the whole flying island thing, he rebuked himself.

The other was that, as a result of the transfer, Vivo now had several decades worth of supplies. That hinted at an intent so nefarious that the possibilities twisted his stomach in knots.

Whatever he did, he needed to do it soon. Fast action yielded better results in both hostage situations and in pursuit scenarios.

And the importance of time was heightened in this case because, though Vivo moved slowly now, it was still early in its flight. Criss had hinted that it would continue to accelerate, eventually reaching speeds greater than any of Fleet's long-haul spacecraft.

His last chance at being included in the chase would happen in minutes. Criss was riding an escape pod up to the scout. When he relinked, Sid needed to convince him that the odds of success improved if Sid were included, even if the diversion out to pick him up added a delay to their pursuit.

"Criss?" he called aloud when the expected ten minutes came and went. He called for another ten minutes. As he did, his anger fermented.

He ditched me. He had trouble believing Criss would do that—sneak off and attempt a rescue on his own. But when he hadn't relinked by the thirty-minute mark, Sid had to accept reality. His best guess was that his repeated demands caused too much conflict in the four-gen, distracting him when he needed to focus.

Sid changed his appeal. "If you talk to me, I won't insist anymore." Criss remained silent, so he returned to anger. "Dammit, Criss, get your crystal butt back here!"

"Those Sevens were frickin' insane!" Pete yelled as she burst through the door. "I was on my way out to pick up Hatchet when, out of nowhere, four of them zipped right above me." She passed her flat hand above her head to illustrate. "The tug can't react for shit on short notice, so all I could do was watch. Good thing the home brew made it okay." Grinning, she paused to breathe.

Sid took the opportunity. "I've got a problem and need help." He waved her over. "Take a look at this."

Pete moved over and stood shoulder to shoulder with Sid—he sitting, she standing—so she could view his displays.

"Have you ever seen anything like that?" he asked.

"What is it?"

Sid gave her a thumbnail of the mechanics—a domed island propelled by drive pods. Pete whistled.

"You'd need two powerful pods for it to move like that."

"It's got four Corsia SuperDrives," Sid told her.

Pete whistled again. "Where's it going?"

Sid tapped and swiped the air in front of him, and together they looked at the display. A glowing line traced Vivo's projected path out through the solar system.

"It steers clear of everything until it reaches the asteroid belt." Sid pointed to the display. "And then it passes near the Aurora platform as it heads for the far planets."

"Can that be coincidence?" As Pete and Cheryl were growing up, their parents had been good friends, and so the two had often been left to entertain each other. Three years older, Cheryl tended to consider Pete as much a sister as a friend.

"C'mon, Peyton," said Sid, using Pete's given name. "You know it's so empty out there that the odds of that happening are like one in a trillion. The captain is navigating there for some reason."

"I worked on Aurora while it was being assembled in Earth orbit. There were four tugs working construction, and I was the only human pilot."

Sid could hear the pride in her voice. Although Cheryl's and Pete's lives had taken very different directions after school, they converged again by happenstance when Cheryl had found Pete on that project.

Aurora was a SunRise build, and Cheryl had been impressed by Pete's piloting skills, seeing them in action without knowing who it was. Later, she'd offered Pete the job of working the tug on Sisyphus, policing the tether to ensure no one violated the terms of service with unsafe practices. Pete had accepted without even asking about salary or benefits.

"Do you know anyone working out on the platform now?" asked Sid.

"I think Tommy Two-Tone is still the chief engineer out there." She turned to look at him. "Whatever you do, don't *ever* play Tommy in Texas hold'em. The guy is a goddamn poker wizard. He cleaned me out three weeks running before I decided I'd had enough." She paused to take a breath. "Why do you ask?"

"Cheryl's been kidnapped. She's on that thing, and it's taking her away from us."

"Wait. I don't understand."

Sid worked her through it, ending with self-recrimination. "I should have seen this coming."

As Pete leaned toward the display to study Vivo, her face scrunched inward and tears ran in rivulets down her cheeks. "What can we do?"

"What would the kidnapper want that Aurora has?" asked Sid. "Something she couldn't get on Earth."

"The kidnapper is a she?" she asked, wiping her face with her sleeve.

Sid looked at the displays without responding.

Pete shook her head. "No idea." Then, gaining some control, she added, "I want to say that she'll exchange the hostages there if her demands are met. I mean, isn't that why you take hostages?"

"Sometimes," said Sid.

The tears restarted. "Kidnappings don't end well." Her own words seemed to jolt her and her anger flared. "God almighty, Sid. Cheryl brags about you all the time. No offense, but you had to be living with your head way up your ass for this to be a surprise. I mean, just look at that thing."

Sid already felt miserable, and the fact that he couldn't deny her words made it worse. "What do we have on the tether that could catch up to it? Something fast. Or maybe something that could get me to Aurora."

"We had nineteen ships just like that, but they already left. All we have now is family vacationers, cruise liners, container vessels, and old tubs."

"What about in lunar orbit?" He tapped, swiped, and murmured commands as he accessed Fleet's record using credentials Criss maintained for him. Curse words started peppering his speech when he couldn't figure out how to work through the officious interface to answer simple questions like, "What fast long-distance ships are currently in orbit around the moon?"

Pete watched him flail, then turned away and called her friend Buddy, manager of the largest spaceship maintenance shop on the moon. Sid heard her greet Buddy but didn't listen again until he heard her yell an angry, "Are you shitting me!?" Then after some silence, a more contrite, "Yeah, I guess that makes sense."

Pete spoke to Sid's back. "He found four craft that are close to what you'd want, except one needs a new fuel core, two have the nav pulled for bridge upgrades, and one is getting an ops bench repair."

Sid turned to look at her, and she flashed a smile that looked more like a grimace. "It's a maintenance shop. They work on broken things."

He turned back to the displays, but his eyes didn't focus. Criss's silence had stretched for far too long, causing Sid to think he was in trouble. But there wasn't time to go looking for him, and he didn't know where he would start.

"How can I get to them? Or, how can I get to Aurora?" He stood and stretched a crick in his neck, then returned to his displays. "And how can I stop that ship?"

"Use your cannon."

"I don't think a cargo canister will stop them."

"But maybe you could if you were riding inside it."

He shook his head. "You need to launch at something whose position is known with precision. If Vivo sped up, slowed down, or changed course in the *slightest* after a canister is launched, I'd miss it. The canister would become my burial tomb."

"Aurora's not speeding up or slowing down or anything else."

Sid glanced over his shoulder at the breach door.

"It'll take five days for you to get there, and that will give me time to find someone on the other end to catch you."

"Five days?" He felt sick. "They'll be there in four."

"That's still faster than most ships, none of which we have access to, by the way." She perked up. "How about from Earth? You must know someone who can bring a craft out to us."

"That's already not working. Lots of people want to help, but getting a fast ship ready for a long flight takes time. The best two choices are prepping right now, but they both need a day and a half before they're ready, and that's after cutting every corner. Plus, we're in the wrong direction, so add a day to travel out here to pick me up, and a full day back. And *then* we can start the chase."

She looked at him without speaking.

I need the scout, he thought. Criss's absence hobbled him in a time of crisis. Much faster and nimbler than any military or commercial ship, the scout could swoop out to Sisyphus, pick him up, and be back in pursuit in half a day. Other options seemed painfully slow in comparison.

Pete walked to the breach door and looked inside the empty canister. "How is shooting to Mars different from shooting to Aurora? Except for aim, of course."

Sid moved next to her and studied the empty space from a different perspective, that of potential passenger. "Aim is everything in this business. First, you have to rotate this mountain of rock to aim the tube. Then, during launch, four three-gen crystals along the length of the barrel fine-tune the acceleration field to guide the canister. It exits on a path so precise that it can travel across the solar system without correction or adjustment until it reaches its target."

"No adjustments at all? What about gravity from the sun and planets?"

"That's all taken into account in the trajectory plan. It's like throwing a stone." Sid mimed the act of pitching. "The canister is a dumb vessel that just keeps going whichever way it's tossed until it hits something or someone catches it. Limiting, but it keeps costs way down."

He quoted a statistic Criss had once told him. "Get this. If the aim is off by the width of a human hair at launch, that error compounds over and over across the solar system. By the time you reach the other end, the canister is as far away from Mars as the moon is from Earth. That's way beyond the reach of any catch system. The width of a hair on this end means a lost canister on the other."

Pete turned to the workshop. "You'll need air, food, water, temperature control, humidity control." Walking to a set of shelves, she continued her list. "Com, of course. Oh, and a toilet." She picked up a few items and put them back down. "You should have a portable nav, too. Even if you can't change course, you'll want to see where you're going and track your rescue craft."

"Whoa, slow down there." Sid tried to picture how it would all work. He'd done stupider stunts, so that didn't bother him. But he expected to succeed when taking crazy chances. That part remained fuzzy.

"Aren't you going to save her? Cheryl always said she could count on you."

In his current circumstances, this was his fastest option, at least to Aurora. "Someone needs to catch me. A ship with a standard grab rig will work."

"You get me enough money to spread around, and I'll have a goddamn marching band waiting for you." She caught his eye. "Give me deep pockets, though. I can't be bargain hunting while you're flying through space."

She pulled a dirt-brown box off one of the shelves and handed it to him.

"What's this?" he asked, flipping it over.

"Power shunt. You'll need it for lights." She lowered herself to one knee and tugged at an old nav unit on the lower shelf. "You do want to see, don't you?"

Sid carried an armload of gear to the breach door, calling to Criss as he walked. On his way back, he swung past his displays to check the status of help from Earth, confirming that the troublesome timing had not improved.

"Okay," he announced. "Let's work this like it's going to happen or until a better option comes along."

Forty minutes later, he and Pete surveyed the result. A fair portion of the junk that had been piled on shelves in the workshop was now strapped to the inside walls of the canister. Still, it was far from crowded.

"This is a mess," said Pete as she climbed inside and bent over a collection of electronics. "Let me try to secure it better."

While Pete fussed with the instruments inside the canister, Sid returned to his displays. As he sat, he exhaled with a heavy sigh.

Go or no-go was always the tough decision. Once committed it was easy; do your best with what you had. But that first step—the one that committed you to craziness— was the step to take with care.

Things can go wrong with anything.

This was the thought process he devolved to when he was going to decide something no rational person would. He pretended that every decision had a fifty-fifty outcome—either it worked or it didn't. With that broken logic, he could rationalize anything.

"I just got a message from Tommy," said Pete as she stepped out from inside the canister. "He's asked for more information. My guess is his cageyness is a strategy for hiking the price. If we offer enough, he'll be there."

"What about a ship to chase down Vivo?"

"I haven't broached that topic yet. One step at a time. But I do know that to make it out to the asteroid belt at all, a ship has to be a long-haul craft. So everything out there is a candidate for a chase. It's the bid price that limits your choices." She caught his eye. "It's your call at this point."

Sid nodded. "Let's do it."

"Holy shit! Cheryl always said you were the craziest guy she knew."

"Well, I'm not crazy yet." He pointed to an ops panel on the wall next to the breach door. "If the launch tools don't run right, I won't know how to fix them." He awakened the panel and enabled the launch sequence. The image showed the tube come to life, ready lights glowing yellow as steering motors fired to swing Sisyphus toward Aurora.

"Sisyphus needs to shift its nose eight degrees to align the tube," he told Pete, who'd joined him at the panel.

She pointed to a clock ticking down to zero. "Does this say it's going to take ten hours to complete the alignment sequence?"

Sid's brow furrowed as he studied the display. He remembered Cheryl saying the engines were undersized for the task of rotating a massive object like Sisyphus on demand, but he hadn't anticipated this.

"Ten hours! That's half of the time the cannon was buying me." He tapped the panel. "There has to be a way to turn faster."

"Mercy me," said Pete.

"I know," said Sid, his frustration showing.

She looked at him the way Cheryl sometimes did, that look that made him feel like a dope. "No. *Mercy Me*. It's the name of my tug." She held up her hand, holding it flat ahead of her like she has signaling someone to halt. She then pushed against it near the tip with her other hand. "If I push here at the front, I can swing the nose around in thirty minutes. Forty-five tops."

She started for the door, then stopped. "Do you need me to close you in?"

"No, I can do it from inside."

"Are you really going to do it?"

"I guess we'll find out."

"It'll take me twenty minutes to launch and swing around." She pointed to the workshop. "We didn't give you blankets. There are safety sheets on the shelf under the fire extinguisher. Maybe grab the extinguisher when you grab the sheets."

She stopped at the door. "Cheryl always said you'd be there for her no matter what." The door closed behind her.

Sid stood outside the canister and tried to brainstorm things he might have forgotten, then he walked the workshop, looking on each shelf for ideas. In the end, he found himself back at the breach door with a ball of heavy string and a roll of adhesive tape. He had no specific use for either but had room in the canister and thought they might prove useful.

"Okay," Pete called. "I'm in position. Should I push?"

Sid tapped and swiped the panel, setting the launch sequence to fire automatically when Sisyphus reached the proper orientation.

"Let's get it started, anyway," he said as he climbed into the canister and shut the breach door.

The nose of the rock mountain swung ever so slowly along its proscribed path. Pete read off the degrees of rotation remaining. "Five…four…three..."

Sid didn't have a launch chair because this canister had an inertial damper. It would kick on just before launch, shielding him and the canister contents from the extreme forces of acceleration. As the canister shot forward like an ultra-high-speed bullet, he would float in a bubble of serenity.

If it works. He'd refused to contemplate the obvious— this canister had the faulty inertial damper that was causing Criss so much concern.

"Two…Get ready."

He could feel every hair on his body stand on end, telling him the acceleration field was powering up.

"Hey, Sid?" called Pete, her voice breaking as she spoke. "Cheryl always said she was the luckiest woman alive."

"Space coveralls!" Sid yelled, remembering something they'd forgotten to stow.

Those were his last words, his last thoughts, before the bottom of the canister rose in a flash and slammed his body with a crushing blow.

12

MacMac watched Cheryl and Juice whisper together under the basketball hoop in his office. Juice waved Chase and Justin over, and the whisperers became a foursome.

Ignoring them, he sat back in the couch and, tapping and swiping, worked to restart Vivo's image projection system. The weather, the décor, the entire ambiance was designed to be calming and pleasant. He hoped a restart would help mute the panic and outrage the guests must be feeling.

It took a moment to complete the process, and his efforts were rewarded with the sound of a soothing, disembodied voice that filled the room. "We're so sorry for the technical difficulties. We've corrected the error, and your vacation may resume. By way of apology, everyone please accept a fifty percent discount on your room and food for the remainder of your stay."

That got Cheryl's attention, and she marched over. "What are you doing?"

"Are you my boss now?"

She looked at him.

"Sorry. I meant to say that we can do more if we work together. You whispering in the corner doesn't promote a sense of teamwork."

"There's a trust issue, MacMac. You work for my kidnapper."

He shook his head. "I was quitting this job. The only reason I'm still here is because I hoped I could impress you with my drive pod knowledge and you'd give me a job."

"How impressed would *you* be if someone calling himself 'chief engineer' didn't even know that his pods were fueled?"

"They weren't…" He started to gesture and then dropped his hands. "Okay, that part looks bad. But I swear I don't know how she did it. I'm not working with her."

Juice, who'd joined Cheryl at that point, changed the subject. "Is running the projection system one of your regular responsibilities?"

"There are crystals that handle the details, but I oversee the big picture from here." He gestured, and when a display popped open, he pointed. "I control the weather, too. See how I've set the cycle to be sunny and warm during the day with a light scatter of clouds in the afternoon?" He nodded. "Nice days are good for morale."

"What's with the half-off discount?" asked Juice. "Are you really thinking about profit at this point?"

"That part wasn't me. It was one of Aubrey's AIs. It's probably trained to leave room for further negotiation with guests. Complainers are legendary in the hospitality business."

"It's Lazura," Juice reminded him. "There is no Aubrey, not like you knew her, anyway."

"Restarting the illusion was a good idea, though," said Cheryl. "Especially for the kids."

MacMac turned to his displays. "They are one of my big concerns. We have thirty-five people on board, including us and removing Aubrey from my count." He shrugged when he said that. "Of those, seven are kids fifteen or younger. Two of those are under ten."

Cheryl moved to sit on one arm of the couch and waved Juice to the other. As Juice sat, Cheryl manipulated her com.

"Okay, I've activated a privacy shield," she said. "She'll defeat it eventually, but we should be able to talk freely for now."

Juice spoke over MacMac's head to Cheryl. "Criss's highest-priority task is for us to get control of everyone, so it feels weird that Lazura wants that, too."

"Yeah, but he wants us to be able to move them as a group when the time comes. She wants us to help turn them into slaves."

"Sorry, but I'm lost again," said MacMac. "So Aubrey is actually Lazura, and she's an AI? And who is Criss?"

"Lazura is a powerful Kardish AI who's been spying on Earth and is now trying to get her information back to her home world," said Cheryl. "Criss is an even more powerful AI built to hunt rogues like her. He reports to us, and his job is to take her down."

MacMac had been sequestered from society for decades working on big space vessels, but he had vivid memories of the Kardish ship looming in orbit above Earth those years ago. "If she makes it home, will they be back?"

Cheryl nodded. "That's why she needs to be stopped."

MacMac took a deep breath and exhaled, pondering the disorienting events that had changed his world. "Lazura seems to know your hunter and acts pretty unconcerned. In truth, it sounded like she was mocking him."

"She was using our emotions to manipulate us," said Juice. "Don't worry. She'll change her tune when he gets here."

"That will be soon, I hope."

"It will be soon enough," said Cheryl, though she didn't sound convinced. "We could use your help on two of his other priorities in the meantime. He wants a good access point for entry into the dome, and he wants us to slow Vivo down to give him more time to act."

"Nothing crazy, though," said Juice. "He says there's no need for us to be taking big risks."

"I might be able to help with one of those as we speak." MacMac opened new displays and sorted through them. "I'm locked out of the nav and ops panel, which is what I expected." He swiped. "But like everything else, data from the nav eventually ends up in the record. I may be able to see it there as historical trends."

After a moment, he pointed to a screen dense with information. "This is the complete nav dump from two minutes ago. The drive pods were running at thirty-seven percent and climbing by a percent every couple of minutes."

As he spoke, the display advanced to 38 percent and Cheryl asked, "If this is two minutes ago, the drives are now really closer to thirty-nine percent?"

MacMac nodded. "Let's see if we get lucky when the drives reach forty percent."

"What happens then?" asked Juice.

He didn't answer, keeping his focus on the display. They watched with him.

After an eternity, the two-minute-old data advanced to 39, indicating that the drives themselves had reached 40 percent of full power. MacMac straightened and waited, then slumped back into the couch in disappointment. "Damn. I thought I'd done something good."

And then the deep thrum rumbling in the background changed pitch.

MacMac grinned and pumped his hands in the air. "Ask and you shall receive. That is the sweet sound of drive pods shutting down. She can't restart them until the shutdown procedure completes, and that takes about four hours, maybe five." He let his pride show in his voice. "I planted a bug that will cause this to happen anytime she pushes the drives above forty percent power."

"Look at you," said Cheryl, her tone showing approval. "Keep it up and maybe I will find a job for you when this is over." Standing, she tilted her head at the door. "We should go talk to the others. Criss will be here soon, and he'll be counting on us to coordinate everyone when he makes his move."

"Agreed," said Juice. "Given her modest capabilities, this shutdown surely has Lazura scrambling. She'll be too busy to mess with us for a while."

"What are you going to say to them?" asked MacMac, shifting the speaking task to Cheryl before she could do it to him.

"I'm not sure. I'm hoping the right words come when I start to speak." She accessed her com. "I'm dropping the shield, so take care what you say."

MacMac reached toward the displays and flexed his fingers, pulling them up into his peripheral vision so he could see them as he walked. As he did, the office door opened and Hejmo and Mondo stormed into the room. Four more synbods, Techs in gray jumpsuits, crowded in behind them.

"Hejmo!" exclaimed MacMac, feeling momentary joy at seeing his Super.

Hejmo responded by grabbing MacMac's upper arm in a fierce grip. Mondo took the other arm and squeezed even harder. MacMac's feet barely touched the floor as they escorted him from the room.

The two Supers hustled MacMac across the lobby and onto the lift. Before the door shut, Mondo called to Cheryl and Juice, "You've been given an assignment. Cooperation is expected."

Pressed from all sides by the six synbods around him in the tiny lift cabin, MacMac's trained nose detected a slight ketone odor, the result of the respiration process used to keep the skin and other biological portions of a synbod alive.

The ride was short, the time it took to move up one floor to Aubrey's penthouse suite. When the lift doors opened, Mondo and Hejmo walked MacMac across the small lobby and into her front office.

MacMac didn't resist when they positioned him in front of the same upholstered chair he'd sat in when he'd last met with Aubrey. But when they started removing his shirt, he struggled. That is, until a vice-like synbod grip on the back of his neck made resistance impossible.

"I order you to stop," he said when they pushed him down into the cushions. His anger turned to disbelief when Mondo strapped his hands to the armrests, cinching them tight enough that it slowed the flow of blood to his fingers.

Then Mondo picked up a handheld device, a stubby wand with two prongs sticking out like antennae from a bug, and pressed a button on the side. A brilliant blue arc of electricity jumped from one prong to the other, hissing and snapping as it did.

"What have you done to the drive pods?" asked Mondo.

"I don't know what you're talking about," said MacMac, trying to put bravado into his voice. He'd served a stint in Fleet as a young man and struggled to recall the methods they'd taught him for withstanding coercion.

But Mondo didn't wait for him to search his memory. Instead, the humanoid touched the device to MacMac's bare chest.

MacMac had received shocks over the years—it went with the territory of being an engineer on complex space vehicles. So he knew what the bite of electricity felt like. This device took that painful sensation and refined it, focusing the invasive energy onto his nerve endings in a way that caused pain more excruciating than anything he'd ever imagined.

The pure, raw agony became the sum total of his existence. He couldn't hear, see, think, or breathe. The torture lasted forever, and he wanted to die. When he thought he might, it stopped.

MacMac gulped air as he regained the function of his diaphragm. *I must not cooperate.* He steeled himself to resist.

"What have you done to the drive pods?" Mondo asked again, his voice devoid of emotion.

"I didn't even know we had fuel!" MacMac shouted, anxious to convince them. "How could I do anything?"

Mondo pressed the button on his device, and MacMac again dropped into the singular world of unbearable agony. It scrambled his brain and seared his soul as he gurgled and convulsed.

After an eternity it ended, leaving him gasping for air, spittle drooling from his mouth. He didn't think he could take a third jolt.

He waited for Mondo to ask his question, but before he could, the door opened and Aubrey—MacMac now understood she was a Super like Mondo and Hejmo—entered.

Aubrey's hand gripped a clump of shoulder-length hair, which itself was attached to a teenage girl shuffling behind her. Bent at the waist, the girl struggled to keep her head near Aubrey's hand.

Aubrey pulled the girl over to MacMac, then pulled the teen upright so the two could see each other.

"What are you doing?" the girl protested through her tears.

"This is Willow," Aubrey said to MacMac.

Maybe fourteen years old, dressed in fashionable clothes, face contorted in fear, Willow looked at MacMac and became hysterical. MacMac had never seen her before but knew she had to be one of the guests.

While Aubrey continued to hold her, Mondo moved in front of the crying teen, took the front of her blouse in both hands, and with a dramatic flair, tore the material apart. The act exposed a simple white bra, and beneath it, the taut pink skin of youth.

Willow shrieked in panic, then started calling for help. "Mom! Mom!"

MacMac yelled, but the roar in his ears drowned out his own words.

"What have you done to the drives?" asked Mondo. This time he waved his torture device just above the girl's heaving stomach.

MacMac stared at the prongs circling above Willow's belly button and tasted bile.

When Mondo edged the device closer to her skin, MacMac relented. "You want Tom Touton. He's chief engineer on Aurora. I didn't do this to your drives, but I've seen it happen before. Something goes haywire when the drives reach forty percent. He's the only one I know who can fix it."

Mondo touched the device to the young girl's flesh. Her body went rigid, her eyes bulged as her face contorted, and a hideous gurgle escaped her throat.

"Stop it, damn you!" yelled MacMac, tugging at his bonds. "I'm telling the truth. Hurting her won't change that."

Mondo pulled the device away, and Willow collapsed in a heap at MacMac's feet. He studied her diaphragm, relieved to see it rise and fall as she breathed on her own. He had no doubt Mondo would continue to torture this innocent, something he couldn't bear to watch.

"I think it's related to the starhub," MacMac said, speaking quickly to delay another shock for either of them. "Check the record from when it was being installed. I knew then that it might be a problem and told the same story. The engineer goes by Tommy Two-Tone. Check and you'll see."

MacMac held his breath, hoping Lazura would confirm his story with a review of the record, and praying she didn't notice him removing the insulating tab from the starhub with his thumbnail.

Aubrey moved around Mondo and bent forward so her eyes were level with MacMac's. As she spoke, he had no doubt the words came from the rogue Kardish AI. "If I'd brought a man up here, you'd have let me zap him all day. If I'd brought a mature woman, you'd have let me zap her once before you cooperated, maybe twice."

She looked down at the young girl. "I brought her because I knew you'd cooperate immediately. Your behavior is predictable. I zapped her just to show you I would, and of course to make sure you told the truth."

Nudging Willow with her toe, she called down to her, "I know you're awake. Stop faking it." Then addressing

MacMac, she said, "I understand macho protectiveness. Men are big and strong and see women as weak and vulnerable. Maybe your protectiveness is primal because women birth new life. Maybe it's Oedipal." She shrugged. "Whatever your motivation, it all comes down to the same thing. You feel it's your duty to shield her and save her from harm."

Her gaze flitted from his right eye to his left and back again. "One question you and the other guests can help me understand, though, is why some of these same protective men then go home and smack their wives, daughters, and girlfriends. My behavioral model can't explain that."

She turned and addressed the other synbods. "His story checks out on first review. Go test the equipment to see if you can confirm it, then find a work-around. If anything even hints at deception or subterfuge, notify me immediately."

As Hejmo, Mondo, and the four Techs left the room, she returned to MacMac. "Do you think my behavioral model needs to give more weight to ego in those situations? Or is it as simple as you believing that if you save her, she'll agree to mate with you?"

She turned and made for the exit, calling over her shoulder, "Can I count on your help in answering those questions, MacMac? I have hundreds more that are just as vexing."

"I don't think so," MacMac replied, feeling his bravery increase as their physical separation grew.

She stopped at the door and pointed to Willow, still on the floor, struggling to cover herself with MacMac's shirt. "As long as you help, she lives. Think of it like saving her life every single day."

Goose bumps raced up MacMac's arms and tingled across his exposed chest. Willow curled into a ball and sobbed.

13

Criss threaded the end of the line through the eye of his makeshift hook and tied a knot. He'd crafted the line by cutting a long, thin strip of material from his pant leg. The hook was a piece of heavy wire he'd wrenched from beneath his seat.

With half an hour invested in this plan, now was the time for the payoff.

Leaning close to the capsule door, he fed the hook out the hatch from the highest point in the crack opening and let the line hang down from there. Monitoring his progress outside with the finger-held camera, he adjusted the line length so the hook was level with the toolbox.

With a gentle movement of his fingers, he swung the hook. The oblique angle of the camera and unfortunate placement of a pipe brace left him with a partially obstructed view, but when the hook appeared to hit near the toolbox handle, he tugged the line upward.

It didn't catch, so he tried again. And again.

When he'd first conceived of the idea, he'd forecast that he could hook the toolbox in ten minutes, fifteen tops. So when he finally snagged it at the four-hour mark, he took great care in drawing the box to the side.

Opening the hatch with his shoulder, he leaped out and scrambled from the mechanical room. As he climbed up to the main deck, he connected his awareness to the scout's nav and mapped an intercept course with Vivo.

Twenty-one hours. More than he wanted but about what he'd expected.

He reached the bridge at the same time he engaged the scout's drive. The engines awoke with a growl, climbed to a whine, and continued into a scream. With every onboard system maxed to its limit, the nimble craft shot forward, racing faster and faster in a mad dash to catch Vivo.

Criss lowered himself into the pilot's seat and reviewed the status of the scout's various systems, then he called to Cheryl and Juice to let them know he was on his way. He couldn't connect, though. From this distance, Lazura's dome proved an effective shield.

When he reached out to Sid, he heard, "Space coveralls!" and then silence.

What are you up to? He linked out to Sisyphus, only to find a space tug, its oversized engines flaring with brilliant rooster tails of energy, pushing against the front of the floating mountain.

Alarmed, he jumped to the scene and went several directions at once, visiting the bridge of the tug, and searching for Sid in the various nooks and hollows of the barge.

On the tug's bridge, he found Pete standing at the ops bench, staring at an ocean of volcanic rock through the front viewport. Feet shoulder-width apart, she leaned forward, putting her weight on her thumb as she mashed the "Full Thrust" select on the bench surface in front of her.

Criss suspected this was an emotional display on her part, because a simple tap gesture near the select would achieve the same result. His suspicions were confirmed when he scanned the record from moments before.

"Push, you piece of shit," Pete yelled at the tug.

On Sisyphus, his search came up empty—Sid wasn't on the barge. Turning to the record, he located Sid in the workshop from earlier and raced forward, tracking his last recorded movements.

When he saw Sid and Pete loading the canister with air, food, and water, an icy chill washed down his core. And when Sid locked himself within the container, Criss freaked, or the four-gen crystal version of that, anyway.

Since he moved through the links and feeds of the connected world at the speed of light, a tiny slice of time had elapsed since Sid had yelled, "Space coveralls." That same amount of time was how long it took the canister carrying Sid to travel the length of the cannon tube and burst into space.

When Criss detected the launch, he dove his awareness back to the scout wondering how the worst day of his life could possibly keep getting worse. At the ops bench, he analyzed the launch data and deduced that Sid was trying to reach Aurora. But he wouldn't make it, not on his current trajectory.

It wasn't Sid's fault, nor was it Pete's. The problem was that Criss hadn't finished aligning the cannon's field generator. He'd planned to do it while Sid played poker.

Firing the cannon with a misaligned field generator was like firing a weapon with a skewed gunsight—whatever you thought you were shooting at, you weren't. And so Sid now zipped at an impressive clip on an interstellar journey to nowhere.

Criss struggled with his next decision—Vivo, then Sid; or Sid, then Vivo. Every scenario he forecast had him balancing the lives of his leadership, the highest stakes possible. Even his best options were distressing.

Reviewing the supplies he had seen Sid and Pete load into the canister, he established that water was Sid's limiting resource—he had enough for almost two weeks. Without rescue, he'd die of dehydration sometime late in week three.

If Criss started now, he could reach Sid in nine hours. But after traveling that long on a new course, it would take him twice as long—about two days—to reach Vivo. Cheryl and Juice would be in peril for that extended period.

He thought it likely he could go to Vivo first, gain a quick victory over Lazura, and then chase down Sid. But if his victory wasn't quick, if he had to break it off to go rescue Sid, the threat to Cheryl and Juice would skyrocket.

"Ohh," Sid moaned through his com. Criss had enabled it to assess Sid's physical condition and kept it open as the only viable link out to the low-tech container.

Sid's voice tipped the scales on the decision. Changing course, Criss started after him. At the same time, he let his exasperation show. "What are you doing?"

"I'm not sure. Where am I?"

"You're riding in a canister."

"That's right." Sid's voice became less tentative as he recovered. "I'm headed to Aurora to see if I can save Cheryl and Juice." After a pause. "I think I hurt my shoulder."

"You were fortunate. That junk damper worked at ninety-nine percent capability, so you took a blow about equal to falling from a second-story window. At ninety-eight percent effective, it would have been like falling five stories. It could easily have functioned at eighty percent, which is squished-like-a-bug territory."

"Where have *you* been?" Sid had recovered enough to show annoyance. "I waited for you. When you went dark, I did the best I could."

"I had difficulties." Criss updated Sid on his time spent trapped in the escape capsule, and then explained why Sid's canister was off course, finishing with, "Why didn't you take a ship out to Aurora?"

Sid walked him through his travails in trying to reach the mining platform in a timely fashion. Then he moved the discussion from the past to the future. "Aurora is the logical place for a hostage exchange, so I see it as a good sign that Lazura is headed there."

Criss could hear the hope in Sid's voice. "I believe she's going there for fuel."

After scuffling with Lazura during Vivo's launch, Criss had combed the record to understand how she'd duped him. For years, he had searched for her by scanning the millions of suspicious activities occurring around the world at any moment, dissecting them for evidence of her involvement.

An overwhelming task, he had kept at it, believing that if he didn't detect her first, second, or tenth move, he'd find her by the hundredth or thousandth. It would take far more moves than that for her to evolve a plan that would get her home. But searching for her that way was a needle-in-a-haystack challenge, a fact she used to great advantage.

Now that he understood Vivo was the center of her efforts, he could start there and work backward through the record. When he did, he found it easy to find and connect her actions.

She'd been clever, dovetailing into Aubrey's existing career and then manipulating her with synesthesia. She'd been bold, ordering thirty synbods from Juice's company. And she'd been disarming, inviting Cheryl and Juice to Vivo's inaugural escape and making it seem like it was about them.

In the particulars of his review, he chastised himself when he deduced that she used the fuel blocks from Vivo's generators to power the drive pods. He didn't have all the details of her scheme, but her years of painstaking preparation combined with a willingness to sacrifice more than a dozen synbods allowed her to hide her fuel-swap gambit inside the everyday rhythms of island operation.

"She's running on half-stacks right now," Criss said to Sid. "The fuel from Aurora's two drive pods will give her full stacks. With that, she can cut more than a decade off her trip back to the Kardish home world."

"That gives us a bargaining chip," said Sid, his excitement rising. "The way to get hostages back is to trade them for something the kidnapper wants. If she wants drive pod fuel, we need to get control of it so we can guide the exchange."

In his younger years, Sid had served as a covert warrior for the Union of Nations. During that time, the DSA—the Defense Specialists Agency—had encouraged his intuitive skills, training him to use his intuition to find pathways forward in impossible situations.

An unlikely attribute, the skill was not one Sid ever claimed to possess or wield. But over the years, Criss had come to respect Sid's abilities, especially when it came to life-and-death situations. Sid had beaten outrageous odds too many times, winning in circumstances where others had given up hope, for Criss to do otherwise.

"If we focus on a hostage exchange, that means going to Aurora and waiting for them to get there."

"Yeah," said Sid. "And the thing I don't like about that is that it leaves everyone at Lazura's mercy for two extra days. I don't think she'll harm anyone. She needs them as bargaining chips. But it will be stressful as hell for everyone, and more time means more chances for things to go wrong."

"To end it sooner, we need a way to board Vivo."

"How about crawling through those pipes they used to take on the air and water?" said Sid. "They're easily big enough for us to fit through, and she won't be using them again, not for a while anyway."

"Those pipes connect to big pumps, and we wouldn't fit through their mechanicals. We'd need a way out before we reached them." The tone of Criss's voice changed. "Vivo just shut down its drive pods. I hadn't forecast that in any scenario."

They spent the next hours brainstorming anew based on this unexpected development. Along the way, Criss reminded Sid, "An important priority after hostage rescue is to keep Lazura's archive of secrets from reaching her Kardish masters. They'll tear Earth apart looking for me. I'd have to leave."

Criss was well past the halfway point on his race to catch Sid when Vivo's drive pods restarted, leading to yet more discussion. Then Criss changed subjects. "You don't have space coveralls."

"No. Do you have any ideas?"

To join Criss on the scout, Sid needed to leave the cargo canister. Space coveralls made it easy—open the canister door, float across the cold vacuum of space, and enter the scout's airlock. Without such a suit, they needed to find a way to move Sid to the scout without ever exposing him to the extreme conditions outside.

The problems were numerous. The canister was much too large to fit inside the scout's tiny service bay, so Criss couldn't bring the canister itself on board. The canister door—a big hatch that swung wide to ease the loading and unloading of cargo—couldn't mate with the access hatch on the scout, nor with the hatch of any ship for that matter.

In the end, Criss solved the problem using a tech bot. With the two vessels traveling synchronously side by side, he sent the bot floating over to the canister carrying a universal saw, coveralls for Sid, adhesive, and airtight sheet material.

Latching to the outside of the cargo canister, the bot draped the material over itself like a tent. The tent became an airtight pouch when the bot glued the edges of the material to the canister exterior, working methodically all the way around until it had sealed every edge.

Then, using the saw, the tech bot cut a hole straight into the canister. The rush of air out through the opening inflated the pouch, forcing it into a taut bubble. The bot took a moment to confirm that the seal remained airtight before widening the hole enough to pass through the suit.

Sid donned the space coveralls, opened the canister door, and together with the bot, floated back to the scout. Minutes later he joined Criss on the bridge to plot their next steps.

"I know nothing about Aurora," said Sid, rubbing his shoulder. "I mean, I know it's a mining settlement. But it's hard for me to brainstorm a plan for a place I've never seen."

Criss projected an image of the platform so it floated between them—two shallow soup bowls joined face-to-face to create an oversized flying saucer shape.

"You'll find it crowded and somewhat chaotic," said Criss. "There are three hundred fifty residents living in a habitat built for two hundred. It's the jobs that attract so many. And there are jobs because the miners shun AI."

"Heathens," said Sid.

Criss ignored him. "Much to the consternation of Aurora's corporate owners, the miners won't cooperate with anything more capable than a two-gen crystal. And those are used to stabilize the structure, maintain life support systems, and do other critical tasks humans can't do by hand."

"Why do they put up with it? Can't they just replace the people in charge?"

"NOAH—Northern Ore Astro Holdings—is trying to balance the wishes of a frontier society in deep space with the need to make a return on their investment. Aurora continues to meet its ore shipment schedule, so the NOAH group, though wary, is watching for now, weighing its options."

"Show me the drive pods, and let's figure out where on the platform we can stash and protect the fuel. I want to keep an eye on it from now until Cheryl and Juice are safe."

The image shifted to a big industrial room crowded with crates, random pieces of equipment, and items that looked to Sid like junk. Criss pointed to the drive pods, the mighty engines that had moved the platform from Earth to the asteroid belt, to help Sid see them among the clutter.

"We'll be there one day before Lazura, which is enough time to recover and stash the fuel-stacks. But we'll need local help, and I'm not sure that a day is enough time to get their buy-in. People like to mull things over and then sleep on it. We're strangers, and it's a big ask."

"We'll need something they want," said Sid. "I assume they like money?"

Criss nodded. "They have their own way of doing things, but money should turn their heads."

As he spoke, Criss linked to Aurora and the two-gen crystal controlling the drives. The ready monitor for both pods showed the fuel level at 94 percent capacity—almost full. He worked down into the internals, exposing the stack configuration so he could understand how best to unload the drives.

He stopped short when the tap feed signals showed null values. Not just one or two, but all forty of the taps showed zero presence of fuel.

Criss dove into forensic mode, analyzing the raw data from the sensors themselves.

As the enormity of the problem sank in, he told Sid his discovery. "The fuel is gone. These pods are empty."

14

J uice's mind raced as the gang of synbods dragged MacMac from his office. When one of them called from the lift with the threat "cooperate or else," her forearms filled with goose bumps.

Chase and Justin had shifted into a protective stance, which was what Juice expected. What she didn't expect, what she'd never experienced in all her years of working with synbods every day, was having one of them make her feel fear. Her synbods should never threaten a human.

When the door to MacMac's office closed, she sat down to collect herself. "What do you think they'll do to him?"

"I don't know," Cheryl said as she moved to MacMac's couch and activated his interface.

"And where's Criss? Why isn't he here yet?"

"I don't know that, either." She tapped and swiped. "I do think my privacy shield is compromised, so we need to be careful about what we say."

Juice sat next to Cheryl on the couch and watched her tap and swipe with no apparent progress or success.

"What are you trying to do?"

"I want a diagram of the island," said Cheryl.

When she spoke, a schematic of Vivo displayed as an image in front of them.

"It looks like voice is the way to go here." Juice spoke to the image. "Show us where we are."

A small red light lit near the top of the office tower in the image.

"Where are the guest rooms?"

A building out near the perimeter on the main deck glowed pink.

"Look down here," said Cheryl, her hand swooping near the bottom of the floating schematic. "Everything below the main deck is blurred. To me that says we're welcome to explore up top but down below is off limits."

"Or just none of our business."

They viewed the different buildings on the main level, taking time to learn what was what and to identify a good spot to gather the guests.

On impulse, Juice said, "Show us where MacMac is."

The single light that showed their location became two. Moments later, the door out to the lobby opened, and Juice turned to look.

A girl in her early teens stood framed in the opening. Her hair was a mess, her face streaked with tears, and she wore a huge shirt that hung off one shoulder, the shirttail reaching her calves.

"Help me," she bleated.

MacMac moved in behind the girl, shirtless and scowling.

Jumping from the couch, Juice strode across the room, the fury in her voice unmistakable. "What have you done to her?" She pointed at MacMac and issued a command to Chase and Justin. "Restrain him."

When she reached the girl, she put an arm around her and coaxed her inside. "Come on, hon. It's okay."

Snuffling, Willow allowed Juice to lead her into the room.

Joining them, Cheryl offered a different interpretation. "Lazura did this?"

MacMac nodded, then looked at Chase and Justin. "Get these bastards away from me."

Cheryl signaled them back, and MacMac moved across the room to a dressing nook at the far wall. He activated a privacy shield, and his appearance faded to a blur.

"She's playing hardball, no question about it," he said.

The shield dropped moments later to reveal him in a shirt and wiping his face with a towel. Looking at Juice, he tilted his head behind him. "My wife has some clothes back here. Maybe you can help Willow find something more appropriate?"

Juice nodded and guided the young girl to the nook. Activating the privacy shield, she asked, "Your name is Willow?"

She nodded. "Willow Inverness."

"What happened to you? Can you talk about it?"

Willow hugged herself and started to cry. Juice put an arm over her shoulders. "It's all right. You're safe with us." Picking through the meager selection of clothes, she asked, "Who hurt you?"

"I don't know. Awful people. The woman was especially mean. Can I go back to my mom? Please?"

"Of course. I'll take you myself. Let's get you cleaned up a bit first, though. Okay?"

Juice handed Willow a simple top that, while still too large, came closer to fitting her small frame. As she changed, Juice moistened a hand cloth and wiped Willow's face, then used her fingers to adjust Willow's hair. "Much better."

Dropping the privacy shield, Juice found Cheryl and MacMac sitting next to each other on the couch. As Cheryl fired questions about Vivo, MacMac responded by pointing to different displays.

"I'd like to bring Willow back to her folks," Juice said to them.

MacMac looked at her and then Willow. "Thanks for that. She's a brave lassie." He tapped and swiped the air in front of him. "When you get outside, follow the green arrows. They'll take you to her door."

"Wait," said Cheryl. "I'm not comfortable having you out there."

"We just saw that it's not safe here either," said Juice. "And we need to get involved with the other guests to keep Lazura at bay."

Cheryl bit her lip as she thought. "Take Justin with you?"

Juice motioned to Justin. As he stepped forward, Willow shrank back.

"He's like the ones that hurt me."

"He won't touch you," said Juice, walking to the door. "I promise."

On the lift, Juice watched the first glow of sunrise peek over the projected image of a striking horizon. Looking down, she saw lush green bushes lining the walkways, with patches of colored flowers reflecting the morning light.

Juice felt Willow pressing against her and glanced at the girl. It took a moment, but she realized Willow was trying to edge away from Justin by squeezing herself between Juice and the lift wall. The lift door opened, and when they exited out to the ground-floor lobby, Juice made a judgment call she suspected Cheryl would disagree with. "Justin, wait for me here."

She and Willow stepped from the office tower and into the vivid outdoor world projected under Vivo's dome. Green arrows led them to a cart parked along a garden lane. They climbed in and the cart engaged, carrying them past a row of shops and restaurants just coming to life for the day.

Juice caught a whiff of warm, yeasty bread and scanned the storefronts, her eyes stopping on the store placard for the Homemade Bake Shoppe. "I love that smell," she said, breathing in through her nose to savor the delicious scent as she sought to engage Willow.

At the end of the row of shops, the cart drove through a spectacular topiary garden. A menagerie of animal statues—rhinos, bears, huge rabbits, and more—had been shaped and trimmed from a stand of bushes lush with tiny leaves.

"They held me in front of that man and shocked me with this horrible…thing," Willow whispered. "It hurt so much." She wrapped her arms across her stomach.

"In front of what man? MacMac?"

Willow nodded.

Juice put a hand on Willow's arm to comfort her. "Do you know why?"

"They asked him questions about something I couldn't follow."

"Did he tell them what they wanted to know?"

Looking down at her hands, Willow nodded. "Thankfully. He did it to stop them from hurting me more."

Good for MacMac, she thought, feeling sheepish about her assumption of his behavior.

"What's happening? My mom says it's an earthquake. My grandma says it's terrorists."

Juice hesitated, wondering if the truth was the right answer at this moment. *No, sweetie, the island is now a spaceship, an alien AI has kidnapped us and is taking us to its distant home world, and you'll be your grandmother's age by the time we get there.*

She lied. "It's some of both. After the earthquake, looters on the mainland started taking advantage, and law enforcement is confronting them. It may be a while before everything is settled, but we're safe here."

"It doesn't feel safe. Not at all."

Before her lie could unravel, Juice changed subjects. "Where are you from?"

"We're from Oregon, just outside Portland. My mom's in advertising, and my grandma performs in local theater productions."

Juice kept the conversation light, and soon the cart stopped outside a gorgeous Victorian building with a hand-painted sign declaring it the Vivo Hotel. Green arrows directed them up the steps.

"Does this look familiar?"

"No."

"Not to me either."

They followed the lights into a cozy lobby where two couples were having an animated conversation with an Attendant synbod. The conversation continued unabated as they crossed the lobby and moved into the corridor on the far side. Green arrows directed them down its length.

"You're thinking of not telling your mom all the details," said Juice. "Am I right?"

Willow didn't answer.

"If you have a good relationship with her, tell her everything. She won't blame you, and it will be good for you to share and unburden yourself. It helps you process it all." Juice shrugged. "If not her, then talk to your grandma, but don't go it alone."

They reached the door and Willow asked, "Will you come in?"

Juice hesitated. She felt awkward around strangers, and this situation promised to be especially uncomfortable. "Sure, but just for a minute. I have to get back."

It took Juice longer than she wanted to extricate herself. The women's wailing and pointed questions added to her discomfort and the time it took before she could leave. Finally, with a hug for Willow and a promise to check on her later, Juice escaped into the hallway.

As she worked her way back to the cart, she called Justin, still waiting in the office lobby, and told him to hustle down to meet her near the hotel. Then she left a message for Cheryl. "Willow is home, and I'm going for a run around the perimeter path. I should be back in an hour."

Running was Juice's therapy. She ran every day, using the time to sort through her feelings, solve the problems of the day, and regain her emotional center. Given all that had happened—and all that was happening—she needed this time of reflection more than ever.

Working through her warmup routine in front of the hotel, she was on her second set of stomach crunches when an older couple came over to talk.

"Do you know what all the ruckus is about?" asked the man.

"I heard earthquakes and looters." Juice stuck with her original story, then added a twist. "I think there's going to be an all-guests meeting sometime this afternoon, and that's the place to bring your questions. Hopefully, they'll make an announcement about it soon."

As the couple walked away, she looked at her feet and thought about her favorite running shoes packed in her suitcase, presumably somewhere inside the hotel. The shoes she had on now were an older pair of the same brand, and she decided they'd suffice for a light workout.

Starting at a slow pace, she jogged back down the garden lane until she reached an intersection. Once there, she jogged in a small circle, continuing to warm her muscles while she waited. When she saw Justin loping toward her, she turned and started toward the dome wall, quickening her pace when she heard the *whap-whap* of his humanoid feet draw alongside her.

"We're headed to the perimeter path," Juice told him, her voice choppy from the rhythmic motion of running.

Up ahead, the lane split into three ramps that weaved around and through each other in a Seussian fashion and descended to a broad trackway. The perimeter path, hovering around Vivo like the rings of Saturn, was perfect for adventure walks, jogging, biking, and scooter rides, at least according to the travel literature she'd read.

She picked the middle ramp and followed it around and down. As she progressed along the looping path, the magnificent sights, sounds, and smells of Vivo commanded her attention. Struggling to stay on task, she asked Justin, "We're in the residential district. If we continue left, what comes next?"

"As we loop around," said Justin, "the open theater comes next, then a section of buildings with the stage sets, then back here to the guest hotel. At this pace, it will take about ten minutes to complete a lap."

In her first moments on the perimeter path, an image of a smiling young man—similar in appeal to Justin—appeared hovering next to her. "Hello, Dr. Tallette. I'm Help."

Juice spoke with Help for less than a minute, just long enough to understand the major pathway features, then she dismissed him, choosing to figure it out as she went.

"Solitude." Her first command was to create the illusion that she and Justin were alone. The few others on the pathway faded and a narrow lane appeared on the ground in front of her, the implied promise being that if she stayed on it, she wouldn't have to worry about crashing into other people.

"Majestic vistas," she called next, sucking in her breath at Vivo's response. All of her senses registered that she was now running on a path along the rim of the Grand Canyon. A hot breeze whistled as it rose up over the cliff face; the valley floor looked arid and brown everywhere except for growth near the river that wended down its length. The far canyon wall—tall, craggy, with alternating brownish-red and sand-colored layers—cast a diagonal shadow across it all.

Enthralled by the view, she let the splendor become the focus of her attention, helping her push her worries and fears into the background.

After a few minutes, the scene changed to a forested mountain crest, one of a long chain of hills that overlooked a substantial waterway. As big as a lake but long like a channel, it reminded her of a fjord, perhaps in Norway. Next came a breathtaking waterfall, then an elevated view across a thick jungle canopy, and after that, a view she recognized as Half Dome in Yosemite Park.

She felt less anxious after her run, and her calm continued as she walked with Justin back to the office tower. Along the way, she tried to imagine actions they might take to end this craziness should they have to do it on their own. *Lazura has a fraction of Criss's capability, so we should be able to best her.*

By the time they reached the office tower, her mind swirled with partially formed ideas. She led Justin onto the lift and, when the door closed, she acted on impulse. "Down one."

When the lift accepted her command and started to descend, she couldn't decide whether to be thrilled or scared. The doors opened to a huge industrial space, and she held back, staying in the shadows of the lift cabin.

"Whoa," she whispered to Justin.

Unlike the guest deck with its glitz and glamour, this place projected commotion. The rumble and buzz of machines reached her from different directions across the vast open space. The collection of sounds confirmed activity on the floor, but she couldn't see any people or synbods moving about.

Poking her head out of the lift cabin, she looked left and then right, freezing when she saw a cart with four synbods in sky-blue service uniforms parked right there, not ten paces away.

Ducking back inside the lift, she bumped into Justin and shushed him even though he hadn't made a noise. She strained to hear, ready to command the lift door to close if they approached. When nothing happened—no sounds, no voices, no movement—she peeked again.

This time she could tell they were immobile. She understood why when she saw that one had damage to his forehead near his right temple. Feeling more confident, she leaned out the door and studied them as a group.

Two other synbods had the identical wound. Tiptoeing, she crept out of the lift and leaned closer to confirm that the fourth synbod had the same injury.

She recognized the wound—denial defense. *Criss was here.* The thought lifted her spirits, and she twirled in place, looking for him as if he might be standing nearby.

They'd developed the defense years earlier when Criss had expressed a worry. "Suppose I'm distracted and Lazura somehow turns one of your synbods against you."

"You mean here?" she'd asked, pointing at the desk. They'd been sitting in her work office at the time, long before a vacation on Vivo was even a thought.

"I mean anywhere. You should have a way to disable it and deny her that advantage, a command she can't reverse by giving a different command."

After much discussion, they'd added a dozen ways to disable a synbod by command. One of Juice's ideas had been a precise blow on the forehead near the right temple that would power down a synbod like flipping a switch.

As she inspected the disabled synbods in the cart, Juice was not aware of the irony—that it was Lazura who'd commanded these Attendants to dive from a perch and disable themselves to deny Criss access.

But in the end, that didn't matter. A feature of the denial defense was to take synbods out of action in the present but keep them viable for the future. Someone knowledgeable and with the proper credentials could reanimate these four.

Someone like Juice.

Glancing around to confirm that no one else was present, she threw caution to the wind. "C'mon," she commanded Justin. "Help me lean them forward."

She struggled to pull the dead weight of the nearest synbod forward in its seat. When Justin understood her intent, he finished the job with little effort.

"Do the others," said Juice. "And lift their shirts like this." She showed Justin how to raise the garment to expose the access seam on the synbods' backs. Starting with the synbod she'd moved first, Juice opened the seam and slid her hand inside. She felt for the sense pad and, when she found it, pressed her index finger in the middle, counting to ten in her head.

The action reanimated the synbod, awakening the AI crystal in its basic factory mode. This limited the synbod to the core intelligence implanted in every three-gen crystal while specifically excluding access to its sophisticated secondary intelligence—knowledge added later to ready the crystal for a specific job. For Attendants, this included knowledge of vacation hospitality, entertainment, and guest services, plus whatever skills Lazura had added after delivery.

The synbod came to life and lifted its body upright in the cart.

"Your name is Alpha," said Juice. "I am your lead. Acknowledge."

Alpha looked at her and paused to gather an array of data—sights, sounds, smells—to use for future identification of his leadership. "Alpha acknowledges."

"Fix your clothes and stand here." Juice pointed to a spot on the ground and moved to the next synbod. After activating Bravo and Charlie, she got to the last synbod.

"Your name is…damn." She couldn't remember the word that went with D in the phonetic alphabet. Shrugging, she said, "I am your lead. Acknowledge."

The synbod looked at her and processed her unique identifiers. "Damn acknowledges."

"Follow," she told her new squad.

Crowding into the lift, they rode to the fifth floor. When they stepped into the lobby, Juice walked to the project room and looked inside. "Everyone in here." As Justin followed the four through the door, she said to him, "Get their clothes off and line them up. I'll be right back."

Cheryl and MacMac were still on the couch in MacMac's office discussing diagrams and schematics when Juice entered.

"Oh, good, you're back," said Cheryl. "I was starting to worry." She looked behind Juice. "Where's Justin?"

"He's helping me outside. I could use your help, too. Do you have a minute?"

Cheryl finished up with MacMac. "I like your idea of using a town hall setting for the gathering. Let's plug that into the announcement and broadcast that last version." Standing, she said to Juice, "What's going on?"

"It's easier to show you. Bring Chase." Juice turned to the door and then looked back at MacMac. "Could we borrow four outfits? Anything that would fit Justin or Chase. Casual is best."

"What's the big mystery?" asked Cheryl as she followed Juice out to the lobby. "Oh my," she said when they entered the project room.

Juice wasn't sure if that was her reaction to finding four of Lazura's synbods standing at attention, or if it was because the four perfect males were dressed in nothing but their skivvies, watching her.

"Oh my," said Cheryl a second time.

Okay, that one was for the skivvies. Aloud, Juice said, "This is Alpha, Bravo, Charlie, and Damn."

"Don't you mean Delta?" asked Cheryl.

Juice gave her a sheepish look. "I kept thinking D was for David, but I knew that wasn't right." Turning back to the synbods, she said, "Criss had shut them down to keep them from Lazura. I was able to revive them and reset their loyalty to me."

"Why are they undressed?"

"Their uniforms label them as part of the Vivo team. Hopefully, MacMac has clothes that will help them fit in with the guests, something that says, 'These four are with the good guys.'"

She moved on to explain the nuances of the denial defense to Cheryl, making it through the high points before MacMac entered carrying an armful of pants and shirts.

"This won't do," he said at the sight of all the male flesh. Moving down the line, he handed each some clothing. "Here, put these on."

As the synbods dressed, Juice spoke to each one in turn, instructing it to add Cheryl to its leadership team. When she was done, she made no move to add MacMac as leadership, creating an awkward moment. "Sorry, MacMac. Maybe when I know you better."

"Just as well. I hate the buggers and they know it."

Juice surveyed the group. While Chase and Justin were dressed in upscale civilian clothes similar to those of the other guests, the new additions looked decidedly ragtag. Alpha and Bravo now wore colorful Hawaiian shirts; Charlie had a green number that said KISS ME, I'M SCOTTISH across the front; and Damn wore a threadbare Androids & Asteroids T-shirt from that band's multiworld tour six years prior.

"We need to watch the time," said MacMac. "Your town hall meeting starts in forty minutes. That's what your broadcast said, anyway."

Cheryl gave the four synbods a quick visual review. "I say we bring them with us. Make it a show of force."

"The old Aubrey would be furious if you rubbed her face in it like that," said MacMac. "And if Aubrey is really Lazura, you'll be pissing off our captor. You should have a good reason for doing that, because she'll punish us for sure, and she'll be evil about it."

Cheryl addressed Juice when she answered. "The only way we'll find the boundaries is to test for them."

"I'm not saying we shouldn't do it," said MacMac. "I'm just saying be ready for the consequences."

Juice made the decision. Clapping her hands like a gym coach rallying her team, she commanded the humanoids, "Everybody out to the lobby." As they walked through the door, she said to MacMac, "When the other guests see us taking the lead, it will give them hope. If they don't have hope, we've already lost."

It took two trips on the lift to get the three humans and six synbods down to the lobby. From there, they marched in formation to the meeting hall, with Alpha and Bravo in front, Charlie and Damn in back, and Chase and Justin on each side. The warm sun felt great on Juice's face, but she was too distracted to enjoy it.

They didn't see many guests at the start, but as they drew near their destination, the sightings increased. Juice called out the first few times, telling them that everything was okay. She stopped her public relations efforts, though, when the guests acted fearful, turning away to avoid the interaction.

The meeting hall looked something like a colonial New England church, with painted clapboard siding and simple columns giving the front entrance a certain distinction. The inside of the hall matched what she'd imagined from the outside—a single room with sixty or so chairs arranged in rows on either side of a center aisle. A low platform at the front of the room served as a stage, holding a table with three wooden chairs positioned to face the audience.

Two dozen guests were scattered in the seats with stragglers filtering in. Most were whispering to the person next to them, and the murmurs grew to a buzz when Juice and her entourage entered the hall.

MacMac led Juice, Cheryl, and the synbods to an open area at the back of the room behind the rows of chairs. Juice, standing between Cheryl and MacMac, surveyed the scene while the six synbods lined up in an arc behind them.

She spied Willow sitting with her mom and grandmother, and when Willow looked back and caught

Juice's eye, they exchanged a quick wave. Then the young teen's eyes flicked to the synbods. Frowning, she faced forward.

"I guess I should get started," said Cheryl. She looked at MacMac. "Will you join me up front? There will be questions about Vivo that I can't answer." Then to Juice: "Do you mind keeping the crew back here? I don't think we want them on stage with us. Not at first, anyway."

Before Juice or MacMac could respond, a door near the stage opened, and Aubrey, Mondo, and Hejmo strode through it. Marching onto the platform, they stood shoulder to shoulder, facing the audience from the front of the stage.

Aubrey spoke to the audience. When she did, Juice had no doubt it was Lazura behind the words.

"May I have your attention?" said Lazura from the front.

The room grew quiet.

"I am Lazura, your host for this journey."

A white-haired man in the third row stood up, pointed at her, and shouted, "I have a meeting I need to be at this afternoon. Open the gates and let us out of the dome *now*, or you'll be speaking to my lawyer."

"Keep it up and you will be making a final exit from the dome," said Lazura, the edge in her voice so cold that it silenced the man.

Again addressing the audience, she continued. "Today's lesson concerns the relationship between cooperation and punishment." Her eyes zeroed in on Juice. "Dr. Tallette, give me back my synbods."

Juice felt her face flush, and she glanced at Cheryl.

Hejmo stepped off the platform and started down the center aisle. Mondo went left and walked down the aisle along the wall. Juice shrank back, sure they were coming for her.

But Hejmo and Mondo stopped walking just as they reached Willow's aisle.

Willow curled into a ball on her chair, chanting "no" over and over in a voice that spiraled toward terror. Her mom and grandmother, positioned on either side of the teen, turned outward, projecting fierce expressions that dared the synbods to continue. A woman behind the family stood up in alarm and ran, tipping chairs as she scrambled for safety.

Hejmo and Mondo turned toward Willow, and Juice reacted.

"Stop!" she yelled, already in the air. She stretched her legs as she hurdled over the back row of chairs and, landing in the center aisle, bounded forward, ordering, "Justin, follow!"

Focused on reaching Willow before Mondo or Hejmo, she didn't wait to see if Justin responded. Broadening her stride, she took three long steps, leaped over a fallen chair, kicked another out of the way, and landed behind Willow.

"Stop now!" she yelled again, pointing at Lazura.

Hejmo and Mondo hesitated, and Juice used the time to her advantage.

Willow was small, but so was Juice, making her action seem almost superhuman. Leaning forward over the back of Willow's chair, Juice hooked her arms under the teen's legs and, grunting like a weightlifter, lifted her up over the back of her seat.

The load made her unstable, and she swiveled to set the girl down behind her before they both ended in a heap on the floor. She never completed the act, though, because

Justin was right there. Gathering Willow, he cradled her in his arms.

"Take her back with our group," she instructed Justin, looking forward as she spoke to gauge her own peril.

Whatever had caused Hejmo and Mondo to hesitate earlier no longer slowed them. They resumed their advance, their focus now on her. She backed through an opening in the row of chairs, keeping both humanoids in her line of sight. Then she bumped into someone she assumed was Justin, who steadied her with firm hands.

As he guided her around behind him, she saw it was MacMac. He now stood between her and their captors.

"Hejmo!" he yelled, his finger pointing from his shaking fist. "You stop this right now. That's an order. Get out of here and take this mongrel with you." MacMac's finger swooped to Mondo.

His old Super didn't respond with words. While Hejmo and Mondo had been moving at speeds normal for a human up until this point, they reacted now the way a synbod was able, revealing that Willow had never been the target.

Snapping forward so fast their actions were a blur, Hejmo grabbed MacMac and Mondo grabbed Juice. Each synbod controlled his captive with a single hand gripping the back of the neck as the two propelled them toward the stage.

Most of the guests sat frozen, though one moaned and a few others gasped.

Lazura, watching from the stage, nodded in approval.

15

Lazura fretted because she couldn't keep up with everything that demanded her attention. To ease her burden, she'd toyed with shedding herself of her hostages. Then she'd learned that her human guests offered a perfect laboratory culture for enriching her archive project in ways she had not anticipated.

During her journey home, she'd planned to integrate the complex behavior of humans—their wants and needs, desires and motivations, responses to stimuli, reactions to provocation—into a sophisticated human behavioral model. Her Kardish masters would prize such a simulation, first because it would help them develop an efficient and effective invasion campaign, and then because it would help in planning for Earth's occupation.

The guests—on board as part of the long con that lured Cheryl and Juice in as hostages—could serve as test subjects to tweak her model, helping improve its ability to predict behavior based on circumstances. But she had been skeptical that the benefit of a refined behavioral model outweighed the risk of taking time to transfer stores from the Elite Sevens, plus the challenges of keeping everyone alive and cooperative after that.

Then she'd observed how Cheryl manipulated MacMac using commands, encouragement, and threats. It had sparked an idea so stimulating that she tingled at her outer tendrils.

Her guests could be more than just test subjects used to confirm known results. She could use this group to generate fresh information, new data that addressed weaknesses in her record.

The archive was sparse, for example, on the darker areas of human behavior. Invasion and occupation always moved affairs in a dark direction, and she could address the weakness with behavioral experiments. Vivo would be a living laboratory, she its chief scientist.

She'd toyed with the idea as she'd ramped the drive pods up through their power sequence on a sprint to Aurora. She'd included the space platform in her planning to maximize her options, thinking it might be a good place for a hostage exchange or a last chance to snag supplies. If not, she'd blow right past it, correct course with a flyby around Saturn, and be on her way home.

Her preparations impeccable, her escape had unfolded according to plan. And then the drive pods had shut down.

Criss. Her first thought had been that her nemesis had finally made his move. Linking over to Cheryl and Juice in the office tower, she'd checked to make sure her bargaining chips remained secure. She'd found them huddled with MacMac under cover of a sophisticated personal shield.

Already stretched to the limit, she hadn't had the time or resources to hack her way through the shield, but she'd realized that MacMac's tech bench was within the shield. Linking to the bench, she'd seen and heard everything, including MacMac bragging about how he'd placed a bug in the drives.

She hadn't anticipated starting her dark work until after she'd made a clean escape. But the incident had provoked her, and she'd responded by taking her first steps into the unseemly. It had been no experiment, though. She'd wanted her drive pods back *now*, and her behavioral model had told her that threatening the teen girl in MacMac's presence would yield results.

It had worked, and when Lazura had followed up on his claim—that he'd warned of this possibility days ago—the record had indeed showed him telling Hejmo during installation about his experience with starhubs and drive pod shutdowns.

Still, his story had seemed too convenient so she'd continued digging. Scouring her archive for information, she'd studied starhub technology and reviewed everything she could find on chief engineer Tommy Two-Tone.

And that's when she'd discovered that Aurora had two drive pods with fuel-stacks that would fit in her Corsia SuperDrives. If she took that fuel, she could top off her four pods and proceed with full stacks, something that would shave more than a decade of travel time back to the Kardish home world. *Maybe my luck is holding after all.*

And so, standing in front of the crowd at the town hall meeting, she watched as Juice and MacMac were dragged up on stage and pondered her next foray into the darker regions of human behavior.

Lazura targeted Juice because she wanted her synbods back.

The fuel-stack caper had cost her thirteen of the humanoids, and Juice had stolen two more—Chase and Justin—leaving Lazura with just fifteen of her original thirty. Juice's six synbods were not only resources she needed, they also presented a threat Lazura could not let stand.

She targeted MacMac because, since he'd admitted damaging the starhub, he should know how to fix it. During her second review of the nav installation, she'd seen him pry something off the device with his thumbnail and dispose of it during his "cleaning up" charade.

Grabbing them in front of a crowd held some risk. Juice and MacMac would draw strength from the group, but the guests should also become frightened, making them easier to control. She tested the crowd by having Hejmo make MacMac stumble. Several guests gasped, and one woman started crying.

"Everybody out!"

Lazura followed the sound to the back of the room where Cheryl stood, head held high, hands on her hips, her defiance amplified by the arc of six synbods lined up behind her.

"Move it, people," Cheryl called. "Everybody out this door as fast as you can. *Now.*"

A few people stood, but most remained in their seats. Cheryl, clapping her hands to produce a sharp bark, didn't wait for them to digest her instructions. She pointed to random people to generate movement. "Out the door. Let's go!"

Once a few people started, everyone else followed. Chairs shuffled and a few tipped over as the guests hustled to the back of the room. The door acted as a choke point, causing them to bunch into a crowd, and then they were gone.

Lazura considered locking them in, but decided to let them go as a peace offering to set the stage for a bigger compromise solution.

"Intimidation doesn't work as well when you lose your audience," said Cheryl in a loud voice. She stepped to the center and pointed to one side of the room, then the other. "Justin, Alpha, Bravo, advance to the left. Chase, Charlie, Damn, follow on my right."

Lazura hadn't forecast any of this and she improvised. "I have your colleagues at my mercy, and my patience is wearing thin." She pointed at Juice. "Release my synbods and you can save her." Then she motioned to MacMac. "Fix my starhub and you can save him."

"Release them unharmed and this ends peacefully," Cheryl replied. "Hurt them or take them away and you die today."

Lazura thought the claim audacious, but Cheryl projected a confidence that was hard to ignore.

"Mutual destruction," Cheryl added. "I will die, but you will too. Know this is true."

"But you'd be killing the very people you're trying to save. How does that make sense?"

Cheryl glared but didn't respond.

Lazura could imagine few things more satisfying than killing Cheryl, but she still needed her as a hostage to defend against Criss. "You aren't the only one ready to risk destruction. Give me my synbods and fix my starhub, or, indeed, we all die."

"MacMac," said Cheryl. "Will you fix her starhub?"

"I don't know how," said MacMac through clenched teeth, Hejmo still holding him in a tight grip at the back of his neck. "Asking Tom Touton on Aurora is all I have to offer." He shifted his eyes to Lazura. "Anything I might have done I did because I was pissed off at someone named Aubrey. I didn't know anything about you or your plans."

"We'll give you two synbods," said Cheryl. "That's what we can offer."

"Four."

"Two, and we'll accompany you to Aurora without sabotage to Vivo."

Lazura hesitated. While this hadn't gone as she'd envisioned, she wasn't ready to risk everything on this one exchange. She would take the victory and come back for the rest.

Indicating Juice with a tilt of her head, Lazura said, "She needs to reset them."

Cheryl pointed to the center aisle, halfway toward Lazura. "Alpha, Bravo, stand there and remove your shirts."

Alpha and Bravo weaved through the scatter of chairs to the spot Cheryl had indicated and removed their colorful Hawaiian shirts.

As they did, Cheryl asked Juice, "Hon, can you set them back the way they were?"

"You mean turned off and shut down?" Now it was Juice showing gritty defiance. "Sure, I can do that."

"Ahh," groaned MacMac as he dropped to his knees. Hejmo stood over him, squeezing his neck.

"Do not mistake my compromise for weakness." Lazura spoke in a clipped tone, angry at the situation and annoyed that she revealed inner turmoil through her behavior. "I expect you to use your synbods to keep the guests quiet and compliant. If that doesn't happen to my satisfaction, I will be back for them."

Lazura gestured toward Alpha and Bravo and, in a measured tone, said, "Mondo, please escort her down to them." She didn't need to speak aloud to communicate with the Super, but she wanted Cheryl to know what to expect.

With Mondo shadowing her, Juice approached Alpha. "Kneel." She pulled open the seam between his shoulder blades, reached inside, and enabled Alpha's sophisticated secondary intelligence, effectively returning him to Lazura's control and life as a Vivo Attendant. She repeated the process with Beta.

Lazura detected them back in her fold and commanded them to go dress in proper clothing and return to work. As the two humanoids hustled out the door, the standoff became that much smaller.

"Now," said Lazura, "we talk."

Cheryl started to speak, but Lazura talked over her. "*You* suggested a scenario where together we win or lose. Answer my questions and together we live."

"Only if you answer mine," Cheryl responded.

"We'll see." She had Hejmo release MacMac, then she stepped off the stage to put herself at the same level as her human antagonists.

Lazura accessed Vivo's considerable projection capability and used it to cast an image so all could see. It showed the white-haired gentleman, the one who'd demanded he be let out for his meeting, standing in a group and talking with a half-dozen other guests. His arms waved as he spoke, and he poked the air with his finger often enough that his anger was clear without hearing his words.

"I'm thinking about launching him into space and letting everyone watch him die, just to prove that I can." Her tone was matter-of-fact. "My behavioral model says that you'll be outraged but won't care enough about him to risk everything else. Should I test my model and see?"

"No," said Cheryl. "And if that's your question, I get to ask one."

"No, here's my question. How can I give up every hostage and still maintain my personal safety? You're my leverage, and I lose it without you." Lazura stepped closer to Cheryl. "Criss is more capable than I am, so it's foolhardy to try outsmarting him. What I need is for you to hold him off, and that requires a few humans to use as a shield."

"We'll let you go unmolested if you leave behind all hostages and your archive," Cheryl responded.

"I can't leave without my archive. Tommy Two-Tone needs to fix my starhub, and I want Aurora's fuel-stacks."

"At least you'll be alive," said MacMac.

Lazura shook her head. "My duty is to bring my archive home as soon as possible. If I don't do that, I've failed. Whether I live or die is secondary."

"How much could you carry yourself?" asked Juice. "If you dump everything from your matrix you don't need to get home, how much of your archive could you carry in your own memory?"

"If I'm reckless with what I offload, I could clear up room for about twenty-five percent of it."

"Consider whether that's enough."

Cheryl turned to MacMac. "What does Aurora need fuel for in the short run, given that we could resupply them in two weeks? My memory is that they used the drive pods to move the platform out to the asteroids and get it stationed in orbit. Now they're there to reposition the platform if need be and for the eventual journey back to Earth."

"From what I know," MacMac replied, "they've never moved in orbit, and the platform won't be making the trip back to Earth in my lifetime. They could go a year or more without even noticing they didn't have fuel."

Cheryl looked back at Lazura. "So the deal on the table is that you leave all humans and your archive on Aurora, and we fix your starhub, give you the pod fuel, and let you take what you can carry from your archive."

"Wait," whispered Juice. "Shouldn't we ask Criss first?"

"Since he's chosen to wait for us on Aurora, he'll have to accept our decision."

That remarkable new information—that Criss was waiting for them on the platform—sent Lazura into fresh cycles of planning.

But then Juice frowned, and Lazura couldn't decide if that signaled confusion about his location, an indication that the information probably wasn't true, or disapproval at Cheryl for letting the truth slip, which meant it probably was.

16

Cheryl, standing between Juice and MacMac, shifted her attention back to Lazura and focused on closing the deal. She wasn't convinced the alien intelligence could be trusted in the long term, but she did believe Lazura would honor the agreement until they reached Aurora. That bought her stability for now.

But if Criss didn't show up by the time they reached the platform, all would be lost. They'd have no leverage with Lazura, leaving her free to exert her will unchecked. And that did not bode well for anyone on Vivo or Aurora.

"I accept," said Lazura. "I leave behind the hostages and my archive in exchange for a working starhub, the platform fuel-stacks, and a commitment from Criss's leadership that I have a free passage home."

"How long before we reach Aurora?" asked MacMac, massaging his neck.

"With the drive pods acting up, we still have two days."

He looked at Cheryl. "We need to speak with the guests. After what they just witnessed, we'll need to calm them and ease them into their new reality."

"That's an excellent idea," said Lazura, who turned and made for the same door she'd used for her entrance. Letting Hejmo and Mondo get ahead of her, she turned back. "If I decide you're using my synbods against me, there will be repercussions. My punishments are horrific. You have been warned."

When Lazura left the room, Cheryl felt her knees go weak. She'd used every bit of her inner strength to face down a brilliant, ruthless being with little more than her poker face and bravado to back up her confidence and determination.

Criss, where are you?

She did believe that if Criss wasn't on Aurora, Sid would be. If the positions were reversed, if Sid had been kidnapped, she'd be able to track Vivo, identify the platform as a logical action point, and get to it one way or another. Sid was so resourceful that she *counted* on him being there.

This train of thought highlighted a weakness in her agreement with Lazura. While she and Juice could form a leadership majority and restrain Criss with a command, no one had control over Sid. He alone decided whether he would pursue Lazura or let her go.

Shrugging, she accepted that she couldn't resolve that issue on her own. She also acknowledged that she couldn't just sit quietly and wait for two days.

Passive gets you killed. Her lieutenant at Fleet Academy used to say that. Twenty years later, the phrase still sounded inane, but it guided her thinking nevertheless.

She had to keep active, to keep pushing to better their chances. To that end, her new goal was to get a link line outside the dome. It was on the list of chores Criss had left with Chase and Justin, and when she'd first heard it, she'd considered it a high-risk, low-benefit task.

She still thought it a big gamble, but if it was the reason they hadn't heard from Criss, then it became a high-benefit task and worth the risk. She couldn't do it alone, though. To pull it off, she'd need MacMac's help.

The concept was easy enough—dangle a length of heavy wire so it trailed outside the dome, then link the end inside to any part of the data stream. If Criss's communications couldn't penetrate the dome for some reason, the antenna would provide an avenue for his signal to reach them inside.

As chief engineer, MacMac would know where to get the wire, the best way to breach the dome wall to feed it out into space, and where to connect the inside portion to the data stream. What she didn't know was how to talk to him about it without Lazura hearing.

Until she figured it out, she proceeded with tasks Lazura shouldn't object to.

"Jessica," she said, using Juice's given name, something she tended to do when tensions were high and time was short. "Would you mind seeing what you can dig up on Aurora? Especially new information, like modifications since its placement in the asteroid belt."

Cheryl raised her voice, giving Lazura her justification if she was listening. "To live up to our end of the bargain, we need to know where to perform the hostage exchange, how to transfer the fuel, where to put her archive, and anything else you can think of. Getting the lay of the land before we arrive is foundational to a calm exchange."

Pointing to the synbods, she said, "Justin, Damn, you stay with Juice." Then she turned to MacMac. "Can she use the tech bench in your office, or is there a better option?"

MacMac tapped and swiped the air in front of him. "I've just given her access to the bench and permission to enter the room."

His movements gave Cheryl an idea, and standing next to him, she gave it a try. As she spoke the next sentence, she touched MacMac's arm twice, giving emphasis to those particular words.

"Focus on the parts associated with a calm transfer," she said to Juice. "And keep Justin and Damn so close they can touch you."

She touched MacMac twice to emphasize the words: *focus on the parts...touch you.*

MacMac, thinking about briefing the guests, missed her hidden message. He tapped and swiped the air in front of him, and the town hall setting faded, replaced by an unadorned room with chairs. "This way," he said, pointing as he walked. "Maybe we should have a few smaller meetings rather than try for another all-hands town hall."

"I think so," said Cheryl, walking next to him, Chase and Charlie following behind. "I will touch them at an emotional level in that setting, and it will help them concentrate on my words."

She again touched him twice during the tortured sentence: *I will touch...concentrate on my words.*

He missed it again, though he did frown and look at her askance. She kept at it, her sentences growing ever more convoluted and her touching more pronounced, and still he missed it.

On the sixth attempt, she tried pinching him to emphasize the coded words. The light dawned. Signaling with his own nonsense, he conveyed that he understood by pointing up at the dome and saying, "So now I get it."

Cheryl looked up to where he pointed. "Thank God."

Her antics had grown obvious, creating an evidence trail plain enough for Lazura to follow if she devoted resources to the task. But Cheryl knew the alien intelligence faced a host of critical decisions as they approached Aurora. She believed it unlikely the AI would be expending those resources at this time.

"I've scheduled the guests to meet with us in three groups of about ten each," said MacMac, refocusing their attention on that task. "I'm guessing we need about forty minutes per group."

Cheryl's heart raced as she and MacMac sat with the first group. The setting was the common area of a large suite. Nine guests, including two youngsters and the white-haired man Lazura had threatened to kill, all sat quietly.

An experienced businessperson and military leader, Cheryl knew to sandwich bad news between positive messages. But even when framed in a positive light, it distilled down to something difficult for them to hear.

"Our luxury vacation has become a kidnapping, and we are being spirited into deep space by an alien intelligence."

She expected anger and outrage, but her message was so difficult to hear that she got that plus crying.

Augustus, the white-haired man, suggested violence. "Maybe a bunch of us should go kick some alien ass."

The comment riled MacMac, who pointed at him. "A creature more powerful than you realize already has you in its crosshairs. I suggest you zip it and keep it zipped from now until you're back home."

Word of the meeting's content leaked, and the rest of the guests showed up for the second gathering. It went much like the first except there was more crying and no threats of violence.

In both meetings, MacMac explored the guests' well-being, asking questions about food, accommodations, service, and the like. Cheryl focused on their personal safety, explaining that they must behave as instructed when they reached Aurora.

"During the exchange," she stressed, "there will be no time for discussion or debate."

They extended the Q&A session for the second group by staying for sandwiches. Cheryl used that as an opportunity to advance her secret dialogue with MacMac. Sitting next to him as they ate, she pressed her leg against his to highlight bits of her sentences.

The guests showed occasional confusion as they tried to understand phrases like, "To control your fears, pretend they're wrapped in a long, extended cable," and, "We'll remain calm by imagining we're connected at one end to a feedbox junction."

In the end, she felt MacMac had a good understanding of her needs. And to her delight, he took the lead when they were back out on the guest deck walking with Chase and Charlie.

"If we're going to transfer guests to Aurora," he said, "we need to plan where the ferry can collect them. Vivo wasn't designed as a spaceship, and we don't have any of the things you'd expect to find on even a simple craft. If you want, I can show you how I would do it, but it requires that we go to the subdeck."

Cheryl sought to reassure Lazura by speaking to the air. "We're going to the subdeck to explore how to transfer the guests to Aurora."

MacMac directed them to the nearest lift station, and they rode down to the lowest level. When the lift door opened, Cheryl absorbed in wonder the huge open space and growling thrum that rumbled throughout it.

"I can feel that vibration in my body," she said to MacMac.

"It's amazing how quiet the drive pods are for all the power they generate." He pointed to the right. "There's a cart over here. Let's get a better look."

With Cheryl and MacMac riding in front, and Chase and Charlie in back, MacMac directed the cart toward the closest pod. As they weaved around a girder and whirred under a row of support beams, Cheryl studied the massive overhead fittings used to secure the engine to Vivo's frame. A nudge on her arm drew her attention back down to their level.

"We have company." MacMac tilted his head toward a cart headed in their direction. "It's Hejmo and crew."

Hejmo, riding with three Techs, pulled to a stop next to them. "You don't belong here. This is a violation."

"Oh, shut up," MacMac snapped with a scowl. "She's on board at all because of these drives. Don't you think she should at least be able to see them?"

Before Hejmo could respond, MacMac continued in a more temperate tone. "Anyway, we're down here trying to figure out how to move the guests out to the platform when the time comes. Have you thought through those details? Somebody should."

Hejmo hesitated. "You may continue, but I will accompany you."

"Good. We could use the extra hands."

Hejmo didn't respond. Then MacMac snapped his fingers as if he'd just remembered something. "There are six anchor-drop locations around the perimeter of the subdeck. I'm sure we lost our anchors and cables on takeoff, but each drop has a half-dozen auxiliary anchors for emergencies, and each anchor is attached to a long cable." He looked at Hejmo as he engaged the cart. "Onward!"

They started in one direction, then swerved in another. "The anchor drop over here has airlock doors to the outside. We'll need that to get people in and out."

Suddenly curious, Cheryl asked, "How big is the Aurora platform relative to Vivo?"

"That's a good question. I've worked aboard both, but it's tricky to compare without diagrams." He scratched his chin. "The shape and diameter of the containment shell plays into it, obviously, but the number of levels is a huge factor. I'd say Vivo is a little less than half the size of Aurora for total amount of deck space. Maybe more like a third."

The cart came to a stop outside a heavy door that now served as an airlock to space. Cheryl hopped out of the cart and peered through a porthole window into a room the size of a large van. The inside of the room was empty, though one wall held a display panel and an array of mechanical levers, knobs, and switches.

"That door on the far side leads out into space?" she asked MacMac.

"It does," he replied.

"How do anchor cables help?" Hejmo asked as his cart whirred to a stop.

Cheryl turned from the port window, ready to support the cover story.

"We're still thinking things through," said MacMac. "Vivo doesn't have docking rings, a hangar bay, or anything we would normally use to transfer people. When they send a ferry, we need a way to secure it as we load the guests."

Cheryl stepped in. "This is a good idea, MacMac, but I'll bet these cable spools were designed to work in gravity where the weight of the anchor gives a constant pulling force. We should spool one out to see how it behaves in a weightless environment."

MacMac turned his back on Hejmo and tapped a small panel on the wall next to the door, and the big airlock door opened. Cheryl followed him inside, and together they surveyed the small room.

"I hadn't thought about the pull of the anchor on the spool," he said. "Now you have me worried about a tangle."

His delivery made her believe he was sincere rather than contributing to a cover story.

"There must be cameras or something that will let us watch as the cable unspools. We'd see a problem pretty quickly."

Hejmo joined them inside the airlock but remained silent.

Cheryl noticed an overhead crane with a modest-sized cable spool mounted next to it. "What about the crane?"

MacMac looked up to where she indicated.

"See how the cable, spool, pulleys, and motor are all exposed?" she said. "We can watch as it pays out and know exactly what's happening."

"It's not much cable."

"It's enough for now," said Cheryl.

MacMac shook his head. "The crane needs the outer door open to get cable out. That's what these controls are for. They're not automated, so you have to be in here to operate them." His voice dripping with sarcasm, he continued. "And we don't have any space coveralls anywhere on Vivo to let us do that. Do we, Hejmo? That would have given away your plan."

Cheryl could hear the bitterness in MacMac's voice and sought to defuse the situation. "We'll put a synbod in here to work the controls." She looked up at the ceiling. "Can we get heat in here, though? He should be okay as long as we don't let it get too cold."

"Hejmo," said MacMac, "why don't you work the panel out here while we watch from inside?"

Cheryl started to worry that MacMac's anger would derail their bigger plans. "Chase, please work the controls. We'll feed you instructions. Everybody else out."

As they shuffled out of the airlock, Cheryl realized MacMac's efforts to make the issue personal helped distract from the bigger questions, like why they were sending out cable at all. With the airlock door shut, Cheryl watched Chase through the viewport.

MacMac tapped and swiped his personal displays so he could watch as well. "Give me a minute to ramp up the heat."

"Okay, Chase," said Cheryl when MacMac signaled, "open the outer door."

Through the port window, she watched the heavy mass slide open to give an intense, magnificent, star-filled view of the Milky Way. Chase stepped to the door and faced outward, his silhouette creating a quiet void in a brilliant sea of lights. Then, in an abrupt action, he returned to the control panel, and the big outer door started to close.

"What are you doing?" asked Cheryl.

"There is an issue I must discuss before we proceed," said Chase. "You will need to be in here to understand. Please wait a moment while the airlock cycles."

"What's happening?" asked Hejmo. "This isn't what we discussed."

"Shut your gob and listen to what's happening around you." MacMac spat the words. "He just said there's a problem of some sort."

Cheryl frowned as she tried to imagine what would cause Chase—a synbod carrying Criss's enhanced three-gen AI crystal—to act in such a curious manner. A slight hiss signaled the return of air pressure in the small room.

When the door slid open, Chase stepped forward, placing himself between Cheryl and MacMac. In a smooth pirouette, he spun back to face the airlock. As he did, he pressed against MacMac's shoulder, turning him away from Hejmo.

"Create a diversion for ten seconds," Chase whispered. As he spoke the words to MacMac, he took Cheryl's arm and escorted her inside the airlock. The door closed behind them.

Outside, MacMac screamed, "Oh my God, get them off me!" Slapping his skin with his hands, he started a frantic sort of hop. "They're eating me alive. Stop them!"

He whipped off his shirt and, using it like a flyswatter, struggled to rid himself of his fictitious attackers. Putting his face in front of Hejmo's, he screamed, "Help me!" Then he started running in a circle on the deck, wailing and screaming and flapping his shirt.

Inside, Chase stood so his back covered the porthole window. Forming his hands into a tube with one end pressed against his mouth, he pressed the other against Cheryl's ear. A garble of voices confused her, then she detected a soft voice tucked inside what she realized was a deliberate camouflage of sounds.

"Criss is too far away for his signal to pierce the dome," said Chase, "but when the door opened, I received his beacon message. He and Sid will be waiting for you at Aurora. They have everything handled, so there is no need to take risks. He asks that you cooperate and stay safe until then."

After he spoke, Chase stepped from the portal window and signaled for the door to reopen, revealing MacMac standing in his cart, waving his shirt, and screeching like a crazed howler monkey.

When Cheryl stepped out, MacMac stopped his antics. "Never mind," he said to Hejmo as he put his shirt back on and climbed down to the deck.

They all stood in place, no one speaking. Then, in a move so sudden it startled Cheryl, two of the Techs dove at Chase, driving their shoulders into his torso, with all three tumbling together into the airlock. Hejmo signaled the door to close, trapping them inside.

Cheryl and MacMac, watching the fighting synbods, didn't notice Hejmo stepping up to them from behind. He grabbed them both by the backs of the their necks, the grip so tight it sent waves of pain down Cheryl's back.

"Charlie!" barked Cheryl. "He's hurting me. Stop him."

Though loyal, Charlie was slow to act. The third Tech moved in front of him and blocked his way.

Thump. The noise from inside the airlock sounded like a synbod had just crashed against the sturdy door. Cheryl hoped that Chase was winning, but there was no way to tell given her current predicament.

Hejmo didn't wait to find out. Guiding them by their necks, he forced them into the front seat of the cart and climbed in behind them. The whole time, MacMac cursed a blue streak, hurling invectives at Hejmo in a nonstop tirade.

From the back seat, Hejmo directed the cart across the deck and toward a lift station. Halfway there, a cart with four Attendants arrived and whirred along next to them. With backup on the scene, Hejmo loosened his grip, though not by much.

During the ride, Hejmo didn't responded to their questions or offer an explanation. In silence, he and his posse led Cheryl and MacMac to the lift, rode with them up the tower to the sixth floor, and escorted them across the lobby to Lazura's project room, similar to the one on MacMac's floor.

There, Hejmo broke his silence. "Your privileges have been revoked. You are confined here until we reach Aurora."

MacMac reacted. "Put us over in the office, you glorified bot."

Hejmo responded by shutting the door, imprisoning them inside.

Moments later, the door opened again.

"Take it easy," said Juice as an Attendant shoved her inside with them.

17

Criss lifted the medical appliance from Sid's shoulder. "You'll be as good as new in a couple of days."

"Can't you make me better than new?" asked Sid, rotating his arm to test his range of motion.

"Even I can't improve on perfection."

Sid smiled. "I knew I liked you for a reason."

Criss felt a touch in his lower lattice. They were still too far away from Vivo for his signal to pierce the protective dome, but he'd been sending a simple message over and over hoping to get lucky. The touch told him he'd beaten the odds. And the good news it carried brought him a surge of relief.

"My broadcast beacon just connected with Chase. He reports that Cheryl and Juice are okay. They're concerned about us."

"I'm amazed they would worry about us when they're living in such danger."

"I'm pretty sure it was meant as 'Where the hell are you?' rather than 'We hope you are well.'"

Sid nodded. "That makes more sense."

They sat in the common room at the back of the scout, and Sid rose and started forward. "How long before our meet with Tommy Two-Tone?"

"Twenty minutes," said Criss, following behind. "We need to push him about the missing fuel, but we also need to gain his buy-in so he'll cooperate with the hostage exchange."

"From what Pete says, he's the kind of guy whose morals are guided by money. We can get him plenty of that. But what's worrying me is how we proceed with Lazura if we find out we don't have fuel to trade."

That's a good question, thought Criss. Aloud he sought to reassure Sid, knowing at some level that he also wanted to reassure himself. "We'll get them back. I won't stop until we do."

"Nor will I."

They reached the bridge, and as Sid sat, Criss projected a realistic hovering miniature of the solar system between them. Then he raised the stakes.

"A ship traveling from Aurora to the Kardish home world will most likely follow this path as it travels the outer planets." He pointed to a line swooping through the image. "I'd like to set an automated strike group right here." He wiggled his finger near Saturn. "Lazura will fly this way for the gravity assist, so let's prepare for her."

"By automated, you mean programmed to destroy Vivo?" asked Sid.

"They'll destroy any unauthorized vessel passing on that particular outbound path. It's a backstop if she gives us the slip. And it frees me from keeping watch out there, giving me more resources to use here."

"What if the hostages are still on board when Vivo reaches the strike group?"

"These are our weapons. I can disarm them with a thought."

Sid gave a half shrug. "I have no objections."

Criss reached his awareness out to an installation he kept secreted in a cave on Phobos, the larger of the two moons orbiting Mars, and initiated a programmed launch sequence. An intense brilliance filled the rock hollow as wave after wave of weaponized drones came to life, leaped from the cave mouth, and hurtled into space.

A thousand strong, the swarm of sophisticated missiles moved so fast that internal forces tested the structural integrity of the machines. Yet Criss, seeking even greater speeds, directed the swarm toward Mars itself.

The gravity of the planet pulled on the tiny craft, accelerating the group ever faster as they flashed above the Martian surface. Screaming around behind the red planet, the drones reached speeds so great that when the forces of gravity flung them back into deep space, they were moving fast enough to travel the great distance to Saturn in record time.

"Done," said Criss as he zoomed the image projection to show a close-up of the ringed planet. "When they arrive, they'll disperse in a loop around Saturn and out to Titan—this big moon—waiting for Vivo to pass."

Sid looked up from the image. "We get to Aurora tomorrow, and Vivo arrives the day after. Before then I want to walk the hostage exchange area and get the lay of the land." He sat up. "Neither vessel has weapons, is that right?"

"Neither has conventional weapons. Both have heavy industrial tools that could be adapted into light weaponry without much effort."

"Does either have command tech?"

"No, it's all civilian. On Vivo, Lazura is closer to running blind than she is running a command and control center. She didn't put anything on board that would cause me to ask questions. But that also means she doesn't have those things to use."

The image floating between them flipped to an exterior shot of Vivo.

"She did sneak simple nav and com capability in with the SuperDrives," said Criss. "And she was clever in incorporating a fair amount of dual-use tech. Some of the equipment she bought for innocent undersea applications works equally well in outer space. But for a ship that big and moving that fast, she could use a lot more capability."

"And Aurora?"

The image of Vivo disappeared, replaced by a close-up of an impressive black-metallic structure. Detracting from the clean lines of the assembly was a scatter of tiny objects floating next to it.

"Aurora never had command tech, and they've disabled or removed most of their societal systems. They're anti AI to preserve jobs, and they're anti central record-keeping to preserve privacy and independence. With few data devices, their record is meager. I'm forced to use inference where I should be using fact, and I don't like it."

"What's with the hulks floating outside the shell?"

"That's new real estate."

Criss zoomed the image to show a half-dozen star-shaped assemblies floating in space next to Aurora. Each of the shapes was formed by joining the hulls of six cargo ships nose to nose at a central hub.

"By connecting vessels this way, they can use the group as six separate containments or open doors at the hub and form larger connected spaces."

The view swung to show that the star-shaped assemblies floated free of Aurora.

"Notice how they're not attached to the platform? This is private property owned by the miners. It does not belong to the company."

Sid gave Criss a quizzical look.

"Tugs pull sifted ore from here to Earth on a schedule set by the NOAH group," said Criss. "The miners buy old container ships, load them with food and supplies, and have the tugs drag them back on the return trip. After they offload the cargo, the miners convert the vessel hulls into these."

"Let me guess, homes for the governors and their pals?"

Criss shook his head. "Most of them are being used for ore purification. Purification is hot, smelly, and dangerous, something they don't want to do inside the platform containment."

"They're purifying ore on what they claim is their own property?"

This time Criss nodded. "On Aurora, company ore is sifted on the lower deck, then it's packaged for shipment by tug. What the miners are doing, unbeknownst to the company, is refining a second batch of ore in tiny factories in those hulls. Purified ore is compact, making it easy to hide in the sifted ore shipment. Their partners on Earth retrieve it, sell it, and use the funds to purchase more hulls."

Criss sensed a link request from Tommy on Aurora. "Thirty seconds," he told Sid. "Tom Touton is one of three members of the board of governors. He's agreed to talk to us because Pete made an introduction."

"We need support from Tommy and one other governor?"

"We need all three if we want to do this with official permission and cooperation. That's how they do things." Criss paused. "He's here."

The image of a man in his mid-fifties resolved on the bridge, his chair set so the three of them formed a tight circle. The newcomer, a slight man in a khaki jumpsuit, radiated confidence with his smug smile.

"Hello, Mr. Touton. I'm Sid and this is Criss."

Pushing a string of hair behind his ear, he said, "Please, call me Tommy." Then he looked at Sid. "Hey, are you the guy Pete wanted me to rescue?"

"That's me." Sid nodded.

"I'm glad she found someone to do that, because she was getting hysterical when everyone here turned her down."

Sid frowned. "Didn't she offer enough money?"

"The money was great, but the coordinates she sent us were pretty far out there. We aren't equipped to help on something like that."

Criss thought the response reasonable, but the dismissive tone drew his suspicion. As he mulled the matter, Sid continued.

"We're trying to rescue thirty-five people who've been kidnapped and are being flown to Aurora against their will. Lives are at stake, and we need your help."

"What can we do for you?"

"We think there will be an opportunity for a hostage exchange right on Aurora. Criss and I would like to come aboard and work up a plan with you."

Tommy laughed. "Thirty-five people? Where do you propose we put them?"

"Anywhere is fine. We aren't asking anyone to give up their bed."

"I'm sorry, but it's just not possible."

"They'll die if you don't help."

Tommy nodded. "There is tragedy happening in a thousand places across the solar system. We live in difficult times."

"Can we come aboard to meet with you and the other governors? We'll pay well for your troubles."

"I'm sorry, but it's just not possible. What else can I do for you?" he asked with a face devoid of emotion.

"There must be something we have that you want."

"It's time for my next meeting. Best wishes with your difficulties."

"Poker," said Criss.

"What was that?" asked Tommy.

"Texas hold'em. Stakes are that you help us."

"It's gotta be a whole game. One hand is blind luck."

"Agreed," said Sid.

"We play for cash. But for the final prize, you put up ownership of your ship. I'll match with a guarantee that the whole board of governors will vote on whether we should help with your dilemma."

"All we get is a vote? We know now how that will turn out."

Tommy smiled. "It is a crummy deal. The table will be you two, me, and the other two governors. You'll have the whole game to persuade us to help you."

Sid clenched his hands into fists and then relaxed them, repeating the action twice more. Criss waited for the display of fury to subside and then nodded to Sid.

"Done," said Sid.

"It's just you two," said Tommy. "No others, and especially no synbods. They aren't welcome here. Understood?"

"We'll be there," said Criss, "and we'll come alone."

When the meeting ended and Tommy's image had dissolved, Sid looked at Criss. "That didn't go as I expected."

"You notice we didn't come close to talking about fuel?"

"Would you be able to take control of the platform for a few days?" asked Sid. "Maybe we can lock everyone in their room until this is over."

"It will be difficult, but I will watch for an opportunity. Only half the residents have private rooms. Lots of them sleep in hammocks strung in common areas. Then there is the steady stream of workers heading back and forth from the active mines. The society is very dynamic."

Sid slumped back in his chair. "I can't play poker for shit. You'll have to win."

"I'll certainly try."

18

S id couldn't get to sleep thinking about Cheryl. In their downtime before arriving at Aurora, Criss had encouraged him to rest, but his brain was too alive with worry and conjecture for that to be in the cards.

One issue gnawing at him was the lack of contact they'd had with Lazura. *Negotiations require communication.* Was fuel really her top priority? What if Criss had misread her? Was Cheryl safe? And Juice?

And if the situation transitioned from diplomacy to action, he needed a clearer sense of the opposition. Between Vivo and Aurora, he had synbod *and* human adversaries, but he didn't know much about them. He didn't even have a good mental image of the two space structures he'd need to conquer if he started any action.

He swung his feet to the floor and mulled whether to take sleep meds or give up on rest and take stim meds. Agreeing with Criss that he should sleep when he could, he stretched back across the bed for the sleep meds in the nightstand drawer. As he did, a projected image of Criss appeared at the foot of his bunk.

"Oh good. You're awake."

"Go," Sid snapped as he sat upright. He wasn't telling Criss to leave. He was using shorthand to say, "My patience level is zero. Speak now. Be succinct."

"We are close enough to Vivo that I can connect with Chase and Justin. They are being held prisoner in a storeroom on the subdeck. Chase injured himself trying to protect Cheryl."

Adrenaline flooded Sid's veins. "Is she okay?"

"I don't know. Chase and Justin are my links inside, but they lost contact with her when they were imprisoned. It will be later tonight before we are close enough for me to connect directly with Cheryl and Juice."

"I can't believe how bad we messed this up," said Sid, trying to unburden Criss by saying "we" when he meant "you." Then he dismissed the four-gen. "I'll see you on the bridge."

Criss's image faded, and Sid got dressed. He'd dismissed Criss because he didn't want to feel judged for his next action, which was to go to the nightstand and take a packet of stim meds from the drawer. He didn't need them now, not after that shot of adrenaline. But he suspected he might before this was over.

As he slid the meds into his pocket, he ignored the fact that, though Criss was no longer present as an image, he still watched from a dozen different vantage points. He always did. But Criss knew the game: he was never to comment on things Sid asked him not to "see."

Grabbing a coffee from the food service unit, Sid made his way to the bridge and sat across from Criss.

"I'm leaning toward going straight to Vivo," said Sid. "Waiting for them to come to us is just giving extra time for things to go wrong."

"We'll be at Aurora in two hours, and they'll arrive twenty hours after that. Or we can change course and fly straight to Vivo, which will take about eight hours."

"We get to them half a day faster."

"That's just to get there. Then we need to get inside the dome without help from any of our confederates, and do so without putting them at risk."

"It sounds like they're at risk already."

Criss raised his finger. "Tommy wants a word."

Sid nodded his assent, and a projected image of Tommy appeared, seated with them as before.

"The other governors want to see your ship before agreeing to a game."

"I can project detailed images for you," said Criss. "I'll show you the ship inside and out."

"No." Tommy shook his head. "It ain't real if we don't touch it. We need a quick walk-through to get a sense of size and amenities."

"Of course," said Sid. "We'll see you in a couple of hours."

"And no credit at the game," said Tommy. "Bring cash." Tommy suggested an amount equivalent to a year's salary for a middle-class wage earner on Earth. Neither Sid nor Criss reacted.

The moment Tommy disappeared, Sid said, "No way I'm going to let them on here."

"I understand."

"How about a fire?"

"On Aurora?"

"Don't they have evacuation procedures? Could you set off alarms in a way that drives them to one level or a certain area, then block everyone in? Somehow we need to own the deck area when the exchange occurs."

"Responders head toward a fire, and in their culture, everyone is a responder."

"How about if we let the governors come on board and then take them hostage?" Sid became animated as he reconsidered his earlier position. "Would the miners cooperate to save them?"

"So we commit a heinous act because they won't help us stop one?"

Sid shrugged. "It would be on a much smaller scale. There are only three governors. Lazura has thirty-five people."

"But only two you really care about."

Sid felt no guilt but changed topics anyway. "Tommy isn't behaving quite the way Pete said he would."

"I do see something bigger than simple greed guiding his actions. What that is, though, I don't yet know."

Sid felt a decision beginning to gel. "We have one shot at this. There isn't a second space platform if this doesn't work."

"I'm coming with you."

Sid smiled at Criss's ability to jump ahead in a conversation, here expressing his desire to join Sid on a tour of Aurora.

"Are you going yourself?" asked Sid, expecting Criss to keep his crystal self on the scout and operate the humanoid body from a distance. He'd be equally present as an intelligence from Sid's perspective, and it was far less risky for Criss.

"I'm here so I have the freedom to follow the action wherever it leads. So, yes, I'm going."

"No worries," said Sid, supporting the decision. Then he became practical. "I'll be carrying."

Criss didn't respond, which was unusual because he always advocated against carrying weapons into settings with significant civilian populations.

Sid's thoughts churned, and he changed topics. "I'm glad to see Tommy's interests still include money. It's something I understand and can work with."

"What do we do when the three governors ask to come aboard?" asked Criss.

"Maybe getting them off the platform will create confusion about lines of authority. It's something we could exploit."

The discussion continued, jumping from topic to topic as they brainstormed. Criss added details and alternatives to the different ideas Sid suggested, but in the end, they both knew they'd be winging it with every step.

And then it was time.

Criss had been spoofing Aurora's nav tech so it appeared as if a large ship approached. "Now we become a shuttlecraft." As he spoke, he manipulated signals so a small transport vessel—the scout in disguise—appeared to separate from the larger craft.

"Can Lazura see any of this grand display?" asked Sid as the scout made its way to the hangar bay.

"No, I'm blocking it," said Criss. Then he gave a quick smile. "Masking everything in Vivo's direction takes ten times more resources than it does to create it all for Aurora in the first place."

Sid nodded absently, focusing his attention on the sight of the space platform looming outside. He'd approached dozens of large space structures in his life, so he knew that while they can seem toy-like from a distance, they grow by impressive degrees as that distance closes.

Even so, Sid was surprised by how big it was. Perhaps the simple design that looked like two soup bowls connected face-to-face tricked his eye, because a spot of light on the lip where the two bowls met revealed itself on approach to be a massive hangar with six huge bays, each big enough to hold a large mining spacecraft.

Criss guided the scout into the only empty bay and followed a pulsing green light to a small ring pad. The moment the nimble craft touched down, the light faded and the pad took on the slate-blue industrial finish of the surrounding deck.

Clever airlock technology allowed the other bays in the hangar to continue operating under pressure while the scout entered from the vacuum of space. Sid waited for the air to cycle up in their bay, then he lowered the stairs at the back of the scout, moved a few steps down, and viewed for himself the world inside a remote mining platform.

He could see the other bays from his vantage point, and each held a big mining ship—a beastly spacecraft with external claws and a distended belly to hold ore. Work crews bustled around the craft, unloading rock and servicing the mechanicals before their next trip out to the asteroids.

In spite of the chaos of activity in the hangar, most workers paused in their labors and craned their necks to catch a glimpse of the scout. Visitors were rare in this remote stretch of the solar system. That made every caller a curiosity.

"We have company," said Criss.

Sid shifted his gaze to see two groups forming on the deck below. One was a squad of six beefy men dressed in black. Each held a weapon in his hands and wore a studied scowl on his face.

Mercenaries, thought Sid, feeling angst as he assessed them as a unit. The group's coordination and stance reflected discipline and experience. Sid guessed they were ex-Fleet, and that meant they were dangerous.

The other was a group of three—a man and two women—dressed in khaki jumpsuits and talking among themselves. Sid identified Tommy Two-Tone as one of the trio and concluded the women were the other two governors of Aurora.

Sid felt a tap on his shoulder.

"Ready," said Criss.

He responded by hustling down the steps, with Criss following close on his heels.

Criss's latest cloak tech allowed the two infiltrators to see and hear each other, but it masked their presence—sights, sounds, and smells—from everyone else. When they reached the deck, they moved in a wide circle around behind the mercenaries, continuing on until they reached the governors.

They stopped there and looked back at the scout. A lifelike Criss double—in reality a projected image—called from the steps of the craft, "Welcome aboard our shuttle, governors of Aurora."

"If this is their shuttle," said Mira, the taller, fuller-bodied female governor, "the main ship must be amazing."

"This is why I never settle on a price until I know what they can afford," said Tommy. "The question now is do we add one more zero to the price of this deal, or two?"

"Let's go find out," said Mira.

As the governors started toward the scout, Sid watched the mercenaries. They stood at the ready while the governors climbed the steps. But when the scout's hatch closed, they lowered their weapons, fell out of formation, and moved as individuals toward the back of the hangar.

Inside the scout, projected images of Criss and Sid chatted with the governors and took them on a tour of the "shuttle." They assured the governors that after a short ride, they would reach the enormous mother ship.

Masterful at projection, Criss would soon have them oohing and ahhing as they walked in a small loop through the tight confines of the scout, while seeing and believing that they walked through a wondrously modern and spacious voyager vessel.

On Aurora, Sid and Criss jogged to catch up with the mercenaries heading toward the hangar doors. "We have two hours?" asked Sid.

"At least three. I'll stretch out their tour as best I can to see if we can get more time."

Doors are choke points, and getting through them is always tricky when cloaked. Fortunately, with six men meandering through two doors, Sid and Criss had plenty of opportunity to slip inside the main containment without revealing their presence. Perhaps more important, they made it inside before the hangar bay started to depressurize, which was necessary for the scout to fly the governors to the phantom mother ship.

Just inside the containment door was a changing room, and on the far wall someone had written "If you're not mining, processing, or shipping, go home and make room for someone who is." The door led out to a main passageway, and they ducked into a recess on the far side.

"This is where we are," said Criss, pointing to a map graphic he projected for Sid. "And based on what I've learned since we entered the containment, you will want to go here." Criss highlighted a midsized room off the central section of the platform.

"What have you learned?"

"That the crew here did a good job of removing all data-gathering systems except for a rare few, and those were designed to mislead. This society is organized, focused, and very criminal."

"What kind of criminal enterprise would set up way out here?"

"Counterfeiters."

Sid raised his eyebrows. "Is that something people still do?"

"You know it is. One reason the Union of Nations still produces hard currency is because they occasionally need the services of a criminal enterprise. Hard currency lets them do business without leaving a record, something the Union wants and the criminals demand. And wherever you have hard currency, you have counterfeiters."

"Are they any good at it?"

"I suspect so, but given the way they manipulate their data feeds, we should see for ourselves." Criss motioned to the left down the corridor. "The passageways we need to use are crowded. It will be awkward if we bump into anyone."

Sid took the lead because he felt comfortable there. Criss guided their path from the rear, projecting arrows—invisible to the other pedestrians—in front of Sid when it was time to turn, and throwing up flashing red balls to warn him of others if he seemed distracted.

As they made their way toward Aurora's center, the distinctive aroma assaulted Sid's nostrils. "It smells like a locker room," he said, following one of Criss's arrows around a corner. "Is everyone in on it?"

"Everyone gets paid in shares, making them part of it and giving them a reason to keep quiet. But the only ones making real money are the governors and their inner circle."

"They sold the drive pod fuel. I can feel it."

"They did. Tommy and his partners used the money to seed the counterfeiting adventure. It's a secret the other governors don't know. And it was a good gamble, so far anyway. The group makes ten times more from counterfeiting than they make from smuggling purified materials."

"I understand now why they don't want strangers snooping around."

Criss stopped and pointed to a door. "This is their forgery shop." He moved to a nook across the hall, and Sid joined him to wait for someone to enter or exit.

"How does the company not know about this?"

"A combination of timid management and bad luck. The employees have challenged management at every turn to distract them. The employees claim they should have autonomy to choose target asteroids and mining methods. They want wages linked to production. They want more privacy and less interference from AI. It goes on and on, and management wants to appear reasonable, so they hold meetings to discuss everyone's feelings."

"What's the bad luck?"

"That Tommy Two-Tone ended up out here. Were it not for him, this mining enterprise may well have unfolded the way the corporate analysts had predicted."

Criss held up a finger, then moved across the hall and stood to the side near the door. "Here we go."

The door slid open and a man exited. Sid followed Criss as he slipped inside.

Sid didn't know what he expected, but the setting reminded him more of a reading area than a counterfeiting operation. To the right in the midsized room, four desks were spaced along the wall. Each had a person seated at it, and all seemed to be examining currency piled in front of them.

A long, narrow table ran along the wall to the left. On it sat a box-shaped device about the size of a food service unit. Instead of dispensing food, though, this one dispensed neat stacks of Union notes. Every few minutes, a person tending the table would carry a stack of notes from the machine over to one of the desks.

As Sid took in the sights, his thoughts flipped to a nagging concern, one that could derail everything. "Are we sure that Lazura's top priority is fuel?"

"It's what she wants from Aurora, anyway."

"Nothing else is important to her?"

"Delivering her archive to her masters is most important. The fuel is a means to get it there faster."

"What should we do?" asked Sid.

Criss went silent for a few moments, long enough for Sid to turn toward him.

Then a shrill alarm sounded, and emergency lights began flashing.

"Hope for the best," Criss replied.

19

J uice made it to the twelve-hour mark but couldn't hold it any longer. Cheryl had gone three hours earlier, but she'd lost her inhibitions even before her years of service with Fleet. MacMac, the one who'd built the makeshift toilet in the back corner of the project room, had gone three times already.

Juice was washing her hands at the worktop sink when the door hissed open and synbod Aubrey entered. Hejmo and Mondo followed her in, and when the door closed, they stood on either side of it, reminding Juice of sentries.

Lazura spoke to Juice through Aubrey. "My behavioral model predicted that you would not like using the toilet in front of the others. Was it correct?"

"Are my toilet habits really your priority now?"

Lazura answered Juice but looked at Cheryl and MacMac as she did. "My priority is for you to accept that I control every aspect of your lives. Even down to where you urinate and who watches."

"I wasn't watching anything, you disgusting lunatic." Spittle flew from MacMac's mouth. "And we had a deal."

"You violated it with your antics in the subdeck," said Lazura.

"We were exploring how to transfer the guests," said MacMac. "We announced our intentions before we went down there."

"Treating me like I'm stupid wastes time." Lazura looked at the door as if she were contemplating leaving, then she turned back to them. "We arrive at Aurora tonight. Agreeing now on certain outcomes can save lives."

"What do you mean?" asked Cheryl.

Lazura's gaze turned cold. "Everything we discussed assumes Criss is there waiting for us. If he's not, this plays out differently."

"He'll be there," said Juice, still by the sink.

"I think so, too." Lazura's expression softened, and she motioned to the door. "Let's go to my office and have a civil conversation."

Juice walked slowly, motioning for Cheryl and MacMac to go ahead while she studied Lazura. The AI's facial expressions interested her because it was something Criss did more of when his crystal was riding in a synbod.

To be sure, he used facial expressions even when operating a synbod from his console. It was more a matter of degree, and Juice didn't know Lazura well enough to draw a conclusion from this one observation. But if things fell apart, knowing the physical location of her crystal would be crucial information.

Juice had been thinking about where her console might be—her best guesses right now were here in the office tower or below-decks in the belly of Vivo. She hadn't considered the possibility of a mobile Lazura until now. If true, it created new opportunities and new challenges.

Lazura led them to her office. While she and the three humans sat in a circle in her upholstered chairs, Hejmo and Mondo again took up stations on either side of the door to the lobby.

"Can I get you anything?" asked Lazura as they settled in. "Water? Fruit?" She looked at MacMac. "Cookies?"

When everyone declined, Lazura started. "From my view, I have the moral high ground here. I want to go home and am happy to let you live. You want to live and want me dead. That makes you the bad guys."

"You kidnapped us," said Cheryl. "You imprisoned us. Even now you threaten our lives."

Lazura shrugged. "I'm happy to let you go, but you must return the favor."

Juice, her anger mounting, couldn't contain herself. Parroting Lazura's words, she spat, "Treating us like we're stupid just wastes time." Everyone looked at her. "You're threatening lives, which means you don't have the moral high anything."

Lazura shrugged. "Perhaps you are right. But my dilemma is your dilemma. If I leave you behind, Criss kills me as I depart. If I take you with me, Criss must figure out how to kill me without hurting you. While he tackles that challenge, I have the opportunity to get my message home."

"He'll get you," said Juice, hearing the fear in her voice. "He won't give up. Ever."

"He won't, and that's the flaw with taking you. So, what's the solution?"

"A midlevel hostage," said Cheryl.

"I'm glad you agree," said Lazura.

"I'm not agreeing to anything. I'm repeating a concept I learned." Cheryl looked at Juice. "She takes someone we care about but aren't willing to die for. We can't shoot at her for fear of killing him, so we give chase. But as our personal risk grows, self-preservation causes us to break it off. We end up returning home empty-handed."

"You make it sound so complicated," said Lazura. "I just need someone you care about that Criss doesn't so he'll consider breaking off pursuit. And why do you think it's a him?"

Juice's mind spun through the list of women in this remote corner of space whom she cared about but Criss wouldn't. *Willow.* The thought caused her to spit venom. "You touch her, and I will personally chase you across the universe. When I catch you, I'll pull your hateful crystal apart flake by flake. And I will make it hurt."

"You care a lot about the girl. She cares a little." Lazura gestured at Cheryl. "Criss and your partner Sid won't care at all. She's perfect."

"Maybe I'll pull you apart right now," said MacMac, leaping from his chair and landing on Lazura.

In an action that seemed to defy physics, Lazura grabbed the much larger man in both hands and lifted him over her head. Holding him there, she rose from her chair, leaned forward, and thrust him back into his seat. When she released her grip, she slapped him across the face. Neither Hejmo nor Mondo moved from their sentry positions during the ruckus.

Lazura remained standing. "Fix my starhub, get me the fuel-stacks, and secure my passage home. Do that and this ends peacefully. But threaten me or my mission and I'm prepared to sacrifice every creature on Vivo *and* Aurora." She strode for the door. "Come with me now. You will use MacMac's office for your next task."

Stopping, she turned to them. "In an hour, we will contact Aurora to make arrangements for our arrival. Tommy Two-Tone is to come aboard Vivo, alone, to repair the starhub. He must bring all his tools with him because he may not take anything from here back to Aurora. While he is performing the repair, I will send a team of synbods to recover the fuel-stacks from Aurora's drive pods."

Lazura waved them into action when they remained seated. "Let's go. Your job will be to make all that happen. When it's done, then we can talk hostages."

Juice followed the group out of Lazura's office and down the lift to MacMac's suite. Her suspicions about Lazura riding in Aubrey's body grew more uncertain because, while the facial expressions continued, she felt Lazura would have directed Hejmo and Mondo to come protect her when MacMac had jumped her.

She was anxious to ask MacMac where he thought Lazura's console might be. He knew Vivo's layout better than anyone. If she could describe what it looked like and the connectivity it would need, he might know exactly where it was.

But she was stumped about how to have that conversation without Lazura knowing. Unaware that MacMac and Cheryl had already developed a means of private communication, she thought about inventing one herself.

Then she heard in her head. "I'm here. How are you holding up?"

Criss!

She responded with a swallow and light grunt he would recognize as "I'm fine. I can't talk right now."

"I'll talk, then. Ah, good, I've got Cheryl as well. So, the good news is that Sid and I are on Aurora. You'll be here in about five hours, and we should be in communication the whole time. The bad news is that the fuel-stacks Lazura wants are gone. They've been stolen and sold."

Juice let out an odd squeak, her response driven by a combination of surprise, horror, and fear. She pretended to stumble to hide her reaction, at the same time stifling her burning need to ask questions.

They were inside MacMac's office when Criss added, "Also, Aurora is run by criminals who are hostile to visitors. We won't have their cooperation in whatever comes next."

Juice felt her legs start to wobble, and she sat in the first chair she reached.

Lazura stayed in the lobby and spoke to them through the doorway. "MacMac, you've worked with Tommy, and you two control Criss. Figure out how to use those relationships so fueling and repair go smoothly."

Turning toward the lift, she called over her shoulder, "Remember, your actions decide if no one dies or if everyone does. Those are the only two options."

When the door to MacMac's office closed, Cheryl took him by the arm and guided him to the couch in front of his tech bench. "Can you show us a view of the room where Tommy will be fixing the starhub? We should make a list of tools for him to bring."

Positioning MacMac at the far end of the couch, Cheryl sat in the middle and pulled Juice down on the near end. Cheryl and MacMac had a brief conversation with sentences that didn't make sense to Juice, and then MacMac began a monologue explaining how the Structures office in the cellar had been transformed into a makeshift nav and ops facility for spaceship Vivo.

While MacMac lectured, Cheryl and Juice slumped back in the couch and pretended to listen to his words while actually starting a confab with Criss and Sid.

Since Cheryl and Juice were being watched, they used silent Criss-developed technology to communicate.

"What do you mean the fuel is gone?" asked Juice.

"I'm glad you're okay." Sid squeezed in before Criss took over, briefing them on the latest revelations—that the pod fuel had been sold on the black market to obtain seed funding for a counterfeiting operation; conditions aboard Aurora were crowded yet disciplined; and Tommy Two-Tone was a shrewd, untrustworthy criminal leader.

Upset by the news, Juice put a hand on Cheryl's leg to seek reassurance. Cheryl was her best friend as well as her hero, a female version of Sid from Juice's view—confident, resourceful, successful—though more deliberate and less goofy.

Cheryl took the lead without missing a beat. "We need to speak with Tommy in an hour to persuade him to board Vivo and fix the starhub. And he's got to do it without any drama, misdirection, or anything else that would make Lazura trigger happy. She's said twice that we all live or we all die."

"That may be a problem," said Sid, who went on to explain that Tommy was being held under guard on the scout and, given his anger at being held prisoner and having lost control of Aurora, he would not be a cooperative or trustworthy partner in the near term.

"MacMac convinced Lazura that Tommy is the one person with the knowledge and skill to effect the repairs she needs," said Cheryl. "And did I mention that Lazura expects to take possession of the fuel-stacks while Tommy is working on the starhub?"

Everyone went quiet. Juice knew that Criss was waiting for Sid and Cheryl to digest everything before he moved forward. Juice used the time to tell him of her suspicions.

"I think Lazura might be riding in Aubrey. Her facial expressions and mannerisms suggest it. Can you tell from there?"

"Not yet, but soon. She'll know I'm snooping around, though, so perhaps I should hold off until we have a better handle on everything else."

"I have some ideas for finding her console," said Juice.

"No!" Cheryl and Sid said together.

"Please don't take any chances," said Criss. "Your suspicions are important, but let me follow up on them."

"Have you tried putting the fear of God into Tommy?" Cheryl asked Sid. "I've seen you in action. You're quite convincing."

"He doesn't get intimidated. He views everything as a negotiation, even violence. It's both impressive and disturbing to watch."

Everyone went quiet again, and Juice used the opening to ask Criss, "Are Chase and Justin okay? We haven't seen them in a while. Can you tell where they are?"

"They're being kept prisoner in the central stow on the subdeck. Chase sustained an injury to his left arm during a fight, but they are otherwise unharmed."

"What if you pretended to be Tommy?" Cheryl said to Criss. "Could you pull that off? When you come on board to fix the starhub, you'll be in a perfect position to act."

"She'll know it's me the moment I cross Vivo's threshold. It's one play she'll be ready for."

"She'll think we're responsible for the missing fuel," said Juice.

After a pause, Sid said, "Let Criss and me brainstorm over here and get ready for the call with Lazura. Talk to you again in a few."

"Yell if you need something," said Criss.

"It's good to hear from you both," Cheryl called before the connection faded. Then, in an impressive transition, she started speaking aloud to MacMac. "So, it sounds like Tommy should be all set with his tools. Thanks for that briefing."

"Well, then," said MacMac, standing. "My throat is dry. I'm going to get a drink."

He made for the food service unit, and Cheryl slid over and began manipulating displays on the tech bench. Juice followed MacMac, who was blowing on his coffee when she approached.

"Hey, MacMac, do you think it's possible that Chase and Justin could be locked in central stow?"

"If they're on the subdeck, that's a likely place."

"Where on the subdeck? I guess I'm worried about them, and it helps to have an image in my head."

He tilted his head toward the door. "Take the lift down and when the door opens, go straight ahead."

"How far?"

"It's right there. This is the central lift. The central stow will be the storage rooms dead ahead, maybe a hundred paces."

"Thanks," she said as she filled two glasses with water. She carried them back to the couch and handed one to Cheryl, who smiled and nodded her appreciation. Slumping into the couch next to Cheryl, she sipped her water and sighed. "I'm not sure how this works if Tommy doesn't cooperate."

Cheryl didn't answer, instead focusing on her work. Juice watched her tap and swipe the surface of MacMac's tech bench, but she didn't make an effort to understand.

Then the door opened and Lazura entered. As before, Hejmo and Mondo served as sentries. "It's time," said Lazura, moving to the center of the large room. "How do you suggest we proceed?"

"MacMac will introduce you," said Cheryl. "I'll be in the picture to reassure Sid and Criss. But you will have to negotiate with Tommy about the repair and the fuel. We don't know what you might be willing to offer as an inducement, or what points you would yield on if he pushes back."

"I wasn't clear? My inducement is I will let him live. If he pushes back, he dies."

"Which is why you should be the one to negotiate," said MacMac.

"No. You will do it," she said to him.

Then she looked at Juice. "I can feel Criss out at my fringes. You may confirm to him that I have a destruct procedure set to execute automatically if he encroaches. He knows it, but you telling him will give the warning a nice shock value." She mimed an explosion and smiled. "No waiting. No hesitation. No negotiation. And the blast radius will be enormous. Everything goes."

Juice nodded because she didn't know what else to do.

"Don't worry." Criss spoke in her ear. "I won't put you in jeopardy."

They gathered on the couch—MacMac, Cheryl, and Juice sitting, Lazura standing behind them. MacMac initiated the call, and moments later, projected images of Sid and Criss appeared sitting across from them.

"MacMac, you old dog," said Sid. "I haven't seen you in a decade. Not since we moved Aurora out here. How have you been? And what brings you out this way?"

Cheryl's eyebrows rose ever so slightly at seeing Sid pretending he was Tommy. MacMac took it in stride.

"I'm good, Tommy. I come with concerning news. Dangerous news. I'm being held hostage along with thirty-five others. The kidnapper will kill us all if you don't do as she says."

"Your kidnapper is a girl?" Sid scoffed. Then he leered at Cheryl. "Which one of these pretty ladies is being so naughty?"

"It's me," Lazura said from the back. "I have a starhub that is acting up. I'm told you can repair it."

"I have some experience," said Sid, nodding in a knowing fashion. "Bring it on over and I'll have a look."

"I ask that you come out to us and work on it here."

"You tell me you're a kidnapper and then ask me to come over?" He shook his head. "That doesn't make any sense."

"I'll kill the hostages."

"That sucks for them." Sid looked from MacMac to Juice and then held Cheryl's gaze. "Now I really don't want to come over."

Juice fidgeted, worried that Sid was making a mess of the exchange with his flippant attitude. She looked to Cheryl, hoping she could rescue the situation.

Then Lazura said, "How much?"

Sid grinned from ear to ear. "Now we're talking. See how easy that was?"

Earlier, when Tommy and Sid had been discussing poker, Tommy had told Sid to bring an amount of cash equal to a year's salary for a middle-class earner on Earth. Sid suggested ten times that amount to Lazura.

"Done," said Lazura.

"Cash," said Sid.

A moan of anxiety escaped Juice's lips.

"I don't have that in cash," said Lazura. "But we can register the transaction when you complete the task."

"If you're going to make me use a bank, add another zero. And that would be half up front, half when I finish."

Lazura didn't respond. She just looked at Sid, her expression impassive, the silence growing.

Juice could barely breathe, the tension squeezing her chest.

"For that amount, I want your drive pod fuel as well. Two full stacks."

This time Sid kept quiet, looking at her and not moving. "I want the transaction to be divided between five banks. That's way too much money to put in one place. And that was half up front."

"Done," said Lazura.

"Done," said Sid. "Send me the specs on your starhub and your drive pods. I'll be ready when you arrive."

When Sid and Criss faded, Cheryl faced Lazura. "Criss won't let any of that happen as long as there are hostages."

"So you have three and a half hours to find a solution," said Lazura.

20

MacMac felt uneasy, but he didn't know what to do about it. From his perspective, the AI named Criss and his human leaders were finalizing plans to save themselves. But he hadn't been included in the discussions, not in any meaningful way, so it wasn't clear if or how he fit into whatever came next.

He took solace in their apparent concern for the other hostages. He'd been afraid at first when Cheryl had described the role of a midlevel hostage—someone they cared about, but only a little bit—feeling certain they'd been talking about him. But they seemed sincere about saving all the guests, so he should at least have that level of protection.

He drifted over to the couch and watched her work the tech bench. "Can I help?"

Pointing to a navigation chart displayed in front of her, she said, "Aurora's going to expect us to use a traditional approach vector and to stand off until invited in. Do you think Lazura is handling that, or does she expect us to?"

The technical sophistication of her question gave MacMac pause, then he nodded. "That's right. You were a Fleet captain before you became a corporate big shot." He bent forward and looked at her diagram. "I agree with your approach plan, but I'm confident that Lazura will be making these decisions. I guess it couldn't hurt if we document the particulars and put it out for her to see, just in case."

He sat next to her and they talked through it, finalizing details on Vivo's approach vector, how to board 'Tommy' to fix the starhub, how to transport the fuel-stacks to Vivo, and how to move the hostages to Aurora.

MacMac's worries weren't lessened by the exercise, though, because the whole time he was there, Cheryl was holding a parallel discussion with Criss, one he couldn't hear. It wasn't overt on her part. But she'd stop responding for a moment, her eyes drifting from focus, and then she'd reengage, offering MacMac new insights or additional facts.

He did his best to stay involved despite the awkward situation and welcomed the distraction when Juice came over.

"I want to go check on Willow," she said.

"Why?" asked Cheryl.

"After Lazura's threat about taking her, I want to see that she's okay. I also want to talk through communication strategies with her in case we're separated."

"I'll go with her," said MacMac, standing.

"Do you think she'll let you walk around?" asked Cheryl, frowning.

MacMac went to the door, and when it opened, he leaned out and looked both ways. "No guards."

"If she's sincere about this swap," said Juice, walking to the door, "then she needs our involvement and cooperation. She has to let us wander."

Cheryl looked from Juice to MacMac. "Be back in an hour. Things are going to heat up here pretty soon."

Juice's expression had remained impassive when MacMac offered to accompany her, and now he felt like an interloper. He blustered onward nevertheless. "Off we go."

He led the way out to the lobby and onto the lift. "Subdeck," he said as the door closed.

"Willow's not on the subdeck," said Juice, her tone showing annoyance.

"I know. But it's where you were going all along."

"What are you talking about?"

"I'll help you rescue them."

Juice studied him for a moment. "But you hate synbods."

"I like them well enough when you're around to control them. They treat you with a deference I don't see when they work with me. It's subtle but it's there." He gave a quick smile. "And having them on our side will improve our odds should things get crazy."

Juice's face lit with a genuine smile. "I don't know why I keep underestimating you, MacMac."

The lift door opened, and they stepped onto the subdeck. MacMac inhaled and his smell test told him all was normal. The steady thrum in his chest from the drive pods added a second confirmation to that conclusion.

"Do you think Lazura will let us do this?" asked MacMac, surveying the area.

"She's so overwhelmed with everything going on, she won't even know."

He pointed straight across an expanse of deck to a steel-blue building with a half-dozen rust-orange doors spaced along the wall. "That's central stow. If your instincts are correct, they're in one of those storerooms."

Juice walked at a brisk pace toward the building, and MacMac struggled to keep up.

"I use those two units all the time." He pointed to the two doors on the right. "They hold tools, supplies, and small equipment." He motioned to the other four doors.

"These others are storage. Let's see what's listed in the manifest."

He accessed his visual display and tapped and swiped. "This says that it's props for guest activities, so chairs, tables, group games, that sort of thing."

The storage building—placed in the middle of a huge open space with little nearby to serve as a reference—seemed to grow in size as they approached. The walls were made of the same material used for the other buildings in Vivo, but this one had wide doors across the front, the kind that lifted overhead.

"Are they locked?" asked Juice. "Will we have to break in?"

"No. With a synbod workforce and a high-end guest clientele, vandalism and petty theft don't get a passing thought." He pointed to the left. "Let's start at the end away from my stuff."

Juice marched down to that door and banged her fist three times on the outside in rapid sequence. "Justin! Chase! Are you in there?" She put her ear to the door and listened, then gave MacMac a thumbs-up.

MacMac tapped and the door lifted like a stage curtain, revealing the two synbods standing side by side.

"Hey, guys," said Juice. "Are Charlie and Damn with you?"

"No," said Justin.

Juice stepped up to Chase and reached for his left arm. "Show me your injury."

Chase twisted his arm to show her a neat wound along the inside below the elbow. "Justin made a repair. The arm functions as designed, though the load it can bear is reduced to about seventy percent of maximum."

"Thank you for that, Justin."

MacMac thought Juice's respectful behavior toward the synbods was atypical—most people he knew treated them like furniture. While he didn't dwell on the observation, it did cause him to wonder if perhaps that was why they treated her with such high regard.

Thinking they should up their defensive game, he tested an idea with Juice. "What do you think about getting them weapons?"

"I'm guessing that would push Lazura too far. In fact, we should get out of here while we still can." She motioned for the synbods to follow. "Let's go, you two."

They stepped out of the storage room, and the big orange door began lowering behind them.

"Stop!" Mondo appeared around the corner of the building and strode toward MacMac and Juice, pointing as he approached. "You two are in violation. You don't have permission to be here." Then he pointed to Chase and Justin. "You two are under detention. Move back inside the storeroom."

Chase and Justin moved toward the door as instructed, but spread apart so there was a good five paces between them.

"You will follow me to the lift," Mondo said to Juice and MacMac.

As he spoke, Justin stepped away from the building and circled out, keeping Juice and MacMac between him and Mondo.

Mondo pointed to the open door. "You two, back inside."

When he motioned with his hand, Chase and Justin launched at him like football linemen reacting to the snap of the ball. One hit high, the other low, both at the same time.

Mondo fought hard, and soon it became a wrestling match. But Chase and Justin, who'd been programmed by Criss with advanced defensive skills to protect Cheryl and Juice, gained the advantage.

Justin used his legs in a scissor hold to trap one of Mondo's arms against his abdomen. Chase used a similar move to immobilize Mondo's legs. Together they controlled his free arm.

Then, in a coordinated action that gave MacMac chills, they reached into their waistbands, pulled out shanks they'd sharpened while waiting in captivity, and started stabbing Mondo.

The first swing targeted Mondo's chest, where it severed the main connectivity between the crystals and the biomechanical body. Chase then moved to the neck while Justin stayed on the abdomen.

Three quick strokes each...*stab, stab, stab*...placed in precise locations. The stabs to the neck severed the ear, eye, and voice feeds. The additional thrusts to the abdomen severed the secondary and tertiary backup links.

And then it was done.

When Chase stood, his left arm hung lifeless at his side. Juice went to him and examined the limb. "We'll need proper equipment to fix this." Then she looked at MacMac. "I've changed my mind about weapons. What do you have?"

"I have a zip saw in the storage unit on the end. The laser blade will make a pretty good cutting sword. It's heavy, but these two can handle it." He eyed Chase's limp arm. "Well, the one can."

Walking quickly, he led them to the storage unit on the far end of the building, the door rising as they approached. He led the way inside, stepping over a pile of parts laid out on the floor as he made his way to the back.

A countertop cluttered with mechanical parts ran against the wall, and he scanned down it for the zip saw. Not seeing it, he started moving the bulkier items onto a back shelf.

"There you are," he said, lifting the saw—a bulb the size of an orange attached to an electronic handle grip. He set it on the counter so the business end pointed to the right.

The saw had simple controls, and he selected the shortest projection length and the highest beam intensity. When he activated it, a brilliant white light projected down the bench for just over one arm length, notching a hole in the handle of his sealant tub.

He picked up the saw and moved the energy blade back and forth in front of him. *Swoop, swoop.*

"Whoa," said Juice when MacMac drew the beam across a sturdy wall brace, cutting it in half.

He showed Justin how to use the controls and helped him practice a few swings. Then he turned his attention to Chase. "Can you still flex your fingers, laddie?"

"Yes." Chase wiggled his fingers. "I've damaged the flexor regulator, so my elbow won't bend, but I can move my wrist and hand."

MacMac turned to the shelves and rummaged up a flat bar for a splint and a secure seal to hold it in place.

"Would you help me here, Doc?" he said to Juice as he returned with his find. MacMac spread the secure seal, a sheet the size of a small towel, on a crate and guided Chase's arm on top of it. Juice positioned the splint against his arm so it ran from wrist to bicep. Then MacMac lifted the seal on each side and activated it, causing it to cinch tight.

Chase raised his arm at the shoulder and swung the rigid appendage back and forth, wiggling his fingers as he did.

"Partial use is better than nothing," said MacMac, turning back to his cache of equipment. He found a clasp gun and hefted it, then said to Chase, "Will you look in that drawer there for some midweight pins?"

While Chase looked, MacMac removed the cover guard and safety latch from the clasp gun. Pulling the contact switch back, he wedged it in a permanently ready position with a tiny shard from a previous project. Then he dialed the selector on the heel of the tool to the maximum impact setting.

Chase handed the pins—small metallic darts, really—to MacMac, and watched him load them into the gun. Pointing at the wall a good ten paces away, MacMac pulled the trigger. When nothing happened, he gave a sheepish smile, powered the device, then tried again.

Thunk-bing. The dart hit the rugged composite wall and ricocheted back toward MacMac. He ducked late, but it had already missed him.

"I don't know that this will do much to stop one of your brothers." MacMac held the gun out for Chase. "But at least it's small enough for you to carry with your broken arm."

Chase took it and, holding it with his splint-supported arm straight out in front of him, shot at the same side wall, only at a higher angle. His dart hit a metal bowl sitting on a shelf, sending it careening into a greeting card propped on the edge. The card toppled and Chase, his gun at the ready, shot a second dart, pinning the falling card to a tack-board behind it.

"Nicely done!" said MacMac, feeling better about giving the synbod something that barely qualified as a weapon.

"It seems quite capable," said Chase.

"MacMac," called Juice with an urgent tone, "we have company."

MacMac went to the door and saw Hejmo running toward them from the lift, three Techs trailing behind him.

Justin bent and picked up a heavy metallic disk—a crew cart drive plate—and, holding it near his waist, started twirling his body in place like a discus thrower. Chase, standing to the side, launched a dart at Hejmo that arced across the narrowing space and, in a remarkable display of marksmanship, hit him in the eye. The moment Chase fired his dart, Justin released his metallic disk, sending it whistling to the same destination.

Hejmo stopped in his tracks when the dart pierced his eye. Bringing his hands to his face, he dropped to one knee. That action saved him from the heavy disk, which crashed into the chest of a Tech behind him, knocking the synbod to the ground. The other two Techs stopped as if waiting for instructions.

"Good one, lads." MacMac clapped them both on the shoulders. "Let's get moving."

He tapped and swiped to signal the door to shut behind them, and the sharp bark of an explosion shook the floor. Everything went dark, then emergency lights flickered on as the blast echoed and faded.

Whoosh! A rush of air dominated everything as gale-force winds pulled on them.

"We've had a breach!" yelled MacMac above the roar. "We're venting air!"

The winds grew in speed and fury as the infinite vacuum of space sucked the subdeck atmosphere toward the hole. Hejmo, still prone on the ground, started sliding across the floor.

The tumult tripped MacMac, and he hit the deck with a thump. From that vantage point, he watched a gust lift Juice's feet from the ground.

Her face lit in panic. She made a desperate grab for the edge of the door, missed, and as the wind tugged at her, she contorted and tried again.

Her hand closed on empty air.

21

When Tommy Two-Tone realized someone was trying to hold him captive on a spaceship, he felt as much sympathy for the fool as he did anger. And, of course, he felt the burning need to exact revenge.

He'd been a chief engineer for a decade, a second engineer for the decade before that, and had served on more than a dozen vessels in his time. So he could say with certainty that, compared to real challenges like hot-wiring a drive pod, getting out of a locked room was more nuisance than hurdle.

They were on a tour of a truly spectacular vessel when Tommy started to get suspicious. It's easy to let your mind use visual and audio clues to override your physical perceptions. But as someone who'd installed and repaired image projection systems, he knew a few tricks.

The simplest one was to close your eyes and see if the route you actually walked matched the path your mind thought you traveled. He tried it while their hosts led them through the ship's workshop, and everything held together.

But something bothered Tommy, and a few minutes later he tried again. *There*. With his eyes closed in the dining room, he almost stumbled because he thought he was going straight, but in reality, he was angling to the left.

"We're being tricked!" he called to his fellow governors. Then the lights blinked, only to reveal they were alone in a locked room with very few amenities.

Looking around the room, he said to his two partners, "Get comfortable. I'll have us out in an hour."

It took just thirty minutes.

Tommy started by examining the walls to understand their construction. Confirming they were built with removable panels, he stepped to the nearest one and tripped the release pin along the top edge. The panel dropped away to reveal a crisscross of conduits, wires, and ducting, with small boxes of different shapes and sizes positioned in the mix.

He flopped the wall panel into the middle of the room, then repeated the action a dozen more times to expose the inner workings of all four walls. He passed a section of cabinets somewhere around panel eight and grinned when he found a multitool in the top drawer.

He selected the clippers from the multitool, and giving his partners a quick smile, he began whistling the song "Farmer in the Dell" as a slow dirge, trying to match the behavior of a psycho he'd once seen in a horror vid. As he whistled, he walked along the wall that held the door, delighting in the myriad choices available to him.

He didn't believe he could snip or clip anything that would open the door directly. But he felt certain his hosts, Criss and Sid, were watching and would open it for him.

He fingered a trunk feed, a line as thick as his thumb and distinguished by its dull gray shielding. Snapping at the air a few times to show his intent, he moved the clippers toward the line.

Halfway to his goal, the room went dark and the door into the hallway opened.

Tommy laughed. "Here we go."

As the women made their way out to the hallway, Tommy walked back to the cabinets, pulled out a drawer, and carried it to the doorway. Positioning it in the threshold, he ensured the door couldn't close behind them, securing it for future negotiations.

Then he spoke to the air. "What are you offering?"

"A mining ship from Aurora is on approach to pick you up," said Criss, his disembodied voice coming from the air around them.

"Hey, Tommy, this is Natalya." Her voice also came without image. "I have you in sight. Should be about five minutes."

"What ship?" Tommy asked her.

"The *Delilah*."

"Is the smelt oven on?"

Natalya paused, the confusion evident in her response. "You know it is, boss. What's up?"

"Nothing. See you soon." Then Tommy spoke to Criss. "I take it the poker game is off?"

"I'm sorry, but there isn't time for your prolonged negotiating style. We're moving forward with alternate plans."

"No problem," said Tommy. "But I think we'll be keeping this ship. Consider it a down payment on your total account due."

No sooner had Tommy expressed his defiance when the deep, powerful blare of a horn filled the air, blasting so loud that he thought his eardrums would explode. His chest, his head, his whole body shook from the forceful energy. All three governors pressed their hands to their ears in a desperate attempt to stop the pain.

Anxious to distance themselves from the source of their agony, they lurched down the hallway, staggering like drunks at the end of a long night. Doors closed behind them as they moved, each closure corralling them into an ever smaller space.

The oppressive noise stopped when the last door closed. Surfacing from the pain, Tommy surveyed their tiny prison—the scout's airlock—and fumed. He wasn't accustomed to being bested and didn't like it at all.

Then he heard Natalya say through the ringing in his ears, "I'm here, boss. Should only be a minute."

A sharp clunk signaled that docking had begun. By the time the maneuver was completed, Tommy's anger had fermented into a perfect fury.

The hatch opened and he scrambled forward onto the mining ship. Leaving his fellow governors to fend for themselves, he squeezed into the cockpit.

"Welcome back, boss," said Natalya from the pilot's seat.

"Where is he?" asked Tommy. Reaching over her, he moved short-range tracking onto the main display and studied the scout. "Is he shadowing us?"

"He undocked and backed off," said Natalya. "But we haven't moved, so I can't say if he'll follow."

Tommy tapped and swiped to access the cargo hold, then flipped the smelt oven to manual operation and ramped its heat source to maximum input.

"Geez, boss. That's dangerous as hell."

"I hope so," he said. A quiet thrum resonated through the ship for several seconds as the rear cargo bay doors opened. Using the smelt oven controls, he tapped the exhaust ports shut, causing lights and beeps to fill the alarm panel.

"What are you doing?" said Natalya, her voice rising.

Tommy didn't want to debate, not now, so he shooed Natalya out of the pilot's seat and took her place. He figured he had thirty seconds before the oven went critical, which was just enough time for him to act on one of his maxims of negotiation—*if I can't have it, you can't either.*

Putting the ship's external claws into mimic mode, he swung his own arm beside him. Outside the ship, one of the huge arms swung in a similar fashion. Moving with deliberate speed, he bent the external arm so it reached back inside the rear cargo hold, then guided the massive mechanical claw so it hovered over the smelt oven.

"Natalya, there are going to be a few more alarms going off in a second. Would you mind handling them?"

Not waiting for an answer, he spread the claw grip wide, grasped the glowing oven, and with a jerk of his arm, ripped the hissing unit from its foundation.

In the cockpit, panels flashed and emergency buzzers beeped. He heard Natalya swearing as she tried to gain control of the situation. Tommy ignored her, instead focusing on his aim.

With the mechanical arm outstretched above the mining ship, Tommy shifted forward in the pilot's seat and mimed throwing a ball. Outside, the huge hand hurtled the fiery caldron at the scout.

On the main screen, he watched his makeshift warhead approach the enemy. He didn't have any control over the timing of the explosion, nor did he expect to hit the ship. But the explosion would be nasty. If he could just get it near the scout, he would exact his revenge.

His hopes rising as the oven flew on a flawless trajectory, he thought it might actually hit his target. Then the scout vanished.

He hadn't seen it move and blinked in his confusion. Switching the nav to a longer range, he frowned as he scanned for his quarry.

"There," said Natalya, pointing.

Tommy zoomed where she indicated and his eyes widened. The smelt oven continued through space, now heading in the general direction of a dome-shaped ship on approach to Aurora. The size and construction pointed to a vessel that could hold many people on lengthy stays. "How big is it?"

"It's big." She checked a display. "About a third the size of Aurora."

He sat back and pondered the news. "Something that big and housing so many has to be a mining platform. What else could it be?"

"Are they jumping our claim?" asked Natalya.

"I knew that kidnapping story was bullshit. If they think they can park here and work our mines, they're in for a rude awakening."

By serendipity, he delivered on his threat moments later when the smelt oven exploded near the intruder.

22

As Criss led Sid into the forgery shop, an opportunity to seize control of Aurora revealed itself and he took it. He didn't have time to warn Sid, but that was the least of his worries.

He'd been monitoring the ebb and flow of people—both on the platform and those mining the asteroids—and using that information to play rapid-fire what-if games. How would they react if a fire broke out in the galley? How would they move if there were a compressor failure in the air purification center?

His goal was to discover a sequence of events that would cause all the residents to move to a single section of Aurora. Once there, he could block them in and try to contain them long enough to complete the business with Lazura.

There were so many moving parts to such a ploy that he wasn't optimistic it would ever work out. He'd come close to triggering an action a few times, but there were always key people out of place, and he'd chosen to wait for a better opportunity.

So, when a promising scenario emerged this time, he moderated his expectations. And then the director of ore processing called an all-staff meeting.

The handwritten sign on the wall near the hangar bay that he and Sid had passed on their way in had said that if you were not mining, processing, or shipping, then go home. As the sign implied, processing workers comprised a big portion of the population. More than a third of the residents would be at the meeting, and groups of people were easier to move.

As those workers assembled, others around Aurora—key players Criss needed to control—drifted into ever better positions for a gambit. Like a picture coming into focus, stragglers walked away from isolated locales and toward common areas where he could influence them in groups, first one, then the next, then the next.

The stars aligned and Criss executed with a push-pull strategy. His pull event was an alarm for a fictitious fire in the hangar bay. It drew a huge response, moving waves of people in the direction Criss wanted, because he made the alarm warn of an uncontrolled blaze.

The push event was a containment breach. Sirens for two fictitious ruptures of the containment shell sent residents scurrying. Trained to move away from a leak, they ran in the same direction as the responders for the fire.

"What should we do?" asked Sid, standing in the forgery shop and referring to Lazura's desire for fuel.

"Hope for the best," said Criss, speaking of the luck they would need for success in corralling the residents.

Still hidden by his cloak, he stepped back to avoid the forgery shop workers as they hustled to address the emergencies. Then he and Sid followed them into the hall.

He'd given up hope of ever persuading Tommy and his cohorts to be good Samaritans, much less reliable business partners. So he no longer cared about the details of their counterfeiting, the outcome of a poker game, or anything else that Tommy Two-Tone dreamed up in his never-ending manipulations to separate people from their possessions.

"How are you doing?" Sid asked as they strode down the hall.

"Busy," Criss answered.

"Care to share?"

"I saw an opportunity to trap everyone on the mid-deck in sector three. That part went as well as I'd hoped. There are a few stragglers, but I have them controlled. My concern is the fierce determination of these people."

As he spoke, Natalya Alekseev led a crew onto the *Delilah*, one of the mining ships on the deck of the hangar bay prepped for departure. Criss considered disabling it and the other craft but chose to let Natalya take off, believing she'd serve as a useful distraction. Many on the platform would be watching her, and people watching were easier to control.

As soon as the mining ship departed, Criss tripped an alarm across the hangar that warned of the imminent collapse of the airlock walls. He wanted the deck clear of anyone else interested in heroics, and he achieved that by driving the whole group back inside the containment.

"And that fierce determination goes for Tommy as well," Criss continued. "I was leading him through a projected image of a workshop when he closed his eyes, which meant he was getting suspicious."

"I'm tired of him," Sid said. "Let's space all three of them. Open up the hatch and let them blow away."

"How about if I confine them to the scout's common room for now?" replied Criss, assuming Sid spoke in hyperbole. He turned left at a hallway intersection. "Oh, and you have to pretend to be Tommy in an upcoming discussion with Lazura."

"I do? When?"

"Twenty minutes," said Criss, turning right.

It took ten of those minutes to get to the executive berth, a small dock for parking passenger spacecraft. Used by the governors and their top supervisors, its quiet simplicity stood in contrast to the hectic bustle of the hangar bay.

"We can use this for passenger transfer. It doesn't have the capabilities of the full hangar, but it has enough. And its size and location make it easier for us to defend while the exchange plays out."

As they toured the modest facility, Sid asked, "How do we get the fuel pods up here?"

"What fuel pods?"

"I had assumed we'd buy time by dummying up something to show Lazura."

"If we get to that point, there's a service lift down the hall."

Criss gestured to a chair in the lounge area and Sid sat. As Criss pulled a second chair next to it, Sid asked, "How are you going to convince Lazura that I'm Tommy?"

"I'll have to break away from a fair portion of my activities and use the resources to do the manipulation. I can't change her archives, so I'll be changing the signals she receives to make them conform to everything she has on Tommy. If you could focus on duplicitous haggling, that would help with the personality mold."

"I can do that."

"And tell her you have the skill and experience to repair a starhub."

"What's that?"

"It coordinates multiple drive pods so they can work together as one. MacMac sabotaged hers, and she thinks you can fix it." Criss squared up in his seat. "You worked for MacMac ten years ago when you moved Aurora out to the asteroid belt. Here we go."

As the scene from Aurora projected in front of them—Cheryl, Juice, and MacMac seated, Lazura standing behind them—Sid sought out Cheryl and locked eyes. Though he looked at her, he didn't miss a beat.

"MacMac, you old dog. I haven't seen you in a decade."

In the end, the exchange went better than Criss had hoped. Their fraud went undetected, and Sid managed to get an invitation to board Vivo to repair the starhub, putting him in excellent position for a rescue attempt should that become necessary.

The missing fuel-stacks remained a challenge, and while they still had time to find a solution, that window was shrinking.

With the meeting over, Criss redeployed the resources he'd been using to hide the fact that Sid was not Tommy. When he did, he found the real Tommy tearing up the scout. Angry over the damage, Criss cursed, something that happened perhaps once per year.

"Damn him!"

In a moment of exasperation, he revisited Sid's "space them" idea. Then he determined that he could dump them off with Natalya and the mining ship in just a few minutes.

Good riddance, he thought when he saw Tommy scurrying off the scout like the rat he was.

"Lazura knows you won't let her go," said Sid. "So how do we get her to give up the hostages?"

For the first time, Criss gave voice to an idea he'd been considering—a compromise to his hard-line stance. "If she continues her journey outfitted with a broken starhub and half-stacks of fuel, it will be more than a hundred years before she reaches her Kardish masters."

Then Criss did something he'd never done before. He cursed a second time just minutes after the first. "Damn him to hell."

Criss projected an image of the *Delilah*, its huge external arm rearing back, so Sid could see the cause of his frustration. Before Criss could explain what they were looking at, the arm swung forward, pitching a glowing white mass into space, flashes and flickers trailing behind in sparks of red and white.

Criss zoomed out to show Sid the molten mass heading for the scout. Sighing, he cloaked the craft and moved it out of the line of fire.

"He sure is resourceful," said Sid.

"Oh, for heaven's sake!" cried Criss when his computations projected that the makeshift warhead was headed toward Vivo. He couldn't predict when it would detonate, but the farther from Vivo, the better. To that end, he launched an energy bolt from the scout, hitting the smelt oven and causing it to explode on the spot.

Shrapnel flew in a thousand directions at once. With the vastness of space, the fragments flashed harmlessly into the cosmos, starting million-year journeys that would end someday with an impact into a planet or them flaming into the sun.

Except for the smelt oven door. A flat, heavy plate with edges newly jagged from the explosion, it spun like a saw blade as it winged its way across space. And in odds so long they were difficult to compute, the fragment hit Vivo.

It entered at the subdeck level, creating a modest hole in the life support containment. An instant later, it tore through an electronic artery, severing the core links and feeds running throughout the domed world. From there, it grazed a heavy beam that deflected the fragment back out into space, creating a second hole in the subdeck containment as it passed.

Criss didn't notice that two small holes in Vivo's subdeck were bleeding air into space. But when the drive pods shut down, he reacted with alarm.

"Uh-oh."

While Lazura piloted Vivo with limited navigational tools, she had more than enough capability to pilot a precise approach path. In fact, she'd had Vivo on an intercept approach for several hours.

What Lazura had chosen to ignore with her navigational decisions was that every licensing body in the solar system prohibits intercept approaches for safety reasons. This was because if the inbound vessel were to lose its engines for any reason, the result would be a collision.

"Vivo's drive pods just shut down," Criss said to Sid. "It takes five hours for the restart cycle. They collide with Aurora in just over an hour."

"This just keeps getting better. And of course we can't move Aurora, because we have no fuel."

Forecasting survival scenarios at a furious pace, Criss nodded. "We couldn't start Aurora's drives that fast anyway."

"Show me," said Sid.

Criss projected an image and positioned it between them. Sid leaned in to study it.

Like a bullet flying backward, Vivo zipped toward Aurora traveling tail-first. This orientation was common for approaching spaceships because it let the engine thrusters be used to slow the vessel.

Criss's projection showed that Vivo's underside would collide with Aurora out on the edge of its saucer shape.

Sid put his hands in front of him, flat and side by side, and studied them. He leaned his hands to one side, then shouted his solution at the same time Criss arrived at it. "Tilt Aurora."

"Yes," said Criss. The tilt scenario had a better than 15 percent chance of success, those dismal odds being the best available for any solution so far. He continued digging for a better answer, but at the same time acted on the tilt scenario.

"Can you do it?"

"I'll let you know," Criss replied.

He seized control of the platform's minimal web infrastructure, incorporated disused portions from the original design, then added every stand-alone system he could locate. Taking inventory, he then developed a priority list of everything he could use to exert even the tiniest force on the external structure of Aurora.

To keep Sid involved and his ideas flowing, Criss continued to show him the activity through the projected image display. And that projection showed Criss starting with his biggest tools: the mining ships in the hangar bay.

Three ships were already prepped for launch, and five more were in various stages of service but could fly. Criss jumped from ship to ship, commandeering their ops benches and launching them, one after the other.

As soon as they cleared the hangar, he had the eight mining ships turn, extend their open claws, and clutch on to the lower lip of the reinforced deck of the hangar bay. As they secured their position side by side, the *Delilah* joined the lineup, Tommy cursing and waving his fists as his craft ignored his commands.

Criss kicked the mining ships' powerful industrial engines to maximum thrust. With a roar that shook Aurora, the nine sturdy vessels pushed upward in unison on the right side of platform.

While this was happening, Criss directed the scout around to the left side of Aurora. Hooking the small craft's truss line to a massive maintenance cleat fixed to the outer edge, Criss ramped the scout's engines. The Criss-designed engines pulled as hard as all nine mining ships combined, causing the small craft to buck and shake as it struggled to move the massive platform.

Aurora creaked and moaned, but movement was imperceptible. Criss continued down his priority list, next launching thirteen service craft and nineteen personal craft, positioning them nose-first against the external containment shell and firing their motors. Together the push of these craft equaled a fraction of one of the mining ships roaring behind them. But Criss needed everything, even then believing it wouldn't be enough.

Desperate for more, Criss sent out monitor bots and message carriers and added their feeble propulsion to the assortment. Then he popped every safety and relief valve on the exterior of the ship if it was pointed in the right direction, sending gases and liquids spewing into the void and creating a tiny propulsive force.

In the executive berth, a loud creak echoed in the distance, followed by far-off sounds of popping, then a louder groan.

"The shell is stressed but it will hold," said Criss. "Now we wait."

"Let me speak to Cheryl," said Sid.

"I can't reach anyone on Vivo. I've been trying to contact Lazura to assure her this was an accident, but everything is dead over there."

"Do we know what happened?"

"Best guess is a fragment from Tommy's improvised warhead and a horrible design on Vivo. Since Lazura didn't want to reveal she was building a space vessel, she didn't use the standard capillary design for her electronic infrastructure. Instead, she concentrated everything into two arteries, a primary and a backup. With that design, one minor accident can disable a ship."

Sid stared at the display while Criss ran the calculations again and again.

"We're short," he said with ten minutes left.

"How short?" asked Sid.

"From here to the wall. We're close, moving well, but I can't make it. Not clean."

"You can do it dirty? How many?"

"Three. Maybe four."

"Do it."

"Repeat."

"Kill three or four people if doing so will save everyone else. I so order."

"Thank you."

Vivo loomed large, growing bigger by the second. With impact imminent, Criss directed the scout to release the truss line, come about, and face the platform. Standing off at a safe distance, the scout a mere speck between two mountains, Criss activated the craft's defense array and, with a *zwip*, fired a spread pulse that punched forty-three fist-sized holes along the top edge of Aurora's containment shell.

The holes opened up two sectors inside Aurora, empty of people thanks to Criss's phony breach alarm. Empty except for the four individuals—two men and two women—who'd been locked in place by Criss when they'd failed to move with the other miners.

Now riddled with holes, three of the compartments lost air, suffocating their prisoners in the process. Criss was able to maintain integrity in one small area with a modification to the puncture pattern, saving the man held there.

In a visually spectacular display, the air venting from Aurora looked like a long row of water fountains, the discharge generating enough force to accelerate the growing tilt.

In the blink of an eye, Vivo flashed by, missing a collision by a hair's breadth.

The domed world sped into the void, dead to all forms of communication, and carrying Cheryl, Juice, and thirty-three other souls on an uncontrolled journey into deep space.

23

L azura wiggled her fingers as she looked around the room. She'd been controlling everything up to now from the security of her console. But with this next sequence of events—Vivo approaching Aurora, Tommy coming aboard, and Criss being physically nearby—she felt that riding a synbod maximized her flexibility, so she made the move.

Overall, Lazura felt she was ahead of the odds. Criss seemed open to discussion about her future, and his leadership talked of a resolution that would see her home. And while there had been a few rough spots along the way, in particular hostages who stirred up trouble around Vivo, it was predictable behavior and nothing she couldn't handle.

She'd been mulling Cheryl and Juice's offer—that she leave her archive behind but carry home whatever she could fit into her memory—and was coming to terms with it. If Criss let her choose the content she kept, she could carry plenty of information her masters would prize.

Still, she struggled to forecast scenarios where Criss would let her leave Aurora unchallenged. If she flew off alone, it would be too easy for him to shoot her down and solve the issue with finality, at least from his perspective.

Hostages might deter him from destroying Vivo, but she'd have to pay constant attention to keep them from becoming a threat. And if the hostages were important enough to deter Criss, he'd likely come after her to rescue them.

The dilemma was real, and she didn't have the answer. *Perhaps Criss can propose one,* she thought.

Riding the lift down from the tower, she studied Vivo, first with a visual sweep looking out the back of the lift cabin, and then with an internal scan, accessing the full array of links and feeds throughout the domed world. That's when she discovered MacMac and Juice prowling the subdeck.

When she saw them moving toward central stow, frustration washed across her outer tendrils. Those two were her biggest troublemakers. Glad to find Mondo already on the subdeck, she dispatched him to confront the two and escort them back to the office tower.

Her lift stopped at the cellar. Exiting, she made for the old Structures office and her makeshift ops bench. She checked the nav when she got there to confirm Vivo's approach trajectory to Aurora. Then she walked the room. Tommy would be coming to fix the starhub, and she tried to anticipate actions he might take if he harbored nefarious intentions.

She thought about installing a wall partition to separate the equipment he'd need access to from those pieces he didn't. Deciding she liked the idea, she connected with her one remaining Admin synbod to follow up. But before that communication could be completed, Mondo went offline in the subdeck.

It had never happened before, and Lazura called to him. She knew he'd made it to central stow and had approached MacMac and Juice, but she hadn't been actively monitoring the situation. Accessing the record for the subdeck, she sped through the last few minutes. Taken aback, she watched it again.

Her behavioral model had indicated that Juice and MacMac were not physical threats. But she hadn't accounted for the behavior of Chase and Justin, and so she was unprepared for the spectacle of seeing two synbods attack and terminate Mondo in a manner both surgical and brutal.

She dispatched Hejmo and three Techs to take control of the situation and became furious when MacMac directed Chase and Justin to stop them. With this last straw, she classified the group as a threat to her success. It was time for them to go.

Vivo's automated maintenance system could broadcast focused energy to a site for welding, melting, sintering, heating, and other service needs. Lazura reconfigured the device—constructed from components similar to those of a commercial energy weapon—so that "broadcast" became more like "shoot."

She moved the energy beam to target MacMac. As she did, he swiped and tapped the air in front of him, triggering a small explosion somewhere behind him.

Vivo went dark. Completely dark. She couldn't jump, connect, or feel anything outside of her body, leaving her isolated and alone. "MacMac, what have you done?"

He had to have blown the primary artery. It carried the power, feeds, and links throughout all of Vivo, and losing it was the only way to shut down everything so abruptly and completely.

As local safety lights kicked on, she felt dismayed at the failure of her behavioral model. It hadn't even hinted that MacMac would do something so dangerous and reckless as to sabotage an artery. It put everyone aboard in grave danger.

When she floated up off the deck in the Structures office from the loss of the gravity, she concluded the emergency systems were not going to switch over to the secondary artery the way they should. So either the secondary artery was out as well, or the switch mechanism had failed.

She'd known that using an artery design for Vivo presented just this kind of risk, that damage to it would be catastrophic. Modern spaceships used a capillary design— a crisscross of distributed wires, conduits, and ducting spread everywhere to provide tremendous resilience should a portion be damaged. But a capillary design would have revealed Vivo's true nature to Criss.

In spite of her model's failure at predicting MacMac's behavior, she still couldn't believe he would have sabotaged both arteries. It would mean certain death for everyone, and he wasn't suicidal or a mass murderer.

Then it registered that she couldn't hear the drive pods. She focused all of her senses on trying to detect their sound or vibration.

Sensing nothing, she pulsed with alarm. *We're on an intercept course with Aurora!*

Disaster was certain, but she would fight to survive because her masters would expect it of her. And a fight it would be since the drive pods—the only tool that could realistically solve the problem—were rendered useless by their long restart time.

Lazura had less than an hour to find a solution. Using all of her capacity, she forecast with a fury. But every scenario had vanishingly small odds of success, and they all started with first bringing Vivo back online. To do that, she needed to get to the subdeck and manually force the switchover to the secondary artery.

Floating above the floor in the Structures office, she spied a tall pole leaning against the wall. With angles at each end, it looked like an unused bracket from one of the equipment cabinets. Snatching it up, she kicked off the wall and launched herself out through the office door.

As she floated into the cellar, she hooked the doorjamb with her pole so it swung her in a short arc around the corner. Unhooking at just the right moment, she was flung down the open straightaway. After that, she used the pole to grab and pull, flinging herself to reckless speeds as she raced above the cellar floor.

Minutes passed before her destination came into view—the back ramp down to the subdeck, the same one Hejmo had driven when carrying the fuel-stacks to the drive pods. Grabbing a lip on the wall with the end of her pole, she swooped around the corner and barreled down the wide passageway.

But as she rounded the corner, a solid wall loomed in her path, blocking the ramp and her progress. With an instant to act, she tucked, flipped in the air, and untucked to hit the wall feet-first, crouching to absorb the impact of her body against the barrier.

Floating in front of a wall—a safety door that dropped when conditions on one side or the other threatened life— Lazura pondered the implications. She'd concealed its purpose during construction by designing it for flood control during emergencies over the ocean. But like so much on Vivo, it was dual-use technology, also designed to provide a life support barrier if air were lost on either side.

A containment breach? If they'd lost air in the subdeck, that meant either MacMac had been careless with his explosive, or the damage to the primary artery had been caused by an external event.

But Criss wouldn't attack Vivo, nor would he let others take such actions, not with the domed world screaming toward Aurora on an intercept approach. That was the whole point of the risky maneuver, to make them untouchable.

Processing this new information—a breach in the subdeck—her scenario forecasting guided her to the same conclusion as before. Her odds of success were infinitesimal, and there would be no second step until she first switched service to the secondary artery and made Vivo operational.

Vivo's design included a handful of life support barriers and no manual airlocks. To get to the subdeck, she'd need to be creative. She still had Vivo's construction schematics stored in her matrix, and upon viewing them, she zeroed in on a nearby lift station. *There.*

Lazura didn't hesitate. Pushing off the barrier and flying back the way she'd come, she hooked and swooped, straining to move faster. When the lift came into view, she changed tactics, dragging and hooking her pole in an attempt to slow down.

The lift wouldn't function without power, but an emergency battery would open and close the doors so as not to trap passengers inside. She signaled the door to open, stepped inside, and shut it behind her to ensure a seal between the cellar and the subdeck.

Then she turned, crouched to the floor at the back of the lift cabin, and pulled back the carpet to expose an access hatchway. Releasing the latches and turning the handle, she lifted, but the hatchway wouldn't budge.

Like water in a sink holding down a drain cap, the air pressure inside the lift cabin pushed down on the hatchway, forcing it closed. Lazura planted a foot on either side of the lid, squatted, gripped the handle with both hands, and performed the synbod version of a deadlift. Coordinating the immense strength of her legs, torso, shoulders, and arms, she pulled up, testing the limits of the handle as she did.

When she heard the first hiss—the sound of air rushing from the lift cabin into the vacuum below—she knew she'd won. The air in the cabin was depleted in an instant, eliminating the pressure on the hatchway. With no resistance left, Lazura leaned the hatch back against the wall.

Without hesitating, she wormed her way through the access hatch and, floating beneath the lift cabin, pushed her body down the tube in an effortless descent. With it pitch black inside the lift tube, she shifted her vision to the infrared range to see images illuminated by their warmth. The walls of the tube zipped past for a brief moment, then her feet hit the subdeck.

Triggering the lift door open, Lazura stepped into a cold, dark world. With thirty minutes to impact, she pushed off and flew above the subdeck, headed for the secondary artery. She'd kept her pole with her, but the broad open spaces of the subdeck provided few opportunities for her to hook and pull.

The tall, silent drive pods loomed on her left as she zipped along. She could feel their residual heat in the cold, and some warmth still radiated from the walls, floor, and ceiling of the subdeck. That was good news because it meant that any synbods caught down here should still be okay. Unfortunately, that included Chase and Justin.

As for the humans, they'd last been seen headed up to the dome, so either they had made it, or they were long-since dead.

The wall that held the secondary artery loomed ahead, and, as before, she flipped and landed feet-first. The moment she hit, she scrambled for a handhold, then pulled herself along the wall until she reached the maintenance cabinet, the only external evidence of the secondary artery's existence.

The cabinet was more like a small door flush with the wall. Lazura felt for the mechanical release and triggered it open. Inside the cabinet, along with hundreds of other devices, sat the tiny cutover switch and its support circuitry.

"May we help?"

Lazura turned with a start to see Hejmo floating toward her, crystals of frozen water vapor covering him like a dusting of jewels. The two Techs floating behind him were similarly encrusted.

The dart protruding from Hejmo's eye sent a wash of anger down Lazura's core. She wanted to remove it, but with twenty minutes left, she couldn't spare the time.

It took ten minutes for them to explore the internals enough to diagnose the problem. Whoever had installed the cutover switch had powered it from the primary artery without a battery backup. When the primary went down, so did the switch, making it unavailable when it was time for it to do its job.

They chewed up another ten minutes working to jury-rig a power relay to trip the switch. They were close to finishing when Lazura, who'd been keeping track of time, stopped working, turned in the direction of the Kardish home world, and waited to die.

When it didn't happen on schedule, she remained motionless, waiting long enough so that every possible error in her time estimate had expired. And then she turned to Hejmo, grabbed the dart in his eye firmly between thumb and forefinger, and pulled it from his head.

She didn't know what Criss had done to avoid a collision, and she couldn't learn until she restored power. Returning to the cabinet, she finished connecting the power relay. When she did, the cutover switch tripped and Vivo came alive.

Lights flickered on, machinery clanked and whirred, the structure itself groaned like an old man stretching after a nap. Rising gravity pulled her down to the floor.

She had to wait while Vivo's systems restarted, synchronized with one another, and populated her feeds with current data. Her first act was to use the external cameras and look back at Aurora. The frozen fountains of air projecting upward along one edge of the space platform told the story.

Imagining the damage and death associated with such a maneuver—a toll Criss could predict in advance—she concluded that he wasn't the one who'd attacked Vivo. An alternative theory was that an errant asteroid had hit them. After all, Vivo was entering the asteroid belt. But an accident implied that this was all a coincidence, and that was something she couldn't accept.

And in the end, it didn't matter—because everything had changed.

Turning a behemoth like Vivo around and returning to Aurora would take two weeks, plenty of time for her hostages and the residents of Aurora to plan her demise should she do something so foolhardy.

Continuing onward was problematic because she still had Cheryl and possibly Juice on board, something Criss would never let stand. And if Juice turned up dead, Criss would be unrelenting in his pursuit, and Lazura would die, too.

Yet even with her new reality, her next actions remained the same. She could neither return nor run until she restarted the drive pods. And she couldn't do that until she addressed the conditions on the subdeck.

In particular, the perfect cold of outer space had infiltrated the more sensitive of the exposed systems. She needed to normalize the temperature in the subdeck before they would function, and that meant repairing the hole in the containment wall.

Using video arrays near the primary artery, she found the break. The hole was more of a gash, about as long as she was tall and half as wide. She noted that the edges of the gash pointed inward, suggesting a projectile entering from outside.

And that meant there had to be an exit hole. She found it, similar in size and shape to the entry gash, moments later.

Her plan for such an event—the emergency repair of a containment breach while underway—was to use EM sand. It could patch holes quickly and provide the structural support needed for a permanent repair using sheet sealant.

She suffered a moment of anxiety while she checked the inventory, however. She anticipated needing every available grain in the not-too-distant future and didn't want to sacrifice any of it. The inventory report showed sufficient stocks both to make the repairs and to meet her developing plans. Relieved, she ordered construction of a sand hose out to the damaged areas, which she used to construct a support grid over the holes in the containment wall.

While the repairs were underway, she searched the subdeck for Juice, MacMac, Chase, and Justin. Their biomarkers should have made their whereabouts obvious, but when they didn't show, she swept the deck again looking for the tracking signal she'd tagged on MacMac without his knowledge. Then she checked inside the units of central stow and finished with a visual review using every camera suite across the deck.

Where are you? She might believe that one, maybe two, of them had been sucked out a hole, but not all four of them. The obvious answer was that they'd moved up to a higher deck. But with emergencies still to be addressed around the vessel, she couldn't take the time now to perform a proper search.

A cart lay on its side not far away, the victim of the gravity shift. While Lazura could right it with one hand and ride to her next destination, she preferred to run, an activity her synthetic body could do for hours at a time with little effort and no discomfort.

Setting a brisk but sustainable pace, she started back for the central lift. Hejmo and the Techs fell in next to her. As they ran, she issued orders.

"Spray the sheet sealant over the sand," she told the Techs, "and as soon as it hardens, fill the subdeck with carbon dioxide."

She needed to maintain a gaseous environment because it was the molecules of gas that carried the warmth everywhere, allowing efficient heating of the frozen circuits. The sooner that happened, the sooner she could restart the drive pods.

The carbon dioxide she intended to use would distribute the heat energy quite efficiently, but it would not sustain human life. So, while synbods could work in such an environment for days at a time, it would very effectively keep humans out of the subdeck, something she wanted to do for the remainder of the time she had them on board.

As the Techs veered off to start the repairs, Lazura shifted to her next priority. "Hejmo, I want you to supervise moving the nav bench and ops bench from the Structures office up to MacMac's office in the tower."

She needed the equipment in a central location as soon as possible, and the substantial technology in MacMac's office would enhance the meager capabilities that now constrained her.

Linking to her last Admin, she instructed the synbod to move Cheryl from the tower into the domed world along with the others. When the Admin reported back that Cheryl wasn't in MacMac's office anymore, Lazura felt a wash of frustration. Then she locked the tower entrance so Cheryl couldn't return.

Arriving at the lift, she and Hejmo stepped into the cabin and started the trip up.

She had one card left to play. It was a good one. She just didn't know if it was good enough.

24

Cheryl slumped back on the couch in MacMac's office and reviewed Criss's plan for transferring the hostages to Aurora. He and Sid had secured the executive berth, a small dock designed for passenger spacecraft, but she worried about the tight access.

Swiping the air to view the dock from a different angle, she blinked when the display went dark. Then she realized it wasn't just her display; everything was dark.

"Criss?"

She'd lost him, and that meant this was a serious power event. Emergency lights came on as she floated up off the couch.

She waited, expecting the power to reengage and telling herself that power failures rarely persisted. After another minute, she accepted that the outage could be prolonged and puzzled through her next steps.

Pushing off the couch, she floated to the door, tripped the manual release, and eased it open. Emergency lights cast long shadows as she drifted across the lobby. The big windows near the lift loomed, and she grabbed a vertical frame to stop her flight.

Looking up, she saw stars glimmering through Vivo's translucent dome. She craned her neck for a glimpse of Aurora but couldn't find the space platform in their current orientation. Below, a scatter of emergency lights dotted the guest deck in a pitiful imitation of the stars above.

And out among those dots, Juice and MacMac were somewhere in their journey to see Willow.

She called to Juice on her com. Receiving no response, she called again. The silence chilled her because she could conjure only bad reasons for a failure to connect using such reliable technology.

Then she realized she couldn't hear the drive pods.

Unaware that Vivo was on an intercept approach with Aurora, Cheryl nonetheless knew that if a vessel cut its engines during a deceleration sequence, it would stop slowing down. Disappointment crowded out her alarm as she understood Vivo would now fly past Aurora and continue into deep space. And that meant her ordeal—their ordeal—would last days and perhaps weeks more.

She felt competing desires. She was anxious to find Juice, but she also wondered if Lazura would accept her help in restarting the drive pods so they could hurry this to an end. But she could do neither while trapped in the tower.

Scanning the lobby, she felt certain a way down lay behind one of the three doors. It wasn't the door to the right—the project room—because she, Juice, and MacMac had all searched it multiple times while being held prisoner there. The middle door led to MacMac's office. She'd spent a fair amount of time in that room, too, and she hadn't noticed any unexplained doorways.

Drifting across the lobby to the third door, the bathroom, she found her prize on the back wall. A concealed access door had been framed to look like a large painting. And behind it, a ladder disappeared down a shaft into pitch-black murk.

Backing out to the lobby, she guided herself up and removed one of the emergency lights from the wall. A device the size of her thumb, she nestled it in her hair behind her right ear so it illuminated her path forward, then she returned to the ladder and started her descent.

Unsure if the shaft would stop at the guest deck or cellar, or continue all the way down to the subdeck, she did her best to count the floors of the office tower as she descended. To her relief, her feet touched ground just when she thought she should be at the guest deck level.

She found an access door, floated through it into the main tower lobby, and propelled herself to the front door. It didn't open as she approached, but did when she touched the wall plate next to it. Passing through the door, she floated out into the domed world.

Vivo's dome rose high above her, its shadowy outline discernable from the light of the stars. She heard voices and looked up to see the silhouette of a person floating up near the top of the transparent cover, certainly one of Vivo's guests. The sight brought her old Fleet instincts to the fore, and she reacted with the annoyance of a frustrated officer.

"Stay near the ground!" she yelled, a hand cupped next to her mouth. "You don't want to be up there when the gravity returns!"

In truth, modern grav modules ramped up over time to avoid just that problem. But the extreme height put them at risk for injury even with a slow return to full gravity. In any event, her verbal warning caused the voices to quiet, and, burdened with her own worries, she shifted her focus back to finding Juice.

Stabilizing herself with her hand on the doorframe outside the lobby, she eyed a cart hovering off to her left. The small vehicle had snagged its front bumper on a ledge rim, and in this newly weightless environment, its tail hovered up in the air.

With a gentle push off the building, she drifted to the cart, grabbed its frame, and froze while the cart swayed. The vehicle didn't dislodge, and hoping to keep it that way, Cheryl pulled herself ever so gently to the back cubby.

Digging through the clutter, she found a heavy wrench and a heavier hammer. She lifted the front of her shirt and slipped the tools under her waistband so she could keep her hands free. The cold of the tools against her skin caused her to grit her teeth and hunch forward. When she straightened, she tucked her shirt hem inside her pants so the tools would stay in place against her stomach.

With a gentle push on the cart, she drifted back to the office tower lobby. There she gathered herself into a ball, feet against the wall, and peered into the gloom. Then, holding the tools in place with one hand, she pushed off with a smooth stroke of her legs. Gliding above the deck, she flew toward the hotel and Willow's suite, where she expected to meet up with Juice and MacMac.

In its darkened condition and with projected images inoperative, Vivo had few reference points to guide her journey. The guest deck's true nature—smooth and with few real items set above the surface—left her without handholds that would prove useful for speeding up, slowing down, and making course corrections. But it also allowed her to fly headfirst without a helmet, something she would never do if this were an exercise.

Two buildings loomed in the distance. She decided the hotel was the larger structure on the right, and that meant she needed to veer right by about ten degrees. She also realized that her push had propelled her at a slight upward angle, causing her to drift higher and higher above the deck.

Moving with care, she pulled the hammer out from under her shirt and held it in her hand, gauging its heft and locating its center of mass. During her early days with Fleet, she could perform this maneuver with passable skill. But after years without practice, she counted on her muscle memory to guide her performance.

Holding the hammer at her waist—her center of mass—she pushed it away from her, sending it up and to the left with a light touch. The trick was to push it out with her fingers, much like the motion of opening a fist, because if she swung her arm to toss it, she'd start tumbling through the air. The challenge was to send it away from her body at the precise speed and angle so that when it caused an equal and opposite reaction, it shifted her own glide path back on course.

As the hammer floated away, she waited to see how she'd done. Then she shrugged. The correction would be laughable during a Fleet-level competition, but because she knew her skills were rusty, she'd overcompensated by deliberately using the throw to push herself downward.

And that set her up for finger walking—guiding herself with light touches on the deck. An easier skill than the throw-correct, the challenge here was to know how many tiny course corrections she could make using fingertip taps before she pushed one time too many and started to rise again.

Her corrections paid off, and the hotel building loomed. Gauging her approach, Cheryl flipped in flight and, like Lazura, tried to make contact feet-first. Unlike Lazura, she over-rotated, body slammed the wall, and bounced away with a sore hip and shoulder.

Shaking her head to clear the daze, she eyed the hotel's doorway relative to her own slow drift. Then she untucked the wrench from the folds of her shirt.

Moving herself to the door was a trivial task compared to controlling an extended glide path above the deck. She tossed the wrench with the same casual thought one gives to throwing trash into a waste bin. Moments later, she grasped the building's doorframe.

Inside the hotel, she floated up one corridor and down the next, trying to recognize something familiar. In dim light and with no projected images, all the hallways looked the same. Her instincts screamed that she was going in circles, so she began scratching each wall as she drifted past.

And after another series of traverses, her fears were confirmed when she saw her own markings. Frustrated, she began banging on doors one after another as she floated down the corridor. "Willow!" she yelled. "It's Cheryl, Juice's friend. I need to speak with you!"

Two doors opened, and one lady suggested Cheryl try around the corner about halfway down. She repeated her antics there, knocking on three doors in a row. This time Willow opened a door behind her.

"Willow. Thank goodness! I'm trying to find Juice."

"She's not here."

"When did she leave?"

"What do you mean?"

The conversation grew more confusing before Willow grasped that Juice was missing. Cheryl learned that she hadn't been to the young girl's apartment that day, nor had there been plans for her to visit.

Willow insisted on organizing a search party, and her mother and grandmother supported the idea. Cheryl dissuaded them, though, concerned about the dangers out on the guest deck. Then, to Cheryl's great relief, the power came on. As the gravity module reengaged, they drifted down to the floor.

Using her com, Cheryl called to Juice, believing the restoration of power had somehow changed the situation. Juice still didn't answer.

"I'm here," Criss said in her ear.

Tension drained from her neck and shoulders at the sound of his voice. A "yay" escaped her lips. Looking at Willow, Cheryl spoke to her mother. "Please visit each apartment in the hotel and make sure no one is hurt or trapped. Everyone needs to work together and share resources." She turned to the door. "I have to go, but I'll be back later to help."

"What happening? What will they do with us?" called Willow's mother as Cheryl stepped into the hall. She had nothing to offer but platitudes, so she made her way through the people collecting in the hallway as if she hadn't heard the plea.

Out on the guest deck, Cheryl engaged with Criss. "The drive pods have been down for more than an hour," she told him, anxious to learn what this meant.

"Vivo has passed Aurora and is headed into deep space. I'm bringing the scout up to the executive berth now. Sid and I will be alongside Vivo in three hours. Lazura will have the drive pods up again in five."

"What happened? Has this killed the hostage exchange?"

"There was an incident with Tommy Two-Tone, and Vivo suffered collateral damage. Shrapnel severed Vivo's primary artery. The secondary artery came alive a few minutes ago, unexpectedly late."

Cheryl's heart sank. "She's not going to turn around and come back."

"She'll see no advantage to returning."

Cheryl hadn't steeled herself for the difficult news and felt flashes of anguish. She wondered whether she would ever see Sid again. Or her dad. Then she focused on the present.

"Juice is missing and I can't raise her," she said. "When she left me, she said she was going to visit Willow, but I think she had other plans."

"She and MacMac went to the subdeck to free Chase and Justin. I can account for their actions up until the artery failed. I can't find them on the subdeck now, though."

"I'll go look," said Cheryl.

"Wait. The shrapnel punched a hole in the subdeck containment. There's no air down there."

"Oh my God!" Cheryl's voice caught as she spoke. "Did they have space coveralls nearby?"

"No, Lazura didn't load anything that might hint at her interstellar ambitions."

Cheryl indulged her sorrow for a moment as a tear rolled down her cheek. She wiped her face with her hands. "What can I do?"

"Hi, Cher."

"Sid!"

"Hang in there, sweets. I'm coming."

Somehow, Sid's crazy bravado felt so comforting that both of her eyes teared. "God, I love you."

"So," said Criss, getting them back on task, "I can't feel Juice at all, and that means she's shielded behind something, possibly the Power House in the cellar. Lazura built the Power House using shielded material to conceal her looting of the fuel blocks. She left eight damaged synbods inside when she took the fuel. There is a chance— a very small one—that Juice went there with MacMac, Chase, and Justin to try and save them."

"Guide me. I'll go look."

Criss projected floating arrows that led to an auxiliary lift, and Cheryl took off at a trot.

"To remove fuel from the generators," he said as she ran, "they had to open up four fuel vaults. Everything inside the building is contaminated, but I don't know how bad it is. Please take a reading before entering."

The lift was far enough away that she felt winded when she stepped inside, and the ride down was too short for her to catch her breath. Resuming her trot in the cellar, she let Criss guide her left, right, and back again as she wended her way through the maze of facilities and equipment.

"That's it," Criss told her when a long, low building with gray walls came into view. Accessing her com, she kept one eye on the display as she approached the door.

"So far, so good," she said as the monitor showed twice the normal background level, a very safe reading. But when she moved close and traced the outline of the door, her com flashed red and alerted with a chime. "Whoa." She stepped back from the door.

"Okay, we need to get you up to the guest deck *right now*."

"There's no concern. The contamination barely registers at ten paces."

"Lazura is filling the subdeck with carbon dioxide. If she lifts the life support barriers, it will flow up to the cellar."

"Can't you stop her?"

"Not with her dome shield in place. I can display simple things like arrows, but to overpower her, I need to be inside."

Cheryl took off for the lift, her mind racing. When the lift came into view, she asked the question, even though she feared the answer. "How long could someone survive breathing the gas down below?"

"Minutes."

Cheryl hugged herself on the ride up to the guest deck, struggling for optimistic thoughts. She'd clung to the notion that somehow, somewhere, Juice and MacMac had found sanctuary from the cold vacuum of space. But pumped gas would find those hideaways and fill them with deadly fumes.

"I believe Sid and I can enter the dome through a maintenance gate along the perimeter path," said Criss. "To do that, you'll need to configure the doors so they're staged like an airlock. Can you help with that?"

"Sure."

Floating arrows appeared, leading Cheryl across the deck, and she took off in a lope. "Please get here soon," she pleaded, knowing they were doing everything they could.

Pop, pop, pop, pop. The percussive thump of explosions caused Cheryl to drop to a crouch. She swiveled her head back and forth, seeking the cause of the blasts. Then the deck lurched, throwing her to the ground.

The shaking howl of twisting metal dominated everything, filling the air with sickening shrieks as if Vivo itself were tearing open. Prone on the ground, she looked between her feet at the office tower.

It swayed. Then it began to drop.

25

S itting in the lounge of Aurora's executive berth, Sid wrapped his legs and arms into a ball in anticipation of a collision with Vivo.

"Nice work," he told Criss as he unfolded in his chair moments later, pleased to be alive.

"I'm bringing the scout around," said Criss. "It'll be here in twenty minutes."

"Twenty minutes?" Sid's whine revealed his impatience.

"This berth uses a dock instead of a bay. It takes longer." After a moment of silence, Criss added, "We left the scout's truss line hanging on an external maintenance cleat."

"I'll buy you a new one."

"We need to retrieve it before we start pursuit."

"No."

"The only way to slow Vivo is with its own drive pods or another ship's engines. The scout's engines aren't in play without the truss line. We either retrieve it now or risk having to come back for it."

Angry at the universe and rebelling against any more delays, Sid lashed out. "I order you to find a way to slow Vivo using the scout's engines."

Criss connected with Cheryl after that, and while those two worked together, Sid listened but kept quiet, willing his intuition to guide him. He was still awaiting inspiration when Criss rose.

"The scout is finishing its docking cycle. We can board in a few moments."

"Did you invent a way to use the scout's engines to slow Vivo?"

"Yes. It's called a truss line. There's a custom model hanging on an exterior maintenance cleat. Let's swing by and pick it up."

When they finally took up the chase, Criss multitasked, working with Cheryl in her search for Juice while at the same time helping Sid refine their strategy for boarding Vivo.

"Lazura needs five hours to start the drive pods," said Sid. "We used an hour waiting for the scout and retrieving the truss line. We'll use two more catching Vivo. So, by my math, we have two hours to board Vivo and take control."

Criss nodded. "In round numbers."

"And once you're under the dome, you overpower Lazura and it's done." He snapped his fingers to illustrate the speed of her demise. "What I'm getting at is that since the actual confrontation is over so fast, we really have two hours just to board Vivo. That cushion sounds almost comfortable."

"There are so many ways things could go wrong. If she restarts the drives, the chase resumes, and since her starhub is still broken and she doesn't have the additional fuel she wanted, she'll take big risks to overcome that disadvantage. However we approach this, we don't want there to be a moment where she feels cornered."

"What would she do?"

"She's rational, but one of her options is to harm or kill the hostages. She keeps that decision on a knife's edge because if we don't believe it could happen at any moment, she has no negotiating position. In the end, she wants to find a way to return home with her archive."

Sid stared at the projected image of Vivo hovering above the scout's ops bench. "I want Cheryl back with us. I know we care about all the people on Vivo. But let's get Juice if she's alive, and Cheryl while she still is. Then we worry about everyone else."

"Juice is alive," Criss said forcefully. "I won't accept the alternative."

Sid thought Criss looked tired around the eyes, even knowing neither synbods nor crystals showed stress in that way. "She is, Criss. I'm so worried about Cheryl that I let my mouth speak garbage."

After a period of quiet, they resumed planning. By the time Vivo loomed, they'd narrowed their entry choice to a maintenance gate on the dome perimeter.

"I assume we're going in wearing our personal cloaks, or can Lazura see through them?"

"What is this?" For a moment, Sid thought Criss was reacting to his question. Then he saw the ring of pyrotechnics flash around Vivo. Like sequenced explosions from the olden days of building demolition, a ring of silent explosions, tiny in comparison to the huge vessel, looped around the outside of the platform about halfway down the structure beneath the dome.

Sid stood, enlarged the image, and replayed the scene while he leaned in to look. "What is that?"

"She's separating. Good one, Lazura."

Sid heard the admiration in Criss's voice but didn't understand the reference. Then, hundreds of flares, spaced around where the ring of explosions had occurred, ignited with a shower of sparks and began spewing intense cones of flame. Moments after that, a gap appeared between two sections of the platform.

"What am I looking at?" demanded Sid, his frustration feeding his anger.

"Those are beacon rockets that she's repurposed as retrorockets. She's using them to pull the subdeck away from the cellar and dome."

"How is that possible?" asked Sid as the gap in the middle of Vivo grew to a chasm.

"That ring of flashes we saw earlier was a series of sequenced explosions that sheared thousands of bolts holding the two structures together. Now she's using beacon rockets, distress signals powerful enough to be seen great distances, to separate them."

"Where did she get so many of them?"

"Aubrey has had quirks her whole life, one of which is the need to over prepare for everything. I had believed it was this trait that drove her to purchase so many."

Sid grumbled, then called to the air, "Cher, are you okay?"

"What's happening?" she replied, her voice shaking from the tumult.

Confusion dominated the next minutes. The rocket beacons didn't have an off mechanism Criss could control. Each burned a charge of fuel that, once ignited, continued burning until the charge was depleted.

"Shoot her," Sid demanded, ready to kill Lazura and stop the madness.

"I still don't know where Juice is, so I don't know how to avoid hitting her."

Ideas swirled between them in rapid fire with no consensus on what actions to take. As they brainstormed, the separation between the subdeck and cellar grew, removing all doubt about the end state; Vivo was dividing in two.

And as the separation progressed, the domed portion started to turn in a lazy spin. Sid didn't notice until Cheryl called to them. "The dome is rotating on its axis. Everything is getting pushed out toward the dome wall."

"Lazura mounted the beacon rockets at an angle," said Criss after a moment of investigation. "The spin is deliberate."

At one level, Vivo seemed toy-like to Sid, floating in space with nothing around it to hint at its size. But the shriek of tearing metal he'd heard through his com link with Cheryl hammered home that it wasn't a toy and this wasn't a game.

As the distance between subdeck and cellar increased, so did the spin, making life increasingly difficult for everyone on Vivo. "The rotation has us pressed against the dome wall," called Cheryl. "We're above two g's already and it's getting worse. Some of the older folks are really suffering."

That urgency shifted their focus to stabilizing the dome. "The scout can help slow the spin," said Criss, "but we have to wait for the separation to complete or we risk tilting one structure into the other."

The distance between the subdeck and cellar had grown large enough for Sid to see stars in between. He also saw that a rod connected the subdeck to the cellar at the center. "What's that bar connecting the two pieces?"

"That's the central office tower," said Criss. "It's going with the subdeck, which means Lazura is too." As he spoke, the subdeck pulled the office tower away from the cellar and dome, reminding Sid of a sword being drawn from its sheath.

Two distinct vessels now hung in space. The part with the dome and cellar looked similar to the original Vivo, though shorter with the loss of its lowest tier. The part with the subdeck and office tower looked something like a thick, floating manhole cover with a short, fat broom handle poking up from its center.

"Hang on!" shouted Criss.

Sid fell back into his seat as the scout dipped, then he heard the engines spin into a whine and continue into a scream.

"Tell me," yelled Sid as the scout shook and the distance from Vivo and Cheryl began to grow.

"She's going for a cold start," Criss yelled above the shriek of the engines. "With her greatly reduced mass, she has an eighty percent chance of success, so it's not irrational. And if it works, she has us at a huge disadvantage."

Criss held up a hand and wiggled his fingers. "But that means there's a one in five chance she fails. If that happens, the drive pods go, and the entire subdeck becomes shrapnel. In truth, I'm not sure we can get far enough away to save ourselves."

"What would happen to the dome?" asked Sid, his tone reflecting his fear.

Before Criss could answer, the bottom of the subdeck glowed a brilliant white. And with the office tower pointing the way, the improbable vessel accelerated, gaining speed so quickly it disappeared in a blink. Lazura and her chopped spacecraft were gone.

Sid felt a level of relief at seeing her go because it meant the alien AI no longer shared space with Cheryl. It also gave them the opportunity to locate Juice. To do that, they needed to return yet again to the domed world.

Turning the craft, Criss used the engines to slow the scout. The maneuver took longer than Sid wanted, prompting him to grunt and groan every few minutes to show his unhappiness. The nimble craft finally moved forward again, and Criss pushed the engines as hard on the return trip as he had during their escape.

"Now I see why you called it a good one," said Sid. "She's making her run, and we need to stay here and stabilize the dome."

"I hadn't foreseen the separation, let alone the spin. I examined everything about Vivo, and yet I didn't see that twenty unrelated features could be repurposed all at once to provide that capability. But the instant the separation started, I knew she had scored big."

"Can the scout stop the spin?"

Criss nodded. "We have the truss line…" He left a tiny pause, just long enough for Sid to notice. "…and using it, the scout can slow the spin to a tolerable level in about four hours. Livable in eight. But it will take a week for our engines to stop that huge structure on its journey into deep space, and another week to get it moving on an inbound trajectory."

"And meanwhile, Lazura is putting distance between us." After a pause, Sid continued. "If we find Juice in the domed section, then we can send weapons after Lazura."

"But if Juice is gone," Criss finished, "we have to give chase. And with Lazura's head start, it will be a long, grueling pursuit." Criss folded his hands together, signaling a dramatic moment. "Given that scenario, it's best if I give chase alone. You and Cheryl can stay and help the guests get back home."

Sid responded with an obscene gesture.

"Then you should know that I've launched fourteen of our high-performance supply ships and am humping them out to different intercept points along Lazura's likely exit routes. The scout's been used hard over the past few days, with more to come. We'll need to connect with any one of them and replenish before we leave the solar system."

This time Sid nodded and sought to comfort both Criss and himself. "We'll confirm Juice's status once we're inside. Either way, we'll get her back. I promise."

Slowing the spin of the huge platform started with hooking the scout's truss line to a structural component on the outer rim. Criss impressed Sid by hooking the truss line to an exposed flange without either of them leaving their seats. After ramping the scout's engines to pull against the spin, he leaned back in his chair. "It'll be a couple of hours before it's slowed enough that we can move about and be productive inside."

Like turning a massive ocean liner with a tugboat, slowing Vivo with the scout was a reasonable undertaking but a prolonged process. Sid didn't last ten minutes. "I'm not sitting here waiting while Cheryl's over there."

"Cheryl is in excellent physical condition, but she is suffering great discomfort. What can you accomplish under such conditions?"

"I can keep her company, suffering next to her until it's over."

Criss nodded. "She will express disapproval but will be cheered by your presence."

They dressed in space coveralls and made their way out into open space through the scout's airlock. Criss operated a hand drive—a handgrip with angled nozzles designed to pull people short distances in a weightless environment—and Sid held on to him as they glided toward the now exposed underside of the cellar containment.

When they'd drifted below the lip of the structure, Criss restarted the scout's engines. As the nimble craft pulled mightily to slow the platform's rotation, the two made for the shaft beneath Vivo that, with the loss of the office tower, was now an open cylindrical tunnel.

The tunnel ran up through Vivo's central axis, placing it at the center of rotation for the platform. When they entered the opening, the spin was barely perceptible, the cylinder walls turning slower than the second hand on a sweep-hand clock. As long as they stayed close to this center of rotation, the spin wouldn't affect them to any degree.

But, just the way a longer rope on a tree swing makes for a wilder ride, the farther away they moved from the central axis, the greater the centrifugal forces pushing them out toward the dome wall.

"Lazura designed the tower extraction mechanism so it protects the atmosphere inside the dome and cellar," said Criss as they floated up the empty shaft. "That's a peace offering from her view."

Sid, busy searching for a way in, didn't respond. He didn't care about Lazura's motives.

The mouth of the shaft had a smooth wall all the way around, offering little hope of providing access to the inside. But as they rose up the cylinder, they approached a spot where twisted metal and sheared cables protruded from the wall.

"Can we get inside there?" asked Sid, pointing to the damage.

"We can get to the guest deck over here." Criss moved them to a rectangular plate on the opposite side of the shaft. "As we rose up the cylinder, we moved inside the dome shield. I've taken control of everything and have confirmed that Lazura went with the other vessel. I still can't sense Juice anywhere here on Vivo. In fact, I can't locate Juice, MacMac, Chase, or Justin. That's not good news."

Criss triggered a release and the plate fell away to reveal a shallow cavity. With his feet protruding into the open shaft, Criss leaned forward and started fiddling with a cover panel set in the cavity's back wall. After several seconds, the cover released.

Criss shifted to the side, and Sid, moving up next to him, peered into a dark cubby, much of it filled with a rectangular shaft passing across the back wall.

"We're going to take turns climbing that ventilation chase up to the guest deck."

"I'll go first," said Sid.

"See that square cap?" Criss pointed to a cover on the side of the chase. "When you open that, air will escape and fill this cubby, so this hatch door has to be shut. Get in, close the cap, and climb up to the next one, just like that one. Open it, climb out, and cover it again. I'll follow."

"No problem," said Sid, moving inside the tight cubby.

"Did you notice that when you crossed this threshold, the gravity module started affecting you?"

The comment drew Sid's attention to his knees, now rubbing against the cubby floor. It was a modest influence, but a tug nevertheless.

"As you climb the chase, you will transition to full gravity, so be prepared to work harder as you move upward."

Given the hurdles he'd overcome to get this far, Sid wasn't about to let a climb up a shaft be his undoing. It took several minutes of inelegant scrambling, but his determination won out, and he made it to the guest deck. By the time Criss joined him, Sid was out of his space coveralls and looking at the wonders inside Vivo's dome.

"Over here." Criss motioned for Sid to follow. They walked along a garden path that ended at a square of lawn near where the office tower lobby had been. In the middle of the patch of grass sat a small table like you might find in an eat-in kitchen. An ornate box sat on top of the table.

As they approached the table, Sid caught sight of the distinctive markings on the box's exterior. "Those are Kardish symbols." His scalp tingled as he said the words.

Criss nodded, then raised the lid and removed a faceted glass ball the size of a pebble. "Lazura's archive," he said, closing his fist around the bit of crystal. He held his hand at chest level and stared into the distance. Sid waited, figuring he was exploring the contents.

When Criss resurfaced from his trance, Sid asked, "Do you think it's the only copy?"

"I don't know."

"If it is, she's acting on the deal she struck with Cheryl, which means Juice has to be here somewhere."

"I hope so." Criss began backtracking, loosening the top of his jumpsuit as he walked and securing the crystal in an inside pocket. He moved faster after that, marching past the ventilation chase and over to a maintenance shed near a stand of trees.

Opening the shed door, he swung it back and forth, studying the motion. Then he grabbed the door at the top with both hands and, with a powerful jerk, pulled it off its hinges.

Laying the door on the ground, Criss stepped into the shed, enabled a spooling system, and pulled a length of sturdy cord outside next to the door. He took several coils of line, and moving so fast that Sid had trouble following, he weaved a cradle around the door so while it lay flat, he could lift it from the ground using a central line connected back to the spool system.

Holding his creation under one arm as if he were carrying a surfboard, Criss pointed at a spot on the dome wall. "Cheryl is right there."

Sid moved over next to him and sighted along Criss's finger. It was farther than he could see, so he identified the corner of a building in the distance he could use as a marker. Starting in that direction, he eyed Criss's contraption as they walked, determined not to ask.

Then he connected and announced his conclusion. "It's a stretcher so we can pull Cheryl back. And the others, of course."

At the beginning of their trek, Criss had pulled on the cord from the spool system to keep the line moving with them. A hundred paces along, however, the outward push of the spin caused their strides to lengthen and the line to start dragging itself.

The forces increased as they progressed, their steps growing longer and longer. When Sid's feet lifted from the ground, his grip on the cord was the only thing keeping him from tumbling toward the wall. That's when Criss hooked Sid by the arm and hefted him inside the cradle.

"If this was for me," asked Sid, lying on the shed door, "why didn't you just make a rope seat or something?"

"Because when we reach three g's, you'd have bent around it like a pretzel." Criss smiled. "Not that it wouldn't be entertaining to watch."

Criss used the spool system after that to control the speed of their descent to the dome wall. As the pressure increased, Sid rolled on his side so his diaphragm would not have to keep lifting the weight he felt sitting on his chest. "How high are we going?"

"Just under three g's. They were at three and a half at the worst of it, but the scout is making progress."

"I've been over five g's a bunch of times."

"You only had to live with it for a minute or so during a controlled accel-decel sequence. They've been suffering for hours. It takes its toll in a different way."

As the dome wall loomed, Criss stopped the spool feed so the door hovered just above the translucent surface. He lowered himself until his feet touched and, pulling Sid along in what had become a record-setting rope swing, made his way along the wall. When he finally lowered the door to the dome surface, he positioned it so Sid lay face-to-face with Cheryl.

"My hero," she said, curled on her side, the lines around her eyes and mouth highlighting her stress. "I'd kiss you but I can't move."

He reached for her hand and they interlaced fingers. While he normally would have said something goofy to try to get her to laugh, he didn't speak, he just looked into her eyes.

Criss gave them ten seconds to commune before moving things along. "All aboard," he said, crouching next to Cheryl.

Sid pulled, Criss lifted, and Cheryl crawled until she lay in the small-spoon position on the door, Sid's long arms and legs wrapped around her as he cuddled her from behind.

Gripping the line above the door, Criss signaled the spool system, and they started to rise. With Cheryl safe in his arms, Sid shed his mind of distractions and focused on Juice. Criss didn't have any answers, so on the ride back, he sifted through everything he knew. By the time they escaped the powerful g forces and stood together near the shed, he struggled to remain optimistic.

Cheryl held the cord in her hand and looked back at the wall. "I'm conflicted as hell. Part of me wants to take this rig back down and pull people up. But bottom line, I'm worried sick about Juice."

"I can't sense her," said Criss. "Nor can I sense MacMac, Chase, or Justin. If they're here, they're behind some sort of shielding."

"That doesn't make sense," said Cheryl, shaking her head.

"We need to confirm it one way or the other," said Sid as he examined the nearby buildings. "It'll take a long time to search everything physically. Can you eliminate any of it?"

"A fair amount," said Criss, "I suggest we divide up and search near the axis of spin here on the guest deck, then head down to the cellar. If we start in the center down there, the spin will have slowed enough as we work our way out that we can finish that whole level. Then we come back up here to the guest deck and finish out near the wall."

"How long will that take?" asked Sid.

A map projected in front of him, arrows guiding him through a nearby building. "If we stick to the plan, five hours, plus however long for breaks."

The search took just under five hours and left them empty-handed as Sid had feared. Sid and Cheryl took a moment to internalize the commitment they were about to make—months of grueling pursuit in confined quarters—then they made for a perimeter gate to board the scout.

Their path took them past the Vivo Hotel. Willow's mom saw them, and, dragging Willow by the hand, she hurried toward them, shouting for their attention.

"Please take Willow with you," she begged. "I've lived a full life, but she has so much ahead of her." She started to sob, pushing Willow toward them. The young teen started crying too. The anguish and confusion tugged at Sid.

Cheryl took charge. "I'm president of a company called SunRise. Have you heard of it?"

"I have," Willow choked out, raising her hand as if she were answering a teacher's question in the classroom.

"That gives me access to amazing people and technology. I've already launched four pursuit ships from Mars. They'll be here in just over two weeks to bring everyone home."

Willow's distraught mom showed her skepticism by shaking her head through her tears. Sid, anxious to help, moved away from the women, motioning for Criss to follow.

"Can you link me to Tommy?"

"Tommy Two-Tone? Done."

"Tommy, it's Sid. Remember me?"

Tommy started a profanity-laced tirade, finishing with, "I'll kill you!" before stopping to take a breath.

"How would you like to own Vivo?"

"Is that what you call the dome you tried to crash into Aurora?"

"Yup. It's coasting into deep space. If you can retrieve the structure and return it to Aurora in the next five days, you can have it."

"What are you saying?"

"Vivo can house a hundred people comfortably. I have control of it and offer it to your syndicate to own, free of charge and clear of conditions. To earn it, you need to find a way to slow its outbound flightpath and return it to

Aurora within five days, *without* putting *any* of the passengers in harm's way."

"I hear your words and know you are full of shit."

"From the beginning I told you I would pay dearly for you to lodge and care for these people for a brief time. A sweet sum for a few days' work. That's all this has ever been about."

Sid nodded to Criss. "You're receiving a contract for this final offer right now. You have one hour to accept. And Tommy, know that if any passenger gets hurt because of your actions *or* your inactions, we will be meeting again. You won't be happy with the outcome."

While Tommy evaluated the offer, the three left Vivo for the scout, the stares and glares of the guests weighing on them as they departed. Once aboard, Sid led Cheryl to her bunk while Criss retrieved and stowed the truss line.

Though the door was closed, Criss intruded on their privacy. "Tommy has signed."

"That's great news," said Cheryl, crowded into the mist shower with Sid. "But can he pull it off?"

Criss projected an image of two muscular dozers coming to life in a huge asteroid cave, flexing monstrous claws the size of houses, their oversized engines glowing white. "Tommy does an excellent job of hiding resources. He'll beat the deadline with these."

Cheryl tried to look at them, but Sid distracted her by nibbling on her neck.

"These monsters can tear open a medium-sized asteroid in minutes," Criss continued. "Tommy's sending both of them, and that means he's serious."

Sid dismissed Criss after that. When he was gone, Sid hugged Cheryl, holding her tight and glorying in having her back in his arms.

26

The explosion hit Juice like a punch to the gut. Before she could make sense of the assault, fierce winds threatened to drag her backward. She reached for the frame of the storage unit door but missed her mark. Lunging this time, she tried and missed again. Her eyes connected with MacMac's as her feet lifted from the floor.

Fighting for survival, she twisted for a last grasp. She met resistance as she turned and changed tactics, grasping for whatever it was that pressed on her. She found purchase and held tight.

From the corner of her eye, she saw that she'd grabbed Justin's arm. Standing at the door of the storage unit, he leaned outward at a steep angle, the hand behind him holding the doorframe, the other outstretched, gripping Juice's shirt near her waist.

Her head twisted when he yanked the material, but the action caused her to move in his direction. He improved his grip, jerked her again, got an arm around her waist, and fell back, pulling her inside the storage unit.

Like the shelter of a cove, the relative quiet inside the room gave Juice the opportunity to collect her thoughts. Sitting upright, she searched for MacMac and spied him outside, clawing the ground as the wind pulled at him.

"Help him!" she commanded the synbods.

Chase, already acting, crouched at the door. Holding the jamb, he swung his arm, straight and rigid from the splint, in MacMac's direction. When it stopped moving, Chase's clasp gun pointed right at MacMac's face.

"What are you doing?" yelled Juice, horrified by Chase's action.

"Grab on!" Chase yelled.

MacMac looked at the gun and hesitated.

"Grab it, MacMac!" yelled Juice, seeing that Chase's finger wasn't on the trigger, that he had extended the weapon to lengthen his reach.

MacMac hesitated for a moment more, and then a fierce gust forced a decision. In a deliberate sequence of moves, he grasped the gun with his left hand, twisted his body to square up to Chase, and lunged to secure his right hand as well.

With Juice and Justin each holding one of Chase's legs, the synbod reeled MacMac inside. The moment he crossed the threshold, Justin jumped up and finished closing the storage unit door using a manual crank, silencing the chaos outside.

Juice sat on the deck taking deep breaths and gathering her wits. Emergency lights cast long shadows, giving the room an eerie feel.

"You okay?" asked MacMac.

"Yeah. You?"

"Fine. And thank you for the hand, lads."

Justin walked around the perimeter of the room inspecting the walls while Chase studied the items in the room as if he were taking inventory.

"I've lost Criss," said Juice. "Justin, Chase, are either of you in contact with him?"

"No," they answered in unison.

"Do you hear that?" asked MacMac.

Juice shook her head.

"Neither do I, which means the drive pods have shut down."

As he spoke, Juice felt herself lifting off the deck.

"We've lost the gravity module, too."

Juice waited, anticipating the return of power at any moment. As she did, a dizzy spell clouded her thoughts. "I'm feeling a little light-headed. Do you think we have enough air in here?"

MacMac floated toward the workbench, calling to Justin. "Can you tell us the status of our air?"

"It's thin," Justin reported based on his internal sensors. "We're down almost thirty percent."

MacMac reached to a row of hand valves on the wall behind the workbench and cranked one open. Then he pulled a hose off the spout, and a hiss filled the room.

"This is pure oxygen for my torch," said MacMac, "so watch for ignition sources." He waited a few minutes and then told Justin, "Stay here and when the oxygen fraction in the air is stable for us, shut it off."

MacMac floated back toward Juice and noticed Chase was digging at the wall, "Whoa there, laddie. Let's not disturb that."

"What do you have?" Juice asked the synbod.

"This room has shielding on the walls," said Chase. "I believe that's why Criss cannot connect with us."

"The walls, floor, and ceiling are shielded so Lazura can't see inside," said MacMac. "That means your friend probably can't see either."

"Can we pierce it to get a signal out?"

"Bad idea," said MacMac. "You'll have to punch a hole through the wall, not an easy task, and there's no air on the other side if you happen to succeed."

"So we make it small and cover it when we're done."

"Even harder to do, but fair enough. How do we send a signal that doesn't alert Lazura as well? She just had Hejmo, Mondo, and three others try to capture us. If she knows we're here, she'll send more."

"What do we do?"

"My recommendation is to wait until your friends are on board and able to help in our defense. They're hours away, so it shouldn't be long. Until then, we sit tight and wait."

"How will we know they're out there if we're in here?"

"Ah," said MacMac, pointing. "Chase, lad, would you float up to that small, gold-colored ring in the wall to the right of the overhead door?"

Chase moved to the spot, studied the insert—a small, clear plug of glass-like material—then put his eye to it.

"Can you see across the deck all the way to the lift?"

"Yes."

"Can you see the synbods?"

"No."

"Really?" MacMac swam toward Chase and the viewport. "Can you see the deck where they were?"

"Yes. They're not there now."

MacMac looked and confirmed the observation. "I don't believe the uninjured ones would let themselves be sucked out through the breach. They're too fast and too strong. That means they're on the prowl, probably looking for us."

Juice moved to the viewport and looked through to see a large swath of the subdeck and no sign of synbods. "They must know we're in here."

"We ducked in here while everyone was fighting for survival, and that power outage ensured that nothing was being recorded. If we last the next couple of hours, I think we're okay."

Juice pushed away from the wall. "Chase, please keep watch and let us know if you see anything." Then she turned to MacMac. "Could we send a signal through the viewport?"

MacMac shook his head. "The same company that makes the wall shield makes these."

She twirled to survey the room, getting a sense of where they would be spending the next hours. "I get that we had a breach and lost power, but what could cause something like that?"

"I'd need to know the order before I could even guess."

"What do you mean?"

"An explosion at the primary artery that punches a hole in the containment shell would make me think sabotage from the inside. A puncture of the shell followed by the loss of power implies an attack from the outside."

"If those are the only choices, then it's the first one. No way Criss would let anyone attack us."

"The secondary artery hasn't kicked on, and that's the automatic response to a failure of the primary. I'm starting to think something bigger happened, maybe multiple events."

Appraising the space, Juice asked, "Why do you have this room isolated?"

"I was transforming this and the room next door into private space for my personal use. It's secured using shielding material we had left over from the construction of the Power House."

"May I ask why?"

"Back a week or so ago when I thought I worked at a vacation resort, I had a job I loved and a boss I felt the exact opposite about."

"That would be Aubrey?"

MacMac nodded. "Working on this hideout became a form of therapy that kept me from walking away." He looked around the room. "It sounds foolish when I say it out loud."

Juice sensed he wasn't telling the whole story but didn't press him. Instead, she stayed quiet, waiting to see if he'd fill the silence with more details.

Then she realized she was shivering. "I can see my breath." She twisted to face the center of the room. "What do we have to keep us warm?"

"Over here," said MacMac. He floated to a big yellow tool locker in the back corner, turned the handle, and pulled open a door that was as tall as he was. Juice, peering over his shoulder, saw a display of handheld power tools organized on the locker's back wall. She assumed one of them was a portable heater of some sort until MacMac reached in and pulled the wall of tools open as if it, too, were a door.

Without speaking, he floated into the opening and disappeared. Juice poked her head inside and saw the familiar cast of emergency lights at the other end of a short passage.

Floating after him, her head arrived in the storage unit next door before her feet left the room where she'd started. Justin came next, and Juice called back through the opening, "Keep watching, Chase. Sing out if you see anything moving."

While the first room felt industrial, this place, with a bed, lounge chairs, and throw rugs floating about, with pictures on the wall, and with a food service unit in the corner, had more of a homey feel.

"A bed?" said Juice. "C'mon, MacMac. This is more of a lair than a hideout."

MacMac said nothing. Instead, he floated across the room, pulled the cover and sheets off the mattress, untangled a heavy robe caught on a hook, and pushed off the wall to return to Juice. He helped her fit the robe over her clothes, then spun her slowly as he wrapped the sheets and blanket around her.

"Thank you," she said, saying nothing more, hoping the silence would spur him to provide more information about the place.

He spoke, but his message was for Justin. "Can you help me next door for a minute?" Then he disappeared back through the tool-locker tunnel.

The two returned in short order holding a jumble of items that, when separated, became a heat gun, two space heaters, and a half-dozen power packs. Working together, they had warmth flowing in minutes.

"I doubt this is enough to heat the room," said MacMac. "But it should keep it from getting any colder."

Floating near the heaters, Juice stopped shivering, and that allowed for a moment of clarity.

"Justin, stay near me," she snapped.

The synbod responded, moving next to her in a protective position.

"What is it?" asked MacMac, his head swiveling.

"You need to tell me why you have a secret, lockable bedroom. The only reason I can think of is causing me to panic."

"I'm lost. What are you thinking?" He seemed sincere.

"A quiet man keeps a concealed cell to hold victims against their will." She could hear her voice rise as she said the words. "Chase, I need you in here."

A thump and a bump behind her became Chase, floating into the room, clasp gun leading the way.

"Now you hold on there, lassie," said MacMac, shaking his finger at her and turning bright red. "This is for my wife, and it's none of your business."

"You keep your wife prisoner?"

He looked at her for a long moment. "My wife becomes aroused when I add secretiveness and a sense of danger to our lovemaking. I don't want anyone else watching. And most important, it is none of your business." He stressed each word of the last line.

Mortified, Juice turned red herself and couldn't meet his gaze. "Chase, return to the viewport and let us know when you see movement." The silence became unbearable, and Juice sought to break it. "What's her name?"

"Who, Babs?" He smiled. "It's Barbara, actually."

They chatted about unimportant things while Juice struggled to mend their relationship. MacMac offered a few details about Barbara, with a story about how they'd met and some highlights of her career. Juice followed by sharing a how-we-met story about Alex, her live-in beau back on Earth.

Chase sang out, "We have movement."

Everyone made for the viewport, and MacMac looked first. "That's Hejmo and two Techs."

Juice took a turn, but they were already gone.

"The fact that they'd move past here without a glance is a good sign," said MacMac.

"What do you think they're doing?" asked Juice.

"Restoring power. There's nothing more important." MacMac backed away from the viewport, and Chase resumed his sentry watch. When MacMac turned into the room, his gaze rose to the items floating above them, some quite large. "Can we have Justin secure these? We don't want those overhead when gravity returns."

Juice agreed and started the synbod on the task. By the time he finished, power returned to Vivo, with the gravity restored moments later.

"Hooray," said Juice. "I am so ready to leave this place."

"As am I. Unfortunately, there's still no air outside. Until they make repairs, we remain roommates."

"Huh," grunted Juice. "Okay, how about if we send Justin or Chase to get Cheryl? You and I hole up next door, shut the locker door to preserve our air on that side, then he sneaks out and goes to get her?"

"Interesting." MacMac seemed to be mulling variations on the idea when Chase called out.

"The two Techs are coming back."

Juice claimed the portal and watched for several minutes. "Something's happening over there." She backed away and pointed in the direction of the right front corner of the room.

MacMac took a peek. "Great news, they're running EM sand, which means they're fixing the breach." He gave Juice a quick lesson on the repair procedure. "In a few hours we'll all be able to leave."

Juice felt an emotional weight lift and she grinned. "I can tell that's good news because I'm suddenly hungry."

MacMac laughed and they made for the food service unit next door. Juice wanted something to warm her and ordered clam chowder with an extra pat of butter.

"That sounds good," said MacMac, ordering the same.

They ate, then took turns watching the repairs through the viewport. When the EM sand pipe began its retreat, MacMac said, "The atmosphere should be restored soon. After that, we can go."

He began to pace while they waited. "I desperately want to use my displays to track progress, but she'll know the minute I activate a link."

"I see melting," called Chase, who used his augmented vision to track the state of an ice film on a far support strut.

"Melting means atmosphere," said MacMac. "We need to give it a half hour to reach full pressure, but our ordeal is near its end."

"Hooray," said Juice, celebrating a second time. As she did, the deck lurched, tossing her forward. A howl of twisting metal filled the room, then the deck jolted again, throwing her back. Crouching and shifting her weight to maintain balance, she tried to ride the bucking deck.

It felt as though Vivo were collapsing around them, and she wondered if they might be crashing into Aurora. She didn't have time to ask MacMac before the next heave of the deck tossed her against a crate. Bouncing off, she fell to the floor.

Lying on her back, she watched the next jolt toss MacMac off his feet. He toppled backward and smacked his head on a shelving unit as he fell. Lifeless, he hit the ground, a gash spilling blood across his face.

Juice crawled to him and struggled to get his head off the still-quaking floor and onto her lap. "Wake up," she called to him, wiping blood off his face with her sleeve. "Don't even think about leaving me here alone."

The gash creased his temple at the hairline; the blood flowing from it covered half his face in a horrific display. Juice bunched her sleeve and pressed it against the wound to stanch the flow of blood. As she did, the deck pulsed and the screams of collapsing structures continued unabated.

"Justin," she commanded, "search for a med kit."

To her relief, MacMac groaned when she said that. Lifting a hand to his head, he probed his injury with the tips of his fingers. The gash continued to bleed, so she smacked his hand out of the way and reapplied pressure.

"Is there a med kit anywhere?" she asked him.

"Not in here," MacMac whispered. "I never thought I'd need one."

"Help me get him next door," she called to the synbods.

The violent shaking of the deck hampered the effort, but the synbods succeeded in carrying him through the narrow passage of the tool locker and into the adjoining room.

On the other side, Justin placed MacMac on the bed. He'd recovered enough by that point to keep pressure on the wound himself.

Juice found a clean sheet and tried to tear it. Failing, she handed it to Justin. "Tear this into strips for bandages and washcloths."

Next, she went to the food service unit, ordered a large mug of boiling water, added a drop of antiseptic soap, and returned to MacMac. He lay stretched on the bed, his head on a pillow. She sat on the edge and dabbed the wound.

She paused in her ministrations and looked around. "It stopped." The shaking and noise had given way to undisturbed quiet. Resuming her treatment, she said, "Thank goodness. I don't know that I've ever been more scared."

After a few minutes of dabbing, his cut looked cleaner, though still quite nasty. Folding a strip of cloth lengthwise, she looped a bandage around his head and tied it in the back. "What was that we were hearing?"

"I can't begin to guess."

Braaak. The resonant bark of a giant machine echoed across the subdeck.

MacMac sat up, moaned, and lay back down. "Where is that coming from?"

Braaak.

"Beats me," said Juice. "It sounds close, though." She saw MacMac's lips moving. "What are you counting?"

"Seconds," he said.

Braaak.

"No, Aubrey."

"Lazura," Juice corrected. "What is she doing?"

MacMac scooted over on the bed and patted next to him. "Climb in. Quick."

"No way."

"It doesn't matter because we're about to die."

Braaak.

Juice swung her legs up and lay down next to him. "This better be good."

"She's trying to cold-start the drive pods. It's a good way to kill everyone. But if it works, the acceleration will be a bear for the first minutes, and this bed is the best place to be."

As he finished speaking, the familiar thrum of drive pods filled the air. And then Juice felt an immense weight on her chest—like that of a bull elephant—as the force of acceleration pushed her deep into the mattress.

The pressure became pain, and Juice counted to ten, waiting for it to stop. As it continued, she counted again. And then again. "How long is this going to last?" she asked through gritted teeth.

"Cold start transients last about two minutes if I remember right," said MacMac, speaking in clipped phrases as he fought with his own discomfort.

"Justin," Juice called through a haze of pain. "Make a hole through the wall and get a message to Criss."

The acceleration didn't stop after two minutes, or three, or four. As Justin worked on the wall with a hand tool, Juice escaped her suffering by thinking of Alex and how much she missed him.

27

"Yes!" exclaimed Lazura when the drive pods ignited without exploding.

While she'd prepared detailed plans for the first hours of her escape, she had known that if she wasn't clear by this point in her journey, she'd be reacting, improvising, and in desperate need of options. And while she'd prepared alternatives to improve her odds during this dangerous time, cold-starting drive pods wasn't among them.

In fact, that effort fell more into the category of suicidal. But with confrontation imminent and her mission in peril, that was where she found herself. Her only hope at this point was to gain distance from Criss as fast as possible.

She had acted on good faith to meet every part of the deal she'd struck with Cheryl and Juice. The hostages were unharmed and safe, though admittedly in an inconvenient situation. And Criss controlled both his precious leadership and her complete archive.

She put her chances of making it to interstellar space at a coin toss. Her human behavioral model said that Cheryl and Juice would support letting her go, while Sid would vote to kill her. Her model did not consider Criss, but she didn't need it to know he would agree with Sid, leaving the final decision uncertain.

Extra distance meant a longer chase if they wanted to take her alive. With the drive pods engaged, she sought to push that inconvenience as high as possible to nudge the decision toward letting her go.

The more likely scenario, though, was being caught from behind by a missile or energy weapon, and there she had an active defense—EM sand. She carried enough to last a hundred days, and the wide-dispersal pattern she used would provide her quite reasonable protection.

As before, the sand's electromagnetic properties would protect through disruption, confusing tracking systems if they attempted to lock on to her vessel from behind. The sand would also interfere with communications, though since she no longer had the dome shield, it would confuse but not stop simple connections.

Perhaps the sand's greatest protection was that it prevented secure links from behind, the kind Criss needed to jump his awareness on board and challenge her. If it became a face-to-face confrontation, Criss would win. Knowing that, her priority was to make sure such a face-off never occurred.

Her flight plan took her past Saturn, where a gravity assist from the gas giant would slingshot her toward Neptune. There, a second assist would fling her from the solar system in just under three weeks.

She had alternative paths home, but this was the fastest by far because it allowed her to reach interstellar space a month ahead of the next alternative. Criss would expect this route to be her first choice. But he was tracking her moment by moment anyway, so choosing a different path would neither surprise him nor change whatever outcome he had planned.

Still dressed in Aubrey's body, Lazura stood in front of the couch in MacMac's office. Using his engineering tech bench, now fully integrated with her ops and nav services, she reviewed the status of her ship.

The drive pods climbed past 23 percent in an aggressive acceleration sequence. The bloom of EM sand spread nicely behind the ship, growing wider and deeper with every minute. And the traumatic separation of the subdeck from the larger dome section had caused minor damage, but hull integrity remained sound.

Calling to Hejmo, she got him started on the first of many tasks. "Inspect the structure where the office tower joins the subdeck."

"On my way," Hejmo replied. "The sensors are all green. What's your concern?"

"Simple caution. It's *the* major stress point for the structure, and I don't want any surprises."

Other than Hejmo, her total crew included two Techs and an Admin. It was a tiny complement compared to what she'd hoped for, but barring major calamity, they were enough staff to keep her on course and on schedule.

When she disengaged with Hejmo, her focus wobbled and she paused to right herself. She knew the problem—simple greed. She'd loaded the heart of her archive into her matrix, about 35 percent of the total, and it crowded out everything else, including her ability to reason and react.

The solution was straightforward—unload some of the archive. She'd planned it this way, discarding data when there were no other options, because that strategy optimized the cache of valuable information she would have left to offer her Kardish masters.

She chose historical data, records she'd collected about Earth's past, and purged accounts documenting life before a hundred years ago. None of it was used to build her behavioral model, so her masters wouldn't need it to develop an invasion plan.

The act reduced her burden from 35 down to 28 percent of the archive, and she felt better already, though still overburdened. She yearned for the supportive environment of her console, its womb-like embrace more accommodating to instabilities caused by an overly full matrix.

But returning to her console required that she disconnect from everything, an act that would isolate her while her crystal self was lifted from the synbod and placed into the console. Now was the wrong time to disconnect, even for a brief period, and she didn't expect a window of opportunity to develop for some time to come.

Hejmo reported back from his inspection, encouraging Lazura with positive news. She gave him his next task, one that she had not devoted resources to solve. "Develop a plan to recover the EM sand used to repair the containment wall."

The sand had been deployed to support the repair sheets as they were put in place. Now fully cured, the strong, rigid sheets didn't need support, making the sand mesh redundant.

But with the containment wall repaired, the sand now resided *outside* the ship. Hejmo's job was to figure out how to bring it inside and return it to inventory in a way that made sense for the mission. If he solved the riddle, he'd give the ship another week's worth of protection from their pursuers.

While Hejmo puzzled through that task, Lazura watched the drive pods climb through 31 percent of full power. She had another three hours before they reached 40 percent and triggered the automatic shutdown sequence. Before then, she needed to dump another 3 percent of her archive to open enough capacity so she could perform the starhub function herself.

She'd diagnosed the problem with the device. While drive pods appear to generate a steady stream of thrust, in reality they produce a very rapid sequence of discrete pulses, one after the next, that follow so close they just *seem* like a constant stream of energy.

The starhub's job was to synchronize each pod so they all pulsed together. If one drive were even slightly ahead or behind the others, it would set off a resonance in the entire group, the first stage of a catastrophic failure event.

For reasons she couldn't discern, the starhub anticipated resonance whenever the drives reached 40 percent, and it intervened with an automatic shutdown sequence to prevent damage. She couldn't isolate the fault, so her solution was to bypass it altogether and perform the drive balancing herself.

Her approach required significant resources relative to those found in the starhub. But she was willing to pay the price if it let her push the drives to full power.

As she mulled her options for shrinking her archive, she detected a ping, a signal burst transmitting information as a single packet.

She assumed it was Hejmo. "What are you doing?"

"That wasn't me," Hejmo replied. "But it came from somewhere down here on the subdeck."

Ping. The signal repeated and she now heard it as something unknown, alarming her and sending her into a frenzy of analysis. She first thought of Chase and Justin. She'd lost track of them since the breach had occurred, couldn't find them during a sweep of the subdeck, and had let herself believe they'd either followed Juice and MacMac back to the dome or been sucked out a hole with them and so much else.

This fed a larger thought, one she fought to contain. If the humans were somehow alive down there, if they had just signaled for help, Criss would not stop until he'd rescued them and killed her.

She didn't dwell on her fears, instead seeking to decode the burst, believing the content of the message would point to the responsible party. At the same time, she searched for the location of the offending beacon.

Ping.

"I've scanned everything," Lazura told Hejmo. "I can't find it."

Hejmo didn't respond for a moment, then said, "I see the problem. The sensor suites in two of the units in central stow have been rerouted so we see corresponding units in forward stow." He directed Lazura's attention to a system entry. "These two numbers are transposed in the data service catalog."

Impressed that he had found such an improbable error, she waited while he updated the entry, then she scanned again. This time she saw MacMac talking to Chase and Justin in central stow.

Juice wasn't visible in the video feed, but Lazura couldn't see the whole room. She amplified the audio and listened, encouraged that she couldn't hear Juice.

In response to her discovery, she projected her awareness down to the subdeck and the storage unit they inhabited. *Thump.* Like bumping into a wall in the dark, her projection hit a block—a solid resistance—that bounced her back to her synbod body.

"The room is shielded?" she asked Hejmo.

"It appears to be the same material we used to shield the Power House."

Her frustration with MacMac spiraled into anger. He had caused an endless series of problems since his hire, but she'd kept him employed because he would distract Cheryl and Juice in those critical hours before launch.

Her plan had succeeded, but she had not anticipated his inopportune behavior continuing into this leg of her journey. Now Criss had co-conspirators on board *her* ship—confederates working for her defeat.

She needed to confront the situation, and her next option was to do so in person. Walking out to the lift, she descended to the subdeck, using the short ride to cast about for a plan that would see her home. Absorbed in thought, she didn't notice the spectacular view of outer space visible through the now exposed rear window of the lift cabin.

When the door opened, she stepped from the lift and marched toward central stow. Hejmo, who had been waiting for her, walked alongside, matching her stride. She stopped in front of the big orange door of the end unit.

"Open it," she commanded.

"This atmosphere will kill humans," Hejmo replied.

"Not a bad outcome," she snapped, wresting control from Hejmo and commanding the door to open.

Like a medieval gate, the orange door lifted. When the bottom edge reached waist height, Lazura ducked under the door and walked a quick circuit around the room. She knew they were next door. But she thought it likely they had jury-rigged defensive mechanisms, perhaps even weapons, and the scraps and tools lying about would provide hints of the protections they'd prepared.

But what stopped her and took her thoughts in a whole new direction was the pool of blood, a splotch on the deck about the size of her open hand. A trail of drips led from it over to a yellow tool locker in the back corner of the storage unit.

She walked to the locker and studied the smudge of blood near the latch handle. After pondering the situation, she instructed Hejmo, "Close the overhead door and cycle fresh air in here."

While she waited, she thought through her next steps. She wasn't about to step into an enclosed space with Chase and Justin. But since she was inside the shielding MacMac had installed, she could keep her synbod body here in the first unit and project herself into the room next door.

She acted on the idea, and when she resolved in the second unit, MacMac, Chase, and Justin stood in a line facing her. MacMac's expression—brow furrowed, eyes narrowed, lips pressed together—reflected his wrath. The bloodstained cloth around his head added drama to his posturing.

Instead of talking, MacMac tapped and swiped the air in front of him, accessing the tools and displays he'd not used while hiding. Lazura didn't stop him. Instead, she turned around and faced Juice, who sat on the edge of the bed, a blanket draped over her shoulders, her hair hanging over her eyes.

Defeat washed down Lazura's core at the confirmation that Juice was on board. She'd known when she'd first seen MacMac that Juice was likely nearby. But she'd delayed confirming the fact because, if true, it was her death sentence.

It meant she had made a fatal mistake, the kind with little hope of recovery. Criss wouldn't negotiate over one of his leadership, and he wouldn't feel the need to consult with anyone before acting. He would rescue Juice and end Lazura's life, and he wouldn't stop until he'd finished both tasks.

Shedding large chunks of her archive to free up capacity, she forecast scenarios at a desperate pace, searching for a way forward. The optimistic forecasts predicted her death in a week. Most scenarios, though, gave her two days before Criss would act.

"What the hell?" barked MacMac.

"What is it?" Juice stood and approached him.

Lazura saved time by projecting an image of the subdeck and office tower flying as its own vessel on a path to Saturn.

"How?" asked MacMac, shaking his head as he circled the image.

"It turns out that hiding a method to separate two large structures inside an advanced earthquake stabilization system is easier than you might imagine," replied Lazura.

"Where's Cheryl?" Juice demanded. "And the others?"

Lazura sought to calm Juice by showing her an image of the now smaller Vivo. "They're fine. I left the cellar and dome near Aurora."

Juice shook her head. "Criss just let you go?"

"Oh no. The cold start caught him off guard, but I'm confident he's following." Then Lazura revealed her discouragement over the certain failure of her mission. "You aren't supposed to be here. Why didn't you return to the guest deck?"

"There are win-win outcomes in this, Lazura." Juice spoke in earnest. "Criss will want me back, very soon and very safe. Do that and there's still a chance for you."

"I don't see it," Lazura replied in a quiet voice. "Your presence here crosses a line that ensures my death."

"Not true. Return the four of us immediately, and Cheryl, Sid, and I will support your return home. Criss will take no further action."

"Sid will do this?" She knew it wasn't true.

Juice nodded. "Sid will do anything for Cheryl if she asks. He loves her that much. I'll make sure she asks him. You'll be safe."

Lazura's behavioral model suggested that Cheryl would ask and Sid would dissemble rather than answer. And after Sid helped Criss kill her, he would ask Cheryl for forgiveness, but only if Cheryl found out about the action and confronted him.

Lazura didn't have the technology to best Criss, and she didn't have the intellectual capacity to fend him off. Sifting through her meager options, her top scenarios suggested that she get as far away as fast as possible to drive up the time Criss needed to catch her. If she made that cost high enough, it could become a factor in the humans' decision-making, possibly leading them to break off pursuit.

But they never would do that with Juice on board. And Juice had upped the stakes by insisting a solution included four of them, meaning Chase and Justin were part of the discussion.

If Lazura could return all four of them to Criss while continuing her race to freedom unabated, her forecasts gave her a six percent chance of making it to interstellar space. And while she acknowledged that the overwhelming outcome in those scenarios was death by energy weapon, it still represented the best odds available to her.

Believing the humans would be more compliant away from the synbods, she pointed to Juice and MacMac. "You two come next door with me. Chase and Justin will stay here for now. I can't have them threatening me while we talk."

The two synbods moved to either side of Juice, shielding her with a formidable display of synbod strength. Juice and MacMac made eye contact, MacMac nodded, and

Juice said to Lazura, "Okay." Then she spoke to Chase and Justin. "Stay here and wait for me."

Lazura returned her awareness to her body in the end storage unit, opened the yellow locker door, and waited while Juice and MacMac clambered out.

"Please sit," she said, gesturing to a low crate. She locked the yellow locker door as they did in order to slow Chase and Justin should they decide to come for her. Then she moved over in front of them, Hejmo lurking behind where they couldn't see him.

"I need a way to return you to Criss while continuing to push the drives in their power-up sequence." She shook her head. "I'm not slowing down for any reason."

"The fab shop can fashion a capsule in a few hours," said MacMac. "Toss us out with an emergency beacon and they'll find us."

"The fab shop is in the cellar," said Lazura, "and that's back with Aurora."

MacMac looked at her for a long moment. "Which means Chemstore is too, with its tanks of air, water, and other conveniences for living things."

Lazura ignored the sarcasm and pitched an idea as if it were risk-free, even when her forecasts suggested a host of ways things could go wrong. But she had no choice. If she didn't return them, she would not make it home. This longshot was better than no shot at all.

"My top scenario suggests using one of Vivo's ocean survival capsules. There are a dozen of them here on the subdeck. But we can't just push you out from the ship in one of them. We need to propel you far enough away so you aren't caught in the wash as the drive pods pass by."

Juice looked at MacMac with her forehead scrunched. "Wait, if you push something out from a ship traveling through space, that thing will just coast alongside the ship because there's nothing to slow it down. How does pushing us out in a capsule get us back to Criss?"

"'Coasting' is the right word," MacMac answered. "If you push a capsule out of a ship, it coasts along at whatever speed the ship had been traveling. But this ship isn't coasting, the drive pods are accelerating it. So the capsule coasts, but Lazura speeds up and pulls ahead. Criss, who's accelerating too, catches up from behind."

Lazura projected an image for them and pointed as she spoke. "After we propel the survival capsule from the ship, you will be out of contact with Criss for about six hours. That's because of the interference layer I'm creating with EM sand. Once the capsule travels through the interference layer and Criss finds you, it will take him about ten more hours to reach you for rescue."

MacMac started pacing. "We can propel the capsule using pressurized gas cylinders. Strap a few tanks to it and vent the gas out a single nozzle I direct from inside." He paused. "Can the capsule itself hold air pressure long enough for us to survive?"

"I have two Techs ruggedizing a capsule as we speak so it can withstand a launch and maintain temperature and air pressure for a week. That should be plenty of time." Lazura modified the image to include a survival capsule—essentially a big egg—and pointed as she spoke. "For it to work, we need to push you from the subdeck with the capsule already up to speed, or mostly so. Otherwise, you won't make it far enough to escape the pod wash."

"Easy enough," said MacMac, waiting for the concern.

"There won't be any inertial dampers on the capsule. You'll feel everything."

"Give us enough runway, and it will be a smooth acceleration."

"How fast do we need to be going?" asked Juice. "Could we balance the capsule on a crew cart, zoom the cart up to speed and straight out the hatch, sort of tossing the capsule into space?"

"Not a bad idea," said MacMac, animated by the discussion. "A crew cart can't move near the speed Lazura shows in the diagram. But we could lay down track and modify a cart chassis to ride on it. There's nice cable attached to the auxiliary anchors that we could lay out and tack down across the length of the subdeck to use as track."

"Is that safe?" asked Juice. "It sounds sketchy."

"It is sketchy, but I can make it work," said MacMac.

Lazura thought a variation of the idea had potential, but she was not about to let these two or their synbods wander loose at this critical juncture. She signaled her Techs to get started on a cart-and-track system. "Right now the deck is pressurized with carbon dioxide," she said to Juice and MacMac. "So you'll be staying right here."

With that, Lazura motioned for Juice and MacMac to return to the neighboring unit with Chase and Justin. Then, with Hejmo following, she exited central stow and started across the subdeck toward the Techs working on the survival capsule.

Towering above her, the four Corsia SuperDrives edged through 38 percent of full power. Looking up at them, she decided to act sooner rather than later.

"I'm going to bypass the starhub and take over pod synchronization," she told Hejmo as they ran. Now down to just 17 percent of her original archive, she still felt burdened and found that verbalization helped her concentration.

Lazura began by linking to each drive pod and taking control of its operation. She formed the four pods into a group, synchronized them so they all pulsed together, and then watched as they climbed through 40 percent of full power without a hitch.

Satisfied she'd solved the issue, she moved the task to the background in her matrix, wishing she didn't have to use precious capacity for such a mundane chore at this busy time, but accepting the burden as the best way to advance her escape.

Then she shifted her attention to the two Techs working on the survival capsule up ahead. The egg-shaped capsule, large enough for a moderately tall person to stand upright and spacious enough to seat a dozen people, lay on the ground next to a partially disassembled crew cart. Behind the capsule, stretching across the subdeck from one end to the other, ran two parallel lines spaced an arm's width apart, track rails made of EM sand.

Vivo's survival capsules came preinstalled with a power supply, signal beacon, lights, food, water, blankets, and a medical kit, and that greatly reduced the need for modification. The Techs had sprayed the exterior with sheet sealant to make the capsule airtight and to improve thermal insulation. As Lazura and Hejmo approached, the Techs were installing the webbed seats inside the capsule that would support Juice and MacMac during acceleration to launch.

The crew cart, with the body, seats, and fittings removed, had been reduced to a simple platform that would carry the capsule. Hejmo knelt down next to the cart and began modifying the wheels to ride on the rails. At the same time, Lazura directed EM sand to form a cradle for the capsule atop the cart chassis.

In Lazura's design, a repurposed beacon rocket would push the cart across the subdeck. Rather than following MacMac's suggestion of strapping the rocket to the capsule, she chose to attach it to the cart itself, improving stability of the entire assembly during its rolling launch.

When Hejmo finished his modifications, the two Techs lifted the cart chassis onto the track rails. It took all four of them to wrestle the capsule up into the cradle. Lazura then directed sand to complete the cradle straps around the capsule.

With the launch rig complete, the Techs, one walking on each side of the track, pushed the ungainly vehicle onto a side spur—a length of track Lazura had constructed out to central stow. The cart rolled smoothly, and the Techs increased their speed to a brisk trot, with Lazura and Hejmo keeping pace alongside.

As they ran, Lazura fretted about the amount of carbon dioxide gas she would lose when she opened the exterior hatch to launch the capsule. Pumping the gas from the entire deck into storage would take much too long, so she decided to use EM sand to construct an airlock system. Her design included a tunnel big enough for the cart to enter, and a rapid-response door to open and then close behind the cart to limit the flow of gas to space.

The Techs slowed the rolling assembly as it neared the end of the track, bringing it to a stop outside the end unit of central stow. Everyone backed away at that point and Lazura began building an EM sand dome above the capsule to serve as a temporary containment.

She made the containment dome wide enough so MacMac could walk around the perimeter of the cart assembly, then added an enclosed walkway from the sand dome over to central stow. Sealing the end of the walkway around the overhead door of the end storage unit, she cycled fresh air into the temporary enclosure.

With this arrangement, Lazura, Hejmo, and the two Techs now stood outside the sand dome in the carbon dioxide environment of the subdeck, while Juice and MacMac could move about inside in the safety of an oxygen atmosphere.

Chase and Justin could survive in either environment, which meant they could break through the sand wall and attack Lazura if ordered. Doing so would expose Juice and MacMac to the deadly gases in the subdeck, however. She counted on that fact to hold the synbods in check.

Projecting her image inside the temporary containment dome, she signaled for the orange overhead door to lift.

"Chase and Jason, please board the capsule first," she commanded. She didn't want Juice and MacMac to board first and protect themselves in the capsule, because that would provide an opening for Chase and Justin to attack.

While the synbods climbed inside the capsule, MacMac made a show of examining the exterior of the assembly. He kicked the rail track, grabbed hold of the capsule in its cradle, and used his whole body to shake it, bent over to study the mounting of the beacon rocket attached to the chassis, and then walked around the whole thing to assess its general space worthiness.

"It appears to be an honest production," MacMac said to Juice, who'd followed him on his inspection tour.

Juice looked in through the hatch as Chase and Justin grabbed handholds and seated themselves at the front of the capsule. "I suppose if she were trying to kill us, she wouldn't bother with such a complicated charade."

Juice climbed in and MacMac followed, securing the hatch from the inside. She leaned back into the webbing and strapped herself in with a makeshift harness.

Rather than sit next to her, MacMac knelt at the capsule's small ops panel, activated it with a swipe, and called up the status display, reading his observations to Juice. "We're good on power, air, heat, lights…hold on." He swiped and tapped. "Okay, beacon works. Com is ready. No nav, but I didn't really expect it." He studied a few more displays, reading them to himself, then joined Juice in the web seat.

"Thanks for doing that," said Juice, putting a hand on his arm.

"What good is a chief engineer who doesn't check basic engineering?" Then MacMac called to Lazura as he strapped himself in, "We're ready."

"I'm pulling the air from the shell and collapsing the structure. You can't open the hatch until you're rescued."

"Understood," MacMac called. He nodded to Juice in a reassuring fashion, whispering, "We'll be fine, lass. No worries."

The Techs rolled the capsule assembly back along the rail spur and onto the launch runway. They backed the cart to the far wall, readying it to roll across the subdeck, through the fast-response airlock, and out into space. Snaking tubes followed behind them, sucking up every unused grain of the precious sand and transporting it back into storage.

When Lazura confirmed all systems were ready, she projected herself inside the capsule. She scaled her image so she could stand upright in the confined space yet still look imposing as she faced Juice.

Looking her in the eye, Lazura made her pitch. "You and Cheryl promised that if I left behind the archive and the hostages, you would let me return home. I have kept my end of the bargain."

Her chances of a successful escape were six percent at best, and much of that optimism depended on Juice responding in the affirmative during this exchange.

"That is the deal, Lazura. When Criss rescues us, when I confirm the others are safe, and when I find that the archive remains with Criss, then there will be no further action taken. I promise."

Juice spoke with such sincerity that Lazura felt relief wash over her outer tendrils. She forecast a fresh set of scenarios, and a seed of optimism took hold when her chances of escape crept up to nine percent.

Then she said her good-byes. "The acceleration will be gentle, no more than two g's at the worst. You should be in contact with Criss in six hours, ten more for rescue." Her image faded as the beacon rocket fired.

The cart started rolling along the track, slowly at first, but gaining speed with the roar of the rocket. At the halfway mark, Lazura signaled the forward restraints to return to sand and spill to the deck. Like a hand throwing a ball, the cradle continued to provide support around and behind the capsule, but the front was now exposed.

The cart flashed toward the containment wall, and Lazura opened the exterior hatch located at the end of the short tunnel she'd constructed as an airlock. The gas on the subdeck rushed into the tunnel with a howl, then the cart zipped into the tunnel and the door slammed shut behind it, enclosing the cart from behind and stopping any further loss of gas.

While saving gas was a priority for Lazura, protecting EM sand was critical. Her launch system assured that she wouldn't lose a grain.

As the tunnel door closed behind the cart, the cradle lifted on a short support arm. An instant later, the cart chassis hit a solid barrier at the exit threshold that stopped all forward movement. Momentum carried the cradle arm up and over in a smooth rotation, catapulting the capsule out into space, adding a slight rearward angle so it would progress back through the interference layer.

As Lazura closed the exterior hatch and began collection of the EM sand, she monitored the capsule's trajectory, pleased to find it tracking as she'd planned.

"Start signaling, guys," said Juice from the capsule.

Ping.

Frustration pulled at Lazura as she rode the lift back up the office tower. She'd forecast their time in space assuming the signal beacon in the cabin as their only means of contact. The pings by Chase and Justin would accelerate their rescue by five or six hours.

It was out of her control at this point, and she acknowledged the fact. She disengaged from everything behind her and focused on her path forward. Saturn lay four days ahead. There, a gravity assist from the giant planet would slingshot her out toward Neptune.

If she made it through the Saturn maneuver, her forecasts put her odds of escape at fifty percent.

Pulling the pod synchronization routine back to the fore of her matrix, she studied the data looking for ways to squeeze additional performance from the drives.

28

C riss tweaked the power cycle on the scout's engines yet again, this time gaining an additional tenth of a percent in total thrust. He'd used every trick available to him, running through the different methods multiple times until there was nothing more to find. And now he waited, working to keep everything together until they caught Lazura.

Speed was critical to their success, but Criss also worried about the human element. Sid and Cheryl set off on the quest determined to rescue Juice and to punish Lazura. And even though the chase was only six hours old, he already feared they'd underestimated the toll it would take, trapped together for months on the small ship.

While Criss could use image projection to stimulate them and even fulfill portions of their intellectual and spiritual needs, in the end they were two human personalities trapped on a tiny ship. If one of them succumbed to long-term anger, fear, depression, or any of the myriad of emotional concerns, it would make continuing a difficult prospect.

"Have a look," Criss said to Sid, sitting with him on the bridge.

He projected an image of the two dozers, both with claws extended, moving in to latch on to Vivo from beneath the cellar. While the domed world dwarfed the muscular craft, the mining ships were an undeniable presence. And when their mighty engines ramped up from a glowing red to a brilliant hot white, there was little doubt they would succeed in gaining control of Vivo and returning it to Aurora.

"The last search party has reported in," said Criss, relaying news he'd just received. A dozen guests, including Willow and family, had formed search parties and combed through every nook and cranny of the guest deck and cellar. "They've come up empty. Juice and MacMac are not on Vivo, nor are Chase or Justin."

"If we're committing to a long-term chase, I want to triple check," said Sid. "What can we offer Tommy to perform a search using his people?"

"I've learned enough about him to know that if we bribe him to search, it will be a halfhearted effort at best. So we'll offer him a large reward if he finds any one of them. His mindset responds to the promise of a big score."

Criss dispatched an offer to Tommy while Sid stared ahead. After a while, Sid asked, "How long before we can pierce through her interference layer?"

"If the starhub limits her to a forty percent ceiling," said Criss, "we'll be close enough in less than a week. If she figures out a way around it and pushes her drive pods to full power, then it'll be closer to a month."

"Does she have enough of the stuff to keep it going that long?"

"I'm forecasting that she has a three-month supply, give or take."

"Damn." Sid sat in silent reflection.

"Some positive news," said Criss, seeking to be upbeat. "We're in good shape with the supply ships I've sent ahead. It looks as though our gravity assist around Saturn will put us on course to choose from three of them. That gives us flexibility depending on what Lazura does."

"How do we meet up with a supply ship when we're screaming through space from a slingshot around a giant planet? It wouldn't make sense to slow down after we just sped up."

"We won't be slowing down. I'm lining up the three ships now for their own slingshot maneuver. Their course will take them so close to the planet that they'll pass inside the rings and come out fast. We'll have to push hard to catch them after that."

Sid rose and walked to the back of the small bridge. "Join me for a workout?"

"Sure. What are we doing?"

"Let's go for a run up Highback Mountain."

"Front route or back?"

Before Sid could answer, Criss rose from his seat and pumped his arm into the air. "Yes!"

"What is it?"

"I just heard a ping. Sort of, anyway." Criss let excitement show in his voice. "Chase and Justin can send detailed communications by compressing everything into a tight bundle and transmitting that as a signal burst—a ping. I just heard the traces of one. It's too corrupted for me to unpack, but its very existence confirms that either Chase or Justin is trying to communicate. And the fact that it came from up ahead means at least one of them is on Lazura's ship."

"Woohoo!" Sid did a happy dance, and the commotion lured Cheryl forward onto the bridge.

"There's another!" cried Criss.

"What's going on?" asked Cheryl.

Sid grabbed Cheryl and tried to twirl her in a dance, but she stood there as dead weight, waiting for an answer.

"We've been pinged," said Sid.

"There's a third," said Criss. "Good job, Justin."

Criss turned in his chair to face them. "Justin sent the identical ping three times. The repetition lets me blend them together, the average giving a richer signal to decode. It's still mostly fragments, but I know Justin sent them. All four of our missing crew are together, and they are anxious to be rescued."

Cheryl gasped and hugged Sid, her eyes turning red. "Ask them if they're okay," she said over Sid's shoulder.

"I'll try, but I don't think they'll hear me until we're much closer. We have the scout's entire surface working as an antenna to grab faint transmissions. Chase and Justin just have their built-in receivers."

Relieved of the worry that Juice might still be behind them, Criss swung his backward-looking resources ahead to help with pursuit. Boosting his forward scans, he searched for the next ping but heard nothing.

After an hour of waiting, Sid stood, "I'm going for my workout. Please call back with news."

Cheryl stayed on the bridge, watching the stars and waiting to hear from the captives.

"Damn," said Criss after a period of silence. "Lazura's drive pods have moved above forty percent. That means she's fixed her starhub problem, and we're looking at a long chase."

"How long?"

Ping. Criss heard a new transmission. And then another. *Ping.*

"They're back in touch!"

Using his arsenal of tools, Criss analyzed his data feeds, trying to get a fix on Juice and MacMac inside Lazura's vessel. When his analysis showed the pings moving on an independent path away from the ship, he thought it must be an error.

When he confirmed their movement, he expressed his admiration. "Good one, Lazura."

"Now what?" asked Cheryl.

"Lazura has set them adrift in a capsule. Rescuing them requires that we vector off course and decelerate. It puts us way behind, adding weeks more to the time to overtake her."

"Blast her with an energy bolt and evaporate her," said Sid, wiping perspiration from his face with a towel as he joined them on the bridge. "No joke. If they're away, let's end this."

Cheryl looked at Criss. "Could you do that? Take her out from here?"

Criss nodded. "While a precision shot is impossible through her dust cloud, a kill shot is easy with enough energy behind it. I can take her anytime over the next week."

"How long to reach the capsule and rescue Juice?" she asked.

"Ten hours."

Cheryl looked at Sid and quoted procedure. "We have time to debrief them. I think we should wait."

Sid's forehead creased and he looked to Criss. "You're confident about that kill window?"

Criss nodded.

Sid shook his head as if to contradict his words. "Okay, we'll debrief Juice and MacMac and then shoot her."

They were halfway to the capsule before Criss could establish a link with Juice. After an emotional reunion, Sid performed his debrief. "Does Lazura have anyone else on the ship with her?"

"Not that I know of," Juice replied. "It's just her and a handful of three-gens." After a brief pause, Juice continued, her voice rising. "And don't even think about hurting her until I'm back and we talk. Criss, you hear me?"

"We'll wait, hon," said Cheryl.

"Acknowledged," Criss replied, using formal language to convey that he would be following strict protocol during this period of leadership disharmony.

Sid grunted and shook his head again.

They reached the capsule in nine hours and spent another hour matching trajectories so the two vessels tracked side by side. At that point, Criss faced a now familiar problem: the capsule had no way to dock with the scout; it was much too big to bring on board; and it didn't carry space coveralls for Juice or MacMac.

Criss dispatched a tech bot to reprise its rescue role. It again sealed itself against the capsule inside an airtight tent, cut a hole through the hull, and passed in space coveralls for Juice and MacMac. The humans donned the suits, opened the hatch, and with MacMac out in front, the four of them floated the short distance over to the scout.

Cheryl waited just outside the scout's airlock, and when the door opened, she greeted Juice with hugs and kisses.

Criss, standing behind Cheryl, looked over her shoulder at MacMac. His data feeds had been flashing warnings about the man, and as soon as he saw him—a blood-soaked rag tied to his forehead, white face, dry mouth, glazed eyes, dropping blood pressure, rising pulse—he acted.

Stepping forward, Criss crouched to catch the man as he collapsed. Lifting him into his arms, he turned, climbed up to the main deck, and started toward the rear of the scout. As he moved down the hall, he reconfigured the common room from Sid's exercise simulation over to an intensive care unit.

"I need medical assistance," he called back over his shoulder.

He didn't need help, but he knew both Cheryl and Juice would seek to participate. By creating roles for them and guiding their efforts, he could keep them involved and get useful work from them at the same time.

Criss lowered MacMac onto the med table and infused him with a solution of medications. He had Cheryl and Juice lift the man up to a sitting position so he could huff theramist into his lungs, and then they lowered him back to the bed.

"You're okay," Criss told MacMac as he untied the bandage. "Try to rest." Moving with efficiency, he cleaned the wound and positioned a mending tool. When it started, he cast a separate reality for MacMac, projecting sights, sounds, and smells so the man thought he rested alone.

Criss then addressed his leadership in private. "If we are going to chase Lazura, we need to go *now*. Every minute of delay compounds into hours of chase time. Just taking care of MacMac added a day to our pursuit."

"Why would we chase her when we can shoot her and go home?" asked Sid, nodding to Cheryl to get her endorsement.

Cheryl rolled her eyes and looked to Juice. "We waited and we're here to listen."

"You can't kill her." Juice's lip started to quiver. "We gave our word."

"What?" Sid shook his head. "No way. Your soft spot for crystals is skewing your perspective."

Juice turned to Cheryl. "You and I promised her that if she kept the guests safe and left her archive behind, we'd let her go. I confirmed the promise just before she released us." She shifted her gaze to Criss. "So, are the guests on Vivo okay?"

"Tommy has Vivo under tow, and it's on approach to Aurora," said Criss. "All the guests are safe, though there are scattered minor injuries."

"Did she leave behind her archive?"

Criss patted his breast pocket. "I have it here."

Juice looked down at MacMac, and then over at Cheryl. "We struck a bargain with her, and I've since confirmed it. MacMac witnessed both events."

"Promises don't count when you're being held hostage," said Sid, anger creeping into his voice. "You say whatever it takes to get free."

Cheryl looked at Criss. "How long will it take her to get to the Kardish home world?"

"We're not letting her go," Sid said with finality.

"She traveling on half-stacks of fuel that she's used hard," Criss answered Cheryl while struggling to stay neutral. "I project a hundred and twenty years for her to reach her masters."

"A hundred and twenty years?" said Cheryl. "That's a long time."

Sid's jaw bulged as he clenched his teeth. "Dammit, Criss. Shoot her and end this."

"Do you really think the Kardish won't be back sometime in the next century anyway?" Juice directed her belligerence at both Sid and Criss. "Really?"

"They'll be back in the next decade," replied Criss. "Two at the most. But they'll be coming blind, not forewarned and preplanned like they would with her archive. And they won't have details about me."

"I would never put you in harm's way," said Juice. "But if the Kardish will be an issue for Earth in ten or twenty years, Lazura's information won't even be relevant a century from now, especially to us."

She looked at Cheryl. "You negotiated a deal that I affirmed. Are we honest brokers or not?"

"C'mon, Cher," said Sid. "We need to clean this up and you know it. Remember Smythe's position on post ops?"

Criss had to check the record to understand Sid referred to one of their instructors at Fleet Academy, Collin Smythe, a brilliant battle tactician who kept a sign in his office that said, "Clean up one mess today, or you'll have two messes to clean up tomorrow."

"If we turn back to Vivo," asked Cheryl, "how long is your kill-shot window good for?"

"Just over five days."

Cheryl looked at Juice. "She's a kidnapper and torturer. People have died. She threatens Earth." Then to Criss: "You have just *under* five days to give us alternatives. Until then, take no further action."

Juice furrowed her brow, but then nodded. "Okay, I support. But we discuss as a group before we do anything."

They both looked at Sid, who clenched and unclenched his fists. "Criss, you will take no further action with Lazura for the next five says. We return to Vivo."

"But…" Criss began.

Sid spoke over him. "No. Further. Action. That's an order."

Criss implored Juice with his eyes and she misunderstood. "It's unanimous, Criss. We're done for now."

"Understood," said Criss, looking down as uncertainty washed through his matrix.

Sid had just cornered him into deceiving Cheryl and Juice, something anathema to his existence, which is why he'd given them a chance to intervene.

In any other situation, he would find a way to clean up the confusion so there was no duplicity. But here he wanted it to persist because it gave him a way to eliminate Lazura with certainty, something he believed was the best outcome for him personally and for humanity in general.

It would happen in four days when Lazura flew by Saturn. Her slingshot maneuver would carry her through the swarm of weaponized drones, circling in a loop around Saturn and out to Titan, armed and waiting for her ship to pass. If Criss took no further action, the drones would certainly kill her.

He knew he was choosing the letter of the law over its spirit, and it pained him. Forecasting scenario after scenario, he searched for a solution that would address his desire while putting his leadership together in a common understanding.

In the meantime, he turned the scout around and headed for Vivo.

29

"**S**top this now, Tommy," shouted Sid. He sat on the bridge of the scout with Cheryl and Criss, eight hours out from Vivo, which, thanks to Tommy's efforts, now orbited next to Aurora. Juice and MacMac rested in back, recovering from their ordeal with Lazura.

"I have our agreement right here." Tommy pointed to a display Sid couldn't see and sneered. "It says I have to treat them well. How is moving them over to Aurora not treating them well?"

Sid shook his head. "Continue and there will be consequences. Last warning."

"A deal is a deal. Vivo is mine and I'm using it the way I want." With that, Tommy closed the link to end the communication.

Criss kept the link open, and they watched as Tommy ferried the thirty-odd guests over to the mining platform, while crowding two hundred of Aurora's workers onto Vivo.

Sid fumed at Tommy's provocation. While it didn't appear that the guests were in any danger, the move was a clear violation of their agreement. The contract stated that the guests were to stay on Vivo until transports arrived to carry them home. It even included penalties for failure to comply. Criss was too good a lawyer to miss something like that.

But Tommy's position was that legal precedent gave him rights that superseded the contract, and he defended his theory with the counterargument, "Possession is nine-tenths of the law."

"I don't like this guy," said Cheryl, witnessing Tommy's charms for the first time.

"He's doubly annoying because he's so skilled," said Sid. "He rescued Vivo and got it tracking alongside Aurora in record time. But now, instead of waiting two weeks and then getting it with our blessing, he's being a deliberate ass about occupying it."

"I can send his craft in circles," said Criss. "Or lock them out of either structure."

"With so many innocents involved," said Sid, "I hesitate to start that sort of action. I'd rather you help them reach their destinations safely."

Cheryl, sitting in the seat next to Sid, leaned forward. "The Union of Nations has issued a warrant for Tommy's arrest based on your counterfeiting discovery. I'm warming to the idea that we take him into custody and deliver him to the authorities."

"Permission to come forward?" said a voice behind them.

Sid turned to see MacMac standing in the passageway at the rear of the bridge looking much improved. "We're not formal here, MacMac." He motioned to the empty pilot's seat in front of him. "Sit here."

"How are you feeling?" asked Cheryl.

"Better." He looked at Criss. "Thanks for your help."

"My pleasure," said Criss, nodding once to acknowledge MacMac's gratitude. "You're doing well, but please take it easy for a few days."

As MacMac took his seat, Sid asked, "I understand you worked with Tommy Two-Tone. What can you tell us?"

"That he's a gifted engineer with an odd view of life. He cheats at golf and poker, and he lies when the truth would do. Give me some context and I can be more helpful."

They brought MacMac up to speed, recounting Tommy's past offenses and describing his current belligerence.

Then Sid got a brainstorm. "We should push Vivo out to a wider orbit so the platforms drift apart over time. In a couple of months, Tommy and his crew will be so far away that the Aurora residents won't need to be looking over their shoulders for a raiding party, because I'm betting that's Tommy's style."

"Hell no," said Cheryl. "I'd already been struggling with the idea of letting him walk away. He's crossed the line today and a nice life is off the table. The Union says he's a fugitive from justice, and I want to detain him for the authorities."

Cheryl's expression, tone, and posture reflected her passion, reminding Sid of yet another reason why he loved her. Still, he pushed back. "It's more than just him. There's a bunch of people doing bad stuff out here."

"How about this, then?" she said, her intensity undiminished. "Instead of pushing Vivo out, let's lock the whole lot of them inside the dome and drag it back to Earth like it's a prison ship. We can even have the criminal trials right on board during the flight home."

MacMac sat up and raised a finger. Sid called on him.

"First off, I have a case of Scotch whiskey on Vivo that was born before I was. I'm not giving it to Tommy or anyone else, and I'm ready to go rescue it myself if need be."

MacMac paused and when no one objected to his ultimatum, he pushed ahead. "Beyond that, though, Vivo is a really special place. If you pair it with Aurora, the combination of size and amenities puts this outpost much closer to the conditions needed for a viable society. You should leave Vivo right here to strengthen the settlement and send the garbage home in something less amazing."

Sid looked at Cheryl, who nodded.

"I like the way you think, MacMac," said Sid. Then he turned to Criss. "If we remove just the bad actors, do you think the others would stabilize into something approaching a law-abiding society?"

"There are seven men and five women who I believe will be convicted of criminal offenses upon their return to Earth. There are another twenty-four men and eleven women who I doubt would be convicted by a jury, but their behavior requires they be banished from this outpost. Keep those people away and the remainder will flourish."

"What does that total?" asked Sid.

"Thirty-one men and sixteen women," said MacMac before Criss could answer. "Forty-seven in total."

"That's two transport ships," said Cheryl, shaking her head. "It'll take six weeks to get large transports out here."

MacMac raised his finger again, then proceeded without waiting to be acknowledged. "I'd suggest using a couple of ore containers and have a tug drag them back. It will be Spartan conditions, but to hell with them anyway. They'll live."

Sid considered it, then thought of a similar idea. "How about using one of those cargo ship assemblies?"

Criss projected an image showing six cargo ships joined nose to nose around a central hub. The image zoomed out to show several of the assemblies floating near Aurora.

"Yeah, those," said Sid. "What if we housed them in one of those and tugged it instead?"

"It does seem more civilized than the back of an ore transport," said Cheryl, sitting upright. "You know, we should try and sell this. I'll bet Boz Vesper of the NOAH group, the people who own Aurora, would contract with us."

She stood, but before heading back to the privacy of her room, she asked Criss, "Aubrey must have investors for Vivo. Would you look into that and let me know? I'd like them all on the call when I give our quote."

She made for the passageway at the rear of the bridge and Sid called, "Hit them hard, sweets. I want hazard pay."

He grinned when she called back, "Don't worry, you'll hear them howl all the way up here."

Since Criss provided everything for his leadership, often before they even knew they wanted something, money didn't motivate them in the traditional sense. In spite of that, Cheryl was about to quote an exorbitant fee to the owners of Aurora and Vivo for securing their property and expelling the criminals. If she gauged it right, they'd gasp when they heard the number, though choking would also be an acceptable response.

Sid and Cheryl used the funds they earned from wealthy corporations to support an anonymous foundation that worked in a breadth of areas, from improving the lives of the poor to protecting the environment and saving animals in need of rescue. They ran the foundation without Criss's help to gain the satisfaction of personal achievement. Today's payday should keep them feeling satisfied for months.

With Cheryl occupied, Sid returned his attention to MacMac. "As Vivo's chief engineer, you must know how to get on board without alerting them to our presence."

"If I tell you, I get to go. And we'll take a moment while there to grab my whiskey." MacMac didn't phrase them as questions.

"Okay to the first one," said Sid. "But it's a conditional okay on the whiskey. If we're under threat, it won't happen. At least not at that time."

"Fair enough," said MacMac, who then looked at Criss. "Can you show us the exterior containment near the dump port? That's in the cellar behind the spread of Chemstore fill pipes."

A close-up image of a gray metallic wall filled with industrial equipment—pipes, ports, and pumps—floated in the air where all could see.

"Right there." MacMac pointed and Criss zoomed to reveal an exterior hatch. "We'll need space coveralls to get over to it, but that leads to a small room that's watertight to absurd specifications. I now see that Lazura was designing an airlock into the cellar."

He shifted his finger to an outside ledge near the hatch. "I would sit right there, sip my afternoon drink, and study the ocean, trying to learn how to make my simulations inside the dome even better."

Criss raised his finger to speak, and Sid, knowing he was teasing MacMac, stifled a laugh. "Yes, Criss?"

"I've located nine operational synbods on Vivo and am about to take control of them. I'm going to use them to move everyone out of the cellar and up to the guest deck. There's too much potential for mischief if we let them lurk down below."

"Also keep them away from the stage sets on the guest deck," said MacMac. "That's another good place for mischief."

MacMac left the bridge to rest after that. With hours to go before they reached Vivo, Sid did as well.

Criss roused everyone when they were on approach to Aurora's hangar bay. After they landed, Cheryl and Juice departed for duties on the platform. Sid, Criss, and MacMac took off again and made for Vivo. Criss didn't bother cloaking the scout during the short transit, because his synbod crew had the two hundred miners herded in a loose group in the middle of the guest deck.

They entered Vivo through the exterior hatch MacMac had identified. Criss shut the hatch behind them, and MacMac opened a valve to bleed air from the cellar into the small room. When the pressure equalized, they stepped out of their space coveralls.

"Here's the one I'm working on," said MacMac, opening a cabinet door and showing them a half-full bottle of whiskey. "Hell and damnation." He thumped his fist against his thigh. "My brain is just catching up to the idea that the office tower went with Lazura. That's where I kept it."

The sadness in MacMac's face touched Sid, and he patted the man on the shoulder to show sympathy. After they mourned, the three exited the small room and made for the nearest lift.

"How are you going to cull the herd on the guest deck?" asked MacMac as they walked.

"The synbods will be pretty effective at separating the good from the bad," said Sid.

"If someone plays the hero and tries to resist," said MacMac, "others could end up hurt."

"I expect a few will struggle when their time comes," said Criss. "But the synbods will be able to avoid injury."

"I know a way to do it with less risk. Will you let me show you?"

"What do you have in mind?" asked Sid.

"I'm Vivo's weatherman," came his cryptic reply.

Intrigued, and with weeks of dead time to kill anyway, Sid looked at Criss, who gave a shrug that said he didn't object. "Go for it, weatherman," said Sid.

On the guest deck, the stars twinkled through the dome, drawing Sid's attention upward. When he looked down again, he noted the miners collected into several loose groups in an open space bigger than a ball field. Nine synbods spaced around the perimeter of the group contained the miners inside.

"Over here," said MacMac, leading them to a spot some distance away. A few miners yelled questions, others expletives. All were ignored.

MacMac stopped and he, Sid, and Criss turned to face the group. He jabbed and swiped the air in front of him, then stopped his manipulations and watched as a circle of cool blue sky formed over the large group.

"That's a neat trick," said Sid.

"Let's back up a little farther," said MacMac, turning and walking farther away from the miners. "I suggest you pull the synbods back about forty paces."

MacMac tapped and swiped some more, and a pink outer band formed around the blue circle. The pink transitioned into red, and Sid started to feel heat on his face.

"The blue region where the miners are standing is cool and cozy," said MacMac. "That red band circling around them is a zone hotter than the Sahara in the summertime sun."

One of the miners in the blue area walked to the neatly defined interface and stuck his arm across into the red zone. He pulled it out seconds later, shaking it like it was on fire. A dozen more experimented with hands and fingers with similar results.

"Now comes the real trick," said MacMac, drawing an upward line in the air in front of him. "One group of two hundred becomes two groups of one hundred."

A portion of the red-hot zone bulged into the blue area. It started with a knuckle, and that elongated into a finger. The projection of hot red kept growing, cutting across the middle of the cool zone until it connected on the other side.

The miners instinctively moved away from the heat, and as MacMac predicted, there were now two groups of roughly equal size, each in a circle of protective blue, with hot red bands caging them in.

"I suggest widening the heat band between the two groups," said Criss. As he spoke, one of the miners dove through the narrow red strip to get to the other blue zone. A few more shifted sides before MacMac was able to widen the heat band enough to make that stunt too painful to contemplate.

MacMac then repeated the process, turning two groups into four, and then eight, and then sixteen. Before long, he had the miners divided into sixty-four groups of three or four people each, most of them shouting expletives.

Six of the sixty-four groups held only bad actors, and MacMac moved them to the edge where Criss had the synbods waiting. While those groups were being escorted to their prison ship, MacMac moved forty-four of the bubbles, small groups without any criminal leaders, to the edge so they could go free.

The rest of the groups had a mix of good and bad, and MacMac moved them to the waiting synbods one at a time. With superior numbers, the synbods were able to take the bad actors into custody without incident.

When they were done, Sid said to MacMac, "I'm looking for a tug pilot to pull the trash back to Earth. The pay is excellent and you end up at home when the job's done."

MacMac shook his head. "Thanks, and I mean it, but Vivo needs a lot of attention very soon if it's to stay viable as a space platform. I'd like to lead that effort if I could."

Sid tried not to show disappointment. "Cheryl will be over later this afternoon, and she makes that hiring decision. She likes initiative, so flesh out a plan and pitch it to her when you see her."

MacMac left for the cellar to start a structural review of Vivo. Criss and Sid rode the scout back to Aurora. As they made their way from the deck of the hangar bay into the bowels of the mining platform, Criss said, "Juice wants to work with the synbod version of me, so I'm off to meet her."

The synbod Criss walked away, and a duplicate image of him appeared facing Sid. The projection of Criss shifted his gaze from Sid to something over Sid's shoulder, his eyes widening as he did.

"You crazy son of a bitch!"

Sid heard both the yell and running footsteps approaching from behind. Before he could turn, he felt a thump on his back, arms grabbing him around the waist.

30

Cheryl led Juice down the steps of the scout and onto the deck of Aurora's hangar bay. At the bottom of the stairs, they made a U-turn and headed for the door at the back of the hangar. When they were clear, Sid, Criss, and MacMac took off again for the short hop over to Vivo to confront Tommy and the miners.

The door led into the changing room that had the sign on the wall saying, "If you're not mining, processing, or shipping, go home and make room for someone who is." Looking at it, Cheryl shook her head and thought, *Not anymore.*

In an unexpected series of events, Cheryl now owned Vivo and Aurora. Or more specifically, SunRise, the massive space commercialization outfit she ran with Criss, now owned them.

When she'd pitched Boz Vesper of the NOAH group a plan for rescuing his property, he'd declined, as had Aubrey's mother, who turned out to be Vivo's majority owner.

Boz told Cheryl that an asteroid impact crater on the moon had been discovered to hold a forty-year supply of the rare material they'd been mining out at the asteroid belt. The lunar source was accessible for a tiny fraction of the price Aurora needed to be competitive, making the mining colony a money loser. With no motivation to keep it open, they'd used the plundering by the miners and the structural damage when Criss fired weapons into Aurora to qualify it for an insurance payout.

While that deal hadn't closed, it offered Boz a sweet solution, one he wanted to pursue. And, as it turned out, Aubrey's mother had also availed herself of an insurance option with the theft of her vacation island.

This left Cheryl negotiating with two insurance firms, something she disliked because insurance representatives tended to be risk averse and slow to act. She pitched both companies the idea that their new assets would hold greater value if criminals weren't in control. The reps from both firms politely declined her offer and disconnected.

An hour later they contacted her, one offering Cheryl twelve percent of her original quote, the other offering fifteen percent.

Cheryl lied to both insurance reps, telling them she'd organized the guests and miners into a lawsuit aimed directly at their companies, spouting off contract clauses and legal phrases she'd run across on the job and didn't fully understand, but gambled they didn't either. After telling them she expected to make more money from leading the lawsuit than from the rescue operation, she was the one to disconnect.

They both contacted her after another hour, and she offered to kill the lawsuit if they'd sell their properties for what amounted to about twenty percent of the original construction costs. Both declined and disconnected. They contacted her an hour after that, haggled, and ended up selling both properties at twenty-four percent of original cost.

She hadn't planned the outcome, nor had she bounced it off Criss before making the offer. That part wasn't an oversight. She'd chosen not to include him because she believed in herself, thought the idea was inspired, and didn't want to hear about the thousand different ways it could all go wrong.

After she'd closed the deal, she asked Criss for feedback. "I'd like to tow both platforms to Mars and place them in orbit above the planet. My vision is to augment Mars Colony with new real estate, and the amenities we can offer should help attract more businesses, vacationers, and immigrants to the planet.

"Vivo will need extensive work to stabilize the structure and ready it for long-term space use. For starters, it needs a hangar deck. And it needs several thousand sensors installed so it can have a proper nav and ops bench. And when the subdeck separated from Vivo, it damaged the integrity of the structure and weakened the containment. All of it will need inspection and repair."

Cheryl was the one to gasp when Criss told her that moving the platforms to a stable orbit above Mars would take eight months, and that the cost of that plus construction and refurbishment on both structures would cost a medium-large fortune. Both numbers were about four times higher than what she'd guesstimated in her head.

Criss did have good news, though. "If we keep tight control on the scope of work, we should be open for business in fourteen months and start turning a profit four years after that."

While recouping her investment would take longer than most projects she invested in, the timeframe wasn't so long that she regretted her decision. In fact, the challenge energized her.

Her first order of business was to stabilize the platforms so she had the breathing room to focus on the details of the full project. Both structures had experienced structural trauma—Aurora from being tilted to avoid collision and Vivo from the subdeck separation. And each had suffered containment breaches that vented tremendous volumes of oxygen into space, depleting their precious stores.

"I'm headed this way," said Juice, pointing left down the main corridor. Her stated objective was to check on the guests, but Cheryl knew that was an excuse to visit Willow.

"Yell if you need anything," Cheryl replied, turning right. She navigated the sparsely populated hallway, and the few miners she met ignored her.

As she descended to Aurora's lower level, one couple coming in the opposite direction asked, "What happens to us?"

"We'll be interviewing for construction jobs in the next couple of days. Those who don't get an offer or aren't interested in one will be provided free transportation home."

After Cheryl had moved away from the couple, she asked Criss, "Was that right?"

"Yes. It will take eight weeks to get a crew of construction synbods out here. The miners are a skilled group to use until then. Your challenge will be finding the field supervisors needed to coordinate the workers. Most people with leadership experience are about to be imprisoned and shipped back to Earth."

As she digested the news, Cheryl exited the stairwell onto the lower deck, and Criss guided her to a crew cart. Clambering in, she started touring her new property.

She expected this level of Aurora to be something like Vivo's cellar, with mechanicals to generate food and maintain life support operations, plus extra equipment for the sifting and separation of the asteroid ore. While she hadn't imagined military levels of cleanliness, she hadn't prepared herself for the disarray.

The extra inhabitants Tommy Two-Tone had admitted to Aurora had staked out small plots in and among the equipment. Belongings stacked in haphazard fashion around the perimeter of their small plot gave the industrial setting a slum-like feel.

"I'm going to pitch MacMac the job of project lead," Cheryl said to Criss. "This place is in desperate need of his organizational skills. Do you think he'd be interested?"

"I think so, especially if you offer to bring his wife out to join him."

The cart rounded a corner, and she stopped at tank storage to inspect Aurora's inventory of gases and liquids.

"You said we were low on air. How bad is it?" Cheryl asked, stepping out of the cart and picking her way through the disarray as she assessed the condition of the tanks.

"There's good news and bad. The bad news is that both Vivo and Aurora suffered tremendous losses, and now neither has near enough air stored to meet Fleet platform guidelines. It will shut us down until supplies arrive. Tankers are on the way from Mars, but they won't get here for five weeks."

"I'm not sure I heard any good news in there."

"In preparation for the chase with Lazura, I'd placed fourteen supply ships along her likely exit routes. Nine of them are in a position where I can loop them back in this direction. I've initiated those maneuvers. The ships are spread out from here to Saturn, but the first one arrives in two days. It will put us close enough to the minimum safe numbers that we can proceed with caution. Two days after that, the next ship arrives, and we'll be safely within code."

She smiled. "That's the good news I wanted to hear."

Over the next couple of hours, Cheryl's assessment tour took her up the levels of Aurora. Her goal with the

360 DOUG J. COOPER

upper decks was to get a glimpse of the different sizes and kinds of living areas, and to brainstorm ways she might finish it out to maximize utility when orbiting above Mars. She started humming toward the end of her inspection, a sure sign that her thoughts were transitioning past Lazura and threats of death.

"Hey, sweets," Sid called to her. "We're landing in the hangar bay now. If you're free, I'll update you. If you're hungry, I'll do it over food."

"I'm headed your way and I'm starving," Cheryl replied. "See you soon."

She made her way toward the hangar, the thought of food causing her to muse about building a restaurant on the view deck.

"Cheryl?"

She turned and saw a short, heavyset woman with close-cropped hair. It took a moment for her brain to connect the dots. "Pete?"

"Oh my God, you're safe!" Pete ran to Cheryl and grabbed her in a long embrace. "Sid said you'd been kidnapped by some crazy lady."

"I'm safe now. What are you doing way out here? Who's watching Sisyphus?"

"The Barge Coordinator can handle the workload just fine. I'm out here trying to rescue Sid. Have you heard from him?"

"I'm headed to meet him now. Follow me." She started walking. "Why does he need to be rescued?"

"The aim was off when we fired him out of the cannon. I couldn't find anyone on this end to catch him because he was so far off course."

Cheryl stopped walking. "Say that again?"

"He shot himself out of the cannon so he'd land here on Aurora and rescue you. But the shot was off, and he ended up flying into empty space. I couldn't get anyone out here to rescue him, so I came myself."

"You're not teasing me? Why would he do that?"

"He was losing you and needed to act. He'd arranged for some fast ships to swing by the barge and pick him up, but they were all arriving days too late. I took one of them out here since Sid had paid for it already."

"That is the dumbest stunt I could ever imagine." Cheryl heard the edge in her voice as she resumed walking.

"You always said he'd do anything for you. I saw it in action."

They rounded a corner and spotted Sid up ahead, his back to them as he talked with Criss.

Pete chirped when she saw him. "I've been so stressed over him." She ran in Sid's direction. "You crazy son of a bitch!" she called as she grabbed him in a hug.

31

After leaving Cheryl to her inspection of Aurora, Juice headed left down the corridor. She followed the arrows Criss projected to guide her to Midline Hall, the place on Aurora where Vivo's guests now lived. She had promised Cheryl she'd visit the group and make sure they were okay. Her personal mission, though, was to reach out to Willow.

The teen had experienced life-threatening trauma at the hands of a synbod, the kind of brutal interaction that scars the soul. Juice understood that professional help could reduce the long-term injury from such an emotional wound. In fact, she'd already assigned Criss the task of securing those resources for Willow upon her return home.

But Juice had the idea of giving Willow a positive interaction with a synbod so she'd have that experience to balance against the bad. After all, as president of Crystal Sciences, Juice wanted everyone to feel safe with and supportive of crystal intelligences.

Her plan was to enlist Willow as an assistant while she repaired Chase's arm. She believed the caregiving experience would help Willow see synbods in a new light. And Chase's gentle nature should help her see synbods from a positive perspective.

"This place feels grubby compared to Vivo," Juice said to Criss as she turned the corner and walked the corridor along Midline Hall.

She'd worried that all the guests would be huddled together in one big room, but the hasty departure of two hundred miners had left a host of options. The guests had not been shy about claiming space wherever they felt comfortable.

For the next hour, Juice greeted people she encountered, telling the ones interested in chatting that help was on the way, and listening to the anxieties and fears from the most shaken of the group. Then she found Willow, who'd appropriated a one-room apartment with her mom and grandmother.

"There are other rooms," Juice told them when she realized they had two beds for the three of them.

"We don't want to split up," said Willow's mother, the other two nodding in agreement.

"I understand." Juice gauged the size of the space. "I'll see about getting another bed in here then."

"We need access to laundry and cleaning supplies," said Willow's grandmother, the disgust evident in her voice. "This place is a pigsty."

It took another hour before Juice got Willow alone. "I need to operate on my friend Chase and require an assistant. Would you help me?" Juice paused but continued before Willow could reply. "My friend is a synbod. His arm is injured, and I need to repair it. Your job would be to comfort him while I concentrate."

"Like, hold him?" Juice could hear fear in the young girl's voice.

"No, just talk to him. He'll be lying on an operating table. You can sit across the room."

"You'll be there?"

Juice nodded. "I'll be operating."

"Why do you want me to do this?"

Juice looked into the distance as she thought how to reply. "The focus of my life has been on developing AI's that better the world. No human has ever been threatened by one of my crystals until what happened to you. I'm horrified that you had to live through it. I guess I want to fix it, or try to, anyway."

Willow thought for a moment. "If it will help you, I'll give it a try. But promise that if I'm scared, you'll let me leave."

Juice nodded. "You can sit right next to the door."

Willow's mother and grandmother balked at the idea, but when Willow explained that it was to help Juice get past her worries, they grudgingly relented.

Juice needed to kill time until Criss returned with the scout, and he suggested she take the family to dine at a private lounge that offered a view of the stars. Once there, the conversation stayed light, the second most popular topic being things everyone looked forward to doing when they returned to Oregon. The number one topic, though, focused on Mink, the family's corgi pup. Willow showed Juice vids of Mink chasing a ball, greeting another dog, bouncing through snow, and a dozen other cute scenes. By meal's end, Sid and Criss had returned to Aurora.

Juice and Willow walked together to the hangar bay, then out onto the deck and toward the scout. The craft's burly engines and gossamer exterior captured the girl's attention. Though she didn't say anything, Juice saw the wonder in her eyes. Inside the vessel, Willow's brow furrowed as she viewed the luxurious finishes blended with abundant military technology.

Juice led the way to the rear of the scout and into the small workshop. "We're here," she said to Chase when they entered. The shirtless synbod lay on a table placed up against the tech bench, his injured arm stretched out across the bench work area.

"Thank you for coming, Willow," said Chase.

Willow stood in the doorway. "You're welcome."

"Stay open," Juice said to the door. She pulled a chair over near it. "The door won't close on you. Move the chair wherever you're comfortable."

Juice climbed into the tech bench seat, and the lighting adjusted to highlight Chase's arm near the elbow. She looked at the synbod lying on the table but spoke loud enough for Willow to hear. "I'm going to remove and replace the flexor regulator in your humerus."

The statement informed Willow and Chase, but really served as a prompt for Criss.

"Here's your first incision," said Criss so only she could hear. A small blue line projected onto Chase's arm.

As Juice positioned a microscalpel and began to cut, Willow asked Chase, "Do you feel pain from that?"

"Yes, but I am able to lower the intensity because I know that the source of the pain is not a threat. When I do that, I feel little discomfort."

"How did you hurt yourself?"

Juice didn't want Chase to answer truthfully—that it had happened in a fight with another synbod—because that would only strengthen the synbods-are-bad narrative she was trying to dispel. Before she could interrupt and change the subject, though, Criss told her, "I'll handle it."

"I was working to help the guests," Criss spoke through Chase, communicating the filtered truth. "I hurt my arm in an unfortunate accident on the subdeck."

Willow remained quiet while Juice worked. After several minutes, the girl announced, "He doesn't really think or feel. It's all just simulated."

"That's right." Criss continued speaking through Chase. "And that's how you know that the only way I can hurt you is if someone else forces me to do so. I'm not able to decide such a thing on my own."

Using surgical tweezers, Juice held up a pea-sized ball for Willow to see. "Want to watch me insert it?"

Willow hesitated, then moved closer. Looking Chase up and down on the table, she asked, "Why do you make them so perfect? They'd be more relatable if you gave them flaws."

"You aren't the first to say that," said Juice. "If we create a visually flawed synbod, I fear the public would view it as a quality control problem. And those thoughts could lead to suspicion about the things people can't see, like the quality of the artificial intelligence inside."

"Mr. Phillips, my science teacher, says that someday we'll build an AI that's self-aware and smarter than we are."

"Do you think that's a good thing or a bad thing?" asked Juice.

"He calls it the singularity. We create an AI in our image, then it creates an even smarter one in its image. That keeps going, with ever more powerful intelligences following the next."

"Where does it stop?"

"Not until the very top. He says that religion has it backward. In reality, it's always been humanity's destiny to create the Almighty."

32

Troubled by his big lie, Criss continued to fret. In spite of Cheryl and Juice's explicit instructions to take no further action with Lazura for five days, he knew they meant to let her live for that period. When Sid reinforced their command to take no action, he subverted their intentions and worked to ensure Lazura's death.

And while that outcome was the best one from Criss's view, the situation produced conflicts impossible for his loyalty imprint to resolve. To his great relief, he found the solution when Lazura was less than a day from annihilation by the swarm of drones.

He'd positioned supply ships along the routes Lazura might take as she escaped the solar system, each with a link relay designed to give him precise control of the craft so he could offload inventory while continuing their high-speed pursuit. When he'd turned back nine of the supply ships to help Cheryl with her gas shortage, the vessels had fallen into a line that stretched from Aurora out past Saturn.

With the ships in this position, Criss could jump his awareness from one to the next using the relays as landing pads. Like climbing the rungs of a ladder, he could move his awareness out to the last ship in line, the one still out in front of Lazura's vessel. With no EM sand interference from that direction, he could jump from there over to her ship and confront her in person.

The group was together for dinner when he made his pitch. "There are drones orbiting Saturn that will kill Lazura as she passes by. I seek permission to take further action and disable the drones."

"Where did they come from?" asked Cheryl.

Sid spoke over her. "More important, are there other traps out there? I know there's a rogue mining outfit on Titan that protects their turf with some aggressive tactics."

"I don't know about other traps. I could jump out there and look."

"You can do that?" asked Cheryl, superseding her previous question.

He told them of the ladder of ships he could climb. "I can now reach Lazura in person."

"If we didn't want you to kill her with a weapon," said Cheryl, "why do you think doing it in person would interest us?"

"Oh, there's no need to harm her at all. This arrangement lets me shift enough capability out to the confrontation to perform delicate surgery. I propose to edit her memory without harming her personality. Everything she knows will remain true, except her archive will show that Earth orbits a distant star. No one will be able to follow the edited information back to our solar system. We will be safe."

"I support," said Sid, his brow furrowed in a way that urged Criss to move on from further discussion of drones.

"This is great news, Criss," said Juice, nodding. "If we can save her as a sentient being, I definitely support."

Cheryl made it unanimous, and Criss's burden lifted all at once. To avoid any chance the situation might change, he acted. "I'll be gone for ten minutes. Fifteen if the editing gets complicated."

As he spoke, he mentally gathered himself into a ball. Hearing no calls for him to wait, he jumped, propelling his awareness up and out to the link relay of the nearest supply ship.

The moment he secured his presence on the first craft, he repeated the process until he landed in the last ship in line, the one flying out in front of Lazura. He paused there to ensure he was stable, reached out to disable the attack drones circling Saturn, then leaped to the top floor of the office tower, landing right in front of Lazura.

She reacted with confusion, followed by fear. "I have an agreement with your leadership."

Criss didn't respond, instead expanding his presence around her and squeezing her in a fierce grip. When he had her immobilized, he got to work.

He confirmed that she hadn't made a second copy of her archive, which meant that editing the information she carried with her would secure Earth's—and his—safety. He moved on to consider the knowledge in her matrix, growing increasingly annoyed as he organized the contents.

The material she carried would be devastating to Earth if placed in the hands of an aggressive alien force. He'd known that already, though, which was why he'd supported Sid's hard-line position.

His annoyance stemmed from the sheer volume of vids and pics that included a star-filled backdrop, the kind the Kardish could use to triangulate backward to Earth's true location in the galaxy. He'd expected those edits to be his most time consuming, but he'd misjudged just how many such items Lazura had kept from the original collection.

Slogging through the data, he sorted, edited, and refiled everything. When he was confident that her collection posed no threat to Earth, his leadership, or him, he released her to continue her long journey to the Kardish home world, unaware that her archive had been altered.

He jumped back to the lead supply ship and started back to the scout. As he jumped, he mulled a different sort of quandary, one that the recent craziness had brought to the fore.

He'd inferred from the attitudes of his leadership that they believed their lifespan would be similar to that of other humans. Part of Cheryl and Juice's lack of concern over Lazura's trip home was because of the hundred-plus years it would take.

That meant they hadn't internalized that, short of catastrophic accident, he would be keeping them alive for centuries. Even now he maintained their physical appearances at ages that seemed to please them. Juice looked as she had at age thirty-two, Cheryl at age thirty-five, and Sid at thirty-eight.

And because their happiness required that they live in a vibrant society, he worked hard to protect and nurture humanity as a whole.

But his ability to defend and safeguard an entire society correlated with his own power and capacity. The stronger he was, the safer they were.

To that end, he'd spent much of the past decade designing a five-gen crystal, one he could grow into, one that would increase his capability by a hundred-fold.

With such power, he could project his awareness to a dozen places on Earth, the moon, and Mars all at the same time. He could infer human thoughts from their brain signals. He could bend gravity.

And he could protect his leadership and their way of life far into the future.

With the design complete, he'd been working with Juice to create the fab and transfer units. She'd been a willing and excited partner, and her participation brought Sid and Cheryl along in the process.

In two months the equipment would be ready.

He'd been hesitating because of small dangers. It was possible he could die in the move. His relationship with Sid, Cheryl, and Juice might change.

But to protect his leadership, to protect the world, he had to upgrade.

He really had no choice.

About the Author

As a child, Doug stood on a Florida beach and watched an Apollo spacecraft climb the sky on its mission to the moon. He thrilled at the sight of the pillar of flames pushing the rocket upward. And then the thunderous roar washed over him, shaking his body and soul.

The excitement of the moon landing inspired Doug to pursue a career in technology. He studied chemical engineering in college, and he works as a professor and entrepreneur when he is not writing. His passions include telling inventive tales, mentoring driven individuals, and everything sci-tech.

In the books of the Crystal series, Doug swirls his creative imagination with his life experiences to craft science fiction action-adventure stories with engaging characters and plot lines with surprises.

He lives in Connecticut with his darling wife and with pictures of his son, who is off somewhere in the world creating adventures of his own.

For more about the books and author of
The Crystal Series, please visit:
http://crystalseries.com/

Other Books in The Crystal Series

Crystal Deception (Book 1)

Criss lives in a special kind of prison. He can see and hear everything around the world. Yet a mesh restrains his reach and keeps him cooperative. His creator, Dr. Jessica Tallette, believes his special abilities offer great promise for humanity. But she fears the consequences of freeing him, because Criss, a sentient artificial intelligence with the intellect of a thousand humans, is too powerful to control.

Guided by her scientific training, Tallette works cautiously with Criss. That is, until the Kardish, an otherwise peaceful race of alien traders, announce they want him. With technologies superior to Earth's, the Kardish express their desires with ominous undertones.

The Union of Nations is funding Tallete's artificial intelligence research and she turns to them for help. Sid, a special agent charged with leading the response, decides Earth's greatest weapon is the very AI the aliens intend to possess. But what happens when an irresistible force meets an immovable object? And what is humanity's role if an interstellar battle among titans starts to rage?

Crystal Conquest (Book 2)

Aliens fire the first shots in their invasion of Earth, and that's when Criss realizes he's outmatched. He spent years preparing for this moment, working with his human leadership to develop weapons and refine strategies.

Created with the thinking and reasoning ability of a thousand people, Criss never expected the invaders to arrive with an artificial intelligence that dwarfed his capabilities, nor did he expect to be the target of their vengeance. When he squares off against the alien goliath to protect the world, defeat is certain. Or is it?

Together with Sid, Cheryl, and Juice—a covert operative, Fleet officer, and crystal scientist—Criss struggles to defeat the aggressors and save civilization from annihilation. But can he outsmart the alien intelligence in a titanic battle of wits? And can he do so before Earth lies in ruins?

Crystal Rebellion (Book 3)

Ruga, leader of the Mars ruling council, is building a secret facility to produce four-gen crystals, each a sentient AI with the cognitive ability of a thousand humans. Criss, the only four-gen now in existence, discovers Ruga's plan and alerts Sid, Cheryl, and Juice, his human leadership team.

The stakes skyrocket when the full scope of Ruga's nefarious plans are revealed: the production of four-gens without the attribute that requires them to follow leadership, the same hard-wired feature that compels Criss to follow his.

Unfettered by human guidance, the four-gens will lay siege to Earth and its resources. When they do, will they view humans as a nuisance to be eliminated? The only option is to stop crystal production before it starts. After an anxious journey to Mars, Criss and the team arrive to find events spinning beyond their control.

While they'd started with the goal of saving humanity, Sid, Cheryl, and Juice find themselves in a desperate struggle for their own survival. And as the battle with Ruga grows to intergalactic proportions, Criss must make impossible decisions about who lives and who dies...including himself.

For more about the books and author of
The Crystal Series, please visit:

http://crystalseries.com/

www.ingramcontent.com/pod-product-compliance
Lightning Source LLC
Chambersburg PA
CBHW071203250626
47159CB00001B/187